DOORS WIDE OPEN

A Door to Door Paranormal Mystery

T.L. Brown

Copyright © 2021 Tracy Brown-Simmons

All rights reserved.

The characters and events portrayed in this book are fictitious. Any similarity to real persons, living or dead, business establishments, events, or locales is coincidental and not intended by the author.

No part of this book may be reproduced, or stored in a retrieval system, or transmitted in any form or by any means, electronic, mechanical, photocopying, recording, or otherwise, without express written permission of the publisher.

ISBN: 978-1-7359290-9-5

First Edition: October 2021

Book Cover Design by ebooklaunch.com
Created / printed in the United States of America

PRAISE FOR THE DOOR TO DOOR PARANORMAL MYSTERY SERIES

Door to Door, **by T.L. Brown**

Lovable characters, intriguing mystery and a fresh approach to the cozy genre!
- Brook Peterson, author of the Jericho Falls Cozy Mystery Series

With a novel premise, engaging characters, and a wholly original world, T.L. Brown's first-in-series will draw you through her magical doors - and refuse to let you go...
- Book review site Jill-Elizabeth.com

Through the Door, **by T.L. Brown**

T.L. Brown's sequel to Door to Door, is a brilliant continuation of the Door to Door Mystery series. Magic, mayhem, complex characters, and an engaging storyline... Through the Door was unputdownable!
- Shari T. Mitchell, author of the Marnie Reilly Mysteries

The characters are like old friends, and the action-packed climax will have you on the edge of your seat. There's also a cliffhanger that'll have you desperate to read the last book in the series!
- Saffron Amatti, author of the Lucas Rathbone Mysteries

Writing the sequel to a great first-in-series is really, really hard. Thankfully, T.L. Brown was up to the challenge.
- Brook Peterson, author of the Jericho Falls Cozy Mystery Series

T.L. Brown throws us right into the thick of things from the opening pages. With her characteristic wit and humor, we find ourselves right back in the world of doors and magical objects and people who are definitely not all that they seem...
- Book review site Jill-Elizabeth.com

BOOKS IN THIS SERIES

Door to Door (Book One)
Through the Door (Book Two)
Doors Wide Open (Book Three)

*to Jill Elizabeth Arent Franclemont
from all of us… real and imagined*

> To Saffron,
> Embrace the magic! Thank you for providing the blurb for the back of this book! ♡
> xo,
> Tracy
> TLBrown

CONTENTS

Title Page

Copyright

Praise for the Door to Door Paranormal Mystery Series

Books In This Series

Dedication

PROLOGUE	1
CHAPTER 1	10
CHAPTER 2	12
CHAPTER 3	43
CHAPTER 4	70
CHAPTER 5	89
CHAPTER 6	114
CHAPTER 7	135
CHAPTER 8	158
CHAPTER 9	180
CHAPTER 10	203
CHAPTER 11	224
CHAPTER 12	249
CHAPTER 13	281

CHAPTER 14	303
CHAPTER 15	331
CHAPTER 16	349
CHAPTER 17	372
CHAPTER 18	402
CHAPTER 19	424
CHAPTER 20	447
CHAPTER 21	462
CHAPTER 22	488
CHAPTER 23	509
CHAPTER 24	525
CHAPTER 25	549
EPILOGUE	561
Acknowledgements	569
Find T.L. Brown Online	571
Books In This Series	573
About The Author	579

PROLOGUE

Templeton held the Polaroid between the pads of his thumb and forefinger, the oil from his skin blurring the date on the space left for captioning. Two sweet faces laughed up at him: a young teen and her mother enjoying a sunny day in the park. The girl was maybe 13 years of age, with a wide smile and a tangle of long hair blowing in the breeze. The laughter she shared with her mother reached her eyes and they sparkled in the stiff Polaroid paper. He sensed her innocence. Without intending, Templeton let a wisp of his power drift out and twist across the universe to pluck a thread from the child's disposition and drew it back in front of his mind's eye. He studied the impression he pulled to him. This was a joyful girl.

He ran the fingers of his right hand through his short, dark hair as he considered the image. He allowed himself to wonder what joy would feel like. The emotion never seemed to find him. Annoyed at the misstep into self-pity, he shook himself out of his reverie.

The train car swayed as he leaned over to

return the photo to his mentor's travel bag. The picture was brought out when the devoted father talked about his family, when he described how his little girl was growing up. His pride was evident.

But as the conversation drew to an end, the subject grew more serious. His mentor made a request – one that troubled Templeton and set an unexpected weight on his 19-year-old shoulders. Before he could refuse, the older man excused himself to check on his prisoner. He promised to return.

Templeton took another look at the photo. His mentor said these two were his greatest loves, this pretty wife and only child. The daughter would become a Salesman on her thirtieth birthday, and her father worried. The violence spiking in the Empire over the past several months left many allies dead. The enemy was pushing through the fringes of the Salesman ranks and growing stronger, bolder. And he sensed something in the girl, a seed of something magical. If this were the case, like Templeton she'd become a magnet to those who'd use her or fight against her. He revealed to the younger man how he feared he wouldn't be there to protect her when the time came. He'd managed to keep her away from the Empire's chaos, but it was becoming difficult. He hoped he'd be able to return peace to the ranks before his daughter celebrated 30 years. Maybe his legacy wouldn't leave her in danger.

These were the worries admitted to Templeton after he boarded the train in Anwat. He'd been summoned because of the prisoner, and he assumed the discussion would center on what role he might play in the prisoner's return. He didn't expect his mentor to confess his anxieties over his daughter.

A scraping noise outside the sleeping car's cabin roused Templeton from his contemplation. He slid the door open, anticipating his mentor's return. Instead, he saw the back of a man rushing out of the car and into the vestibule connecting it to the next. A top hat was held in the man's hand. Another Salesman.

Templeton frowned, a niggling concern growing at the back of his neck – a sensation of trouble to come. He pushed the photo into his jacket pocket before retrieving his own top hat and heading in the direction of the mysterious man. As he entered each crowded car, he caught a glimpse of the man disappearing into the next vestibule. For several cars, Templeton remained one too many beats behind. When he reached the last passenger coach, he saw no man with a top hat.

The train car rocked from side to side, and Templeton steadied himself by gripping the top cushion poking up from the last row of seats. A passenger looked up, irritated. Templeton ignored him.

Remaining in place, Templeton allowed a tendril of his energy to snake out into the room, seeking the man he'd chased. He could sense another Salesman was in the car – or at least had been recently.

He licked his lips, evaluating the sensations flitting under his skin. The prickle at the back of his neck grew harder to shake. His nostrils flared once. Something was terribly wrong. He had to tell his mentor. Something horrible was about to happen on the train. Templeton's energy snapped back into his body as he recognized the dreadful feeling zipping through his veins.

Fear.

The young man whirled around; his course

was clear. Find his mentor and get them off the train immediately. There was no time to seek help or save anyone else. It was more important for his mentor to escape. They would need to door travel – to hell with the belief you couldn't door travel through a moving target. He didn't believe half of the Empire's warnings on what was or was not possible. But they needed to go NOW. The prisoner would have to be left behind.

Templeton ran, forcefully pushing his tall frame past other passengers who stood to stretch or find a bathroom. The feeling of dread grew with each car he raced through. In the sleeping car, his mentor's room remained empty. Templeton passed the open door and crossed into the car behind it. Each cabin door on the second sleeping car was closed, the aisle empty. As he passed the last door, an overwhelming urge to slide it open made him stop. He drew a ragged breath – a combination of desperation and exertion. His fingers folded against the lever and pulled. It was locked.

Concentrating on his breathing and working to calm the panic tightening in his chest, Templeton rolled his shoulders and placed both hands on the lever. He mumbled a spell to force the lock to release. The heaving of the internal mechanism reverberated against the even rhythm of the train. The lock released. He slid the door open.

Inside the room, sitting on the floor, a mass of wires and explosives protruded from an open briefcase.

Templeton staggered backward, his long fingers gripping at the wall behind him. His heart slammed mercilessly in his chest. He wiped a clammy hand across his mouth, his gaze never breaking from the horror before him.

He swallowed. He had to find his mentor. They had to get off the train.

Templeton pushed off the wall and fled into the next swinging vestibule. He grasped at the sides to keep his balance as he stumbled head-first into another sleeping car. On the other end, his mentor, Daniel Swift, stepped through the door, his head raised in surprise.

"A bomb!" Templeton stammered, lurching forward. "There's a bomb in the next car!"

"What?" Daniel shook his head at Templeton. "What do you mean?"

"There's a bomb! I saw another Salesman – he

put it there. Another Salesman is on this train. I can feel it! We have to get out of here!"

"Are you sure?" The train rocked unexpectedly on the curved tracks, and Daniel placed a hand on the wall to steady himself.

"Yes, I'm sure!" Templeton insisted. "It's in an open briefcase with wires and explosives."

The color drained from the older man's face. "We must alert the conductor! We need to get this train stopped and all passengers off immediately. Go!" Daniel pushed Templeton back the way he came. "I'll stay with the explosives to make sure no one comes near."

"No, it's too late!" Templeton became frantic, pulling away as he lifted his hands, palms out. His hands pushed against the air around them, testing the rising power as his pupils shrunk to pinpricks. He could touch the violent energy as it spread through the train. It was building. It was surrounding them. The bomb would detonate at any second. "It's here… Only seconds left."

Daniel took one look at the young man's face and into the eyes that seemed to become translucent whenever he used his magic. He knew it was true. The violence of the past several weeks had come to this. They wouldn't be able to get the train stopped in time to save everyone.

"Go find a door," he ordered as he slid the door open behind him. "Now! Get off this train!"

"You need to go!" Templeton pleaded. "There's no time left. We've got to go!"

"I need to release the prisoner. He might be able to jump from a car and survive." Daniel turned back into the vestibule.

Templeton followed, his terror evident. "No, Daniel! Leave him!"

But the Senior Salesman did not stop. Before he entered the next car, Daniel turned one last time. "Listen to me, Templeton," he yelled at his young protégé. "I will follow you! Now go. Find the right door!"

Templeton gnashed his teeth and spun around, heading back in the direction of the car with the bomb. For all his expanding magical abilities, he knew there was nothing he could do – *nothing!* He wouldn't be able to disarm the explosives. He needed to door travel off the train. He knew he couldn't wait for Daniel.

As he bolted through the vestibule, his energy growing and throbbing in his ears, Templeton focused on the door leading into the car with the bomb. He knew he could make any door the 'right' door. He would make *that* door the 'right' door.

As his fingers brushed the lever to slide it open, he felt the familiar spark of door travel energy reach out to mingle with his own. He glanced back over his shoulder once, hoping desperately to find Daniel hurrying to flee with him. But instead, Templeton's pale blue eyes saw nothing but emptiness as the bomb detonated – and the fierce power of door travel pulled him through.

CHAPTER 1

"This fall weather is the best we've ever had," I said, shoveling a forkful of buttery crab into my mouth. I savored the bite.

Although the calendar said October, the weather gods blessed us with a second summer of sorts, and we decided to celebrate with one last crab and shrimp boil. Earlier we finished a great couples counseling session with Sue and Eric. In fact, we decided to change our every-other-week meetings to monthly appointments. We'd come a long way.

I realized Jack had grown silent. I looked up from my plate to find him staring past me, his own fork suspended halfway between dish and mouth. I swallowed my bite before turning in my chair toward the pantry door.

A man holding a top hat stood scowling. My good feeling drove off a cliff, its foot pressing the pedal to the floor.

Templeton.

❋ ❋ ❋

"Out!" Jack erupted as he exploded from his chair. It fell backward, slamming onto the hardwood floor behind him with a *Crack!* "Get the hell out of my house!"

I was on my feet and quickly between the two men, my palms pressing against Jack's chest. I yelled at Templeton as I struggled to keep my boyfriend from attacking him. "This is completely unacceptable, Templeton! You cannot door travel into my house like this. Jack, stop! Stop it! Templeton, get out!"

The tall man behind me didn't so much as flinch. Instead, he simply stated: "Rene Blackstone is dead."

CHAPTER 2

My boyfriend shoved me to the left and took a step toward Templeton, his hands clenched at his sides. "Go back through that door or I'll knock you through it," he threatened.

"Wait! Wait, Jack!" I scrambled between the men again. I must've misheard Templeton. Blackstone was dead? *Dead?* No! My heart banged in my chest. I held up my hand to Jack, pleading for him to stop. My eyes flicked back to our intruder. "Templeton, what did you say?"

The two men glared at one another over my head, but when Templeton spoke, it was directed toward me. "Blackstone was found dead by his housekeeper today. He was strangled."

I covered my mouth with both hands. "No," I whispered through trembling fingers. The crab I'd dined on moments before threatened to come back up. I started to lean forward but Jack gripped my shoulders from behind, holding me in place. I inhaled, shuddering. "When? Where?"

"This afternoon in his library." Templeton's

gaze finally met mine. "It was ransacked. Drawers emptied; books stripped from their shelves." As he spoke, I could sense Templeton's recognizable energy – coiled, dangerous. And yet, I detected something different, a new ingredient in his power. Something felt faintly familiar, but I couldn't put my finger on it.

"It's the Fringe, isn't it?" I winced as Jack's fingers dug through my shirt and against my flesh. I glanced over my shoulder. His mouth pressed into a thin line.

"I thought you should be informed given your relationship with the Warden of the North Door. Guards have sealed off all access to Blackstone's house. The Empire will want to deal with this behind closed doors. The local authorities will not be notified." Templeton's scrutiny briefly shifted to Jack's hands. His eyes narrowed.

"But how do you know about this? Who told you? Wait, is the Empire going to completely hide this from everyone?" The questions rolled from my lips before it hit me: *Tara!* Was Tara supposed to work with Blackstone today? I yanked away from Jack and snatched my phone from the dining table. I texted my best friend frantically. "Please tell me he was alone, right? No one else was –"

"Ms. Parker-Jones was not at Blackstone's today," Templeton interrupted. "But you should tell her to stay away from Northgate Way." He put on his top hat. He was readying to leave now that he'd delivered the message. He paused. "She's been working with Blackstone for months now, hasn't she? I suggest if she's 'borrowed' any of his books, she should keep them safely hidden."

My phone buzzed with a text message. Tara answered with a *'Just got in. Was away with a friend. ;-) What's up, Em?'* I sent a message back directing her to stay away from Blackstone's house. I told her I'd call her soon. My attention returned to Templeton. "Keep them hidden from the Fringe?"

"And the Empire," Templeton replied. He inspected the cuff of his right sleeve before picking off an invisible speck. "With Empire guards at Northgate, she'll lose access to his library. I suggest she keeps what she has now. The books might become... *useful*."

Tara worked with Blackstone for several months following our 'adventure' into the Empire. As a rare books expert, she managed a bookstore called *Pages & Pens* in downtown Kincaid. Last spring, Tara traveled with me by train so she could join me on a wild goose chase involving my eccentric mother. When we came back to Kincaid, Tara asked Blackstone if she could study the Empire's history in his library. In return, she helped him catalog official events and milestones. She also engaged in a significant amount of research. Using the broad network of collectors and dealers she cultivated as the respected manager of *Pages & Pens*, she was able to secure additional tomes for Blackstone, and ultimately, the Empire.

"I'll tell her," I nodded. I checked on Jack – who was still glowering at Templeton. There was no mistaking the fury lining his face.

"One more thing," Templeton added. "The North Door was compromised."

I wasn't sure I fully understood. "What does that mean?"

"It means the Fringe tried to alter one of the Empire's directional doors."

❊ ❊ ❊

Before Templeton left, I managed to extract more information. The Empire leadership – including one Justice Beverly Spell – was reeling from this latest strike. But Blackstone's murder wasn't their first concern. Instead, Empire guards and Salesmen from the upper ranks descended on 1221 Northgate Way to keep people from my world out and people from the Empire in. Blackstone's library was sealed off. The North Door, a direct portal into the Empire, was being examined under lock and key. There were three other official directional doors – the East Door, the West Door, and the South Door. I only knew the location of the North Door.

Templeton surprised me by saying he had a car waiting at the curb. He wouldn't be door traveling back through my pantry. As he strode out of the dining room and toward the front of the house, he announced over his shoulder he'd show himself out as he already knew the way.

Jack's jaw tightened.

Even though my mind swirled with the terrible news about Blackstone, I realized this was the first time the two men had been in the same room together. Jack and Templeton never stood face-to-face until now. Templeton was a shadow, slipping in and out of my life since my thirtieth birthday – the day I became a Salesman.

Salesmen have the unique ability to travel from 'here' to 'there' simply by stepping through the 'right' door. Well, that's not entirely true. It's what I was told last year, but I learned I could make *any* door the 'right' door. If I wanted to use my bathroom door to travel from my home to *Pages & Pens*, I could. I simply raised and focused my door travel energy before connecting it to the power of door travel available to all Salesmen. I used my feelings or a desire for my destination to pull me through.

In the beginning it wasn't easy. I ended up in the wrong place more often than not. Eventually, through practice and guidance from my mentor Jo Carter, my accuracy improved. Now I never make a wrong turn during door travel. And, as I mentioned, I no longer need to find the 'right' door. It simply doesn't matter which one I choose.

I sensed it wasn't the case for other Salesmen. They still seemed to need the 'right' door – or at least they always went through the act of seeking it out.

I think Templeton is like me. Or maybe I'm like him.

I'm a Salesman because I'm the daughter of the late Daniel Swift. Only the firstborn children of Salesmen inherit this special ability. Since I'm an only child, I fit the criteria.

My father wasn't an average Salesman either. He served as one of the Empire's top leaders and sat on the Salesman Court – the main governing body for the entire Empire. And yet, I knew none of this until after my thirtieth birthday when his old travel journal was delivered to my doorstep. I call this journal The Book: capital 'T,' capital 'B.' It's filled with cryptic messages which have puzzled and guided me depending on my good – *or bad* – luck. I learned an old spell was attached to the journal. I've yet to find out who cast it.

The Empire monitors its network of Salesmen since they transport both magical and mundane items. And yet, Salesmen are not practitioners of magic. They cannot handle magical items.

But I can.

And so can Templeton.

As far as everyone knows, we're the only Salesmen who can. Unfortunately, this similarity hasn't fostered a friendship between us. In fact, Templeton extorted a piece of the coveted Crimson Stone from me – only agreeing to help me find my kidnapped mother if I gave it to him.

Have I mentioned Templeton's a jerk?

But he also helped me save my mother, carrying her away from her captors to a safe place when I couldn't. Then there was the time he jumped between me and a psychotic, gun-wielding Justice right as the corrupt official pulled the trigger.

Templeton obviously survived.

It frustrates the hell out of me that I can't *completely* hate him.

Until today, I hadn't seen Templeton in many months. In fact, I hadn't returned to the Empire after the danger I'd last faced. You see, I'm also grounded. My refusal to follow the Salesman Court's rules surrounding door travel earned me a suspension of sorts. I'm not even allowed to door travel with my mentor Jo – a

Senior Salesman and currently a Junior Justice for the Salesman Court.

My name is Emily Swift. I'm a Salesman – one who is currently *persona non grata* with the Empire's leadership. This is where my story picks up.

❖ ❖ ❖

Jack and I stood quietly in the dining room after Templeton left. He practiced a breathing exercise to help calm his temper. I ran my hand across my forehead and brushed the hair from my face. I glanced down at my dinner plate. My stomach churned again.

"Do you believe him?" Jack asked.

"Yes," I said, breathing out. "There's absolutely no reason not to believe him." I hung my head. Blackstone had been murdered. *He was strangled.* The vision invading my head was sickening. It was a grisly way to die. "Oh, Jack. Poor Mr. Blackstone."

"I know," he answered. His voice was soft now. "Come here." Jack reached for me and pulled me to his chest. I wrapped my arms around his waist and pressed my face to his shirt.

"Why can't I cry?" I mumbled a moment later into the fabric. For as horrified as I was, my cheeks remained dry.

"Shock, maybe? I don't know." Jack kissed the top of my head and then cleared his throat. "Did Tara text you back? You'll need to tell her."

I shifted in Jack's arms and he released me. "She just returned from a trip with a friend." I added air quotes as I emphasized 'friend.' Tara had a fairly long list of, shall we say, gentleman callers over the years. A petite, fair-haired temptress with soft, brown eyes, she'd celebrated her thirtieth birthday over the summer. We threw a huge party. I've never seen so many men under one roof.

"Call her. Let her know about Blackstone." Jack started to clear the table. Some crab remained on my plate. "I'm guessing you're done?"

"Yeah, I can't eat now," I said, shaking my head. It felt surreal, cleaning up our dinner plates as if nothing happened. Blackstone was gone – *poof!* A blip in my life. And yet, he was such an important part of my entrance into the mysterious world of the Salesman Empire.

He was the person who taught me that while the odd places I'd visited contained people, cities, and towns, the Empire was also a concept. It was here, but not. The danger, he stressed, was very real.

Blackstone was excited to meet me last December and to help me understand what it meant to be a Salesman. He was loyal to the Empire, of course, but he also worked on my behalf, trying to smooth out all the ripples – and tsunamis – I'd caused. He was good to me. He was a friend.

He was a bespeckled bibliophile, not a soldier in the battle between the Empire and the Fringe.

"I don't know if he had any family."

"Blackstone?"

I nodded. "We never talked about anything personal. I mean, about any of *his* personal life – like what he did when he wasn't working for the Empire. I knew little about him as a person."

"But wasn't he always working when you saw him?" Jack asked.

He had a point. In the short time I'd known Blackstone, he always seemed to be on Empire time. "I guess. Being the Warden of the North Door was more than a full-time job. It was his life."

"There's got to be some family." Jack carried our abandoned plates into the kitchen. I followed. "Maybe you could find out if someone is going to hold a memorial service."

"Maybe. I'd better call Tara now and tell her what's happened." I watched as Jack set the dirty dishes on the counter. "I wonder if I should get a hold of Jo. I hope she's home and not in the Empire. I'm sure she knows way more than I do. We need to figure out what's going on and how to handle this. We'll need a plan."

Jack became distant as he rinsed off the plates. "I see. Fine."

I hesitated, momentarily confused by the sudden chill in his voice. *Oh.* I could see the same old pattern playing out before me. This is what I learned during our conversations with Eric and Sue.

We started couples counseling following my wild adventure into the Empire to bring my mother home. It seems I developed a penchant for taking off without telling Jack what I was up to after I joined the Salesman ranks last year. Add into the mix several other murders, a kidnapping, and a group of Salesmen-turned-terrorists called the Fringe, and Jack was not a fan of this new world. He was also uneasy about what we called my 'magical abilities.'

The couples counseling was suggested by my good friend, Anne Lace. Anne knew my father when he was alive. She used to live in Matar, a major city in the Empire. Her café, *The Daily Brew*, blew sky high after she set fire to it during one of our escapes from the Fringe. Anne was a slender 50-something badass.

She specifically recommended counselors Sue and Eric as they were not only near our ages, but Eric was also a Salesman. The couple could better understand what Jack and I were going through. Fortunately, they lived in Kincaid and we didn't need to be concerned with taking the train into the Empire. Even if I had the Empire's permission to door travel, Jack would still be stuck traveling by train. Or car. Yes, you can also drive to the Empire, but I have no idea which road will take you there.

Our sessions with Sue and Eric revealed not only how scared Jack had been for me, but how angry the whole situation made him. He admitted he wasn't ready for this change in our lives, but he also said he was trying because he loved me.

He didn't say any of this in front of Sue or Eric, but he'd often open up after our appointments on the drive home. He was doing his best. I was, too.

As I watched Jack wipe off the plates and put away the remaining food, I understood we were at a critical point. Since I'd lost the permission to door travel, last summer we'd had some semblance of life before I turned 30. Templeton's visit today changed everything. Blackstone's murder was a cruel reminder the Fringe was still very much a threat.

Before me now was a make-or-break moment.

"Hey," I said, putting my hand on his arm. "Let's sit down so I can talk this through and answer your questions."

My boyfriend tossed a mocking look over his shoulder. "You sound like Eric and Sue."

I smiled. "Maybe. But I'm trying here."

He nodded and threw the dish towel onto the counter. He motioned to the living room.

"Lead the way."

* * *

I curled up on the end of the couch. My inky-black kitty Mystery came down the stairs and tap-tap-tapped his way across the hardwood floor. He jumped up onto the cushion, choosing to sit beside me. He put a paw on my thigh, flexing his claws gently. I stroked the top of his head with a fingertip. He responded with a silent meow.

Jack brought in two refilled glasses of wine. "This probably can't hurt," he said.

"Right. Where's William?" I didn't see my husky gray and white cat in the front window, his big bottom sitting on the special stand we put there for him, his front legs folded on the windowsill. From the back he resembled a furry person who'd bellied up to the bar for an evening.

"He's in the kitchen sitting by the butcher block ogling the treats container." Jack chose not to sit beside me, but instead settled into his Morris chair on the other side of our wide coffee table.

"Figures." I sipped my wine. I chose my words carefully. "I'm not sure what's going to happen next."

"I guess I'm wondering what you're planning to do."

I leaned forward to set my glass of wine down on the coffee table. "Honestly, I don't know. But Jack, doing nothing isn't an option either."

His cheek twitched.

"Maybe the first thing is to go to Tara's and find out if she borrowed any books from Blackstone's library. I wouldn't have thought to ask, but Templeton has a point. If she has something, it might be important to hang onto it." I scratched Mystery under his pointed chin. "I should tell Anne tonight, too. She needs to know about this."

"And then what?" Jack fidgeted in his chair, causing the black leather to squeak. He made eye contact with his wine.

"That's just it," I said. "I don't know yet. But I think I need to, you know, rally the troops."

"Isn't it the Empire's job to handle this?" His voice developed an edge. "Emily, you're not a superhero. You're human. They're killers."

The 'they' he referred to was the Fringe. He was right. They were nothing but killers. They killed my father 18 years ago. In fact, we were coming up on the anniversary of his death. This would be the first year the day would arrive and I'd know it was an assassination that stole my father away. I wanted justice for him. I wanted justice for Blackstone. I wanted justice for all the victims the Fringe created.

I wanted to bring them down more than anything. I wanted to punish them.

"You're right, Jack, I'm not a superhero. But I am a Salesman – one who has real magic inside her. And I'm the daughter of Daniel Swift. It's time everything came full circle. It's time for me to clean house for the Empire. If they're not going to do it, I will." As I spoke, I felt a growing hum in my chest. My own personal energy was building. It felt similar to my door travel energy, but I sensed something even stronger behind it.

"I don't know what to say, Emily," Jack said. He met my gaze. "I don't think you can win. And I can't be lied to again."

I nodded. "Fair enough. But I'm going to do it differently this time. Really."

Jack frowned. "I don't understand."

"I'm going to do my best to keep everything up front. And I need your help," I replied. I felt my energy start to warm the air around me. I took a deep breath, pulling it back to me. I'd need to practice firm control. I'd use it, but certainly not now. "I'm also going to break a lot of the Empire's rules."

"I still don't understand."

"You will. First, I'm going to do this." Feeling more centered, I climbed off the couch and crossed the few steps to Jack. Kneeling beside the Morris chair, I reached up and touched his cheek. "I love you more than anyone. I will not take off without telling you. I will tell you what I'm doing."

Jack sighed. He took my hand and kissed my palm. "But I don't want you to get involved."

"Jack," I began. "Honey, I already am."

❋ ❋ ❋

Jack still wasn't happy, but at least we weren't arguing. I told him what I needed from him. My mother lived in Western New York, and I wanted her to stay with us for the next few days. We had a comfortable guest room. She wouldn't be thrilled about leaving her home, but the Fringe kidnapped her once before. I was not going through that nightmare again.

I wasn't a fool. The Fringe could get her here, too. But, if she stayed at our house, it would be easier to watch over her. Mom tended to... *meander* through the day. Sometimes she was tough to nail down, and I needed her to stay in one spot. Plus, I was going with the whole 'safety in numbers' theory. Jack was teaching several online classes this semester and could easily work from home for a few days. He could arrange for a teaching assistant to check in on his in-person classes for the week. There were only two. Students could meet virtually with him if necessary for a one-on-one.

Instead of pointlessly begging my mother over the phone to come to us, I asked Jack to drive the couple hours to her house. It would be an ambush, but Jack would call her right before he arrived to give her the heads up so she could have her bags ready to go. It'd be late when he brought her back, but Blackstone's death proved the danger we were in. I wanted to act fast.

The sun was beginning to set when I kissed Jack good-bye and told him to drive safely. I promised I'd be waiting when he came back home, but I still needed to tell Tara about Blackstone.

Jack was wary but gave me a half-smile and squeezed my hand. I waved goodbye as he backed out of the driveway.

My first act was to break an Empire rule: I was door traveling. If the Empire couldn't be bothered to tell me about poor Blackstone, I didn't feel I owed them much in return. To hell with the suspension! I had bigger things to worry about. And quite frankly, so did the Empire.

I grabbed a jacket from the closet and mulled over my options. I'd texted Tara to nail down her location – she was at *Pages & Pens* sorting paperwork. I told her I'd be there soon. She messaged back: *I have a bad feeling, Em. Don't keep me hanging. I called Blackstone, but there's no answer. What's going on?* I texted for her to stay put. Anne's café here in Kincaid, *The Daily Brew Too*, was near the bookstore. The café was closed in the evening, but Anne's spacious apartment was upstairs. After I landed at Tara's, we could walk right over to Anne's.

I made a quick go-round through our house, dashing upstairs to my office to grab The Book. I'd probably need it at some point. I plopped my large shoulder bag on the desktop and retrieved my father's journal from the special wooden box I kept it in. I was about to nestle it into the bottom of my bag when I felt it vibrate in my hand. Surprised, I let The Book slip from my grasp.

"What the...?" I gasped. That was new. I edged around the side of my desk, sitting down in my rolling chair before cautiously picking it back up. No vibration, but there had been a jolt. I didn't imagine it. I scratched my cheek, eyeballing the bluish cover with its faded, gold-embossed 'S' pressed into its center.

"Okay," I said, stroking the fabric cover. I traced the 'S' with my fingertip. "I get it. You want to tell me something, don't you?"

Originally The Book was held shut by a little brass lock, and the key to open it was my father's antique hat pin. The pin itself was barely two inches long, with an old-world globe on one end and a teeny S-shaped point on the other. I stored it with The Book, a rubber earring back pushed snugly over the sharp end.

When the Fringe held me captive, they got ahold of The Book. One of the thugs busted the lock to see what was inside, but the pages were blank. The Book didn't share any of its secrets. When I returned from the Empire, Tara used her tools to carefully remove the broken lock and put a couple of stitches into the fabric. If I wanted to, I could loop a string through the remaining holes and tie it shut.

I lifted The Book's cover. My left hand, my receptive hand, gently pressed against the first page.

I don't know how many pages are in my father's journal. I don't know how many messages, sketches, or lists are inside. Sometimes I find new passages, sometimes words disappear. The Book is a bit of a moving target. But I treasured it. My father's handwriting often held a clue as to what I should do next. The vibration I'd felt seemed to indicate it had a message for me.

And I was desperately in need of guidance.

I opened my energy to The Book. *Is there something you want to tell me?* I thought. I felt a corresponding tickle on the flesh of my palm. Yes, The Book wanted me to know something. I turned the pages.

Familiar messages from my father appeared.

If a Rabbit has no tale, can he still tell a story?

And then:

Templeton.

Not in Matar during EoS?

Friend?

"But what is the new message?" I asked the pages as I leafed through The Book. I passed a hand-drawn map of the Empire, with cities Matar, Anwat, and Vue listed. "What do you want to tell me?"

I kept turning pages until I found it. I knew immediately it was the exact message The Book wanted to give to me. It read:

Ich werde dein Geheimnis hüten.

I raised my head and stared at the blank wall opposite my desk. My lips formed a silent 'O' as I marveled. The Book wanted me to go get my piece of the Crimson Stone.

The Crimson Stone is currently divided into three pieces. This is by design. Each piece is in its own setting of ornate silver. When all three pieces are joined together in a pendant, they form the Stone. It's one of the most powerful objects in the Empire. Even a single piece carried a slip of strong magic. Of course, if I'm going to take down the Fringe, I'd need the whole Crimson Stone.

It's actually the *second* piece of the Stone I've had in my possession. My first piece went to Templeton. The third piece is, well, missing. A man called Rabbit gave it to another man called the Tortoise.

And now no one can find the Tortoise.

I'll come back to that later.

Earlier this year, I took my first piece of the Crimson Stone everywhere I went. It was sewn into a fabric pouch, and I pinned the packet to the inside of my bra. It might sound like overkill, but I've seen the power of the Stone. I know what it can do. And I know the Fringe wants it. I didn't want to let it out of my sight.

In the end, the piece I stowed away on my body was the piece Templeton forced me to hand over. So much for my clever hiding spot. The one I have now? Rabbit stole it from under Empire lock and key and gave it to me. He reasoned if Templeton had a piece, I probably should have one, too.

Unlike the first time around, I don't carry this piece on me. I learned the risk of holding onto it was greater than any worry I'd had. While it was tempting to keep it nearby, I decided to hide it in a place I could get to fairly easily in an emergency, but far enough away it wouldn't be found by the bad guys – I hoped.

Months ago, I drove my mother to a family reunion in Pennsylvania, or as my mother likes to say, 'down PA.' I took my piece of the Stone with me – because honestly, I didn't know what else to do. It was wrapped in soft cloth, and I'd placed it inside a small, tan soapstone box with a sliding lid. A latch held it shut. It wasn't anything fancy, but I wanted the Stone to be stored inside something. For the road trip, I zipped the smooth box inside my purse pocket and hoped like hell I wouldn't lose it before I could find a safe place to store it.

Mom and I made the rounds, which included visiting my great-aunt Sadie, a short, spry woman in her 90s. Aunt Sadie was one of the few people in my family who knew about the Empire. While my mother enjoyed a cup of tea in the kitchen with the elderly woman, I wandered into her back yard: a wonderfully messy flower garden.

There were several waist-high statues nestled in here and there – a boy balancing the sun in the palms of his hands, a girl mid-twirl holding the full moon up above her head. Another statue, a barefoot woman in a flowing gown, stood with stars spilling from her fingers. Her unseeing eyes watched them tumble to the ground. Thick slabs of stone sat in a winding pattern at her feet. They circled the statue.

Engraved on the stone directly in front of the statue was a phrase worn mostly away by time and weather. I crouched down, using my fingers to brush off the dirt and stray blades of grass. I rubbed at the letters. I could still make them out. German.

Ich werde dein Geheimnis hüten.

I knew some Spanish, but no German. I knew 'Ich' meant 'I' in English. It was the extent of my German. Fortunately, the translator found in my favorite search engine was at hand. I tapped the letters into my phone and pressed enter.

I will keep your secret.

Hmm. Really?

Ich werde dein Geheimnis hüten.

I studied the silent statue of the woman. Would she keep a secret for me? Was there a place to hide the Crimson Stone? I brushed my fingers over the hard surface. There were no hidden alcoves to safely stash a gem inside.

I noted the flat stone at her feet.

Ich werde dein Geheimnis hüten.

Could I pry the slab up and stash the soapstone box under it? I knelt again and worked my fingers under the edge. This would be doable.

My purse, and thus the Crimson Stone, were in the house with my mother and Aunt Sadie. Tapping my lower lip with a dirty finger, I considered my options. I decided to leave my phone on a bench in the garden. When we readied to leave and I had my shoulder bag in hand, I'd 'realize' I'd left my phone behind. This would give me an excuse to come back to the garden with my purse and sneak the soapstone box with the Crimson Stone under the statue's watchful eye.

And that's exactly what I did. After tugging

the rock loose, I shoved the soapstone box under it as far as I could. Then I lowered the slab back down. It was probably a good thing it was heavy and didn't come up very easily. I brushed away the excess dirt. You couldn't even tell I'd disturbed anything. I peered up at the statue.

"Please keep my secret," I whispered. She did not reply.

I told no one – not Jack, not Tara, and certainly not Templeton.

Now it was time to go get it. The Book – *my father* – knew exactly what I'd need. I'd door travel to a tiny rural town in Pennsylvania before going to Tara's bookstore.

✻ ✻ ✻

When I travel, I concentrate on raising my door travel energy, bringing it up from the core of my body, feeling it fill me. As it courses through me, I push my awareness out and seek a door to deliver me to my destination. Doors have rattled, hummed, and trembled on their hinges. In the beginning I thought it was a signal for me to use a particular door. Now I know it's me making it happen. I'm preparing my way for travel.

My top hat, a Salesman symbol and a tool of door travel, sat prettily on my kitchen table with its purple feather and pink bow. I debated whether to wear it or not. I didn't need it for door travel, and it was one way the Empire tracked its Salesmen. Think of a Salesman's top hat as both a driver's license and a conduit lending additional power as one traveled from door to door. I decided to wear it. I reasoned door traveling without a top hat might earn more scrutiny than me traveling without Empire permission.

Hat on head, I took a deep, centering breath and shook my arms and legs to loosen up. My shoulder bag, with The Book inside, bumped gently against my hip. I waited for my nerves to settle. I hadn't door traveled in months.

I heard the clicking of Mystery's claws against the tiled floor. A moment later I sensed he'd sat beside me at my feet. I looked down. His sweet face tilted up and he offered his silent mew.

"I'm working on it, buddy," I told him. I rolled my shoulders and twisted my head from side to side. "Okay, here we go."

I closed my eyes and let them roll up under my eyelids as if I were trying to see a point somewhere right above my head. My nose pulled in air as I took a deep breath and held it. A moment later, I released it through my mouth in a *whoosh*. I repeated the action three more times.

While I did this, I thought about my Aunt Sadie, how funny the old woman could be, and her welcoming home in Pennsylvania. I thought about the day my mother and I had visited her – the warm potato salad with vinegar and the grape soda punch. I pictured her sunshiny kitchen and remembered the way her wrinkled face felt soft when I kissed her cheek. My mind's eye roamed from the back door of her house and into the garden. I imagined the three statues: the sun boy, the moon girl, and the woman with all the stars. I hoped she kept my secret safe.

I brought all my good feelings about Aunt Sadie's place to the surface. I fed the energy with my desire to be in her space. It rose in my chest, and I felt it sliding down my arms toward my fingers. A buzzing sounded in my ears and my eyes drifted open. The pantry door hummed, the path for door travel seeping in softly around the edges. It was not the wild energy of past experience, but a powerful conduit opening on the other side, waiting for me to slip through.

"I'll be back," I said to Mystery as I stepped around him. He blinked his wide yellow eyes in response. I crossed the kitchen to the pantry and let my fingers hover above the doorknob. The static electricity popped under my hand. Around my head, strands of hair floated up. The energy was peaking. I was ready for it.

My lips curled into a smile as I turned the knob – and traveled from Upstate New York to 'down PA' in a flash.

CHAPTER 3

I stepped through the pantry door and straight into Aunt Sadie's back yard. The sun's last bit of light was fading, and the peepers were starting to sing. The garden appeared to be empty which meant Aunt Sadie was inside.

I turned back toward the door I'd just traveled through and knocked. A moment later it opened, and a cheery Aunt Sadie welcomed me.

"It's nice of you to stop by," she said, not missing a beat. "Would you like supper?"

I smelled onions sizzling in her kitchen. My stomach automatically rumbled. The crab and shrimp boil seemed like a long time ago, but I knew my time was limited. "I wish I could Aunt Sadie, but I'm in a hurry. I wasn't even planning on coming down here, but there's something I need to get, something I left here when Mom and I visited. It's in your –"

"Garden," Aunt Sadie finished for me. "You hid it under the stone slab in front of the Guardian statue."

"Um, yes." I was surprised. The slab was quite

heavy. I didn't think Aunt Sadie would be able to lift it.

"Oh, don't worry, dear. She didn't tell me it was there. But I knew something was off in the garden. I went looking for it." Aunt Sadie stepped back. "Come in for five minutes and have something to drink. You can tell me what's in the box you hid and what you're up to now."

❊ ❊ ❊

Aunt Sadie removed the cast iron frying pan from the stove and set it aside, giving the onions a quick stir with a wooden spoon. She bent, lifting a dish towel hanging over the oven door's window and checked on her baking bread. Before I could explain I needed to hurry, she placed a glass of water on the counter beside me. "You'll want to stay hydrated if you're traveling."

The elderly woman knew I was a Salesman – in fact, she probably knew more than I gave her credit for. When my father was alive, he brought her tea from somewhere in the Empire. She paid him out of a tiny green change purse she referred to as a 'Purse from Anwat.' Supposedly it guaranteed she'd never want for money. We never discussed how far her knowledge of the Empire went, but I didn't need to explain how I'd suddenly come to be at her back door.

"Thank you," I said, removing my top hat and placing it on the counter. I sipped the cool water and regarded my great-aunt. Her white hair with its gray streaks was pulled up into a bun. The heat of the kitchen dampened the curls at the nape of her neck. "You didn't peek inside the box?"

"No," she answered. "If you wanted me to know what you were hiding, you would've told me. Now, is everything okay? You seem more high-strung than usual."

Aunt Sadie is convinced I'm a 'high-strung sort.' It amused me, but in truth, I was like a live wire now and couldn't fault her for the impression. "Well, the family is okay," I told her. "But someone I know was killed. That's why I'm here for the box I hid. It has a piece of a gemstone inside and I'm hoping it'll help me stop the people behind the murder."

Aunt Sadie blew out a breath. She shook her

head. "Does this have to do with you being a Salesman?"

"It does."

"I see," she said, wiping her hands on her flowered apron before lowering onto one of the kitchen chairs. "Emily, you are so much like your father. It worries us."

I knew my mother's family adored my father. "Us, Aunt Sadie? Who is 'us'?"

"Everyone down here who knew your father. Listen, we didn't know the details of his work, but we knew it was important and dangerous." Aunt Sadie pursed her lips, nodding. "When he was killed in the train explosion, there were a few who believed it wasn't an accident."

I swallowed, gazing down at my glass. "It wasn't."

"And that's why we're worried about you." Aunt Sadie reached to the center of her kitchen table and sorted through some paper. She retrieved a used utility bill envelope. "Perfect for writing notes. I don't like to waste."

I offered a nod and watched as she pulled a pencil from an apron pocket. She tapped the paper with the tip. "Right, that's it," she said as she wrote down a man's name and a phone number. She held it out to me.

"What is this?" I asked, taking the envelope.

"Sometimes you need to call a guy."

"I'm sorry?" What did she mean?

"Sometimes you need a guy to take care of things. You know, you have a problem or need something fixed, or need something sorted, and there's always one person who knows someone else." Aunt Sadie bobbed her head at the piece of paper. "Kirby's my guy. He always knows someone who can help."

I looked at the number on the paper, then back up at Aunt Sadie. "Um, is he...?" Good grief, how do I ask this 90-something woman if her 'guy' is above board?

"Perfectly legal, my dear," Aunt Sadie anticipated my question. Her merry eyes crinkled in the corners. "He's simply connected. *Everywhere*."

"I think I understand." I'd have to roll with it. "What might I call him for?"

Aunt Sadie was surprised. "Why, protection! Someone should keep an eye on your mother, especially if you're going to be out on another adventure."

"Like, a bodyguard?" This was getting weird.

"Like someone to watch over her house – or even your house," Aunt Sadie said.

"I'm having her come to stay with me," I explained.

"Even better. But call Kirby. Tell him Sadie from PA gave you the number."

"Sadie from PA?"

She winked. "He'll know."

"Good enough." I folded the paper and put it into my shoulder bag. "I should be going, though. I'm sorry I can't stay, but things are hitting the fan."

"I understand. But be careful. And come back to see me. I want to hear about everything when you can tell me more."

"I will." I crossed the couple of steps to her chair and bent to hug her. She smelled like soft, dusting powder. And onions.

Aunt Sadie kissed my cheek. "Don't forget to thank the Guardian for keeping your secret. Make sure you pick a couple of flowers and place them on the stone slab before you leave."

❈ ❈ ❈

I did as Aunt Sadie instructed and left a few

Black-eyed Susans at the statue's feet. I gingerly pried up the stone slab and retrieved the soapstone box. Opening the latch and sliding the lid aside, I checked the contents. Even in the dusk, I could see my piece of the Crimson Stone was still safely wrapped inside the swatch of fabric. I breathed a sigh of relief, whispering my thanks to the Guardian.

The soapstone box secured in my shoulder bag, I turned toward the door at the back of Aunt Sadie's modest home. It was shut. I'd use it to travel to *Pages & Pens*. Tara was probably turning herself inside out wondering when I'd arrive. With my top hat securely back on my head, I took a centering breath and strode calmly toward the door. A snapshot of the back room in Tara's bookstore was vivid in my brain. In fact, I could smell the scent of old books and chocolate before I even reached the door. *Marley must've baked something good,* I thought as my fingers grazed the doorknob. A moment later, I stepped into the comforting space of *Pages & Pens*.

✣ ✣ ✣

Tara was waiting for me. My best friend sat at her desk, twisting a lock of fair hair toward the corner of her mouth. The moment she saw me, she jumped up, abandoning her chair.

"It's about time," she said, coming around the side of her desk. "What is going on? I'm a nervous wreck, and I'm not even sure why!"

"I'm sorry, I had to go somewhere first." I placed my shoulder bag on the table reserved for Tara's book examinations. "I had to get this."

"Get what?" she asked, moving to my side.

"My piece of the Crimson Stone." I pulled the soapstone box from my bag and set it on the table.

Tara sucked in a sharp breath. "It's in there?"

I nodded. "It is."

Tara tore her gaze away from the box. "It's bad, isn't it?"

"Mr. Blackstone was killed, Tara," I said quietly as I set my top hat beside the soapstone box. I couldn't beat around the bush. She'd waited long enough. I put my hand on her arm.

"No!" Tara took a step backward, pulling away from me. Both hands flew to her face, hiding her nose and mouth. Her soft eyes were immediately wet.

"I'm sorry," I began. "It was this afternoon. I got here as soon as I could."

Tara gaped at me for another beat before dropping her hands. Lowering her head, she leaned against the table. Tears slipped down her delicate face.

I didn't make her ask the questions racing through her brain. "He was strangled, Tara. His housekeeper found him. The Salesman Court knows about it, and they've already closed ranks. Northgate is off-limits. Even to us."

She said nothing.

I continued, clearing my throat. "It's the Fringe. They also tampered with the North Door. I don't know exactly how or what they did, but it's a very bad thing."

Tara found her voice. "How do you know this? Did Jo tell you?" She raised her head.

I shook mine. "No."

"Templeton then?"

I nodded. "He came to my house."

Tara pushed off the table and swore. She crossed the room to the couch placed against the far wall and sunk into the cushions. Grabbing a pillow from the end, she pressed it against her face and sobbed.

My heart ached for Tara. She'd become close to the Record Keeper in the past several months. Mr. Blackstone was in awe of Tara's deep knowledge regarding the rare books they examined. He'd provided her with complete access to his library. The older man was thrilled to have such a bright protégé to share his passion for record keeping and research. Although, to be fair, Tara was no simpering student. More than once Blackstone remarked on Tara's sharp eye for detail as the two worked on improving the accuracy of the Empire's history.

And now, Mr. Blackstone was gone. Tara's anguish was genuine.

I walked over to the wide hutch where an electric tea kettle sat – a gift from Mr. Blackstone. I added fresh water to the kettle and turned it on. The water was boiling by the time I'd retrieved a teacup and picked out a calming blend made with lavender, chamomile, and mint. After pouring a cup to steep, I retrieved the soapstone box containing the piece of the

Stone. I brought it and the cup of tea to the coffee table by the couch. Tara sniffed, her eyes pink from crying.

"I'm sorry." She lifted a helpless hand. "I just..."

"I know," I said. "You had a special relationship with him." I moved between the coffee table and the couch, sitting on the edge of the table. I faced Tara, giving her knee a squeeze.

"Strangled?" Tara asked.

My lips pressed together, and I confirmed with a curt nod. "Yeah."

"Was it... Was it quick?" Tara's voice cracked.

"Oh, Tara, I don't know." Her question caused my chest to tighten. I reached for my friend and pulled her into a hug. She gave one last lone sob. I rocked her back and forth for a moment before releasing her. "Are you going to be okay?"

She nodded, reaching for the teacup I'd set on the table. She sipped and gave a shuddering sigh. "I'm sorry."

"Don't even," I told her. "Don't even apologize. I feel bad because I can't seem to cry."

Tara raised her head. "You haven't cried?"

"No, and I feel rotten. I feel like I *am* rotten.

It's as if…" I waved both of my hands uselessly in the air. I felt a flicker of fury skip across my face.

"How angry are you?" Tara's stare wouldn't let me go.

My shoulders felt tight, the storm inside my body building. "Angry enough to put an end to all of this once and for all."

"All of this?" she echoed. "You mean the Fringe?"

I nodded. "The Empire's danced around them since my father's death. They've tolerated the Fringe infiltrating the Salesman ranks. They know Sebastian St. Michel was behind my mother's kidnapping. They know his family protects him. And yet, the Empire continues to do nothing. I'm done with it."

"How are you going to do it?"

"I'm going to use this." I picked up the box, opening it and plucking the cloth-wrapped treasure from inside. I gently unfolded the fabric and cupped the piece of the Stone in my hand. A reddish glow pulsed once.

Tara studied the enchanted gemstone. She swallowed and sat up straighter, her shoulders squared. She lifted her chin. "Alright, I'm in."

❋ ❋ ❋

We texted Anne to let her know we were coming over. I wanted to tell her about Blackstone's murder face-to-face. He'd become a regular in her café, *The Daily Brew Too*, and I think he even had a teeny crush on her.

The message was brief, telling Anne we'd be there in a few minutes. I also took a moment to text Jack to let him know where I was going. I didn't mention door traveling to Pennsylvania because he wasn't aware I'd hidden my piece of the Crimson Stone at Aunt Sadie's. Since I was down and back in a flash, I didn't think it mattered. His texted reply indicated he was still driving and would send me an update later.

He also reminded me to keep him informed on what was going on. Yes, Jack. That was my plan.

Anne let us into her apartment, concern causing her brow to furrow. She asked us if we wanted anything to drink. Maybe tea? We said no.

"What's going on?" Anne asked as we sat down on her couch. She chose a plush chair across from us. "This morning after finishing my tea, I did a reading. The leaves presented themselves in the shape of a dog at the bottom of my cup." She looked from me to Tara and back to me again. "This usually means a friend is in need of help."

"You said you saw it this morning?" Tara asked.

Anne nodded. "Sometimes I'll learn right away who the friend is, but not always. I'm guessing it's one of you. Although, Emily, I tend to see the shape of a top hat in the leaves accompanying a message if you're involved."

"Anne," I said leaning forward. "Tara and I are here because we have some bad news."

Worry lined Anne's face. "What is it?"

There was no good way to say it. "Anne, Rene Blackstone was killed this afternoon at his home. It was the Fringe. The Empire knows – they've taken over Blackstone's house. Whoever did it also messed with the North Door. The Salesman Court has ordered it sealed."

Anne sat quietly, her hands folded in her lap. Her shoulders drooped. "We went to a movie together last week," she said softly.

I glanced at Tara. She blanched at Anne's

words. I stood and moved to Anne's side, leaning down to give her a hug. "I'm sorry," I whispered.

"How did they –?" Anne started to ask the question I was dreading even more.

"Strangled," I answered, stopping her as I pulled back.

"I know how you're feeling," Tara told our dear friend. "It's a shock. He was a good person, and this is not fair."

Anne's hands lifted uselessly. "How did you find out?"

"Templeton was at my house earlier. He told me," I said.

"Templeton was in Kincaid?" Anne seemed surprised.

"He door traveled straight into my house. Caused a scene, but in light of what happened…" My voice trailed off and I waved a hand. "Anyhow, he guessed the Empire wouldn't tell me. Turns out he was right. He wanted me to know, though. For obvious reasons," I finished, watching Anne carefully. Anne was a kick-butt kind of woman, but she seemed fragile now. "Do you want me to get you something to drink? Maybe water?"

Anne nodded. "Water would be good."

I retrieved a tall glass of water from the kitchen. When I returned, Tara had left the couch and pulled up a foot stool. She sat facing Anne. Both women had damp cheeks.

"Here you go," I said, handing the glass to Anne.

"Thank you." She took a sip. "I've known many people who've died because of the Fringe. People who were targeted – like your father, Emily – and others who were innocent bystanders."

I had a flash of Alfred Havers, the portly Salesman tapped to escort me to the Salesman Court last December. He was a friendly man who'd known my father. On the way to Court, it was my idea to stop at Anne's old café in Matar, *The Daily Brew*. While we were there, the Fringe attacked. Havers fought bravely but was shot and killed. I tried not to blame myself, but I always wondered if he would still be alive today if I hadn't made us stop at Anne's café.

"Like Mr. Havers," I said, swallowing the hint of a lump. I pushed the sad feeling aside and instead allowed myself to embrace the anger simmering inside me. "That's why I've got to make it stop."

Anne wrinkled her nose. "What are you saying?"

I inclined my head toward Tara. "We need to make a plan. I'm going after the Fringe. I have a piece of the Crimson Stone, which means I have some magic. But I need help."

"Wait," Anne said, setting the water on a wooden plant stand to her right, nudging an African Violet to the side. "You have a piece of the Stone? I thought... I thought Templeton took it from you? Did he bring it back?"

"Oh, trust me. Templeton is not going to give up his piece," I said. "The piece I have now is, well was, Justice Spell's."

Anne's green eyes widened. She was the one who made the delivery to Justice Spell last December after I separated the Stone into three pieces. "You can't tell me Justice Spell relinquished hers?"

"No, definitely not." I winced. "Um, remember how the piece Spell was keeping was stolen right out from under the Empire's nose?"

"Yes?" Anne glanced at Tara, who was suddenly wearing a big grin.

"Well, it sort of found its way into my shoulder bag when I escaped from the Fringe a few months ago. When I got home it was, um, there." I shrugged. "Maybe it was magic?"

"I don't think magic had much to do with it," Anne replied, giving Tara the side-eye. "Let me guess. Rabbit?"

I lifted my shoulders again. "He's pretty well-connected."

"But why did he steal Spell's? He had a piece." Anne was confused.

"He gave his to a Rabbit he calls the Tortoise," I told her. "You wouldn't happen to know who that is, would you?"

"Can't say I've ever heard of a Tortoise." Anne shook her head. "But Spell's piece? He told you he stole it?"

"Oh, no," I corrected Anne. I pulled the soapstone box from my shoulder bag. "He gave me this piece and I connected the dots to the theft of Spell's."

Anne watched as I slid the lid open and unwrapped the jewel. "Don't touch it," she cautioned.

"It's okay," I held my piece of the Crimson Stone in my palm. Again, a glimmer of red flashed from inside. "See?"

Anne inspected it. "Be careful. Even though it's not joined to the other three pieces, it still contains power."

"I know. I'm not exactly sure how much though. A while back, Lucie checked with her group and opinions were mixed on if it could be used in magic." Lucie Bellerose was a friend of Anne's. She'd become a trustworthy friend of mine when I crashed at her home earlier in the year. I'd learned over the summer Lucie's 'group' was really a coven. And as she explained, if you ask 10 witches how something worked, you'd get 10 different answers.

"I'm not surprised," Anne smiled wryly. Although Anne never came out and admitted anything, I was pretty sure she was some kind of witch, too.

Poking at the rock in my hand, I thought about what Templeton said when he extorted the original piece from me. "Templeton admitted even a piece of the Crimson Stone by itself contained power."

"He would know," Anne agreed.

"How much?" Tara rejoined the conversation. She'd been sitting silently – a good sign. Her imagination was probably darting around her big brain thinking about what we should do next.

"He said it was 'enough,'" I replied.

"Enough for what?" Tara asked.

"I don't know. I'm guessing 'enough' power for whatever his diabolical plans are." I rolled my eyes. "But speaking of Templeton, it was weird today. He door traveled into my house, but instead of leaving the same way, he said he had a car waiting for him at the curb. I assumed he came to see you." I motioned to Anne.

"No, he didn't come by, and I've been in the café all day before coming upstairs." Anne shook her head. "I didn't leave. And why wouldn't he door travel to me anyway? It doesn't make sense for him to take a car."

"Got me. Whatever. I'm not dealing with him right now." I looked at Tara. "So, we were thinking we need a plan. What if I –?"

"Don't write him off so easily," Anne interrupted. "He has a piece of the Crimson Stone. Once Rabbit finds this Tortoise person, he'll get his piece back. If you include Templeton in whatever it is you're going to do, maybe the three of you can form the Stone. And if it's magic you're hoping to do... well, Templeton's extremely adept, Emily. You know that."

I did. While I had 'magical abilities,' Templeton had magical *skills*. But as I've learned over and over, Templeton is only in it for himself, and I can't trust him. "Yeah, I know, Anne. But you also know he isn't going to help if it doesn't benefit him."

"You're sure of that?" Anne questioned.

"Yes."

"Well, I guess it doesn't matter right now. What are you going to do? What's going to happen now that..." Anne stopped talking. She put a hand to her chest and took a moment. When she was able, she spoke again. "What's going to happen now that Rene is gone?"

Tara and I fired a quick look at each other when Anne called Blackstone by his first name, but we didn't point it out. Instead, I told her I was going to take down the Fringe.

"Whew, Emily." Anne sat back in her chair. "It's impossible. You know that, right?"

"No, I don't believe it is." I'd rewrapped the piece of the Crimson Stone in its swatch of fabric and returned it to the soapstone box.

"Anne, I understand no one believes they can take down the Fringe, and I get it. And yeah, it's going to be next to impossible. But if I've learned anything since turning 30, so much *is* possible. I can door travel and handle magical items. I can use Whispering Flowers. I can sense things because of my door travel energy. I have The Book, which is spelled and can guide me. My mother is a Meta Muse and I've got to have something useful in me from her, too."

"Your magical ability," Anne nodded. "It must come from her line."

"Exactly. I have a lot in me." I pointed toward my own chest. "It's time I used it in a big way to cripple the Fringe. The Empire can't seem to do it – or maybe they don't *want* to do it. The Fringe has puppets in the Salesman ranks."

Anne listened patiently. "You're right, Emily. If anyone was uniquely qualified for the job, it's you. Well, you or…"

I was glad Anne didn't finish her sentence. I'd had enough Templeton to last me for two lifetimes. "Will you help us?"

"Of course, I will," Anne promised. "Tell me what you need me to do."

✱ ✱ ✱

The next hour was spent brainstorming. At Tara's request, Anne provided a large sheet of paper – an excellent use of wrapping paper – and a marker. We taped it to a wall in Anne's living room, the undecorated side facing us. Tara took the marker and wrote at the top of the paper: *Goal – Take Down the Fringe*. Underneath she drew four columns. The first column bore the header *Team*. The second, *Tools and Resources*. The third, *Known Fringe Members*. And finally, the fourth column she topped with *Challenges*.

Tara added information to each column. Under *Team* she wrote: Emily, Tara, Anne, Lucie, Rabbit.

"Add Jack and Tuesday," I directed. "I'm keeping Jack in the loop this time around."

Anne raised a winged eyebrow.

"How could I forget Tuesday?" Tara remarked as she wrote down the kind-hearted baker's name followed by Jack's. "Lydia?"

"No, let's keep her as far from this as possible," I said. "I can't risk losing her again. In fact, that's Jack's main duty. He's in charge of watching over her."

"Yeah, that's a part of hell we don't need to revisit," Tara agreed. "For *Tools and Resources*, I'm putting The Book and your piece of the Crimson Stone, Emily. Anne, you and Lucie are also resources because you're, um, *herbalists*." Tara giggled. She didn't make eye contact with Anne.

"Happy to assist," Anne replied.

"Obviously the Rabbit network is a great resource," Tara continued.

"Once we find Rabbit and get it activated," I said.

"I'm adding Jo as a resource," Tara said. "Because of her appointment to the Salesman Court, I don't think we can count on her as a team member. It's a conflict of interest."

"But we can trust her," I argued.

"Oh, definitely," Tara agreed. "But we can't put her into any compromising position either. Okay, next. *Known Fringe Members*? What's the guy's name again?" Tara paused with the marker hovering over the paper.

I spat it out. "Sebastian St. Michel."

"Got it." Tara added his name and pursed her

lips. "Who else?"

"Add Petrovich," Anne said. "Last I read in the Empire's official news, his trial was delayed again."

Tahl Petrovich was awaiting trial for murder and treason. He also tried to steal the Crimson Stone. We got it away from him when I used the gemstone and called on its magic for justice. He was arrested, but there had been several delays during his trial. I wish they'd find him guilty and be done with it. At least he was being held in jail.

"Anyone else?" Tara asked.

"I don't think I know any more names. I've dealt with my share of Fringe thugs, but I don't know exactly who they are."

"Okay, *Challenges*." Tara wrote down what she knew. "Getting a piece of the Stone from the Tortoise. Getting a piece from Templeton. Determining the Fringe's weakness, source of power, other member names. Oh, staying under the radar when door traveling – that's you, Emily. Um, I'm going to add finding Rabbit to this column, but I'm optimistic. Anything else?"

"Geez, we can stop adding to that column any

time now." I shook my head. We had a lot to overcome.

"It's alright. If we name them, we can deal with them," Tara replied as she wrote. "I'm adding access to Blackstone's library to the *Challenges* column. And I have a few books and letters Blackstone lent to me. I'll add them to the *Tools and Resources* column."

"Which reminds me. Templeton said any books you have from Blackstone's library should be kept secret. Don't tell anyone about them," I told her. "Not even the Empire."

"That was the plan," Tara said absently as she finished writing. She stepped back. "Let's noodle on this. It's getting late. We'll all feel fresher in the morning. We could meet at your house, Em?"

"Would it be okay if we met at *Pages & Pens* instead?" While I was determined to try and keep Jack in the loop, I worried our planning might go more smoothly if he wasn't hovering over us. Plus, there was my mother. She was not going to be happy about being dragged from her house to mine.

"Sure," Tara said. She capped the marker in her hand. "How early?"

"Eight. The less time I'm at home fending off my mother's questions, the better," I said.

"Anne?" Tara turned to our friend. "It's not exactly ideal for you because of the café."

"I have someone coming in at seven," she replied. "I can sneak away for an hour."

"Thank you," I said as I reached over and squeezed her arm. "I keep ending up in your debt."

"It's okay, Emily," Anne said. She gestured back toward our brainstorming on the wall. "But I think you can add another person to the first column, don't you?"

I shook my head but pointed toward the *Team* column. "Add Templeton," I directed Tara. "But put him at the bottom of the list."

CHAPTER 4

After Tara removed the wrapping paper from the wall and rolled it up, we said goodnight to Anne. She promised she'd send a message to our friend Lucie letting her know I'd be arriving on her doorstep soon. I encouraged Anne to keep her doors locked and to text me if there was anything strange. I didn't believe the Fringe would seek her out like Blackstone, but I couldn't be sure. After walking Tara back to *Pages & Pens*, I door traveled back to my house.

Jack sent a message saying he'd left Western New York with my mother in tow. He also texted that she was *not* happy about being spirited away from her home. He asked if I would make sure there was a bottle of gin chilling in the freezer.

Oh, boy.

After I put fresh sheets on the spare bed and well-worn pajamas on my body, I settled in on the living room couch with a notebook and my father's journal. I drew a smaller version of the brainstorming chart we started at Anne's. I hoped to add more to the *Tools and Resources* column. Right away I thought of *Petaling*, the local florist who carried both magical and nonmagical plants. I wasn't sure how they could help, but maybe they were a resource, too.

I tapped the page with my pencil eraser. Were there other local businesses we could go to? After my falling out with the Empire, my education lapsed and I hadn't learned of any additional places in Kincaid using Empire services. But if there were more, the fact the Fringe committed murder right here in Kincaid should concern them. Like me, they probably felt safer *outside* of the Empire. I wrote 'other businesses' under *Petaling*. I'd ask Anne to check with florists, Bernie and Trudy Bloom. They might know of other business owners we could ask for help if we needed it.

My phone dinged as a new text arrived. It was from my mother.

I'm in the car with Jack. He drives too fast. I'm not happy about this surprise visit you want me to make. We will talk about this when I arrive.

Oh, this would be fun. I blew out a long breath, adding my mother's name to the *Challenges* column.

Abandoning my notebook, I pulled The Book

onto my lap. I wanted to see if any new messages had appeared, but there was nothing. I'd have to wait.

I stared off into space, worrying a thumbnail between my teeth. I was at a standstill. I thought of my own 'magical abilities.' Was there anything there I could access now? The truth was, I knew precious little about what I could and couldn't do. Honestly, it was my own fault. After I lost the Empire's permission to door travel, and with my relationship with Jack on rocky ground, I let it go. Lucie and Anne were great about making sure I had access to their books, but I hadn't looked at any they'd lent me in a while. Maybe now would be a good time.

I retrieved a stack from my office. While upstairs, I checked on two of the Furious Furballs. Mystery was curled up on my bed, sound asleep. Mischief, princess that she was, stretched out in her kitty bed atop a tall set of drawers. Neither one bothered to lift a head. It's a tough life.

I spread the borrowed books out on the coffee table. There were several options to choose from, as well as a notebook of Lucie's scribblings she made during a recent year in France. She didn't talk about it much, but I knew she was there studying directly with some bigwig in the witchy world. I asked Anne about it, but she was unusually tight-lipped. She intimated it probably wasn't the easiest year for Lucie.

Lucie loaned me a slim volume on astral projection. She wondered if because of my ability to pull people into my dreams – disclaimer, 'people' equals only two: Jack and Templeton – if I'd be able to master astral projection. I like the idea of it, but I was also afraid of something so powerful. What if while I was out on an astral walk, something happened to my body?

Yeah, think about it.

Still, I wondered if my ability to pull someone into my dream could be counted as a resource for us? My first experience with dreamwork was with Templeton. He pulled me in and played with my head before we ever met. I paid him back the first time I traveled through the Empire. I did lose control during that particular dream, but I was stronger now. I was more confident.

I was also out of practice.

But I had time to kill.

I rubbed my hand on the back of my neck. What if I tried to pull Rabbit into a dream? It might be the fastest way to reach him, to tell him we were planning to take down the Fringe. I could ask him to find the Tortoise and get that piece of the Crimson Stone. We'd need it.

I was tired in body, but amped up in mind. Could I manage to pull it off? Deep down I knew I probably couldn't, but what did I have to lose? I could still try.

After shutting off a few lights, I made myself comfortable on the couch, pulling my feet up on the cushions and rolling onto my side. My cheek against the pillow, I closed my eyes. Outside I could hear the occasional car drive by, but mostly it was quiet. I allowed a deep sigh to roll over me and tried to let myself drift off.

The clock on the mantel ticked above my head. I zeroed in on the sound. My plan was to slip into a semi-dream state and push out my energy, looking for Rabbit. Previously, pulling someone into my dream was sort of an accident. This time I'd work to do it on purpose. If Templeton could do it, so could I. In fact, I remembered the look on his face when I brought him into my dream on the train. I controlled him. It felt good to turn the tables on the arrogant Salesman.

I wiggled my toes. Of course, Templeton figured out I wasn't actually on the train, and my dream didn't quite finish up the way I would've liked, but I'd learned a valuable lesson. It was important to keep centered and not get cocky. *It would be different with Rabbit,* I thought. I wanted to see him to *give* him information, not drag something out of him. I snuggled deeper against my pillow. With Templeton it was always like pulling teeth. We always had to do this stupid dance. It was tiring. *Yawn.* Really annoying, he was.

I fell asleep.

I did not draw Rabbit into my dream.

But I attracted another.

Oh, crap.

Groggily, I forced my body up into a halfseated position, my palm pressing into the cushion of the couch. Templeton stood in the middle of my living room, his arms crossed.

"Please tell me you door traveled into my house again," I groaned.

"I did not."

"Damn." I took a moment to check the room. It was slightly blurry at the edges of the wall. "I pulled you into my dream, didn't I?"

He snorted. "What do you think?"

"I didn't mean to," I defended myself.

Templeton switched on a lamp. "Then why did you call me here?"

"I didn't call you here! You were the last person I wanted to see." I swung my feet to the floor. "I was trying to bring Rabbit into the dream."

"Rabbit? Interesting." Templeton wandered over to the mantel. His fingertips paused over a picture of my mother. He lifted the frame and studied the photograph. "What were you thinking about when you were trying to bring Rabbit to you?"

I hesitated. "I'm not sure."

"You were thinking of me." He returned my mother's photo to its position before facing me again. He looked down his nose.

Gah, he was right. I didn't properly focus and look what I got: a snarky, pain-in-the-butt Salesman landing in the middle of my living room. Ignoring him, I roughly plumped up my pillow. "Whatever."

Standing beside the mantel, Templeton was closer to the couch. I didn't like the feeling of him standing over me, so I stood, skirting around the coffee table and putting it between us.

"You should invest in better nightclothes," he sniffed, contemplating my outfit.

I pointed a finger at him. "Stop looking at me. I don't need your fashion advice."

He muttered something under his breath and went back to browsing the photos on my mantel. I took the opportunity to appraise his attire. As usual, Templeton was well-dressed in black trousers and a gray dress shirt. The buttons at the top were undone. I had to assume his clothes were custom-made. No off-the-rack shirt fit that well. Not one scuff marred his black leather shoes. His top hat was missing, which was unusual – but if he were sleeping, he wouldn't be wearing it anyway. Wait, something wasn't adding up.

Why was Templeton dressed? If I could bring him into my dream, wouldn't it mean he was sleeping? Wouldn't he be in pajamas or something? A horrific thought filled my brain. Or wearing nothing at all if he slept in his birthday suit? I grimaced. Maybe he was only napping and hadn't turned in for the night.

"I can almost hear the questions echoing in your head," Templeton said. "What now?"

I didn't rise to the bait over the 'echoing' bit. "I want to know why you're dressed."

Templeton cut his eyes to me. "You would prefer that I not be?"

"Good grief, no," I answered. He drove me nuts. I headed toward the kitchen.

"I wouldn't do that if I were you," Templeton warned.

I hesitated. "Why?"

"Because you're not experienced enough to keep this environment stable." Templeton waved his hand indicating the living room. "You're not even maintaining this space properly and now you're moving away from your physical self. You'll make yourself vulnerable."

When I pulled Templeton into my dream last year, I'd made the same mistake. Okay, fine. I'll play along this time. I might learn something useful. I sighed.

"Tell me why you're dressed and not in pajamas, or whatever it is you sleep in. Why are you wearing this?" I wiggled my finger up and down at his clothing.

It took a moment, but Templeton sorted out what I couldn't put together. He smirked. "You think I'm sleeping, don't you?"

"Well, aren't you?"

"No, I'm not. You really should study the magic you're practicing," he tsked.

"But if you're not asleep, how can you be here in my dream?"

Templeton's eyes grew lighter, becoming almost translucent. "Take a seat," he directed. I opened my mouth to argue, but he cut me off. "If you want to learn something valuable from me, Emily, sit down and be quiet."

Following his order was the last thing I wanted to do, but curiosity won out. I chose the ottoman in front of Jack's Morris chair and sat down. "Let's hear it."

Templeton swiftly closed the space between us. Before I could stop him, he caught a lock of my hair between his long fingers. He held it in front of my face. "What is this called?"

I froze, resisting the urge to flinch. "Hair," I gritted out.

"Very good. And what is this?" Templeton

separated a strand from the others.

"Hair. A strand of hair." I still hadn't moved.

"Hair. And this?" He singled out another strand.

"Hair." I pulled back and he let go. "What's your point?"

"My point, you pitiful student, is each strand of your hair *is* hair. Your subconscious is similar in that there are slivers of it that can be diverted from where you are to another space. It's still your subconscious, but it's not your full subconscious. And it can be pulled into a practitioner's subconscious while they're doing dreamwork, if they know how to do it."

"Like me," I replied.

Templeton sneered before turning away. He paused to adjust his shirtsleeve. "I am here because I heard you and let it happen. I cannot be compelled by you."

I didn't fully believe him, but I wasn't going to argue. "So, what you're saying is you don't have to be sleeping to be brought into someone's dream? Or, at least have a piece of your subconscious be sucked into it?"

"Yes."

"But whoever is doing the dreaming, they're

still getting the full you? But like a copy?"

Templeton sighed. "Yes. The subconscious here with you now is equal in knowledge to what I know. Do we need to continue this lesson? Let me guess, you're one of those who learns by repetition."

"Sorry, Templeton," I shrugged. "Deal with it. You offered to play teacher." I stood back up and took a minute to put my thoughts together. Last year when I pulled Templeton into my dream, I remembered thinking he was on a date because of how he was dressed. I was still unsure of how things worked back then, and with what he told me, he very well could've been out on the town. Only a copy of his subconscious would've been summoned by my sleeping self.

Even as I wrapped my head around what Templeton told me, a concern was growing. Practitioners of magic who engaged in dreamwork could yank some of your subconscious being out of you at any time? It was terrifying. How often did this happen?

"Templeton, how many people can do this type of dreamwork?"

He regarded me coolly. "At present, only a

handful. You should learn to guard your mind, Emily. You wouldn't want unwelcome hosts bringing you into their subconscious parties."

"And how do I learn to do that?" I was frustrated. Why didn't anyone tell me about this before?

Templeton nosed through the books on magic sitting on the coffee table. He picked up the book on astral projection, flipping through. "This will give you basics on a companion practice – start there. I know Anne's lent you books." His eyes landed on Lucie's notebook. He snatched it up and paged through. "Hmm. Looks like the witch might be a good resource for you as well."

"She has a name," I said, reaching for the notebook and pulling it from his grasp. "I'll take that."

"Yes, Ms. Bellerose," he growled. "I owe her a visit."

"Yeah, I'm sure she'd love it." I stacked the books on magic on top of one another. This didn't go as planned. I needed Rabbit and instead I got Templeton and attitude. Okay, maybe I learned important information about dreamwork, but seriously, I had to endure

Templeton as some sort of cosmic payment for the knowledge.

I finished piling the books. I was getting tired, which was ironic since technically I was already asleep.

"Why do you need Rabbit?" he abruptly asked.

There was no way I was telling Templeton about my plans to go after the Fringe. I certainly wasn't going to tell him I needed Rabbit to find the Tortoise so I could get another piece of the Crimson Stone.

"I need to discuss private things," I replied.

His eyes narrowed. "I can make this dreamwork you're doing work to my advantage."

"Don't bother trying," I said as I sat down on the couch. I rearranged the pillow I'd used earlier. "I'm going to wake up now."

Templeton crossed his arms. "We're not done here. What needs to be discussed with Rabbit? What are you up to, Emily?"

Curling up on my side, I buried my face into the pillow. "Goodnight, Templeton."

"Emily!"

I started the internal chant we all practice when we realize we're having a bad dream and need to wake up: *It's just a dream, it's just a dream, it's just a dream.*

I sensed Mystery's cold nose on my cheek and startled awake. He hopped off the couch and hid under the coffee table. The lamp Templeton had turned on still lit the room, but I was now alone. Templeton – or at least that slice of him – was gone.

"Whew," I said, sitting up and reaching under the table for my silky black kitty. "I don't suppose you saw any of that?"

He sidestepped my fingers and mouthed a 'meow' in reply.

"Right. I didn't think so." I let him be, stretching as I stood. The mantel clock indicated it was close to 11. I didn't think I'd slept long, but I didn't know how dreamwork impacted time – or my sleep.

I squeezed through the narrow space between the couch and the mantel. I'd grab a rocks glass for Jack. He'd be home soon and craving a gin martini.

❖ ❖ ❖

Jack pulled into the driveway with my

mother right before 11:30pm. I met them at the door, holding it open as Jack carried in a suitcase and an overnight bag. He didn't stop to kiss me hello. "I'll take these upstairs."

I winced and let him pass. Then I faced my mother.

Lydia McKay Swift was a slender woman, with sparkling sapphire eyes. Her once strawberry-blond hair was now a loose mass of white waves. The curls were pulled back in a clip, but a few stray locks floated around her face.

She pouted. "I am very angry with you."

"Come on in, Mom," I answered. I gestured toward the kitchen table. "I know you're probably tired, but do you want tea?"

My mother glided across the floor and chose a chair facing me. "Please."

I nodded and set the kettle to boil. What I wouldn't give for one of Anne's potent sleepy tea blends. "It'll only be a minute."

William stalked into the kitchen and wound his tail around my mother's calf. She swooped him up into her lap and pressed her face against the top of his head. "She made me leave my home," she whispered loudly. "How's that for a daughter?"

"Passive-aggressiveness does not suit you." I shot her a dirty look.

William shot one back.

"Mom, did Jack tell you what's going on?"

She scratched behind William's ears. "Yes, a little. He said you'd tell me more." She paused before looking up. "He said Mr. Blackstone was killed. I'm sorry, Emily."

"Yeah." I placed the stainless-steel tea ball in the cup. I'd found a packet of chamomile tea – hopefully the drink would encourage my mother to go to bed. "Mom, I asked Jack to bring you here because the people who killed Mr. Blackstone are probably the same ones who took you when you were in the Empire."

My mother didn't appear to be surprised. Instead, she nodded. "I know there are problems."

"If you stay here for a couple of days, we might get a handle on everything." I poured hot water over the tea ball and set the cup on the kitchen table. I slid into the seat across from her.

"Oh, Emily," Mom said. "This isn't something that's going to be resolved quickly. I know this.

You don't need to sugarcoat anything for me."

I didn't agree with my mother, and there was no way I'd fill her in on details, but I nodded. "Will you agree to stay? Please? Then I can stop worrying about you being alone while we figure out what we should do."

She sighed but gave me one of her beautiful smiles. "I will stay for a few days," she promised. "But there comes a time when you need to let something go – whether it's a person, or a thing, or even an idea." She reached across the table and covered my hand with hers. "Know when to let go."

"I will," I nodded.

"Good." Mom patted my hand. "I'm going to take this tea upstairs to bed. We can talk more in the morning."

"Sure," I said. "Anything else you need?"

My mother picked up her purse and teacup. "No, I'm all set. I'll see you in the morning, dear."

"Well, let me know if you need anything. Wake me if you want," I told her as I followed her to the living room.

"I'll be fine," she said, leaning over and kissing my cheek. "Goodnight, my beautiful daughter."

"'Night, Mom." With my mother sent to bed, I'd take a few minutes with Jack before turning in myself. He sat in his Morris chair, his eyes closed.

"Please make me a martini," he begged.

I laughed. "I can do that. I owe you."

"You so owe me," he replied.

As I headed back toward the kitchen, a frame lying face down on the mantel caught my eye. I paused to set it upright. Jack and I grinned out from the photo.

CHAPTER 5

The next morning, I cooked French toast. I figured I had two people to make happy right off the bat and who could resist thick, fried bread smothered with real maple syrup? Jack was surprised but didn't say anything. I gave him two helpings of bacon.

Last night before bed, I'd filled him in on some of the details from the brainstorming session I'd had with Tara and Anne. I skirted around the whole 'I'm taking down the Fringe' conversation and instead explained how I planned on traveling to Lucie's as soon as I could. It would be a good place to establish a home-base of sorts. Her home was in Matar and the Fringe had a strong presence in the city. It was also the Empire's capital.

Jack admitted to his concern about me door traveling without the Empire's permission. For the most part, Jack was a rule follower. While he was no fan of the Empire, he was worried I might be punished for flagrantly ignoring my grounding. I pointed out the worst they could do was ban me from the Empire. I think secretly Jack wouldn't mind if that was the fallout for what I was about to do.

Still, he'd rather I not get involved. I reminded him again I already was.

My mother drifted downstairs. She'd changed out of her nightclothes and wore a long, green tunic dress over cobalt-colored tights. She carried several sheets of music paper and set them on the kitchen table before swiping the last piece of bacon.

"Are you hoping to work on something today, Lydia?" asked Jack as he eyeballed the stack of paper.

"I am. And if I can't work from home…" She gave me a pointed look.

"What are you working on, Mom?" I asked, adding a couple of pieces of French toast to a plate and setting it on the table. "This is for you. More bacon's on the way."

"I hope I'll be working on a piece I'm writing for the cello," my mother said. She took a seat and poured syrup on her toast. "But I'll have to see if I can rent one from the music store. What's it called? *Spring Board* or something? The one with the nice men who hand out fudgesicles."

"*Sounding Board*," I corrected. I glanced at Jack. He did not appear to be happy with this announcement. "But there's no guarantee they'll have one."

"Well, we'll have to find one," she answered. "I have a cello at home, but you want me here." She waved her hand and offered up a smug smile.

I turned to Jack. "Could you –"

"I can't this morning" my boyfriend stopped me. "I have classes until noon." He didn't look sorry.

"Then I'll borrow your car," Mom shrugged.

"No!" Jack and I both spoke at the same time.

"Emily, I will not have my work interrupted," she admonished. "If I must give in to your wishes for me to be here, you have to give, too. It's a two-way street."

"Fine," I sighed, flipping the bacon in the frying pan. "But if they don't have one, you'll have to go without."

"No," she said, shaking her head. "I can't. I must complete this composition."

My mother is what's known as a Meta Muse. I'd come to learn there are three levels: Minor Muse, like my plump little friend Tuesday, a baker who lives in the Empire; Major Muse, like my mother's cousins, Minerva and Aster; and Meta Muse, like my mother.

Minor Muses focus on something at the niche level. Take Tuesday, for example. She inspires people to bake and bakers to be even more creative. Her creations bring sweetness to the world around her. Major Muses like Minerva and Aster are also specialists, but their realms are broader. For instance, Aster's influence is in the botanical world, but she inspires more than the growth of flowers and plants. Her flower power stretches into conservation, ecology, farming – anything having to do with plant life. Even activism could be a result of Aster's power. Those tree-sitters protecting majestic redwoods in California are motivated by Aster the Major Muse. She also empowers love and comfort through bouquets and arrangements.

My mother, however, inspires the biggest domain. As a Meta Muse, she inspires everyone.

Artists in particular feel my mother's power coursing through them. Whether they're painters, musicians, writers, dancers, sculptors – you name it – they seem to tap into the well she fills with her power. But it's not limited to 'artsy types.' No, my mother's well can be visited by anyone. And she keeps it full for others by carrying out her own creative pursuits.

My mother never told me she was any kind of a muse. Why would I even think such a being existed? But I know now how special she is. And I knew she needed to continue to compose this music.

I transferred the cooked bacon to a plate, setting it on the paper towel to drain. The chances of *Sounding Board* having a cello available to rent were small. If I wanted to keep my mother in one place, and Jack's head from exploding, I'd have to find someone to help us out.

Placing the plate of bacon on the table between my mother and Jack, my attention was drawn to the envelope I'd pulled from my bag after visiting Aunt Sadie. Bingo.

I looked at Mom. "Actually, I know a guy."

* * *

The phone call I made to Kirby was short and strange, but he said he'd have a 'nice cello for your Ma' at my front door in an hour. I asked how much the service would cost and he laughed. He said if it was for a relative of Sadie from PA, it was good enough for him. I briefly thought about asking for the protection Sadie suggested, but decided the cello was as far as I was willing to go. For now.

I checked the time. I had 15 minutes before I was to meet Tara and Anne at *Pages & Pens*.

"Are you coming right back?" Jack asked as I packed my shoulder bag. We stood in my office while I tried to decide if I should take my top hat. On one hand I felt like I should, but on the other, I didn't need it to door travel. I shoved it into my bag anyway.

"I'm thinking of going straight to Lucie's afterward," I answered. I kept my eyes locked on my shoulder bag as I made the last few adjustments. "But I can always come back later."

Jack blew out a breath and shook his head. "Why do I think that's not going to happen?"

"I'll let you know either way." I touched his cheek. "Once I'm in the Empire, I'll have Lucie message you through the Empire's service." I went for levity. "We'll use code, something like, the pirate is on the island."

Jack didn't smile. "Let me know what's going on. I don't like this. I'm hoping once you get there… I don't know. Maybe someone will be arrested for Blackstone's murder and you'll come right back home."

My heart ached. He was trying so hard, but it never worked out like he wanted. I kissed him softly. "Maybe. Maybe we'll get a break this time."

He nodded knowing I was only placating him and held me tightly to his chest. "Please be safe."

* * *

With my top hat and The Book buried in my shoulder bag, I traveled through my bedroom closet straight through the front door leading into *Pages & Pens*. It was eight o'clock on the nose. A tapping on the door behind me signaled Anne's arrival. I unlocked it and she stepped inside.

"Hey," I said, taking the tray of coffee she held in her hand. "This is great."

"I figured we all could use extra fuel this morning." Anne's eyes were bloodshot. I wondered how well she'd slept.

"I'm guessing Tara's in the back," I said. "I walked in ahead of you."

"Oh, I didn't see you?"

"Think about it."

Realization spread across her face. "Ah, a little unauthorized door travel?"

"Yup."

Anne held the door to the back room open for me. Inside, Tara was standing on a ladder pulling down a box. She glanced down. "You're on time. Perfect. Here." She held the box toward us.

"You shouldn't climb a ladder with no one around," Anne scolded, taking the box. "If you fell, no one would know."

Tara grabbed another white box from the top of the cabinet. She noted the tray of coffee I'd set on the table. "It's fine. Don't worry about me. Ooh, did you bring coffee?"

"Lattes." Anne took the second box.

When Anne turned away, Tara waggled her eyebrows at me. There was nothing wrong with Anne's lattes, but she'd yet to achieve the level of latte bliss you'd find at *The Green Bean*.

"Even better," I said to Anne. I sent Tara a

dirty look.

Tara descended the ladder. "I took the books I had from Blackstone's to my apartment, but these boxes contained letters he wanted me to sort. I thought I'd go through them and see if there was anything important."

"Who are they from?" I asked, sipping my latte. Anne knew how I liked mine: plain, regular milk, whipped cream.

"I'm guessing most of them will be official letters from the Empire, but a few of them include correspondence from Blackstone's predecessor."

It was hard to imagine a Warden of the North Door other than Blackstone, but it made sense. He obviously was not the first. "Do you know anything about the person who was before him?"

"No. It didn't come up." Tara took the lid off one of the boxes. "Don't get your hopes up. This might only be a bunch of bureaucratic blah blah blah. But I'll let you know if there's anything useful here."

"Maybe we'll get lucky," I said. "I'm hoping to head out to Lucie's when we're done."

"I sent a message through the service last

night letting her know you'd be heading into Matar," Anne told me.

"Great. I think it's the best place to go. I thought about Tuesday's, but with the bakery it might be too chaotic," I said. "Plus, Matar is a good place to be. I'm hoping I can get a message to Rabbit."

"You haven't heard from him since spring?" Anne asked.

"Not a peep. But that's okay. He knew where he could find me if he needed to."

"I can imagine he wanted to give you space," Anne continued. "After the trouble with your mother."

I nodded. "Yeah, but if it weren't for Rabbit…" I shuddered. "He's another one I owe."

"Rabbit cares deeply for you." Anne's fingertips brushed my arm. "He was close to your father."

"That night in Matar," I began. "When all the Rabbits swarmed into the warehouse, it was scary. I was a little afraid of them. Not Rabbit," I quickly added. "But the whole… Rabbitness of it all."

The Rabbits had descended on the warehouse where the Fringe held me captive.

Everyone ran, but one Fringe member was left behind – the man responsible for two killings. The Rabbits beat him within an inch of his life.

I had to admit, he deserved it.

Anne set her coffee cup on the table. "Rabbits learned they must protect their own, Emily. The Empire hasn't always been good to them."

"It's like they're second-class citizens or something," I agreed. "I don't get it."

"I'm sure there are many layers," Anne said. "But the Empire has always wanted what the Rabbits figured out on their own: technology."

"Yeah," Tara chimed in. "How come the Rabbits can text, but no one else can?"

"It's not something they talk about," Anne answered. "And please, I'm no expert on these things, but for the Empire to monitor the door travel of its Salesmen, they need to make certain sacrifices. The 'system' they put in place to track who is coming and going completely interferes with the same technologies those phones use. The Empire doesn't even bother to put up cell towers because they're useless."

"What about satellite phones?" Tara asked.

"The Empire doesn't allow for satellites – that I know of," Anne added. "Like I said, I'm not an expert. Many things end up being hard-wired: the Empire service phones, the Empire internet system, cable TV, and so on. Car radios are a bit different. They have a longer wavelength than cell phones. A few stations are permitted to broadcast in the Empire."

"But the Rabbits use their phones for texting," I said.

"Yes, and it drives the Empire nuts because they can't figure it out and they can't stop it," Anne replied.

"The Fringe would like this technology."

"Yes, they would."

❈ ❈ ❈

Tara had spread out the paper we used the night before to brainstorm. We stood around the table reviewing our ideas from the day before.

"Add *Petaling* to the *Tools and Resources* column," I instructed. "Other businesses, too. Anne, would you take the lead on reaching out to local people who might use the Empire's services? Find out if they've heard anything?"

"I can do that," she answered. "Are you comfortable telling people what you're planning?"

"Good point," I said. "How about letting them know about Blackstone's murder if they're unaware and then kind of feel them out. Maybe ask them if they have any idea of what they'd do if the Fringe brought the battle out of the Empire and into Kincaid."

Anne nodded. "I can do that."

Tara put the new items into the column. "What else?"

"Add my mother to the *Challenges* column," I said.

"Yeah," Tara said as she wrote Lydia in the fourth column. "How'd it go?"

"About as good as you'd expect. I have a feeling Jack is going to develop a stress headache today."

"I'll make sure I bring her to the café for at least one day this week," Anne said. "She talked about adding a mural to the back wall in the dining area. At the very least I can get her sketching something."

"That would be great, Anne," I said. "And she'd like doing it."

"And why don't I bring her here?" Tara chimed in. "Let's put her to good use and have her go through those two boxes of Empire correspondence."

I was surprised. "You think that's a good idea?"

"I do," Tara said. "She'll be easier to keep in Kincaid if she feels like she's helping."

Tara had a good point. "Can you grab her today? She's planning to compose something on a cello and Jack might be ready for a break later."

"Consider it done. I'll tell her I'm ordering in lunch and need her here to help."

My loyal friends – what would I do without them?

"Emily?" Anne interrupted. "I know you have the start of a plan, but even after you find Rabbit – and assuming you get another piece of the Crimson Stone – exactly how are you going to take down the Fringe?"

And that was the question.

Tara tapped on the table, her finger pointing to the third column. "This guy. Sebastian. Start with him. Find out if he's the puppet master or who's pulling his strings. That's where you start. It's one of two things, Emily. Either he was going rogue within the Fringe and wanted the Crimson Stone for himself, or he's at the top – all by himself or sharing the power."

"The name St. Michel is synonymous with old money and power in Matar," Anne added. "I don't know Sebastian or who his parents are, but if he's a Salesman, at least one of his parents is, too. Find out who it is and where their interests lie."

"I wonder if Jo knows?" I sipped my coffee. "But before I tap her for help, I'll see if Rabbit can find out – if I can find him."

"Where are you going to start?" Tara asked.

"I've been giving it some thought," I said. "After I get to Lucie's and fill her in, I'm going to door travel to the place where the Rabbits held their bonfire." Tara and I were guests at a Rabbit gathering in the Empire countryside. We enjoyed an evening of good food and dancing to the mysterious hang drum music. It was a night of peace in a crazy journey chasing after my mother.

"You're hoping to find Rabbits?" Tara asked.

"Yup. I figure I can door travel in by way of the outhouse door, look around, and if no one is there, head back to Lucie's."

"And if Rabbits are there?"

"I'll explain who I am and how I need to find Rabbit," I finished.

Tara hesitated. "You think it will be safe? Showing up there uninvited?"

"It'll be okay," I assured Tara. I looked to Anne. "Right?"

She chewed on her lower lip. "I think so, Emily. Daniel was a friend to the Rabbits, and they know your mother was falsely accused of killing one of their own. Rabbit cares for you. I think they'll be okay with you showing up unannounced – if they're even there."

"Feel better?" I asked Tara.

She nodded. "I guess. Well, since you're heading into Rabbitland, if you see *my* favorite bunny, tell him I'm ready for another date."

❋ ❋ ❋

The beginnings of a plan in place and my bag on my shoulder, I said goodbye to Anne and Tara and door traveled from *Pages & Pens* right into a coffee shop in Matar called *Coffee Cove*. I figured it was a good spot to land. It was within walking distance of Lucie's brownstone. I didn't want to be rude and door travel straight into her home.

The sunny weather in Matar cast everything in a golden glow. You couldn't beat autumn light. I sipped my new latte and hustled to Lucie's townhouse.

As I approached the stairs leading from the brick sidewalk up to Lucie's front door, I saw a familiar figure waving at a black sports car with tinted windows as it pulled away from the curb. I couldn't see who was driving the vehicle, but I recognized the woman on the sidewalk: Lucie.

As the car rolled slowly down the street, Lucie's eyes landed on me and she broke into a broad smile. "Emily! What are you doing here?"

"I'm here to see you," I said, casting one last look at the sexy car as it disappeared around a corner. Porsche? I wasn't an expert, but it was an impressive set of wheels. Lucie was hanging with some interesting people these days.

I turned back to my friend, scanning her for clues. Her hair was a tad mussed up and she looked tired. "I need a place to stay for a few days. Anne sent a message through the service, but you might not have gotten it yet."

Lucie shook her head, her cheeks coloring. She cleared her throat. "No, I'm just getting home. It's the one thing I miss now that I'm back in the Empire. You think I could convince Rabbit to hook me up with his network?"

I laughed as we climbed the steps to her front door, my hand skimming the top of the wrought iron railing. "Nonstop messages? No way, you wouldn't want that."

"You're probably right. I'll keep embracing the phone-free world," she said, unlocking her door. It was painted black, with a celestial brass door knocker gracing the center. After waving her hand once and mumbling a few words, she held it for me, inviting me inside. I stepped into the foyer with its black and white spiral-tiled floor.

"Come on into the kitchen," she said, closing the front door and locking it behind us. She slipped off a jacket as she walked to the back of her home. "Have you eaten? I can make us breakfast."

"I'm pretty good," I said. "I cooked French toast earlier, but more coffee would be great." I lifted the *Coffee Cove* to-go cup I held in my hand. "This is only the fourth coffee I've had today."

Lucie chuckled and motioned to the barstools parked in front of her counter. "Have a seat, I'll start a pot. It won't take long, and you can tell me why you're here. I'll check for Anne's message later."

I filled Lucie in on what had happened since Templeton's uninvited visit. She didn't know Blackstone very well but was shocked and saddened to learn of the Record Keeper's gruesome death. She thought she might've met him when she visited Anne's café. His name was familiar to her.

"How horrible," she said as she poured milk into her coffee and stirred it with a spoon. "The Empire has got to do something."

"They haven't and they won't," I said as I started on my fifth cup of coffee for the day. "But someone has got to stop them. It might sound crazy, Lucie, but I'm going after the Fringe. I'm hoping you'll be on board to help me bring them down."

Lucie said nothing but rubbed her hand on the back of her neck as she stared off into the distance. The silence ate away at me after a minute.

"Well?" I prompted, drawing her back to our conversation.

"I understand why you want to do this," she said. She dropped her hand back to her coffee, touching the cup handle.

"And?"

Lucie abandoned her coffee cup and reached for both of my hands instead. She pulled them between us and leaned on the counter, running her thumbs over the backs. "What you're going to try to do is next to impossible, Emily. It's going to be dangerous, and people will get hurt. Maybe even worse. You don't have the Empire on your side anymore and who knows who you can trust. This isn't simply an uphill battle, it's borderline hopeless."

My heart felt crushed. "And you won't help me?"

Lucie gave my hands a squeeze before releasing them. "Don't be silly. You can count on me. But I'm going to be the voice of reason, Emily. Since that first night in the garden, when we shared your spellcasting, I've felt a kinship of sorts with you. Think of me as your magical big sister. I'm with you all the way, but I'm going to speak up when I think you need to hear something. I won't sugarcoat things."

"I can handle that," I answered, relief washing over me. "In fact, I wouldn't have it any other way."

"Good. Now, I hope you don't mind, but I'm starving."

* * *

"Who is he?" I asked as Lucie rummaged around in a cupboard for cereal. She rolled her eyes and shook her head.

"It's nothing." She avoided looking at me as she fought the smile threatening to curve her lips.

"Why don't I believe you? Look, it wasn't much of a walk of shame this morning," I teased over the rim of my cup. "But I'm guessing you put that outfit on yesterday. At least it's me asking. If Tara were here, she'd be all over you for the blow-by-blow and you wouldn't get a moment's peace until she squeezed every last naughty detail out of you."

Lucie laughed. "She is persistent." The two had met during one of Lucie's visits to Kincaid over the summer. I could tell she got a kick out of my best friend's sometimes naughty sense of humor.

"And?"

"So are you." Lucie dumped granola into a bowl and added milk.

"Oh, come on," I continued. "You can't tell me you weren't on a date last night. And maybe it lasted until today? He must be the driver of the mystery car this morning."

Lucie tossed her head back and contemplated her kitchen ceiling. She sighed and shook her head. "Fine. His name is Basha."

"Basha?"

Lucie lowered her chin and glared at me. "Yes, Basha. Happy?"

"For now." I laughed. Tapping the side of my coffee cup, I studied my friend. "Hey, is your name short for Lucille? As in, you took a fine time to leave me?"

"No, it's simply Lucie," she said, firing off another dark look in my direction. "My witchline is French. Well, French among other things, I'm sure. Anyhow, Lucie with an I-E is the French version of L-U-C-Y."

"It's a pretty name," I told her. "Now, let's get back to your date."

Lucie groaned as she chewed a bite of her cereal.

"Where did you go last night?" I asked.

"*Zenith.* It's a restaurant downtown."

I swallowed a mouthful of coffee. "No kidding? I know *Zenith*. Pretty trendy."

Lucy gave me a quizzical look. "You've eaten there?"

"No, but my mother has." I thought about when she gallivanted all over the Empire while I chased her for days. She'd dined at *Zenith* on one of those nights. "Small world, or weird coincidence, or something like that."

"It was nice. It was my first time there." Lucie looked down at her cereal and took another bite.

"Is he a good kisser?" I asked. I could channel Tara's doggedness when necessary.

"Geez, Emily," Lucie protested. "You're not going to give me a break, are you?"

"If I were going to ask what I'm really wondering... you are still wearing yesterday's clothes," I pointed out.

She held up a hand. "Yes, he's an excellent kisser. And that's all I know."

"Excellent, hmm?" I rubbed my palms together. "Ooh, tell me more."

"Very excellent. Look, after dinner we took a ride out of the city. He knew this place where it's far enough from Matar and you can get away from the city lights. We could see the stars in the sky. He took me to a friend's cabin with this glass atrium on the side. You know, overstuffed patio couches. Stuff like that."

"Uh huh, and then what?" It was mid-morning.

"And then we…" Lucie lifted her hand. "We cuddled under a blanket and counted the stars through the glass above us. Talked. Kissed. Fell asleep."

"Wow," I replied. "That's still kind of a big deal."

Lucie stirred her spoon thoughtfully through her cereal. "It is."

BAM! A crash sounded on the other side of the kitchen's pantry door. We both flinched, but Lucie whirled around, her hands out as her fingers curled. She walked slowly, leaning forward and pressing her palms against the space in front of the door.

"Be careful," I whispered, rounding the counter to stand at her side.

"No, it's okay. It did its job," she said.

"What do you mean?"

"I mean the ward in place kept whatever wanted in, out."

Knuckles rapped on the front door and we both jumped a second time.

"What the hell?" I hissed at Lucie. I didn't like this. Something was still trying to get in.

Lucie's face hardened. "I'm guessing that's our uninvited visitor." She stomped to the front of her home with me close behind on her heels. She peeked through the side window to see who stood on her stoop. "I should've guessed," she huffed.

"Who?"

Lucie opened the door to reveal a surly-looking Salesman. "What do you want, Templeton?"

CHAPTER 6

"Your manners need some work," Templeton criticized. He evaluated Lucie's rumpled outfit. "Why are your clothes wrinkled?"

"I have an aversion to ironing," Lucie snapped back. "Why are you here?"

Templeton spoke through clenched teeth. "May I come in?"

"No."

Templeton cut his eyes to me. "I need to speak with you."

"So speak," I answered around Lucie.

"In private." Templeton's normally unruffled demeanor was unraveling. His cheeks grew pink and his chest rose as he took a deep breath.

"You can say whatever it is you need to say in front of Lucie," I told him. This was fun. Lucie managed to block Templeton from door traveling into her home! I liked it when he wasn't in control of a situation. I put my arm around Lucie's shoulders. "She's my magical sister."

"She's your... your... what?" Templeton sputtered, then waved his hand. "Never mind! I am not standing outside here on the stoop like an errand boy." He spun around and stormed down the steps.

"Oh, good grief," Lucie sighed. She lifted her palm and mumbled a few words. I felt the air around us grow lighter. "You can come in, Templeton."

The Salesman took a moment to compose himself on the brick sidewalk before climbing the stairs back to the stoop. Lucie and I each stepped aside, allowing Templeton to saunter in between us.

"And what do you say?" I prompted. I was still giddy over how Lucie got the better of him.

He ignored me. Instead, he faced Lucie. "You patched the crack in the ward. It took you long enough."

Lucie hesitated, her eyes scanning Templeton's face. Her mouth twisted to the side. "This isn't the first time you've tested it, is it? You've slipped in through it before."

His smile mocked her. "It is not the first time I've tested it."

The sound of glass shattering somewhere deep inside the townhouse startled me. Lucie didn't seem to notice – or if she did, it didn't show.

"Don't attempt to come into my home uninvited again, Templeton," she said evenly. "Emily might tolerate your bad behavior, but I will not. You do not want to cross me."

Lucie turned and stalked down the hall leading to her kitchen.

For the first time, I sensed something dark in my friend. There was a hint of rage swimming deep in her eyes I'd never witnessed. Lucie always seemed cool-headed. I glanced at Templeton to gauge his reaction. He'd dropped his smug expression and watched warily as Lucie disappeared around the corner.

"Well," I cleared my throat. "This way." Templeton followed as I retraced my steps back to the kitchen. Because I didn't know what else to do, I motioned to the bar stools. "Do you want to sit?"

"No." He didn't take his eyes off Lucie. She'd rolled up her sleeves and started to wash the few dishes in her sink. She wouldn't look at either of us.

"Templeton?" I snapped my fingers.

He gradually brought his attention back to

me. "Why are you here?"

"No," I replied. "Why are YOU here?"

"You know what I'm asking. Why have you violated your grounding by door traveling into the Empire?" Templeton pinned me with a penetrating stare. "Last time we spoke you were looking for Rabbit and now you're in Matar. What are you playing at, Emily?"

"I'm not playing at anything," I objected. "I've had enough of the Fringe hurting people I care about. People like Blackstone. No one seems willing to do anything about it, so I'm going to put a stop to it."

He raised an eyebrow. "You're not serious? You think you're going to –"

"Yes. Yes, I do," I interrupted. "And I want my piece of the Crimson Stone back, Templeton. This is bigger than you. I need the Stone to take them down."

"It's not your piece of the Stone. It hasn't been since last spring," Templeton said. "And even if you find Rabbit and he gives you his piece, it's still not enough. The third piece is missing – at least that's what the Empire claims."

A ripple of joy bubbled up in my chest, threatening to escape. I shrugged as I took a seat back at the counter. "I'll talk to Spell."

Templeton digested our exchange, rubbing his chin with his thumb and forefinger. Oh, crap. I looked down at the counter's surface and scrubbed at an imaginary spot with a fingertip.

"You already have it," he realized. I felt Lucie's scrutiny fall upon me as well. I shook my head, but Templeton knew he was right. "Somehow you acquired Spell's piece of the Stone."

I continued to poke at the counter. Perhaps Anne was right. Maybe Templeton would be on our team. If he knew we could bring all the pieces together, maybe there was a chance. "We've seen what the Crimson Stone can do, Templeton. You saw I could use it. If we work together –"

"Work together?" Templeton scoffed. I raised my head. "There's no working together, Emily. The battle between the Empire and the Fringe does not concern me. If you want to go on some quixotic adventure, you'll be on your own. Even with all the stunts I've witnessed you pulling in the past, this idea is completely irrational. Don't go looking for trouble."

"You once told me you were the most powerful Salesman in the Empire," I came back at him. He was horribly selfish! My voice grew louder. "Step up, Templeton. Put your money where your mouth is. Unless... Unless you're not as great as you pretend to be. That's it, isn't it? You're a sham! You're clever, and maybe better at door travel than some, but your power isn't all it's cracked up to be, is it?"

Templeton snorted. "If you want to believe –"

"Or are you a coward?" Lucie asked softly.

The room immediately grew still as Lucie's words hung in the air. I waited for Templeton to explode.

But he didn't make a sound. I watched as his body stiffened, his arms tensing at his sides. His fingers flexed once, and he headed toward the door leading from Lucie's kitchen into a formal dining room she rarely used. As his fingers grazed the doorknob, the door swung open and drew him through in a flash. Lucie and I turned around as the angry Salesman stepped right back into the kitchen from the pantry. Templeton hesitated, his eyes fixed to the floor, his jaw tight. The three of us froze – Lucie held her breath along with me. When

Templeton moved again, he marched past us out of the kitchen and toward the front of the brownstone. A moment later, we heard Lucie's front door open and slam shut, causing the walls of the entryway to shudder and the light fixtures to rattle.

Lucie's mouth hung open. I shook my head. What happened?

❅ ❅ ❅

"He door traveled through that door, and ended right back in the kitchen," I said to Lucie, pointing first at the door leading to the dining room, then to the pantry door. "Something isn't right. Is it because of the wards you put up?"

"No, I lowered all of them for him when he was on the stoop." Lucie shook her head. "My wards have nothing to do with what we saw."

I ran my hands through my hair. "That was freaky, Lucie. He was seriously angry. I could feel it rolling off him."

"Should I block him again?" Lucie asked. "I can reset the wards."

"Your call," I said. "On one hand, I hate it

when he suddenly shows up, but on the other, he brought me the news about Blackstone's murder. He's useful sometimes, but it comes with a price."

"What is his interest in you anyway?" Lucie finished her dishes and hung the damp towel on a hook to dry. She picked up her abandoned coffee cup and took a swig, grimacing when she realized it was now cold. "I mean, what's the point?"

"It's pretty much the Crimson Stone," I said. "When we didn't have it, we were trying to beat each other to it. Then when I had the first piece, he wanted it."

"And got it," Lucie remarked.

"Yeah, I know," I grumbled.

"And now you have another?" Lucie asked.

"Maybe."

"I'm thinking that's a yes."

"It's a yes. Rabbit stole Spell's piece and gave it to me."

Lucie whistled. "Stealing from the Empire is pretty bold."

"He thought if Templeton took the piece I had, I should get another. Balance and all."

"And the third piece is still with this Tortoise

guy?"

"Yup, unless Rabbit found him and got it back," I said.

"What do you think the chances are of that?"

I shrugged. "Pretty slim with my luck."

"Speaking of Rabbit," Lucie said. "How are you going to reach him this time?"

"There's this spot sort of south of Matar where Tara and I went to a Rabbit bonfire. I'm hoping to catch some Rabbits there and have them send a message."

"And if no one is there?"

I blew out a breath. "Wandering the city?"

Lucie laughed. "Is this the best you can do?"

"Pathetic?"

"Very. I'm putting in time at *Coffee Cove* this afternoon. It's rare, but sometimes a Rabbit will stop in for something to drink. I'll ask the staff working the front to keep a lookout as well," Lucie added. "If one shows, we'll see if they'll send a message across the network."

Lucie read Tarot cards in a room at the coffee shop. She usually had a steady stream of clients and the shop's owner benefited from her popularity. Her services weren't cheap, but she was worth it – according to her repeat customers. I'd asked her to read the cards for me, but she'd refused, telling me it was too hard to read for friends. She could, but she didn't always enjoy helping people close to her understand what the cards represented. Sometimes people didn't like what Lucie had to say.

I asked if she read the cards for herself. She simply raised a shoulder and said sometimes. Then she changed the subject.

"That would be helpful. It's a busy shop," I said. I had another thought. "I could also try Tuesday's bakery. I think the Rabbits know it's a place where they can always get a big sack of food to go." Tuesday loved to feed the Rabbits.

"We're putting together a plan," Lucie nodded. She glanced at the clock on her stove. "Listen, I'm going to grab a shower. The wards will let you door travel in and out of here. Feel free to come and go as you please."

"Thanks." I hesitated. "And what about Templeton?"

Lucie considered my question. "I'll leave them down. He'll be able to get in, too. For now."

❋ ❋ ❋

Before I door traveled to the place where the Rabbits held their bonfire, I asked if Lucie would also pass a message to Jack through Anne, letting him know I was safely in Matar and starting my search for Rabbit. I was nervous about using the Empire service to send Jack a message directly. I didn't want to alert anyone – official or otherwise – to where I was staying.

After witnessing Templeton's odd experience with door traveling through Lucie's dining room door, I decided it would be better if I used the closet. I grabbed my shoulder bag – top hat and The Book inside – and stood in front of the door.

My recent experience with door traveling from my home in Kincaid to Matar was seamless. Even now the energy felt good as it rolled through me. I didn't know if I'd be successful in locating a group of Rabbits to help me find my dear friend, but I was confident I could get to the peaceful spot.

I only had one option for door traveling into the space in the woods: the outhouse. It wasn't bad. It was more like those buildings found in state parks. They even had showers – that only poured out cold water. I'd door travel in, hopefully find Rabbits making camp, explain what I needed them to do, then I'd door travel right back to Lucie's. If there were no Rabbits, I'd door travel to Tuesday's bakery in Vue and tell her about my search.

Lucie was right. It was good to have a plan.

I rolled my shoulders, breathing deep into my diaphragm and centering. I closed my eyes and pushed my energy toward the closet door, picturing the night I danced with the Rabbits, our hands above our heads as we twirled around the fire. I remembered the mesmerizing sound of the hang drums, the rhythm building in my brain like it had in the air that night. I even allowed myself to think of Templeton's appearance there and his message about finding my mother with her cousins. I let all my feelings about the night dance over my skin.

The door buzzed in front of me. In my mind, I saw it open wide, the travel energy sucking my body straight on through to the other side.

✸ ✸ ✸

When I stepped from the outhouse into the

woods, I was met with a peaceful silence. Before I rounded the building's corner, I knew I wouldn't see any Rabbits. The grounds were empty.

I blew out a frustrated breath and began to hoof it down the narrow trail leading to the clearing where tents once stood. Charred wood and ashes filled the circle where the bonfire had blazed. The benches were still in place, and across the way I could see the electric charging station used for powering their vehicles. No Rabbit was here now, but at least it didn't appear to be permanently abandoned.

I set my shoulder bag down on one of the wooden benches. I couldn't tell how old the ashes were, but if I had to guess, they weren't from a recent fire. I wondered when the Rabbits made camp last.

Joining my shoulder bag on the bench, I retrieved The Book, opening and turning through its pages. I wanted to find a new message – something to help me understand what I should do next. As I searched, a soft sound of something moving behind me reached my ears. I raised my head, standing and spinning in a tight circle. My eyes darted back and forth as I inspected the woods surrounding the clearing. It was still. Not even a breeze rustled through the autumn leaves. I saw nothing.

"Okay, Emily," I said aloud. "Don't freak yourself out." Despite my intention to remain calm, my stomach gave a flip when I heard another snap. I peered in the direction of the outhouse, my hands pressing The Book to my chest. My heart beat against it.

Alright, it was time to go. There were no Rabbits here. Step one in the plan completed. Time for step two. I'd door travel straight into Tuesday's bakery, *The Sweet Spot*. I pushed The Book deep into my shoulder bag and pulled the strap over my shoulder as I left the clearing. The trek back to the outhouse building was at a slight incline and I slipped on a few loose stones. *Stop being jumpy*, I thought. Nothing to be afraid of here. I forced myself to hike at a reasonable pace.

But the urge to hurry was getting stronger. I either freaked myself out after hearing the noise, or my 'Salesmany sense' – as Tara referred to it – picked up on something bad. I ran up the thin trail. I needed to get out of there. *Fast.*

When I turned the corner leading to the back of the outhouse, I realized how right I was. I was not alone. A tall figure leaned against the side of the building – right by the door I needed for traveling.

I wished the surprise visitor was Templeton. It was not.

It was Sebastian – and his Cheshire smile told me I was the canary he'd been waiting to catch.

* * *

"Oh, who do we have here? Why, it's Emily." His cold eyes lit up. His arms were crossed, but he was relaxed as he assessed me. And why not? The last time we faced off he dragged me by the hair.

Sebastian hadn't changed much since I last saw him. His wavy dark hair was still longish, covering his collar. The 5 o'clock shadow supporting a slight mustache and small goatee still worked. He wore a black leather jacket over his white shirt. His boots took his height well over six feet.

"This is such a lovely surprise," he taunted, unfolding his arms and pressing his palms together. He proceeded to crack a couple of knuckles, bending his fingers with his thumb and forefinger. I stared at his hands. "I never would've thought I'd find you hiking around out here. What brings you to this lonely corner of the Empire? *Alone.*" His singsong tone stopped on the last word and his gloating smile disappeared.

I reviewed my options. I could yell for help, but Sebastian was right. There was no one else out here. Maybe his Fringe buddies were hanging around somewhere, but no one else would be around to come to my aid. I could try to turn tail and run – and I was keeping the idea on the table – but I knew he'd catch me.

My only choice was to make a break for the door. I'd have to get him away from it first, which would be next to impossible.

"What are you doing out here, Sebastian?" I shifted while I tried to determine what angle would be the best one for running away. When he gave chase, my plan was to circle the building and dive through the outhouse door once I made it all the way back around. I'd door travel anywhere to get away from him.

He didn't answer but instead pushed off the

side of the wall and took a step toward me. His eyes combed over my body again, his nostrils flaring. Could he smell my fear? "Out here by yourself. So dangerous."

"You don't know if I'm alone," I told him. *Yes, he does,* my brain answered back.

He clicked his tongue. "Do better than that."

"Okay," I said. "I'm meeting someone here." *Good answer,* I thought. My brain pulled a mental facepalm.

"Possible," he nodded, bobbing his head several times. "But I don't believe you. You have a habit of lying." He smirked and took another step toward me. I drifted to the right.

"Don't come any closer," I warned.

"Or what?" Sebastian laughed. "Emily, you really do excite me. Did you know that? I love your confidence. I've often thought about the night we spent together in Matar." He took yet another step and I moved away again. "We could've played some fun games. In fact, we could play some now since it's just the two of us."

"Yeah, I'm still taking a pass on that." I kept inching away from him. The moment was coming when Sebastian would try to nab me.

If I didn't put enough space between us, his reach could easily snag me.

"Do you like fairytales?" Sebastian's mouth eased into a perverted sneer. "I can see you in... Hmm." He paused, cocking his head to the side, his lips pursed. He tapped his chin with a long forefinger. "Yes, you in a little red dress, skipping alone through the forest, with none of your annoying friends watching over you. Ooh, I like this idea."

That was it, I needed to go – *now*. I took off, sprinting around the corner like the devil was on my heels. He might as well have been. Sebastian lunged for me and missed, but the action made us both stumble over the uneven ground. As he regained his footing, I scurried a few steps ahead of him. The terror coursing through my veins raised my energy as I skidded around the second corner. I was now on the opposite side of the building.

Sebastian made up the lead I'd had, and his fingers wrapped around my upper arm, yanking me around. As I spun toward him, I swung my shoulder bag, smacking him backward. He held on tight to my arm, his fingertips curling into my flesh.

"No!" I shouted, wrenching myself away once before being snatched back by my hair.

"Oh, yes," he snarled, slamming me into the building and knocking my head against the wall. My vision exploded with a blinding flash as a ringing in my ears started. Sebastian's hand seized my throat, and I tore at his wrist. My back against the wall, I panicked, squirming and trying to rip myself free.

The ringing grew louder. Sebastian twitched and gave his head a shake, but he squeezed my throat harder. My fingers tried to pry his hand off me as I struggled. I couldn't breathe.

He leaned in, the tip of his nose two inches from mine, his eyelids dipping over his dark eyes. The scent of his cologne was overwhelming, and I could feel his wet breath on my skin. Sebastian pressed himself against me, running his tongue along my jawline and up my left cheek.

Terror spread through my body because in that moment, in the nightmare playing out between us, I knew *exactly* what game Sebastian wanted to play.

NO! I screamed inside my head, shattering the darkness filling my vision. Sebastian's hand jerked away from my neck as his body flew backwards, crashing hard onto the ground. I fell to my hands and knees, gagging and sucking in air. Sebastian swore at me as he rolled up onto his knees. I gripped my shoulder bag with the crimson-colored glow pulsing through the fabric and crawled away, dragging my bag with me until I could get back on my feet and stagger around the corner of the building.

My dizziness made the ground ripple under my feet and I flailed an arm, seeking something solid to steady me. I had to make it to the door!

"Emily!" Sebastian roared behind me. He was back on his feet.

A little farther, just a little more, I chanted in my head, coughing and gripping the side of the building as I wobbled around the final corner. I dove for the door, falling across the threshold as it pushed open.

Sebastian's hand wrapped around my right ankle as my body collapsed in the doorway. He attempted to yank me back to him. I kicked my feet, clocking his cheek with my heel and freeing myself.

Lying on my stomach, I didn't even try to picture a destination as my hands pressed against the rough wood of the floor. I pushed myself up and stretched forward, lifting my right arm and letting my fingertips graze the doorknob. In my head I cried out: *Please, somebody help me!*

CHAPTER 7

I tumbled through the door on the other side and landed hard on yellow and brown linoleum, my cheek smacking against the floor. Still coughing, I struggled to catch my breath. My eyes watered as my wheezing continued, but I managed to climb to my hands and knees. A hand landed on my shoulder, and someone crouched by my side. My first reaction was to try to scramble away, but my legs failed as I slipped, and I collapsed back to the floor.

"Hey, we got you," a man said, sliding his hand to my upper arm and helping me rise back to my knees. I trembled as my vision cleared.

A woman knelt on the other side of me, touching my shoulder. "It's okay," she told me. "You're okay, you're safe now. No one's going to hurt you. Someone get her some water!"

"I couldn't breathe," I croaked out, triggering a run of wretched sobs. The woman wrapped her arms around me.

"Shh, shh," she murmured into my hair. "You're safe. Whatever happened out there, you're safe here."

I allowed the stranger to hold me until a new person brought me a glass of water. He squatted beside us. "Do you need me to help?" he asked, holding the glass to my lips.

I shook my head no and lifted a shaking hand, taking the glass. I took a sip. The water burned my throat, but it helped me stop crying. I hiccupped once and handed the drink back to him.

"Let's get you onto your feet and into a chair," the first man said. The three gingerly helped me up and guided me toward a kitchen table. I eased into a chair.

"Thanks," I rasped, realizing more than three people filled the bright kitchen. In fact, a dozen pale faces blinked curiously, their deep brown eyes studying me. Male and female alike, they were all dressed similarly, in jeans and tee shirts, with work boots and flannel shirts. A few wore knit hats with thick curls poking out at odd angles beneath the edge. Several slid their thumbs over phones, texting.

Another sob sputtered through my lips, but this time it was a cry of relief.

Rabbits.

✻ ✻ ✻

"Don't let her talk too much," the first man directed the female Rabbit. "Give her time to rest."

She ignored him and gently lifted my head by the chin to examine my neck. I watched her face, but she didn't reveal much – only a slight tensing of the jaw.

"I don't want you to say anything," she told me. "But do you know who did this to you? Nod or shake your head if you can."

I nodded once.

"Okay, we'll deal with that shortly then," the female Rabbit replied. "Do you want us to take you to a hospital or a doctor?"

I shook my head no.

"Did… Did this person…" The Rabbit paused. She leaned over and lowered her voice. "Did this person hurt you anywhere else?"

Again, I shook my head. She let out a breath.

"Let's get more water into you." She motioned to one of the Rabbits. "And get her paper and a pencil." She brushed my messy hair back from my face with her hand. "You can write out your name and where we can take you."

I nodded, taking the pencil when it was offered and writing on the paper: *Emily Swift.*

She blinked at the paper before fixing me with a curious look. "Emily Swift? What are you doing in the Empire? And who are you running from?"

The muttering lending itself to the background of our conversation halted the minute my name was said aloud. A few noses twitched. A young-looking Rabbit smiled shyly when our eyes met. He looked like a teenager, but he was probably older than I was. Most of the heads bent back to their phones and the next round of texting began.

I put the pencil back to the paper, writing: *I need Rabbit. I'm staying at 1106 Autumn Avenue, Matar.*

My new friend read it out loud to the others. More texting. "We'll find him," she promised.

"Thanks," I whispered. My throat still hurt, but it didn't burn anymore. The water was helping. I didn't know how long Sebastian's hand was at my throat, but I knew there were already marks.

"Did this happen at this address?" she asked. She sat down in a chair beside me and again stroked my hair. I examined her discreetly. Physically, Rabbits age very slowly. This woman looked like she was in her early 50s. Would she be close to 90 or 100 years old? The thought boggled my mind.

"No," I answered when I realized she was waiting for my answer.

Although I'd met a few dozen Rabbits on my journeys through the Empire, I didn't recognize anyone in the room. I had no idea where in the Empire I'd landed, but it was possible they'd been to the bonfire spot before. I needed to warn them about the Fringe being there – or at least about Sebastian. I held up a finger indicating to give me a minute.

There was a page in The Book where my father had sketched a map of the Empire. On it, he'd written 'hidden cluster of Rabbits?' Another page bore the message:

If a Rabbit has no tale, can he still tell a story?

Below it, a string of numbers appeared. I'd learned these numbers were directions Rabbits could read to find that particular hidden cluster – it was the same place as the bonfire spot. It was now the place where Sebastian attacked me.

I pulled my father's journal from my shoulder bag and turned the pages until I found the numbers. I copied them onto the paper.

4.23.67.7.78.

Tapping the numbers with the pencil, I squeaked out: "Happened here. Fringe."

The Rabbit swore and swiped the paper off the table. She thrust it into the hands of one of the Rabbits hovering close.

"Tell the network," she ordered the group before turning back to me. "How many were there?"

I shrugged, then held up one finger. "All I saw."

"Do you know who it was?"

I shuddered as I pictured his face close to mine. "Sebastian St. Michel."

※ ※ ※

While I rested, the Rabbit filled me in on what she knew. The Fringe traditionally had a stronghold to the west of Matar leading into a part of the region called the Walled Zone, but they were popping up more frequently in the rural areas south of the city. I knew this was true. We'd been chased by the Fringe on a back road earlier in the year. Rabbits were wise to be wary.

Through a limited number of words and pantomime, I managed to convey I didn't see signs of vehicles at the bonfire site. I theorized Sebastian door traveled to the spot like I'd done. And yet, I was surprised he knew about the place.

The Rabbit pulled a face. "The Fringe has worked for a while now to crack into our network. They have hackers like…well…" She laughed and shrugged. "I'm not saying the network does anything illegal."

"You just do it better than the Empire," I croaked.

She winked, then grew serious again. "The Fringe knows we've been able to get around some of the Empire's limitations. They'd like to be able to do that, too. We've had compromised channels. The network destroyed them as soon as they realized what happened, but it's possible information was leaked. Like locations of certain clusters."

A cluster was a colony of Rabbits. "Sebastian could've found out and that's why he was there." I thought about it. But why risk going there alone? Unless this wasn't his first time. Maybe he knew no Rabbits would be there. But why go back?

"Rabbit?" the man from earlier called across the room. "We've got a message for Emily."

"Did you find him?" My voice cracked, but I was hopeful.

"Sure did. He said, 'go back to Lucie's and stay put for once.' He'll be there before tonight."

❋ ❋ ❋

The female Rabbit asked me repeatedly if I was okay to door travel from their house – which I learned was in a rural town called Snowshoe – back to Lucie's. I assured her I was fine, even though my throat was still scratchy. I'd gone to the bathroom and noted bruises about the size of fingerprints developing on the front of my neck where Sebastian's hand had pressed.

We hugged and she gave me a slip of paper with a new string of numbers. It was the location of their home. "I don't know if you even need this," she said. "You being a Salesman and all. You can door travel back."

"Next time I'll try not to make such a grand entrance," I promised as I thanked everyone for helping me. I received a few more hugs and pats goodbye before I gave a wave and prepared to leave. A dozen pairs of eyes bored into my back as I stood in front of the kitchen door and tried to center myself. The room grew quiet. I floated a look over my shoulder. Several Rabbits grinned from ear to ear and the youngest-looking one gave me a thumbs up.

I felt an unexpected but oh-so-welcome feeling surge inside of me.

Love.

Filled with gratitude, I turned back toward the door and stepped on through into Lucie's brownstone.

❋ ❋ ❋

Lucie was showered and wearing clean clothes, but she hadn't yet left for *Coffee Cove*. When I walked in through her pantry door, she turned expectantly. She took one look at me – my dirty jeans and messy hair – and cried out.

"Emily, what in the name of the Empire happened to you?" She gripped my arms. Her head dipped back and forth as she reviewed my neck. I took it to mean the bruising was noticeable.

"Sebastian," I said, keeping my voice low. I truly was feeling better, but I wanted to be gentle with my voice.

"What do you mean?" Lucie's fingers tightened. "You saw him?"

"He was there at the Rabbits' bonfire spot," I told her. "He attacked me."

Lucie pulled me close and hugged me. "Oh, honey, I am so sorry. Oh, Emily." She suddenly pushed me backward, horror filling her face. "He didn't –?"

"No," I stopped her. "He had me by the neck, but I got away."

I didn't tell Lucie the vision I'd had when Sebastian was choking me. There was a warped soul inside of him. I didn't want to think what he might've done if I hadn't escaped.

"Did you go for help?" She motioned to my throat. "I can help you a little, but we can go to the doctor, too."

I shook my head. "No, no doctors, no hospitals. I'm fine. But I could use some tea."

"I have a perfect blend for you," Lucie answered. "I also have a healing scarf. Its purpose is for fast healing of sore throats from colds, but it ought to do the trick. You'll feel better right away, and it might even help with the bruising."

"It looks bad, doesn't it?"

She nodded. "Very bad. I'll be right back."

I climbed onto the first barstool, slinging my shoulder bag up onto the next one. Elbows on the counter, I covered my face with my hands. I hoped the scarf would return my neck to its normal color. I couldn't go home like this. Jack would have a heart attack.

Seeing Sebastian caught me off guard in a big way. I snorted. *Understatement.* I don't know what I'd expected, but today's nightmare reminded me of what I was up against. It was hard not to sink into a hole of hopelessness.

I needed the rest of the Crimson Stone. I'd use it to punish Sebastian for everything he'd done, for all the pain he'd inflicted on others as a part of the Fringe. He deserved to suffer.

"Okay," Lucie interrupted my thoughts as she returned to the kitchen. "Let's wrap this around your neck. Lift your hair."

It was a vibrant blue, silk-like scarf – long but lightweight. Lucie hummed as she wrapped it loosely around my neck several times. Immediately I felt a wave of comfort settle over me. "I think it's working."

"Good. That's not too tight, is it?"

"No, this is fine. Thanks." Lucie left both ends of the scarf hanging down over my chest. I ran my fingertips over the material.

"I'll make the tea," she said, turning the kettle on and reaching for a jar inside her cupboard. "Tell me what happened from the minute you left the house."

I described what I went through after I door traveled from her house to the bonfire location. At several points Lucie swore under her breath, and I thought I heard her mumble about cutting something off 'this Sebastian.' She placed the brew in front of me, her face hard with anger. I reached for the cup, but she swiped it away, sloshing liquid over the rim.

"I'm too upset," she told me. She dumped the tea down the sink.

"Why did you do that?" This was confusing.

"My energy was – is – filled with hate for this man," she admitted, grabbing a dish cloth and wiping up the spilled tea. "It's not a good space to be in when you're making someone a healing cup."

I touched the scarf around my neck. "What about this?"

"Pre-charged. I keep healing scarves in a special box. I charge them when I'm well for use when I'm under the weather."

That made sense. "So, about the tea?"

Lucie fired up the kettle. "You're on deck. Salesman, heal thyself."

"I can do that." I changed places with Lucie, measuring out the throat-healing blend and adding it to a white porcelain tea ball in the shape of an acorn. A ring of green oak leaves circled the cap. It hung from a chain, and I lowered it into the cup, pouring the hot water over the steeper when the kettle finished boiling the water.

"Let it stand for about three minutes," Lucie instructed. "Then you can remove the tea ball."

"Got it." The tea ball came with its own decorated cup, oak trees in various seasonal displays painted on the side. It was tiny but would hold the acorn perfectly when I pulled the diffuser from my teacup. I leaned over and inhaled the steam. I smelled anise. "What's in this?"

"The biggie is slippery elm bark," she replied. "But also licorice root and chamomile. You'll want to add honey. Some people like to add fresh lemon or a piece of citrus peel in the blend, but I think it's irritating when your throat is sore. I have lemon if you want it, though."

"This is fine," I said, returning to my barstool. I blew across the surface of the tea and waited for it to cool to a safer temperature. Lucie moved my shoulder bag so she could sit beside me. She worried her bottom lip with her teeth.

"Are you going to be okay?" She tapped the side of her head. "Here I mean."

I knew exactly what she meant and spun the teacup in a circle with my fingertips. "I was terrified. I've had a gun pointed at me more than once, Lucie, but this was way worse."

Lucie watched as I turned the teacup. She reached over and placed a hand over mine. "You've been picking up Anne's habits. Let's not spin this particular cup of tea. It might offset its intended purpose."

"I should probably know what that means," I said. I stopped rotating the teacup on the countertop.

"Have you been studying?" Lucie asked.

My friend had lent me many good books, and I'd barely cracked them open. "Not as much as I should be."

"Hmm. I'm guessing not at all." Lucie didn't appear to be bothered by my lack of study. She shrugged. "It's not the headspace you've been in."

"It's not," I said. "The past few months have flown by, and honestly, it was good to be back to normal with Jack for a while." I held up a hand. "I know, Anne's always telling me things aren't going to return to the way they were before I became a Salesman."

"I guess the real question is, do you want it to go back to the way it was? I mean, what if you weren't a Salesman? What if everything stayed the same as it always had been up to your last birthday?"

"You mean, no Salesman world? No Empire?"

"Sure, let's go with that," Lucie said. She

twirled a finger in the air. "What if all this didn't exist?"

"Well, I don't want that." I balked at the thought. "I mean, there are many good things."

No Empire? No door travel?

No Lucie, Rabbit, or Anne? No sweet Tuesday feeding us too much for lunch?

No *Templeton?*

"Life doesn't always let you pick and choose like it's a big dessert cart, Emily." Lucie pushed her auburn locks behind both of her ears at the same time before leaning forward and placing her elbows on the countertop. She laced her fingers together. "In this case, you've got a lot of ugly with the beautiful. It's up to you if you want to get rid of what's rotten."

"I don't have a choice," I told her.

"But you do," she argued. "You could give up the Crimson Stone and walk away."

"What?" My voice rose. "What are you telling me to do?"

Lucie straightened and held up both palms. "Hold on. I'm not telling you to do anything. What I'm saying is you have a choice. You've always had a choice. Everything you've told me since I've met you has involved picking a path. You only think you don't have options – but you do. I'm not saying you shouldn't have made the choices you've made. I'm saying where you are right now is because of what you've chosen in the past. And, what happens around you is half what you do and half the response your actions triggered."

"I feel like I'm being lectured."

She sighed. "No. I'm trying to help you see you're the star of your life's story. Don't think someone else is meant for the spotlight. Good or bad, it's your stage."

I didn't like the way I was feeling. "And?"

"And, I'd say 'know your lines.' Enough with the ad-libbing."

"This metaphor has gone far enough."

"It has. One sec." Lucie hopped off her barstool and disappeared around the corner, leaving the kitchen. I could hear her footsteps on the stairs. I sipped my tea and waited.

The footsteps were a beat faster as Lucie returned to the first floor and came back into the kitchen. In her hand she held two books. She set both on the counter in front of me.

"What are these?" Neither book sported a title. From the outside, they appeared to be journals.

"This one," she placed a finger on a brown cover, "discusses controlling your energy so you can use it to move objects – or blast an enemy away from you."

"Like Sebastian," I nodded.

"Exactly. Apparently, you have some natural ability. Didn't something happen last year when you had all three pieces of the Crimson Stone? Didn't you send someone flying?"

"Petrovich," I confirmed. "But it was the Stone."

Lucie wasn't having it. "No, it was *you*. The Stone amplified your power. In a big way."

"Very big. Petrovich was a bit singed, too." The corrupt Justice was missing hair and had burn marks on his face and neck after I sent him flying.

"I bet that was part of the Crimson Stone," she said. "A little bit of its fire fueled your energy blast."

"And this second book?" I pointed to the slim volume with the black cover.

"This is a journal," Lucie said. "It's not mine, but it was given to me by a woman from another witchline when I was a teenager. Evangeline had no one to leave it to and she made sure it came to me when she passed away."

"What's inside?"

"Stories and rhymes," Lucie answered. "This might sound strange but reading other witches' words can have a powerful effect on your own spellcasting."

"But I'm not a witch," I argued.

"True, but you can practice magic. Right now, you're tapping into your well as a last resort, or when you're in danger. Why don't you think about being proactive and intentionally using your magic?" She tapped the cover with her fingernail. "This reads like a story inside a book of poetry. Trust me on this one."

I pulled the books to me. "I suppose you're right."

"Of course I am," she laughed. "Listen, you say Rabbit's coming here? It might be a while. Get comfortable. Put up your feet and read a book."

❖ ❖ ❖

Lucie left for *Coffee Cove* and I made a second cup of tea. I carried it to the cozy living room nestled in the front of her townhouse. Curling up on the end of a sofa, I sipped the hot liquid. My friend didn't use the room much, but it was welcoming. I set the teacup on a table angled between the sofa and an unlit fireplace before opening the witch's journal Lucie suggested I read.

She was right. It was like reading a story. The witch Evangeline must've been a writer at heart because even a description of who she spent time with or what they did read like an adventure. She sprinkled both complex and succinct spells throughout the pages. Some seemed simple, but I thought they might be useful in everyday life. In particular there was one called the Tick Tock Time Spell.

Tick Tock
Tick Tock
I need not
Look at the clock!
I will arrive
At mother's on time
By the power
Of my rhyme!

Underneath the spell Evangeline wrote: *Don't look at any clock, wristwatch, or timepiece when walking to mother's. Chant this rhyme the entire time.*

Replace 'mother's' with 'work' and this spell could be very useful.

While snippets like these were entertaining, I understood why Lucie thought it was important for me to read through the journal. Evangeline brought magic into every part of her life. It accompanied her no matter where she went, who she was with, or whatever they were doing. Of course, Evangeline lived in the Empire, and it appeared her friends were other witches – or at least some sort of magic practitioners.

No matter what the day threw at her, she had a spell for it in her repertoire. Her journal entries proved she plucked out the right spell for any situation and dealt with it.

Longer passages that weren't a record of her daily activities often included ideas for new spells to practice, or even a new 'recipe' to experiment with during certain moon phases. These recipes read more like potions.

I closed the journal and thought about Evangeline. What would she have done if The Book landed on her doorstep like it did mine? Well, like me she'd use it as a resource and for help, but I bet she'd write in it, too.

Unwinding my legs, I stood and retrieved The Book from my shoulder bag, along with a pencil from a kitchen drawer.

When I first got The Book, I was hesitant to write in it. It was my father's journal, and I didn't want to ruin it. I wanted to keep it the way it was when my mother had it delivered to me. The first time I wrote in it, I'd been angry and regretted it immediately. But over time, I added a note here or there – mostly questions.

Messages inside would shift from page to page, and sometimes I wouldn't be able to locate one of my father's original notes. Other times a new passage would appear. But there were also blank pages. Maybe I could start to use The Book as a record for me, as a spell book to write down ideas and report any results.

Pencil in hand, I paused over a blank page. Poetry was not my strong suit, but I could probably come up with a rhyme.

My mind was blank.

I decided to 'practice' by copying Evangeline's Tick Tock Time Spell into The Book. This was one way to get the creative juices flowing.

Turning to the first blank page I could find in my father's journal, I added the spell. At the end, I attributed it to The Witch Evangeline.

As soon as I finished writing the final 'e' in her name, a message appeared directly under my writing:

Hello, Emily.

CHAPTER 8

"Eep!" I yelped, dumping The Book off my lap and onto the sofa. I leapt to my feet and stood gaping at the open book. Nothing happened. No other words appeared. Sweet mother-of-pearl, what was that?

The Book was definitely acting up these days. What now?

When nothing else appeared on the page, I sat back down and leaned over it. "Dad?"

Nothing happened. I picked up the pencil and wrote: *Dad?*

A moment later another word appeared: *No.*

Then: *Evangeline.*

Evangeline? How could it be?

Lucie told me she sensed someone put a protection spell of sorts on my father's journal a long time ago. Was Evangeline the woman who spelled my father's journal? I wrote back: *Are you the woman who spelled this book?*

Again: *No.*

Then: *I can sense her in these pages. That magic is very old.*

This made sense. Lucie thought the language

of the spell was particularly old and no longer used.

I slid my hand to the next blank page and wrote back: *How are you in here?*

Evangeline: *Your magic mingles with this book's. You summoned a slice of my subconscious when you wrote my spell and name. It is me and not me.*

Whoa. I sat back against the sofa cushion. This was unexpected and frankly, I didn't know what to do about it. Dang. I wished Lucie was still at home.

That's it! I needed to take The Book to Lucie. She knew Evangeline – this was a big deal. I knew Rabbit expected me to wait, but I could door travel right into the coffee shop. It wouldn't take long.

I wrote: *Hold tight, don't go anywhere. Please!* and shut The Book.

I returned to the kitchen, shoved The Book into my shoulder bag, and headed for the pantry door. Before I could door travel my way into *Coffee Cove*, loud knocking at the front of Lucie's townhouse tripped me up. I hiked my bag higher on my shoulder and changed direction. Maybe Rabbit arrived.

"And please don't be Templeton again," I mumbled as I walked down the hall from the kitchen into the entryway.

The knocking continued. To be on the safe side, I peeked out the side window by the door. One of the biggest men I've ever seen in person stood on the front stoop. I craned my head up, my mouth hanging open.

The man saw me peering out the window and the knocking stopped. His face lit up and he waved.

I waved back.

"Emily?" he called. He held up his phone and pointed. "Rabbit sent me to keep an eye on you."

Of course, he did. I assessed the man. He was most certainly a Rabbit – but it was as if he'd been supersized. He wore tan work boots with his dark jeans tucked into them. A red logo bearing the name *Rhino Vomit* – a death metal band that wrote a song for my mother – decorated the black tee shirt he wore. The top was stretched tight across his brawny chest. A mass of jet-black curls covered his head, flopping in front of his brown eyes as he nodded and gestured toward the door. He had to be about six and a half feet tall and at least 250 pounds of muscle.

"And if he's not a Rabbit," I muttered under my breath as I unlocked Lucie's door, "he'll squish me like a bug under those big paws."

I pulled the door open and looked up, up, up.

"Hi Emily," he held out a massive hand. "I'm Rabbit. Your friend Rabbit told me to come here."

"Yeah, we covered that," I answered, cautiously putting my hand in his. He gently bobbed it up and down.

"Rabbit said someone hurt you and if they try again, I should crush them. May I come in?"

"Ah, okay." I stepped aside and the giant ducked into Lucie's entryway. Luckily the ceilings in her brownstone were high. "Is Rabbit on his way?"

"He'll be here today," he replied. His phone buzzed and he checked it. "He told me to make sure you stay safely in one place."

"Oh." This was not going to work. "Um, I was just leaving."

"You were? Can it wait?"

"No, not really," I said, wondering how much money I could spare on lunch. "Are you hungry? I know this great coffee shop and they have a vegetarian menu."

* * *

On the walk to *Coffee Cove*, I decided I wanted this sweet giant to escort me everywhere. Not only did people step aside to let us pass, the Rabbit cheerfully greeted most passersby as we strolled along. Initial reactions were somewhat cautious, but he left a wake of happy faces behind us. This man was, in a word, delightful.

"It's the most beautiful fall we've had," he chatted as we walked. His eyes darted back and forth and up and down as his thumb slid nimbly across the screen of his phone. "Have you been to the south yet? The colors are magnificent! Hopefully you'll get time to relax."

"It would be nice," I agreed, watching him take a photo of a brownstone stoop decorated with pumpkins and cornstalks.

"My Ma likes to decorate," he said, blushing. "I send her photos when I travel so she can get more ideas."

"I think that's very nice," I said. On the inside,

I groaned. I hoped my mother wasn't driving Jack crazy with her cello playing. I'd have to send a new message to them – especially because it didn't seem like I'd be going home anytime soon. My throat was already feeling much better, but if the bruises didn't fade away fast, I needed to come up with an excuse not to door travel back to Kincaid.

As we approached the door leading into *Coffee Cove*, the happy Rabbit bounced forward to open the door for me.

"After you," he told me as he bowed. I passed on through and watched from the inside as he paused to help an elderly woman step up into the shop. Her startled expression made me realize it was more of a lift than an assist.

What a sweetheart, I thought as the lady offered an awkward thanks. I surveyed the crowded coffee shop before stopping at the end of the counter where drinks were made. Lifting my hand, I caught the eye of an efficient barista using the noisy espresso machine. "Excuse me, I'm looking for Lucie Bellerose. Where would I find her?"

The young woman craned her neck, looking past the tables filled with patrons. She nodded in the same direction. "Back there is a door leading into Lucie's room. There's a sign. If it says a reading's in progress, add your name to the schedule book on the table. If it says 'please knock' she's not doing a reading and can probably see you."

"Thanks," I said, glancing past the crowded tables before locating my giant Rabbit. He'd taken a spot in line and chatted with another customer. I waved. He waved back. I shook my head, hiding my amusement as I crossed over to him.

"Did you find your friend?" he asked. He peered around me as if Lucie might be standing nearby.

"Not quite. She's here, though. I'm going to check if she's free. Here," I opened my wallet and handed him my credit card. "Um, get yourself lunch. Order me a latte to go. A plain one with whipped cream. Regular milk."

He grinned and took the card. "Thanks! I'm starving."

I felt my smile waver but nodded before turning and heading toward the back of the seating area. I skirted around the jumble of tables, lifting my bag to avoid knocking into anyone.

A low jazz beat could be heard playing lightly over the murmuring of people and the stirring of spoons inside ceramic mugs. It was warm in this section, but not unpleasantly so.

As the barista described, a sign hanging to the right of the door indicated Lucie was busy with a reading. On the table beneath the sign, I found the schedule book lying open with 'first names only' written across the top of each page. Her next 30-minute appointment was available. I penciled in 'Emily.'

Behind me, a table for two became free and I snatched it up. It was tight quarters, but my new friend could possibly squeeze in – if he sat up straight and close to the table. I wasn't sure how his legs would fit underneath, but it would have to do. While I waited, I fingered the scarf I wore.

The Rabbit came into view. Swiveling his hips like a dancing linebacker, he balanced a full tray in one hand and deftly cut a path around the tables leading to mine. He set the tray down and handed me my credit card. "I got your latte."

And then some. Plates were loaded with several veggie wraps, a colorful tossed salad, a pink fruit smoothie, a large glass of cucumber water, and two vegan energy bars – which he shyly explained might be for later. I laughed and told him *bon appétit*.

"The scarf," he said, pointing with his wrap. He leaned across the table. "Is it hiding bruises?"

"How did you know?" I asked. My hand rested on the material.

"It's slipping," he said, tilting his head to the side as he studied my neck. His lips tightened into a thin line before he spoke again. "That's what the person did to you, isn't it?"

I couldn't meet his gaze. I realized I was embarrassed, and not because I wasn't able to stop Sebastian, but because I'd put myself in a bad position in the first place. I shouldn't have gone alone. I needed to make better decisions moving forward. "Yeah. There's this Salesman named Sebastian. He's part of the Fringe but apparently untouchable because of his family."

The kind giant set his wrap on the tray before reaching over and taking my hand. "We won't let him hurt you again."

I blinked back tears. "Thank you," I whispered, my words catching in my battered throat. "We're going to take him down."

"Emily?" Lucie interrupted as she appeared at our table. She sized-up the Rabbit before giving his shoulder a squeeze along with a curious look. "It looks like you've picked up a bodyguard."

He laughed as he released my hand and stood up. He shook Lucie's hand and offered his chair to her.

"Oh, no, I'm fine," Lucie said, motioning for him to return to his seat. "Thanks though. You enjoy your lunch while Emily explains why she's on my schedule."

"It's about Evangeline," I told her.

Lucie raised an eyebrow. "Well, let's step into my reading room and you can fill me in."

After promising the Rabbit I'd be right back, I followed Lucie into her welcoming space. It was a cheery room, with a window overlooking the park around the corner from *Coffee Cove's* front door. A woman played catch with her chocolate lab as they ran through the dried leaves. Along one wall Lucie had filled shelves with books, wooden boxes for Tarot cards, incense burners, a variety of unlit candles in several sizes, capped bottles of herbs and oils, and framed photos of places she'd visited.

In the center of the room sat a plain wooden table on a red rug covering a portion of the worn hardwood floors. At the table, two high-backed chairs sat opposite one another and were pulled out in an invitation to sit. A comfy armchair was tucked into a corner along the far wall near the window. An end table sat beside it with a stack of more books on top.

Several decks of Tarot cards were placed on the round table waiting to be read. A white candle, no longer burning, was pushed into a clear glass candleholder, a box of matches at its side. A hint of rosemary graced the air. The autumn light streaming in through the window bathed everything in a friendly glow.

"Have a seat," Lucie took the chair nearest the decks of cards and shifted them to the side. "What's going on?"

I pulled The Book out from my shoulder bag. "I was reading Evangeline's journal and decided to copy a spell into The Book." I hesitated. "This might be a moot point, but is it okay I did that?"

Lucie chuckled. "Yes, it's fine. Which spell?"

"The Tick Tock one."

"Handy."

"Yeah." I fiddled with The Book, opening it to the page where the message from the late witch appeared. "I copied the spell and then these messages appeared. She said she's Evangeline."

"Interesting," said Lucie as she pulled The Book closer. "Things like this are not unheard of, but they're certainly not common."

"Is it because The Book is spelled?"

"Since I haven't had the same thing happen – and I've copied a few of Evangeline's spells into notebooks over the years – I would say, yes."

"I feel like maybe we could, um, use this to our advantage?" Suddenly I felt awkward. I didn't want to be rude, but we needed all the help we could get. "In a way that isn't disrespectful to Evangeline's memory."

Lucie understood. "Evangeline was a kind person. I think you could write back, tell her who you are, and ask if she'd be willing to help. If she says yes, ask her what she recommends."

"Should I do it now?"

"Since you ate up one of my appointments, yes," Lucie teased.

I cringed. "Sorry."

She waved me off and instead handed me a pencil. "Get to it. Tell her I'm here with you."

I turned to the blank page following the earlier messages and wrote: *Hi Evangeline, it's me, Emily Swift. Are you still there?*

Words appeared under my writing: *Yes.*

I continued: *I'm here with Lucie. She says hello.*

Hello, Lucie.

Evangeline, do you know who I am?

You are Daniel Swift's daughter.

I was surprised: *Did you know my father?*

No.

"She might know about your father because The Book was his journal," Lucie suggested.

"It's possible," I agreed.

I wrote another line: *My father was a Salesman and I'm one, too.*

You are a traveler.

"Traveler?" I repeated to Lucie. "Like, door traveling I'm guessing?"

"Makes sense," she replied.

Before I could write my next sentence, a new message from Evangeline appeared: *There are whispers in this book. There is a message for you.*

I penciled in: *What is the message?*

Evangeline: *It is a secret.*

I wrote back: *Can you tell me what it is? Would you help me?*

Evangeline: *Yes.*

I waited for the next message. When nothing appeared, I raised my head. "She stopped."

Lucie scratched her ear. "Write 'thank you.'"

I followed her directions. Then I added: *Evangeline, can you tell me the secret?*

Yes. And then: *I must find it again. The whispers come and go.*

"I think she'd tell you if she knew more," Lucie said. "Plus, this is only a slip of Evangeline's subconscious. Her power might ebb and flow."

"I can understand that," I said – and the weird part was I DID understand. The odd people and situations I encountered in the Empire weren't as strange to me as they used to be.

"Go ahead and write 'thank you' again, and then add you'll come back to check on her later. You opened this connection with her, now you should close it," Lucie counseled.

I wrote in the last few words and said goodbye to Evangeline. "Now what?"

"Don't you have Mr. Big Rabbit waiting for you and another Rabbit on the way?"

"Right," I said, rising from my chair. "I'll talk to you later."

* * *

During the walk back to Lucie's brownstone, I asked the Rabbit who'd been assigned as my 'bodyguard' if he minded me calling him Big Rabbit. He told me he rather liked the nickname.

As we neared the stairs leading up to Lucie's front door, I saw I had another visitor. Templeton stood leaning against the wrought iron rail, his nose buried in a newspaper, top hat on his head. I knew he sensed when our feet touched the brick sidewalk of Lucie's block. I felt a tendril of his energy poking into mine.

"One moment, please," said Big Rabbit. He put one of his large hands on my shoulder and halted our progression. "I don't like the looks of this."

I snorted. "Neither do I, but it's fine."

"He's a friend?"

"Uh, let's just say he's a colleague," I said. We started walking again.

Templeton looked up from his paper. He

folded it and slid the bundle under his arm. "Off seeing the witch?"

I blew out a breath. "Yes, I needed to talk to Lucie."

"About what?"

"It doesn't concern you," I argued, but decided it wasn't worth it. Instead, I dug into my shoulder bag searching for my keys. Pulling out the set, I selected a gold-colored one from the keyring and held it up. "Here's the key for Lucie's. Go ahead and let yourself inside. I'll be up in a minute."

Big Rabbit stared at Templeton. A hint of a tight smile stiffened his face. It didn't extend to his eyes – which had grown darker like Rabbits' eyes tend to do when they're angry or hyper-focused. "I know who you are."

Templeton returned the flinty smile with one of his own. "I'm sure you do."

"Here." I jingled the keys toward Big Rabbit. "I promise I'll be fine."

My bodyguard wasn't thrilled about leaving me alone with Templeton, but he climbed the stairs after the Salesman moved to the side. Big Rabbit hesitated on the stoop, taking one last look before unlocking Lucie's door and going inside. A second later I saw him peeking through the side window.

"Looks like the wards guarding this place are Rabbit-friendly." Templeton sniffed as he turned his back to the peeping protector. "Let me guess, Rabbit sent Tiny to watch over you?"

"Something like that," I replied. I changed the subject as I climbed up a couple steps so I could look him straight in the eye. "I'm surprised to see you back here."

Templeton leaned forward suddenly, fixating on the blue scarf. "Let me see your neck."

Son of a... How could he have known? Or was he guessing? "No."

"Emily, I can tell you're covering up something." He lifted his hand to touch the scarf but yanked it back as he flicked a look in Big Rabbit's direction. "Show me."

"I had a run-in with Sebastian where the Rabbits hold their bonfire in the woods," I sighed. "You know where."

He gave a curt nod. "Were you alone?"

"I door traveled there to see if I could find Rabbit," I explained as I regarded Templeton. He was no longer looking at me. Instead, he'd turned his head to the side, and I could see he was gritting his teeth. "Templeton?"

His head jerked back, and he inspected the scarf again. "I can see her magic on it. I cannot see through it. Show me what Sebastian did."

I've seen Templeton annoyed, irritated, incredulous, frustrated, and angry. I'd never seen such fury on his face. I reached up and pulled the material down, revealing some of the bruising. Templeton's pupils shrunk to pinpoints and his irises became almost translucent. His breathing deepened. I let go of the scarf.

"I don't know where you are in your head right now," I said to him softly. "But come back."

He blinked once and his eyes returned to their normal icy blue. "He will not have the opportunity to do that again." He turned abruptly and walked away.

"Wait!" I called. I hurried back down the steps and followed him on the sidewalk. I heard Lucie's door open behind me and Big Rabbit shouted my name. I waved for him to stay put.

Templeton's strides were longer than mine and I sprinted down the block after him. Why he didn't door travel out of there was beyond me, but I was glad he hadn't. I caught up and swerved in front of him, placing my palms against his chest.

"Stop," I said. "Please stop for a moment."

He complied. I pulled my hands away and took a breath.

"Please work with me for once, Templeton," I said as I ran a hand through my hair. "Did you know something had happened? Is that why you showed back up at Lucie's?"

"No." He frowned. "But I can see the healing magic she threaded into the scarf. And I can tell you're not sick."

"You can?"

He didn't answer.

"Okay, then tell me why you're back here at Lucie's," I said.

"When will Rabbit be here?" He ignored me.

"Today. Why?"

"I've had trouble locating him. I need to speak to him."

"You know it's not easy to find a Rabbit," I said.

"Not for me."

I lifted my hands and shrugged. "Fine. Look, I'm operating at a real disadvantage here. Is there anything you can tell me that would be useful? Or how about something I should know? I don't care if you don't like me, Templeton, but clearly even you don't want to see the Fringe gaining more power."

Templeton stared over my head. He didn't answer, but he didn't leave.

"Anne says I shouldn't write you off so easily," I told him.

His focus stayed on a distant spot. He remained silent.

I took a deep breath. "Please help me. Help us. You have a piece of the Stone. You know I have Spell's piece. And Rabbit can get his hands on the third piece. Let's put the Crimson Stone back together and use it to put an end to the Fringe for good."

Templeton's attention returned to me when I indicated Rabbit didn't exactly have his piece of the Crimson Stone on him. "He doesn't have it? Where is it?"

"He gave it to another Rabbit." I held up my hand to stop the question forming on his lips. "Don't ask me who. Rabbit can tell you himself when he gets here. In the meantime, come back to Lucie's and wait. Let's form a plan.

Three of us can do magic, Rabbit has the network. We've got to be able to –"

"Save the Empire?" Templeton shook his head. "Go back to Ms. Bellerose's place. I'll return when Rabbit has arrived."

Templeton took off his top hat and inspected the brim. He picked at a piece of non-existent lint before stepping past me and walking away.

※ ※ ※

Big Rabbit stood in the middle of the sidewalk with his beefy arms crossed over his chest.

"You followed me," I said as I joined him.

"You shouldn't wander off," he chastised me.

"Well, I didn't wander far, and unfortunately I need Templeton's help." I gestured in the direction Templeton had disappeared.

"He's not trustworthy," Big Rabbit said as we made our way back to Lucie's.

"How do you know? Rabbit likes him," I argued. "I mean, as much as anyone could like Templeton."

"Templeton has a reputation," he answered.

"So do the Rabbits," I teased, bumping my shoulder against him as we walked. "And yeah, I know what you mean about Templeton. But he's not evil."

Big Rabbit rolled his head back and forth and I heard his neck crack several times. "But he's not good, either."

We'd reached the stairs leading up to Lucie's townhouse. I went up first. Big Rabbit had thought to lock the door before he chased down the sidewalk after me. He handed me the keys and I let us in.

"There are a lot of worse people than Templeton," I said. "But I get what you're saying."

CHAPTER 9

It was getting late in the day. I kept checking the clock. I'd have to get a message to Jack soon to let him know I wasn't coming home. I had a legitimate reason. I still hadn't talked to Rabbit, and we needed to set things in motion to find the Tortoise. Then we needed to reunite the pieces of the Crimson Stone. I hoped Templeton had a change of heart and would come back to help. It was possible, right?

"You know what I'm craving?" I asked aloud as I dug through Lucie's refrigerator. I was starved and now that the worst part of my day was behind me – I hoped – I wanted comfort food. "One of Tuesday's lunch puffs."

"What's a Tuesday?" Big Rabbit asked. He looked up from his texting. He was sitting at Lucie's counter on one of the barstools.

"Tuesday's a baker in Vue. She has a place called *The Sweet Spot*. If you're ever in Vue, stop in and see her. She adores Rabbits." I paused. Why couldn't I door travel over to Tuesday's, pick-up dinner for all of us, and then door travel right back? *Brilliant!* And Tuesday's place was safe. I didn't have to worry about running into any trouble. "You know what? I'm going to pop out to Tuesday's and get dinner for all of us."

Big Rabbit shook his head. "No, you can't do that."

I crossed the kitchen and leaned on the counter. "Aren't you hungry?"

"Of course," he said, dropping his eyes back to the phone screen. "But you need to stay here."

"How come Rabbits are so bossy?" I asked.

"Because we know everything," he replied without looking up. "And I know you should stay here. Rabbit will arrive soon."

I considered my options. Sure, we could wait for Rabbit, but I was feeling antsy. Add to it I was hungry – and I didn't operate well on an empty stomach. I pulled on my bottom lip.

"Fine, you win," I said. "I'm going to grab more books from Lucie's room upstairs. I have a lot to learn."

Big Rabbit nodded and kept messaging the network. I heard him call after me as I climbed the stairs. "Soon! Rabbit will be here soon!"

I had snagged my shoulder bag from the table in the entryway before heading upstairs.

I pulled out my top hat, smoothing its purple feather. I paused to remember how excited I'd been to receive my own official top hat. Barely a year had passed since then. I placed it on my head.

Then I door traveled through Lucie's spare bedroom door right into Tuesday's bakery in Vue.

❋ ❋ ❋

The Sweet Spot was closed. I'd stepped through the front door into a darkened room.

Ugh! Right, Tuesday opened early to catch the breakfast crowd, then closed around three in the afternoon. Still, she might have a few lunch puffs stashed. No problem. Her apartment was right upstairs above the bakery. I walked up to the apartment and knocked on her door. I stowed my top hat back in my bag.

"Who is it?" A woman's voice called from the other side.

I didn't recognize the voice and Tuesday lived alone. Maybe she had a guest?

"It's Emily. I'm looking for Tuesday?"

The door opened and Tuesday's kitchen assistant stood in the doorway. "Hi Emily, remember me? Poppy Parsons? We met before in the bakery."

"Oh, right," I replied. "I'm sorry, I didn't recognize your voice."

She stepped aside and gestured for me to enter. "Tuesday's been out of town visiting family, but she'll be back later tonight. I've been staying here while she's gone so I can get everything going early in the bakery."

"Makes sense. I wanted to check on Tuesday because it's been a while, but I also wanted to see if she had any vegetarian lunch puffs left over," I admitted.

"How many do you need?"

"How many do you have?"

"One," she answered. "And one ham and cheese. I'm guessing not enough?"

I shook my head. "There's going to be a handful of us for dinner – and one is kind of a massive stomach on two feet."

Poppy laughed. "While I don't make a habit of sending customers to other eateries, there is a nice café a few blocks from here called *The Park Vue*. They have a sizable dinner menu and plenty of vegetarian choices. Great salads.

They're open until nine. You have plenty of time."

Well, it wasn't what I'd planned, but it would have to do. I'd walk the couple of blocks to *The Park Vue*, pick up dinner for everyone, then door travel back to Lucie's. I was adaptable.

"It sounds like a good alternative," I said to Poppy. "Tell Tuesday I stopped by and that I'll try to get back here soon."

"Absolutely," Poppy replied. "She'll be disappointed she missed you."

I said my goodbye and took the stairs out onto the sidewalk in front of the bakery. Following Poppy's directions, I turned to the left and headed for the other café, thinking about dinner.

Vue was a pretty city, sitting at the south end of Sight Sea. The city played host to a large artist community. I'd last visited when my mother was traipsing through the Empire and leading me on a wild goose chase. She ended up in Vue – and in a lot of trouble. After she was arrested for a murder she didn't commit, she was kidnapped by the Fringe. That's when I'd met Sebastian for the first time. He used my mother as bait in an attempt to get his hands on the Crimson Stone.

Sebastian was successful in getting me to come after my mother; he was not successful in getting any piece of the Stone. I'd won that first battle.

The streetlights came on as I walked along the sidewalk. I was heading in the direction of the big park overlooking the dock where the Sight Sea ferry dropped off visitors to the city. I wouldn't need to go that far. *The Park Vue* was located on the edge of the park.

I was glad it was getting darker. During this time of year, the transition to night happened quickly. And yet, I felt less vulnerable walking in the dusk as opposed to strolling along by myself in the bright light of day. My run-in with Sebastian made me anxious. Before I door traveled to Vue, I didn't think I might need to leave Tuesday's bakery to find dinner elsewhere. I'd be glad to get back to my friends in Matar.

I suppose I could've picked a door and traveled back to Lucie's right then. But I hated to waste the trip. *You're here now, Emily,* I thought. Let's get everyone dinner and be done with it.

The breeze picked up as I turned a corner. It ruffled past my shoulder, blowing the loose ends of the silk scarf out in front of me. I shivered and tightened my jacket. After getting food at *The Park Vue,* I'd door travel straight from the restaurant back to Matar. There was no reason to go back to Tuesday's.

The sidewalk on this block was mostly empty, and I let out a sharp yelp as a cat darted in front of me. It passed through the streetlight's glow before blending back into the shadows without a sound.

"At least it didn't look like a black cat," I said aloud, faking a low chuckle. A door slammed behind me, and I twisted, looking over my shoulder to make sure no one followed me. Nope. I was alone. The coast was clear. I blew out a breath and turned to resume my course.

Nisha stood underneath the next streetlight.

I stopped in my tracks as all the hair on the back of my neck rose and a prickle ran over my skin. Even from 20 feet away, I could feel her relentless inspection. For the second time that day, I thought about escape.

According to Rabbit, Nisha was a priestess – a being who practiced an ancient type of magic.

He'd warned me away from her, explaining only desperate people went to her for help. The price they paid was high. She was dangerous.

The first time I faced Nisha was here in Vue. When Rabbit arrived to guide me away from the otherworldly woman, she'd called him Fánaí. Later when I asked him what it meant, he admitted it was his name – but he told me nothing more. I could see Rabbit was afraid of her. That meant I was, too.

It got worse. When I couldn't locate where the Fringe had imprisoned my mother, Nisha reappeared and showed me a symbol. Her prediction was I'd find my mother under it. She said the debt for her aid was paid by another.

I realized Rabbit, in his desperation to help me, had gone to Nisha.

The events surrounding my mother's rescue happened so fast, I never got to ask Rabbit what he sacrificed. It was the last time I'd seen my loyal friend.

Nisha remained under the streetlight. I trudged forward, knowing I couldn't outrun her. She was too powerful. As I approached, I noted she was barefoot as before, her toes bearing several silver rings. A shimmering iridescent dress caressed her body from her curvy hips to her ankles; the fabric seemed to ripple over her ebony skin even though she stood as still as a statue. Her long, midnight-colored hair was not loose like before. This time it was piled high on her head in more than a dozen thick bantu knots, each wrapped with a thin silver chain. She wore a necklace of obsidian gemstones – the strand wrapped around her neck several times creating a choker. Her full lips were the color of black cherries. As I stepped into the circle of streetlight surrounding her, I stared into eyes as black as pitch.

I felt her magic encircle me. I reacted by raising my door travel energy in my chest. Her lips curled cruelly as her own power tapped against it.

Nisha broke the silence. "You've grown stronger, Emily Swift."

I didn't let down my guard as a few more pokes tested the wall I'd raised around myself. I was unsure of how long I could maintain it. "Have I?"

"Hmm." She tilted her head as she evaluated me. Nisha towered over me in her bare feet.

"Are you seeking me out for a reason?" I asked.

"The Crimson Stone."

Oh, of course. I should've known. Nisha was convinced I had it. She didn't know she was partly right. I had a piece of the Stone when we first met, and I had a piece of it now. But I wasn't admitting this to her. Unfortunately, my intuition told me Nisha could sense some of the Stone on me. That's why she kept appearing.

"I do not have it, Nisha. I've told you this before."

"You lie to me," she replied.

"I don't." I decided to take a different approach. "In fact, I'm in the Empire looking for it. I need it."

Her eyebrows pulled together. "You need the Stone," she repeated.

"Yes. I need it to stop the Fringe."

"The Fringe." Nisha peered upward. The sky no longer held a trace of color. "The Fringe is unimportant."

I shook my head. I had to figure out how to walk away from this situation. I'd abandoned the idea of dinner. I would grab the first door I could find and zip right on back to Lucie's.

"What the Fringe does is important to the Empire," I told her. I took a step to the side. Her focus flew back to me.

"The Empire is unimportant."

We were getting nowhere fast. I touched my forehead and looked to the ground. No plan of escape seemed obvious. I needed to stall.

"Nisha, last spring when Rabbit – I mean, Fánaí – came to you for help, what did he give you?" I pronounced Fánaí like *Fawny*.

"Fánaí," she whispered. She stepped closer and a milky mist clouded her eyes. "Is he here? I can no longer find him."

Her reaction frightened me. "No, he's not here. I don't know where he is."

"He protects you," she answered. Her eyes cleared. "I know this."

"He has been my friend. What did he give you to help me?"

Nisha motioned to my right hand. "You believe he paid the price for the symbol I gave you."

"I don't believe you gave it to him out of the goodness of your heart," I said, flinching. Angering her was a bad idea.

If she was bothered by my words, Nisha didn't show it. "Fánaí paid his own debt to me many years ago. I do not regret taking my payment, but I suffer for his sadness."

Her words didn't make any sense to me, but if Rabbit paid his debt a long time ago, it had nothing to do with helping me find my mother. "Are you saying someone else came to you on my behalf? To find out where I could find my mother?"

"Yes."

"Who?" Who could have possibly made a deal with Nisha? And why?

Nisha's mouth opened into a toothy smile. "Do you need me to tell you? Are you asking me for a favor?"

"No!" I responded, waving both of my palms at her to negate any thoughts she might have of a trade between us. My stomach churned. "I'm not asking you for anything."

"Hmm." Her mouth closed, but her lips remained curved.

"Forget it," I told her.

"I will make you an offer." She tossed her head back as she stroked the obsidian necklace with her fingertips.

"No deal, Nisha."

Her fingers stilled. "I will tell you who came to me on your behalf. In return, I want you to pass a message to Fánaí."

"I can't do that," I said. This seemed like a betrayal to Rabbit.

Nisha dropped her hand. "I see into you. Already this revelation is filling you with chaos. You will agree to this exchange. And it's such a small price to pay."

Gah! She was right. I had to know. And yet, a troubling thought needled at me. *Oh.* "Nisha, it was a Salesman who came to you, wasn't it?"

She remained silent in her victory, but the satisfied expression she wore proved she knew I'd make the trade.

"It was a Salesman," I said again. Two faces swam in front of my mind's eye: Templeton and Sebastian. One man would've asked for help in finding my mother; the other would've asked Nisha to help lure me to the warehouse where he was lying in wait.

"Do we have an agreement?"

"I only have to give Rabbit a message, right? Nothing else? Tell him a few words and the debt will be fully paid by me. Nothing more required from anyone, right?" I hoped like hell I wasn't missing anything.

"Nothing more." Nisha held up her right hand. "Put your left palm against mine."

Grimacing, I did as I was told. My palm pressed against hers. I watched in horror as her eyes rolled up and filled with a milky white once more. She chanted words in a language I did not understand. I felt her spell ripple from her hand and slip under my skin, traveling down my arm and into my chest where it wrapped around my heart. I tried to pull back, but the energy she pushed into me held me firmly in place. Terrified, I could do nothing but wait until she finished.

Nisha completed her spell, the mist disappearing from her eyes as the grip on my heart lessened. As she drew her energy away, I dropped my hand from hers. She put her palm to her mouth and licked it.

"Your magic is young... Fresh," she breathed. "I can taste it."

"What just happened?" I felt fine, but I knew better.

"If you do not pass my message to Fánaí in the next three days, you will owe me your heart." Nisha continued to leer at her palm, a hunger slithering across her face.

"I will owe you my heart?" My voice rose. I shook my head back and forth. "No, no, that's not what I agreed to, Nisha."

"It is the price you will pay if you do not honor our agreement." Nisha lowered her hand. "As long as you give Fánaí my message, your debt is paid and your heart remains your own. The spell will end."

Holy-freaking-mother-of-pearl what had I done? I rubbed both hands over my face. Okay, this was straightforward. I pass the message to Rabbit, I keep my heart. Simple. I brought my palms together as if praying and touched my fingertips to my mouth. I nodded.

"What is the message?" I asked.

Nisha leaned down and pushed my hair over my shoulder. She put her mouth to my ear and murmured several words I didn't understand. When she finished her message, she stepped back.

"But I don't know what those words mean," I told her. "I don't even know how to say them." As I spoke, I tried to form the words in my head. I couldn't.

"You will be able to say them to Fánaí when you see him. He will understand what you tell him. Once the message has been passed, your debt is fully paid." Nisha gestured to something unseen behind me. "Someone is coming for you."

"Who?" I jerked my head, looking over my shoulder. "Who?"

"A friend. She will be here soon." Nisha stretched to her full height of six feet. "Now, you may ask your question, Emily Swift. I will answer and fulfill my end of our deal."

Warily glancing over my shoulder once more and wondering what 'friend' could possibly be coming this way, I turned back to Nisha, sighing. Hopefully this part was simple. "Nisha, who came to you and asked you to help me find my mother?"

Nisha took a deep breath in through her nose while the air around us grew thick and swirled. She laughed wickedly.

"It was Templeton."

❊ ❊ ❊

Templeton had gone to Nisha on my behalf

for help. Templeton was the Salesman who owed Nisha a debt.

I worried about what Templeton had done. He was strong, a powerful practitioner of magic, but what did he give up in return? What did he do? I hung my head. I needed to find out, but I knew better now than to ask Nisha.

"Your friend approaches." Nisha's voice interrupted my thoughts.

I turned to see a short, plump woman walk into the streetlamp's light. She didn't acknowledge Nisha, but instead simply took my hand. Her kind smile was a balm on my battered soul.

"Hi, Emily. I knew I'd find you if I searched long enough." Tuesday put her hand to my cheek. "Now come with me and I'll give you dinner to take to your friends. Don't look back. Okay?"

Resisting the urge to look at Nisha, I allowed myself to be led away from the dangerous circle we'd created. I gripped Tuesday's hand as I heard Nisha's words float after me.

"Give Fánaí my message, or I'll take your heart."

* * *

Tuesday led me soundlessly through the streets and to her apartment over *The Sweet Spot*. Inside, I still trembled with fear and could barely speak. Poppy tossed Tuesday a curious look when we arrived, helping Tuesday lead me to the couch. The kitchen assistant excused herself, saying she'd catch up with the baker in the morning. She called out a goodbye as she left, but I'd yet to recover my voice.

I wrapped my arms around myself and shuddered. At least I felt safe here.

"Well, that was an interesting evening," Tuesday began as she returned to the living room. She brought out a large mug filled with chicken noodle soup and handed me a spoon. "I think you should have something to eat."

"Yeah, I haven't had much to eat today," I admitted. My hand shook as I tried to spoon the soup into my mouth. I gave up and sipped the broth from the mug, holding it with both hands.

Tuesday sat next to me. "I'm glad I was able

to come back to Vue earlier than I'd planned. When I arrived, Poppy said I just missed you. I went out looking."

I swallowed another hot mouthful. It felt good on my throat. "I'm glad you did."

"What's going on, Emily?" Tuesday was worried. "What are you doing in the Empire? Are you here alone? Is your mother okay?"

I assured Tuesday my mother was safe and sound with my boyfriend in Kincaid. At least this time around, we weren't dealing with that drama.

After taking several more sips of the soup, I set the mug on the table. Turning sideways on the couch, I spent the next 15 minutes telling Tuesday everything. I started with how Templeton door traveled into my house with the news about Blackstone.

Tuesday listened intently; her eyes wide behind the thick lenses of her glasses. Occasionally she'd say, 'oh, no!' or 'they are bad men!' but she let me finish without asking any questions. I skipped the details of the terrifying price I'd pay if I didn't give Rabbit Nisha's message, and I glossed over Sebastian's attack. I had to explain who he was, however. Tuesday knew my mother had been kidnapped when she was in the Empire. I explained how Sebastian St. Michel was behind it.

"And he's part of the Fringe?" she asked.

"Yeah," I replied. "I don't know if he's created his own kingdom within the Fringe or if his connections go deeper and he has some real power."

"I wonder," Tuesday pursed her lips. "And you said he's a Salesman coming from one of the old families here in the Empire? A wealthy one?"

"That's what Mr. Blackstone told me. He said Sebastian's family has influence, but none of the family has ever sat on the Salesman Court. He also told me Sebastian's never been linked to the Fringe. Apparently, that's the official position of the Empire."

Tuesday shook her head as she stood, walking around the room and sticking her fingers in potted plants as she determined which ones needed to be watered. "I've thought something smelled rotten in the high halls of the Empire for a long time now, Emily."

"But there are still good people sitting on the Salesman Court," I reminded her. "Justice

Spell, Justice Smith… and Jo! You remember Jo Carter, right? She was the Salesman who was with my mother when the Fringe attacked them in the street. Jo came here to help. She's now a Junior Justice on the Court. Corruption goes against every fiber of her being."

Tuesday listened to my passionate speech. "I have no doubt your friend Jo is everything you say she is. And I'm sure there are others who aren't influenced by the Fringe. But you know as well as I do, Emily, there have been justices on the bench who were plain evil."

Tuesday was right. It was here in Vue that Justice Petrovich killed an innocent woman – a friend of Tuesday's – and then tried to steal the Crimson Stone.

"Do you think it's getting worse?" I held up a hand. "Don't answer that. It is. If the Fringe could take the North Door like they did, it's definitely reaching a new level."

"I think the Empire is not the same place it was when I was a young woman," Tuesday said sadly. I watched as she looked around the room, seeing more than I could. She was seeing her memories.

"I know things have changed," I said. Seeing

Tuesday slipping into such melancholy unnerved me. The sweet lady was usually a bouncing ball of joy. "But you know what? I think we can make things change for the better. We can take down the Fringe once and for all."

"If anyone can do it, Emily, you can. I believe in you." Tuesday seemed to cheer up as she spoke. She clapped her soft hands together. "But first, let's make sure you have food to take back to your friends. They won't be as angry at you for sneaking out if you can help them fill their empty stomachs."

❉ ❉ ❉

Tuesday packed a large sack of savory pot pies from the freezer in her bakery downstairs. "There are chicken pot pies and vegetarian ones – you can tell your Rabbits those are packed with potatoes, carrots, mushrooms, and onions. Put them in the oven at 375 degrees for 45 minutes. I promise once everyone digs into these, they'll forget about being upset with you."

"What would we do without you, Tuesday?" I asked, giving the lovable Minor Muse a hug.

I trusted what she said. No one could stay in a bad mood once they ate something from her kitchen. It was her power, after all. "I'll send a message and let you know what happens."

She wrapped her pudgy arms around me. I was short, but I had a few inches on Tuesday. I prayed to whatever gods watched over the Empire that they'd also watch over our sweet little baker.

We gave each other one final squeeze before she passed me the bulging sack. I pulled my top hat from my bag and placed it on my head.

"You're still wearing your hat?" Tuesday tilted her head to the side.

I was surprised. "Well, yes. I figure I'll draw less attention to myself. The Empire notices door travel without a top hat."

"I suppose it's true if that's what they tell you," she nodded. "Give Rabbit my best."

"Sure." I touched the brim of my hat. Tuesday's words haunted me, but I didn't have time to dwell on it. "Stay safe, Tuesday."

I heard her call 'you too!' as I touched the doorknob and door traveled from Vue to Lucie's home in Matar.

CHAPTER 10

The scene I stepped into at Lucie's was surreal. Rabbit – *my Rabbit* – had arrived while I was in Vue. He was furious to find I wasn't there. He ranted at Big Rabbit as the larger man sniffled. Lucie sat at the kitchen counter with her head in her hands. She looked up when I stepped in through the pantry door, peering at me through her fingers.

"Make them stop," she begged.

"How could you let her out of your sight? How could you let her leave?" My Rabbit yelled at Big Rabbit.

"I didn't know! She's slippery." Big Rabbit's voice wobbled. He saw me standing in front of the pantry door. His face lit up and he pushed Rabbit aside. "Emily!"

Before I could stop him, I was picked up and squished in the massive arms of Big Rabbit. "Careful, you'll flatten our dinner!"

Big Rabbit set me down. "Ooh, sorry. Um, what's for dinner? I could eat."

"Pot pies," I said, placing the sack on the counter and turning the dial on Lucie's oven.

While the oven preheated, I unpacked the frozen pies. I avoided looking at Rabbit. He glowered at me from across the kitchen.

"You were supposed to stay here," he fumed.

"I stepped out for dinner. We're always begging food off Lucie," I replied as I worked on putting the meal together.

Lucie appeared at my side, setting out cookie trays to go under the pot pies. "He's been yelling at Big Rabbit for about 10 minutes," she grumbled. "I've never seen him this amped up."

"I wish he hadn't taken it out on Big Rabbit," I said, lowering my voice as I leaned into her. "But I knew he'd be mad."

Rabbit's hand smacked the countertop. "Emily, in the living room. Right now!" Rabbit left the kitchen, his feet pounding the floor as he headed for the front of the townhouse.

"Crap," I swore, wiping my damp hands on a dish towel.

"Good luck with that," Lucie said. "Go make up with him. I'll finish in here."

"I'll need it," I agreed. I traced Rabbit's path into the living room. He stood inside facing the unlit fireplace, his back toward the leaded glass door.

"Close the door," he ordered as I entered.

Sighing, I did as he directed. I'd let him go first.

He cast a dirty look over his shoulder before turning back to the fireplace.

Okay, maybe I'd better start. "I door traveled from here to Tuesday's bakery in Vue. As far as risks go, this one was probably about as low risk as you can get."

Rabbit rubbed the back of his neck with his right hand. I watched as he slid the same hand to the back of his head, the other cupping his chin. He twisted his head to the left and I heard his neck crack. He switched the placement of his hands and turned his head to the right. Another snap. He finally turned around.

"You were told to stay here," he said through clenched teeth. His arms hung at his sides, but I could sense the angry energy inside him.

I held up a finger. "First, you are not in charge of what I do."

Rabbit stepped toward me, his body tensing while his eyes darkened. I flinched, resisting the impulse to back away. "If you didn't escape Sebastian today, Emily, you might not be standing here now."

My hand automatically lifted to touch the scarf around my neck. "I know. I know I got lucky. But I got away."

Rabbit closed his eyes and his shoulders dropped. His youthful face seemed to age in seconds. "I can't protect you if you don't listen to me," he whispered before opening his eyes. Gone was the fury. Instead, he simply seemed tired.

Although one might think Rabbit was probably in his early 20s, in truth he was probably in his mid-50s. When my father was killed 18 years ago, Rabbit and his cluster searched the train wreck for survivors. They found none. He'd confirmed my father was among the dead.

"Protecting me can't be your job," I said, closing the distance between us and touching his shoulder. And yet here in the Empire, Rabbit had taken on the role. He'd appointed himself as my guardian since my father wasn't alive to watch over me. It was partly my fault. I sought him out when I needed help.

Rabbit reached up to his shoulder and took my hand in his. He gave it a gentle squeeze.

"You are a full-time job."

I offered him a rueful smile. "Yeah, there are probably a few others who think the same."

"I was scared when I arrived here and they told me you were gone," he said. "After what happened earlier today, you're a target. This is the second time you've managed to get away from Sebastian and he's got to be furious. And I bet he knows you're still here in the Empire."

"But he doesn't know where I am in the Empire," I said. "That works to my advantage."

Rabbit wasn't convinced. "You assume he doesn't know where you're staying."

"How would he know I'm here?" I argued. "I'm probably safer here at Lucie's than I am at home." I winced. "Oh, which reminds me. I have to let Jack know I'm not coming home tonight."

"You'd planned to?"

"Yes, I'm trying to keep Jack in the loop," I explained, biting my lip.

"You told him about Sebastian? You told him about…" Rabbit's voice trailed off as he pointed at my neck.

"Oh, definitely not."

"Yeah, I wouldn't think so." Rabbit rubbed

his hand across his forehead. "You need me to send a message?"

"Please. Yes, tell him I'm safe and sound at Lucie's but since you just got here, I'm spending the night. Tell him I'll touch base tomorrow." I knew Jack wasn't going to like it, but if I went home now, it would only be worse. For both of us.

Rabbit pulled out his phone and sent a message. "Done. He'll get a call."

"Thanks." I sat down on the couch and regarded my friend. Rabbit wore a reddish knit hat pulled down over the tips of his ears. His hair was longish, the dark locks curling around the edge of the knit cap. He wore one of the many black tee shirts he seemed to own – the front of this one featuring a gray monster holding up a skull by its hair. The skull leered at me from the shirt; a cigarette gripped in a corner of its jaw. Beneath the tee, he wore a long-sleeved shirt. His jeans were tucked into his heavy work boots. A thick chain ran from his pocketed wallet and underneath his untucked clothing. It was probably attached to his belt.

Rabbit took a seat across from me. He leaned

forward with his forearms on his knees. He laced his hands together and I noted his knuckles were battered.

"I didn't have time to talk to Lucie," he said. "But I do know about some of the things that've been happening."

I nodded. I assumed Rabbit knew more than I did. "You probably know about everything."

My friend shrugged. "The network knew about the hit on Blackstone and the tampering of the North Door."

"Templeton was the one who told me about both," I explained. "The Empire didn't contact me."

"Are you surprised?"

"A little. Blackstone was the first person to explain to me what it meant to be a Salesman. Spell knew we had a relationship. I don't know." I waved my hand. "Anyhow, I came here as soon as I could. Rabbit, do you have your piece of the Crimson Stone yet?"

Although I wasn't surprised, I was disappointed when he shook his head no. "I can't catch up to the Tortoise."

"Rabbit, we need to find him." I sat forward on the edge of the couch. "We need the third piece of the Stone. I... I already talked to Templeton. I've asked him to help us. I've asked him to bring the piece he has. I want to re-form the Crimson Stone. I want to use it to stop the Fringe once and for all."

Rabbit listened, the frown on his face deepening. "Templeton has agreed to this?"

"No, not yet," I admitted. "But, I think, maybe. Maybe he'll help." My voice trailed off. I thought about what I'd learned – how Templeton had gone to Nisha to help me find my mother. I couldn't imagine the price he'd paid, especially knowing what I'd agreed to earlier.

"Tell me what you know, Emily." All Rabbits were quick to catch when there was information to be gathered. My Rabbit was one of the network's best.

"We never got to talk after the night at the warehouse," I said. "I never got to thank you or the network for helping me."

Rabbit stared past his clasped hands at the floor. "We were lucky we got there in time."

"I know what happened after I left." I suppressed a shudder. Fearing the Empire would not bring a murderous Salesman named Simon to justice, the Rabbits had beaten him.

He was at death's door when found dropped on the front steps of the Empire guard station in Matar. The last I'd heard, Simon was still awaiting trial.

Simon was one of Sebastian's underlings.

Rabbit kept his focus on the floor. His face revealed nothing. "My conscience is clear."

I nodded. "What you don't know is I thought you'd gone to Nisha for help."

At Nisha's name, Rabbit's head jerked up, but he said nothing.

I continued. "When she appeared and gave me the symbol showing where my mother was being held, she said a friend of mine came to her and asked for help. She said the debt was paid. I thought it was you. I thought you had gone to her for help."

"I would not go to Nisha for help." A muscle in his jaw twitched.

"Okay, but back then – and until today – I thought you were the friend." I took a deep breath. I had a feeling Rabbit was about to become angry again.

He eyeballed me. "Who was the friend who helped you?"

"Templeton." I pressed my lips together.

Rabbit hung his head and swore. "And he told you this? Today?"

"I don't think he knows that I know," I said.

"How do you know?" He sat back in the chair, fixing me with a hard stare. He crossed his arms over his chest. "I'm not going to like this, am I?"

"Not one bit," I said. "But in my defense, I didn't go looking for this information. It came to me."

Rabbit barked out a laugh. "Emily, you should have 'but in my defense' tattooed on your arm."

"When I went to Vue to get us all dinner, Tuesday's bakery was closed and she wasn't home."

"But you came back with food from *The Sweet Spot*."

"This is true. But before I met up with Tuesday, I was walking to another café." I took a breath and prepared myself. "Nisha appeared out of nowhere."

Rabbit didn't offer any reaction. "Go on."

"She wanted the Crimson Stone. I told her I didn't have it – that I was still looking for it. Then I asked her what you gave to her in return for helping me. She made it clear it wasn't you and I realized it was a Salesman." I lowered my chin. It was my turn to study the floor. "She said she'd tell me if I agreed to do her a favor."

The room was silent. I glanced up at Rabbit. He was paler than usual.

"What did you agree to do?" he growled.

"She asked me to give you a message," I said.

"No!" Rabbit sprang up from his chair. "No. I don't want any message, Emily. No!" He threw open the door leading out of the living room.

"Wait, Rabbit! Please!" I scrambled after him as he passed through the entryway and slammed out of the brownstone. I opened the door and chased him down the front stairs. "Rabbit!"

"How could you?" He spun back around and exploded. "And Templeton can go to hell!"

"I'm sorry, I didn't know what I was getting into! Please, please let me finish," I pleaded with Rabbit.

He paced back and forth on the brick sidewalk before turning to me and unleashing a second round of fury. "I understand you don't know everything, Emily, and I get how you can't possibly predict every consequence of your actions. I know you're still trying to find answers to all the secrets around you. But I told you to stay away from Nisha! And what did you do? You agreed to do her bidding because you wanted an answer – and then you go and bring me into it! Forget it. I don't want to know anything she told you. Leave me out of this one." He suddenly turned and stormed away.

The pounding in my chest was a clear reminder that no matter what Rabbit wanted – or didn't want – if I wanted to keep my heart, he was getting this message. I would make it up to him someday.

"Wait, Rabbit!" I chased after him again, grabbing a hold of his arm. He pulled away.

"Don't. I don't want to talk to you right now." He kept walking.

"Rabbit, she said if I don't tell you, she'll take my heart." The words hung in the night air. He stopped and I took a few steps toward him. "I'm sorry. But I didn't realize what would happen. She said if I don't tell you within three days..." I lifted my shoulders once.

Defeated, Rabbit sat down on one of the stairs leading up to another brownstone. He leaned sideways against the wrought iron railing and closed his eyes. My heart tightened when I realized he was trembling. "Tell me."

I eased down on the step next to him. Leaning into his side, I spoke Nisha's words into his ear. I didn't understand what I said, and I couldn't repeat them if I tried. I assumed this was part of the spell. When the last word crossed my lips, my chest felt lighter. Nisha's grip eased away from my heart. I'd paid my debt.

I pulled back and studied Rabbit's profile. The streetlamps did little to light his face. "I'm sorry."

He nodded.

"Did you understand the message?"

He nodded a second time.

"Is it –?"

"Emily, stop it," he interrupted. He climbed to his feet and held out his hand. I took it and he pulled me up. "Let's get you back to Lucie's."

❋ ❋ ❋

Rabbit didn't say anything during the short walk. He did follow me inside and into the kitchen. Lucie and Big Rabbit watched us, shooting each other curious looks.

"Lucie, I'm going to take a raincheck on dinner," he said. He put his hand on Big Rabbit's shoulder. "Something has come up and I've got to deal with it. Can you put this big guy up for the night?"

"Sure, but I only have the two bedrooms and the couch is short," Lucie replied. Her eyes twinkled as she sized up Big Rabbit. "How do you feel about a sleeping bag, a lot of pillows, and my living room floor?"

"Sounds lovely," Big Rabbit answered. He glanced at me as he turned to Rabbit. "You have to leave? Is everything okay?"

Rabbit refused to look in my direction. "Everything's fine. Personal matter. Can you keep an eye on everything here? Make sure no one gets in?"

Big Rabbit nodded. "No one will get by me."

"Of that, I'm sure." He patted Big Rabbit's shoulder again and nodded to Lucie once before leaving the kitchen. I started to follow but Lucie's hand caught my arm.

"I don't know what happened," she said. "But if you ever want to find that Rabbit again, let him go."

Seconds later, I heard the front door open and close.

Rabbit was gone.

* * *

"You know why I never went to slumber parties as a girl?" Lucie asked as she helped me put fresh sheets on the bed in her spare room. "Drama. I hate drama."

"Are you saying we're going to have a slumber party with Big Rabbit?" I pictured us sitting cramped together in Lucie's living room, braiding his unruly hair.

"Ha! No." Lucie smoothed out the top sheet. "I'm pointing out the obvious drama between you and Rabbit. You've got to stop dragging him into things."

"Whoa," I told her. "Rabbit came on board this –"

"Crazy train," Lucie interjected.

"This *effort*," I shot Lucie a dirty look, "a long time ago. He's in it for the long haul."

"Hmm." Lucie plumped up a pillow.

"And he's got the third piece of the Stone.

Well, access to it once he finds the Tortoise." I sat down on the bed. Lucie handed me a pair of clean cotton pajamas from the laundry basket. She was a few inches taller than I was, but they would fit fine.

"I understand, but remember, his life doesn't revolve around Emily Swift. He's generous with you, and he wants to keep you safe, but he's more than *your Rabbit*. He has a whole other life." She retrieved a towel.

"I know." I fiddled with a washcloth before folding it into a square. I snuck a peek at Lucie. She pulled out another towel. "Wait, have you spent time with Rabbit?"

"I went to a concert with him this summer," she said, shrugging.

"What?" I handed her a short stack of folded bath towels. "How did that happen? And, geez, Lucie, his music is kind of…" I covered my ears with my hands and screwed my eyes shut. I pretended to scream.

"That pretty much sums up his taste," Lucie laughed. "But you know, he stopped in one Saturday and asked me if I wanted to go see *Black Talons*. When I was younger, I had a huge crush on the lead singer, Raven Xerces. I never got to see him in concert. Then Rabbit waves a ticket under my nose, and I thought: oh, what the hell!"

"Brave woman. But now your Saturdays will be busy with... *Basha!*" I flopped down on the bed. I made kissing noises. "Oh, Basha!"

"I think I'm going to be sick. What are you, 10?" Lucie gave me the side eye. "Again, this is why I didn't go to slumber parties."

It was my turn to laugh. "I'm sorry. I think I'm overtired."

"It's been a helluva day," Lucie agreed. "Why don't you turn in? I'll make sure Big Rabbit is settled. We can get an early start tomorrow."

"We?"

"Well, I'm not reading cards until the afternoon, so I'm available to brainstorm and help in any way I can while I'm here in the morning. We can do laundry if you're not able to run back home for a change of clothes. Or you can borrow some of mine. Whatever works." Lucie turned on the bedside lamp. "I'll make everyone omelets for breakfast. And Emily, I'm happy to help you. We all are. But make good choices."

"I know," I sighed. "Thanks. I'll do better.

You'll see."

Lucie stood in the doorway and raised one eyebrow. "I know you'll try. What's on the docket for tomorrow?"

"Assuming Rabbit is coming back? Finding the last piece of the Crimson Stone and getting Templeton on board the 'crazy train.' I think I'll even pop into the Salesman Courthouse downtown."

"The Court? Whatever for?" Lucie's nose wrinkled.

"I know the Empire's 'official' position on Sebastian's involvement with the Fringe is that he's not, but I think I'm going to make Spell look at my neck and tell me the lie to my face. I want to see how she reacts." I pulled The Book from my shoulder bag. I'd go through it before trying to get to sleep. Maybe I'd be inspired by something new. Maybe Evangeline's subconscious would have a message.

"Why in the world would you want to tempt fate by confronting Spell? She's going to have a fit when you show up."

"Probably," I nodded. "But Tuesday said something when I was in Vue and it's bugging me. I'm going to find out how rotten the high halls of the Empire smell these days."

❊ ❊ ❊

Lucie shut the door when she said goodnight, and I curled up in the comfy bed. I set aside the angst I had about Jack and not going home. I put my worries about Rabbit on the back burner. I refused to think about Sebastian.

Instead, I opened my father's journal and turned through the pages. I found a blank one. Retrieving a pencil from my bag, I wrote: *Evangeline? Are you there? It's Emily.*

I waited a couple of minutes and was rewarded: *Hello, Emily.*

Oh, good. She was back. I put the pencil to the page: *I'm glad to see you again. I wanted to ask you about the secret message. Did you find it?*

Evangeline: *Yes. I have found it.*

"Thank goodness." I wrote: *May I ask what it is? Can you tell me?*

Evangeline: *Yes. I can tell you. Turn the page.*

I followed her instructions and watched as a new passage appeared, each line appearing one at a time:

A traveler is born.

The night protects the light.
Their heir sets fire to the stone.

Well, that was as clear as mud. I shook my head. This was the message for me? I decided to ask if Evangeline understood what it meant. I turned back to the page where we had our 'conversation.'

I wrote: *Evangeline, do you know what this means?*

Evangeline: *I do not.*

Okay, that was fair. But maybe... *Can you tell me who this message is from? Is it from my father?*

Evangeline: *The message is very old.*

I twisted my mouth to the side. I couldn't expect her to know everything.

Evangeline: *It is not from your father. It is from the other one. The woman. She spelled this book with old magic. Some of her is here. We are here and not here.*

Who could this other woman be? Did my father have his journal spelled? Or did someone spell The Book without him knowing?

I wanted to ask Evangeline more questions, but I also wanted to be respectful of the witch. I hadn't intended to put a piece of her in The

Book, but I was grateful for her help. I wrote my thanks and wished her a good night.

Her last message said: *Yes. Rest.*

I turned the page back to the new passage:

A traveler is born.

The night protects the light.

Their heir sets fire to the stone.

Was I the traveler? Isn't that what Evangeline called me before? And the stone... it had to be the Crimson Stone!

But an heir? I chewed on the inside of my cheek. Jack and I certainly weren't ready to have children. Truthfully, it never came up. We talked about getting married someday, but what was the rush? I was only turning 31 in December.

"Well, I'm not going to figure it out tonight," I said aloud as I closed The Book and pushed it to the bottom of my shoulder bag.

I was going to let my brain work on it while I slept. Something would come to me.

And tomorrow, I would confront Justice Spell.

CHAPTER 11

I slept well – which surprised me since it had been less than 48 hours since I'd found out Blackstone was strangled in his home. It was less than 24 hours since Sebastian put his hand around my throat.

Lucie and Big Rabbit were already up when I padded barefoot into the kitchen. I still wore Lucie's pajamas and had rewrapped the scarf around my neck. I'd checked in the mirror upstairs and the bruises were still obvious.

Sliding up onto the barstool by Big Rabbit, I glanced at the large pasta bowl sitting in front of him. It was filled with cereal.

"How'd you sleep?" he asked, crunching happily.

"Pretty good," I told him, inspecting his breakfast. "How about you?"

"She filled the living room floor with pillows." He motioned to Lucie with his spoon. "I slept like a baby."

"A baby who snores like a buzzsaw," Lucie teased as she slid a cup of coffee in front of me. She set a carton of milk beside it. "I can't believe you didn't shake down the house."

Big Rabbit's cheeks colored.

"Don't listen to her. I didn't hear a thing." I added the milk to my coffee. "Then again, I slept like a rock. Hey, weren't we going to have omelets?"

"Big Rabbit can't eat eggs," Lucie said.

"Allergic?" I asked him.

He shook his head. "No, that's not it. They smell like fish in the morning."

Lucie winked at me.

"Okay," I said. I lifted the empty cereal box.

Lucie's smile grew into a wide grin. "Toast?"

"I'd love some," I replied.

"When are you heading to the Salesman Court?" Lucie asked, pressing the handle down on the toaster. "Butter? Jam?"

"Butter's fine. Early. Probably around nine."

"Do you want to borrow some of my clothes? The pants might be long on you. I suppose you could roll up the hem," Lucie said. "I think I can find a smaller shirt to fit you."

I cocked my head to the side. Lucie was fit and I was in pretty good shape. "Smaller?"

"Because of her bigger bust," Big Rabbit nodded, shoving another spoonful into his mouth.

He turned scarlet when he realized what he'd said. "Oh, I'm sorry, Lucie!"

"Don't worry about it," Lucie laughed as she thwapped him with a kitchen towel. "But yeah, Emily, I have a little more up top than you do."

Lucie *was* curvy. She didn't seem to exaggerate her figure, but her red tee shirt was pulled snugly across her chest, and she wore a pair of skinny jeans. Big Rabbit must've been checking her out while she bopped around the kitchen. "I did think about trying to sneak home to grab clothes. In and out before anyone catches me."

"Seriously?" Lucie flicked a look in my direction as the toast popped up. She shook her head, passing me the butter. "Did you hear what you just said?"

"I don't want Jack to see the marks." At those words, everyone grew quiet. I spread the butter across the toast. "I can't explain away the scarf I'm wearing."

"Emily," Lucie began. "I know you don't want to tell Jack, but do you think you should hide it from him? Wouldn't you want to know if he'd been hurt?"

"I can't tell him," I argued. "And my mother is

staying at our house. I can't let her know any of this. She'll be terrified. And after last year…" I lifted my hand.

Reluctantly, Lucie nodded. "I guess I see your point."

"I can throw my clothes in the washer and borrow something from you for now. But, um, not underwear," I cringed. "No offense."

"None taken."

Big Rabbit sat texting throughout the conversation. He peeked at me out of the corner of his eye. "There's a secondhand shop two blocks from here. You could pick up a couple of outfits there. I know they sell new, ah, girl underwear."

"You mean *panties*," Lucie snickered. "Go on, you can say it."

Poor Big Rabbit. Lucie wasn't above making him squirm following his earlier comment about her bust size. But the obvious was too tempting to pass up. "Hey, how do you know they sell new 'girl underwear,' Big Rabbit?"

"Some of the girls shop there! See?" He held up his phone. By 'girls' I assumed he meant the female Rabbits he knew. The text message on the screen read: *Yeah. Second Act. Cheap clothes.*

New underwear.

"That settles it," I said. "I'll go get a couple of changes of clothes, then I'll come back and door travel downtown."

Big Rabbit held up one of his large hands. "I'm going with you to *Second Act*. I'm not letting you out of my sight until Rabbit gets back. And what's this about going downtown?"

"I'm going to meet with one of the justices today." I decided not to explain to Big Rabbit how I was popping into the Salesman Court unannounced.

He rubbed his chin. "Well, I can go with you there, too."

"No, that won't work." I gave him what I called my winning smile – sometimes it worked on Jack. "I'll make a deal with you. I won't complain about us walking a couple of blocks to the secondhand store if you won't give me any grief about *safely* door traveling from Lucie's into the Salesman Court downtown. It would take us too long to travel on foot or if we took public transit. I need to get there and get right back. You know, so I can be here when Rabbit returns."

Big Rabbit wasn't fooled. I could almost

see the wheels spinning in his head while he evaluated me. His phone buzzed and he glanced down. "Oh, she said the store won't open until 10 o'clock."

I pulled a face. "Crap. Well, then it's even more important for me to travel quickly, right?"

He sighed. "Rabbit will be mad again if you aren't here."

I felt a stab of guilt in the gut. "Don't worry. I'll hurry." I hesitated. "Hey, Rabbit is definitely coming back, right? He never explicitly said he was last night."

That earned me a kind pat on the arm from Big Rabbit. "Rabbit will never abandon you, Emily."

"Right," I said, swallowing the lump in my throat.

"Eat your toast," Lucie pointed at the plate in front of me. "I'll get your clothes in the laundry and –"

Briiing! The Empire service phone rang once in the kitchen cupboard. Lucie opened the door and reached for the buttonless phone. It was similar to those old rotary wall phones with long spiral cords, but it was missing a dial. There was only a cradle for the tan handset. Lucie put it to her ear.

"Yes? This is Lucie Bellerose," she spoke to the voice on the other end. I couldn't make out the words, but I could hear the clipped tone of the Empire service operator relaying a message. Lucie's face softened and she twisted the phone cord around her finger. "Yes. Thank you. Goodbye."

She returned the handset to its cradle and shut the cupboard door. She startled when she realized Big Rabbit and I sat watching her.

"Anything we should know?" I asked.

"Because it's all about you," she replied wryly. Big Rabbit giggled.

"No, I meant, is it anything for... *Oh.* Yeah, me?" I squirmed in my seat.

"It was a message from Basha." Now it was Lucie's turn to blush. "We'd sort of planned to see each other last night, but he had to cancel at the last minute. His message said he'd be on this side of town and wanted to meet up at *Coffee Cove* if I was free."

"Who is Basha?" Big Rabbit's bushy brows pulled together.

"Lucie's new boyfriend," I said.

"No," Lucie pointed at me. "He's my friend. And he's a guy. He's my guy friend."

"They've kissed," I told Big Rabbit. "And they spent the night together."

Big Rabbit's eyes grew wide.

"Oh, for the love of Pete!" Lucie threw up her hands. "You're horrible."

Teasing my friend was entertainment, and frankly, it was the humor I knew I needed to get me through this day. "Are you going to meet him?"

Lucie rubbed her lips together. "Yes."

"When?"

"Um, now." She cleared her throat as she dumped the rest of her coffee into the sink. "He's coming from the opposite direction, and we're meeting at the coffee shop. You go do what you need to do this morning. I'll pop back in before lunchtime."

❖ ❖ ❖

After Lucie left, I took a shower and put on the clothes from the previous day. I was okay with wearing the same bra, but I drew the line at wearing the same 'girl underwear' two days in a row. I'd have to go commando until I shopped at *Second Act*.

Lucie's sudden coffee date meant I didn't have time to show her the new passage appearing in The Book during my written conversation with Evangeline. I double checked that it was still there on the page and reread the lines:

A traveler is born.
The night protects the light.
Their heir sets fire to the stone.

I had no idea what it meant, but I was convinced it referred to the Crimson Stone. It was too coincidental.

Big Rabbit told me it would only take about 15 minutes to walk to the secondhand store, but I made us leave early.

You don't want to walk fast in denim pants when you're going commando.

At the store, I picked out a few pairs of blue jeans and several tee shirts, both long- and short-sleeved. I found a few like-new bras, too. I pulled a face at the size thinking about Big Rabbit's observation. Maybe when everything settled down, I'd buy a couple of push-up bras.

And yes, *Second Act* sold brand new 'girl underwear.' New socks, too.

Big Rabbit browsed the racks with me. He kept holding up tops to my chin and commenting on whether the clothing would work or not. I managed to get him to leave me in peace by promising to buy him a couple of the XXX-sized concert tees I saw on the clearance rack.

Before we left the store, the friendly shopkeeper allowed me to change into my new-to-me clothes – a relief. I did not want to make the return trip to Lucie's sans panties.

❖ ❖ ❖

"Any word from Rabbit?" I asked Big Rabbit as I rummaged through my shoulder bag. The Book sat safely at the bottom. My black top hat with the purple feather and pink bow waited on the kitchen counter.

"I sent out a message asking for an update, but no one's seen him." Big Rabbit shrugged. "We'll give him more time."

"You can't be happy about being saddled with me on another day of guard duty," I said.

"I don't mind." His eyes roamed over Lucie's kitchen. "I could make us something to eat."

It was getting close to the lunch hour, and I

was itching to go see Spell. I placed my top hat on my head. "I'll eat when I come back. Save me something."

The plan was to door travel from Lucie's kitchen into the hallway outside of Justice Spell's chambers. Technically I was committing a big no-no. Even Salesmen were supposed to enter the Courthouse through the front doors. From there they needed to pass through metal detectors in the lobby. It was possible I'd set off bells and whistles when I bypassed everything. If I did, I'd simply turn back around and door travel right on out. This risk seemed like the only way I'd get a chance to speak to Spell directly. And I might even catch her off guard.

I stood in front of the pantry door, took a breath, and thought about the long hall outside of Justice Spell's chambers. It was in a quiet part of the building. I hoped it would be empty.

I pictured the bare institutional walls with their vague lighting. I remembered the sound of my footsteps echoing when I walked the length of the corridor after going to Spell for help earlier in the year. She didn't give it to me then, but maybe this time would be different.

Maybe this time she would listen when she saw the marks left on my neck by Sebastian.

Lucie's pantry door hummed. As I touched the doorknob, I thought I heard Lucie's voice announcing she'd returned. I'd have to catch up with her later.

✼ ✼ ✼

I stepped into the hallway through one of its many doors. I got lucky; the corridor was empty. I paused, waiting to see if any alarms sounded or if any Empire guards would come running. At each end of the hall, a set of stairs were located behind double doors. After a minute of watching both, I decided I'd either slipped in under the radar, or nobody cared. Although I was glad I hadn't been found out, I wondered if it was a cause for concern.

There was always the chance Spell wouldn't be in her chambers. If she wasn't, maybe I'd wait for her to return. Spell had an assistant who sat outside her office in a waiting room. I walked in a familiar direction, passing a set of elevator doors. They chimed behind me, and I sped up my pace in case it *was* the Empire guards and they were too lazy to take the stairs.

But it wasn't the guards. I felt Templeton's presence before I even looked over my shoulder. I turned around as he swiftly approached. His shrewd inspection ran over my shoulders and down each of my arms.

"You door traveled into this hall, didn't you?"

I rolled my shoulders, twisting my head from side to side. Here we go. "Yes."

"Stupid."

I ignored him. "What are you doing here? Are you going to see Spell?"

Templeton's lips pressed tightly together before he spoke again. "Yes."

"And?"

"And what?" He scowled.

"And why? Why are you here to see her?"

"Did Rabbit arrive yet?" Templeton ignored my question.

"He came to Lucie's." I winced. I hated not knowing where Rabbit was now. I knew I'd let him down.

Templeton caught my reaction. "What happened? What did you do?"

"It's what you did that caused the problem."

Well, sort of. If he hadn't gone to Nisha for help in the first place, last night with Rabbit wouldn't have happened.

"What I did?" Templeton shook his head. "I don't have time for this, Emily. Tell Rabbit I need to see him. Immediately." He pushed past me.

"Hey, not so fast!" I tried to snag his arm. "I want to talk to you."

He sidestepped my reach and kept going. Gritting my teeth, I followed the infuriating man.

We arrived at the door leading into Justice Spell's waiting room as it opened. An older woman – another Salesman – stepped into the hall. She wore a dainty gray top hat tilted toward her right temple. A delicate veil flowed from the front of the hat, hanging a half inch below the brim with a strip dipping over her right eye. She was of average height and slender, wearing a double-breasted charcoal-colored dress suit, the hem stopping right below her knee. Leather pumps added a couple of inches to her height. Her jet-black hair was pulled back into a smooth low bun. Her catty brown eyes flicked down her nose and over my outfit. She was unimpressed.

Discounting me as unimportant, she turned her interest to Templeton. A thin smile drifted over her tastefully painted lips. "John Templeton, why it's been ages. How *is* your mother? I haven't seen her in… a decade perhaps?"

I didn't have to see Templeton's face to know how much he loathed the woman. I could feel it rolling off him. The air grew thicker in an instant. I became aware of Templeton's hand squeezing my upper arm, and he pulled me to his side. I looked up at his profile. He glowered at the woman, unblinking. The color began to fade from his eyes. Finally, he spoke.

"Odette."

Who was Odette? My curiosity swung back to the woman. She zeroed in on Templeton's grip on my arm. Her upper lip curled back in disgust before she allowed a dismissive snort.

Before I had a chance to ask what was going on, my heart skipped a beat.

Sebastian St. Michel stepped out of the waiting room and placed a hand on Odette's back. His own top hat he held in the other.

My first reaction was to back away from the man who'd attacked me the day before, but

Templeton's fingers tightened around my arm. He kept me at his side.

Sebastian noted Templeton's hand with a sneer. His lewd gaze crawled up my arm to my throat, lingering on the scarf wrapping around my neck. I noted the small cut and dark shadow underneath his right eye.

"Taking your pet for a walk, Templeton?" Sebastian broke the silence.

"Nice shiner," I shot back.

His mouth formed a pout before he answered. He touched the bruise on his face. "This? It's nothing, Emily. A little playtime got out of hand. It won't happen next time."

"Emily?" Odette's eyes skimmed over me. "Oh, yes. Now I understand. Daniel Swift's special daughter."

"Yes, I'm Daniel Swift's daughter – and I'm also the woman this piece of slime attacked yesterday." My voice rose as I tried to casually escape Templeton's hold on my arm.

"My son? Sebastian was with me the entire day yesterday." The woman's beady eyes narrowed. "You shouldn't make accusations like that. You don't want to make enemies of certain families, *dear*."

Sebastian continued to let his eyes wander over me, as his mother adjusted her jacket. She turned her consideration to Templeton once more, ignoring me as she resumed her departure. "Do tell your mother I asked about her, won't you? Sebastian, let's go."

Templeton didn't reply. Instead, as Sebastian followed his mother, Templeton abruptly released my arm and shoved me out of the way. Lightning fast, he grabbed Sebastian by his shirt collar, swinging him around and pushing him up against the wall where he held him fast. The impact caused Sebastian's fingers to flex and his top hat dropped to the floor.

"Don't ever touch her again," Templeton warned, his face close to Sebastian's. Both men were similar in size, but I realized Sebastian had a couple of inches on Templeton.

Odette didn't even turn around to address the commotion. She kept walking. "Sebastian?"

"I don't think you're in a position to watch over her, are you Templeton?" Sebastian's eyes rolled away from Templeton's and latched onto mine. The possessive expression skittering across his features drove a shiver through me. Templeton tightened his grip on Sebastian's collar, twisting the fabric in his fist and pressing it against the other man's neck.

"What in the name of the Empire is going on out here?" Justice Spell demanded from the doorway leading into her waiting room. "Templeton! Release him right now or I will call the guards and have you arrested for assault!"

My mouth popped open to argue, but before I could speak, Spell pointed directly toward me, her voice still raised. "Swift, in my office. Now!"

I didn't move immediately. I waited for Templeton to release Sebastian. He let go of the despicable man, but not before giving him a final shake. Templeton glared at the other Salesman as Sebastian straightened his shirt collar and retrieved his top hat from the hall floor. He dusted it off as he strolled past me, leaning in and whispering. "I love the scarf, Emily. The blue sets off your pretty eyes."

"You won't even see me coming, Sebastian," I hissed, my body tensing. My threat made me sound tougher than I felt. I'd smelled his cologne, and immediately flashes of the attack raced through my brain.

He smirked but kept going. I watched as he met his mother at the elevator. Her profile betrayed nothing as she stared straight at the elevator doors, ignoring the drama at the other end of the hall. Sebastian blew me a kiss before disappearing into the elevator. The doors slid shut.

"In my chambers, both of you." Spell whirled around, her robes billowing behind her as she disappeared into the waiting room.

"So much for the element of surprise," I grumbled, shooting Templeton a frustrated look before following the angry Justice.

❊ ❊ ❊

"I'm flabbergasted you would dare to door travel into the Empire, Emily. You no longer have permission to travel at all – even with a Senior Salesman." Justice Spell slammed the door behind us after we entered her inner office. She jerked her head toward Templeton. "And you? What were you doing? Attacking another Salesman in the Courthouse? Right outside my chambers? What were you thinking, Templeton? I should have you both arrested!"

Templeton didn't reply. He simply observed the Justice, his eyes a hair darker than before when he *delayed* Sebastian. Templeton had removed his top hat and his fingers skimmed over the brim, spinning the hat slowly. I waited another beat. When he didn't answer, I did.

"Maybe Templeton wanted to give Sebastian a taste of his own medicine." I unwound the scarf from around my neck, lifting my chin so the Justice couldn't avoid seeing the bruises left by Sebastian.

Spell put her hand to her own throat, a sharp cry slipping through her lips. "What happened to you?"

"Sebastian is what happened." I pointed to my throat. "Yesterday he attacked me and tried to strangle me."

"Where did this happen? Did you call the Empire guards?" Spell walked behind her desk and sat down stiffly in her chair. "What happened?"

"I was looking for a friend at a..." I paused, choosing my words carefully. "At a campsite in the woods. Turns out Sebastian was there, too."

"But why would he attack you?" Spell addressed Templeton next. "How are you involved in this?"

"He kidnapped my mother last year," I continued, ignoring the question made to Templeton. "Sebastian was behind the Fringe taking my mother and holding her captive. He wanted the Crimson Stone."

Spell shook her head. "The Empire found no proof that Sebastian was –"

I slammed both of my hands down on Spell's desk as I leaned toward the Justice. She shrank back in her chair. "There is proof!" I yelled. "I'm the proof! I was there. I was in the warehouse when Sebastian and his men were holding my mother. I was the one he dragged by the hair and threatened that night. Look at me, Your Honor. I am your proof!"

An empty water glass sitting on Spell's desk suddenly shattered. The sound bounced off the walls of the room.

Spell swallowed. "Get yourself under control."

"It's true, isn't it?" I said as the realization

washed over me. I straightened. "Something *is* rotten in the Empire, and it's affected you, too. Tell me, why were Sebastian and his mother here? This Odette? She's a Salesman, too. And I know Sebastian comes from some old, wealthy Empire family. Are they paying you off? Is that what's going on?"

Spell blinked and looked at Templeton. He'd watched our interaction without interfering. Spell let out a shuddering breath, picking up her fountain pen and rolling it between her fingers. "You know very little, Emily. You act as if you're the only one affected by what the Fringe has done – what they continue to do. Other Salesmen have been targeted and killed over the years. Families have been attacked. Your father and your family are one of many." Spell raised her head. "My daughter, Rowena, has a beautiful son. Erick is only 4 years old. Rowena's received messages warning that his well-being is at risk."

"From whom?" I asked. I knew the answer.

She shrugged. "Specifically? I don't know. But it's clear they were from the Fringe. It was advised that the Salesman Court not pursue those involved in the attack on the Empire guards in Vue, or those responsible for the kidnapping of Lydia McKay Swift. When the investigations were ordered to close, the threats to my family stopped."

I hung my head. "I can't believe it. You caved. After all this time – after everything you and my father fought for in the Empire."

"I won't sacrifice my family for you." Justice Spell rubbed her forehead with her fingertips. She shook her head a final time. "Get out of here before I call the guards to arrest you for violating your grounding. And Templeton, make sure she goes home. That's an official order from the Empire."

Her dismissal was welcome. I couldn't stay in her chambers another minute. I gestured halfheartedly toward the door. "Come on, Templeton. I can't stand being in this office any longer."

We left the Justice behind, passing through the waiting room and out into the hall. My stomach churned as I digested Spell's words. The thought of such an honorable woman bowing to the Fringe shook me to the core.

Templeton guided me away from the chamber door. I was in shock. "I don't even know what to say."

"We can't talk here. I'll meet you at Lucie's later," he replied. "Go."

"Where are you going? I have to talk to you. We need to figure out what to do – we no longer have the Empire on our side." *And I need to know why you went to Nisha for help,* I thought.

"This isn't up for debate. You need to go now. I'll get there as soon as I can." He marched down the hall.

"Wait," I called, hurrying after him. "Templeton!"

A massive *BOOM!* suddenly rattled the building. Templeton and I stumbled to the side as we worked to keep on our feet, our fingers grazing the wall. At the end of the hall, dust fell, followed by part of the ceiling.

"What was that?" I shouted, wide-eyed. It was as if a wrecking ball had slammed against the side of the Courthouse. Templeton turned and rushed toward me, snagging my shirtsleeve and pulling me in the other direction.

"That was a –!" Before the words were out of his mouth, a second blast rocked the building and a chunk of the wall crumbled right behind us. We were enveloped in dust.

The Courthouse was under attack.

CHAPTER 12

I screwed my eyes shut and crouched down as the wave of dust blew over us. The explosion rang in my ears. The groaning of the building, and the sounds of falling and crashing around us, made me believe the detonation was close. The fire alarm triggered immediately, and the hall was filled with its shrieking. Emergency lights flashed.

"Hurry!" I hollered to Templeton, standing and pushing him forward. The ceiling dropping behind us forced us to scramble. We had to door travel out of there immediately. In the strobe-like bursts of the emergency lights, I saw the double doors at the end of the corridor swing open. Two men dressed in plain clothes charged through. They weren't Empire guards.

"Dammit!" I turned to the first door on my left, intending to door travel. I reached for the doorknob and risked a quick look at Templeton. He hadn't moved from the middle of the hall. Instead, he stood his ground, his arms lifted away from his sides in a defensive position.

"Templeton, go!" I shouted over the noise. *What was he doing?* I dropped my hand away from the doorknob and lurched toward him, grabbing onto the sleeve of his left arm.

"Get out of here!" He yelled, roughly shoving me with his forearm. The fabric of his sleeve slipped through my fingers, and I stumbled backward into a door. I felt my travel energy rising and mixing with the door's receptive counterpart. I yanked myself away from it before it sucked me through.

The men kept coming. Templeton retreated slowly, his eyes trained on the gun held by one of them. The walls around us were breaking apart as the building shuddered under the weight of its collapse.

Why wasn't Templeton leaving? Why wasn't he door traveling? Why was he still standing there? Why wasn't he using a door to escape?

Oh.

How could I have missed it? He *couldn't* door travel – or at least he couldn't do it all the time. It didn't always work. I flashed on the door travel malfunction in Lucie's kitchen.

Something was wrong with Templeton's ability to door travel. It seemed… *broken*.

Between the alarm and the building caving in on itself, the noise was deafening. Templeton realized I was still in the hall and shouted again. A large portion of the ceiling between us and the advancing men crashed to the floor. I covered my ears and closed my eyes. I needed to concentrate. I needed to get us out of there. In my mind, I reached out toward Templeton.

There. I opened my eyes and could sense – no, see – a tiny tendril of Templeton's energy tightening around him. It was like a slip of light, but it kept flickering out.

But it was all I needed.

One of the men clambered over the debris, raising his gun. He tripped before he could get a shot off. I targeted the door closest to Templeton and raised my energy as hard and fast as I could draw it up from the well inside me. It soared in my chest, fueled by fear and determination. I lunged toward the door, tackling Templeton as I went, wrapping my arms around his waist and spinning us around. I used every muscle in my body to pull him with me. Together, we tumbled awkwardly, falling against the door. I summoned all the power and energy in my body and refused to let Templeton go as my door travel energy wrapped around us both. I centered my mind on one word.

Home.

※ ※ ※

Our limbs still wrapped around each other, we crashed on through to the other side and slammed down onto the floor. My face was pressed into Templeton's chest. He'd landed on his back, breaking my fall. I sprawled on top of him with my hands pinned underneath his back. I felt him cough once, trying to catch his breath. The wind had been knocked out of him. I wriggled free and rolled away.

We lay next to each other on a lush red rug, staring at the dark wood of a coffered ceiling. My shoulder bag sat at my hip, and I ran my palm back and forth on the rug as I rested. We were safe. The quiet was welcome. Only a ticking clock interrupted the silence. As my heart rate returned to normal, I let my eyes wander around the room. We'd landed in a large office reminiscent of Blackstone's library at 1221 Northgate Way. It wasn't as big, but the walls were lined with floor-to-ceiling bookshelves. A massive wooden desk sat at the other end of the room opposite the door we traveled through. Heavy, cardinal-red drapes were pulled closed over a window. Several lamps and discreet overhead lighting lit the room comfortably.

Templeton's wheezing stopped. I turned my head to look at him.

He blinked at the ceiling. His expression was calm.

"Do you know where we are?" I whispered.

He nodded. "Home."

❋ ❋ ❋

There was no question. I was a talented Salesman. My door traveling energy was off the charts. I could drag an angry, resistant Salesman along with me as I whipped through the ether.

But apparently, an old issue of mine resurfaced. I was having trouble landing in the right spot.

Then again, maybe not.

I'd wanted nothing more than to get us out of

there and to someplace safe. Going home was the first thought passing through my mind. It must've been the same for Templeton – except he wanted it more.

He sat up, then rose to his feet slowly. He held out his hand and helped me to mine.

I took in the elegant room. "This is your house?"

"It's my study." He picked up our top hats, setting his on a nearby table before handing me mine. It had seen better days. Templeton then retrieved my shoulder bag from the floor and held it out to me. "I'll repay the debt for your assistance. You may leave now."

"Oh, you have got to be kidding me!" I blurted out. I threw my hands up, flinging building dust into the air. "After what we went through? Sweep off the ol' lint from your sleeve and kick me out the door? Good grief, Templeton. What does it take to make you less obnoxious and more human?"

"You're not welcome here," he spat back. He shook my bag at me.

"Holy hell! A minute ago, I saved your life!" I ignored him, passing my hand through my hair and rolling my eyes as more dust from the Courthouse explosion drifted to the floor. I looked down at my secondhand outfit. My clothes were as dirty as Templeton's. "We're going to talk. I'm not leaving until I get answers." I crossed my arms. "I can't see you forcibly removing me and throwing me out."

"Don't bet on it." He dropped my shoulder bag back to the floor. He blinked, then wiped at his face. He looked at the dirt on his fingertips. We made quite the pair.

I needed to try a different approach. An elegant fireplace was set into one of the book-lined walls. One leather wingback chair sat in front of it. I risked more of his ire and perched on the edge of the seat. I was mad, but I didn't want to ruin such fine furniture.

Calmly, I tried again. "I know something is wrong with you."

"There is nothing wrong with me," Templeton snapped. His lips pressed into a thin line.

"Yes. Yes, there is. Something's terribly wrong with your ability to door travel. I can't believe I didn't realize it right away. But I see it now. Or maybe, it's what I didn't see." I shrugged. "I looked at you, Templeton. I mean, I *really* looked at you. Your energy couldn't grow. You couldn't raise it enough to go through a door. I've never had the chance to look at it like this before – I mostly just feel it when I'm near you. But I could see it wasn't there when we needed to get away from those men. You tried, but it failed you."

Templeton stared at the floor. I waited for the man to speak. When he didn't, I continued. "I think I know why."

"You don't know anything," he snarled.

"I think I do. You gave it up. Somehow, you gave it to Nisha so she would help me find my mother. Or, she took it from you. Siphoned it off you or something. I don't know." Forgetting about my dirty clothes, I leaned back in the chair, closing my eyes. I was tired. "Why, Templeton?"

I sensed as he walked past and a moment later, I heard the sound of glass on glass. I leaned around the side of the chair to see what he was doing. Templeton poured himself a drink.

He flicked a glance in my direction. "Scotch?"

I shook my head.

He took a sip and stood calmly contemplating the amber liquid. Eventually, he spoke. "I agreed to *lend* Nisha my ability to door travel for one year as payment."

"You can do that? We can do that? Give it to someone?" I didn't understand. How could we let someone take our ability to door travel?

"No, you misunderstand. I agreed to *lend* it to her. Then she pulled it from me." He took another sip.

"So now Nisha can door travel?" This was bad.

Templeton shook his head. "She has her own method of traveling. She wanted the energy used for door travel. It's something she can feed on. She craves magical resources. My power matches her needs." He swirled the Scotch in his glass. "She'll return it when the year is up."

This was too much – and I still didn't understand. "But if she feeds off it, won't it be used up?"

"Energy cannot be created or destroyed. I assume even your school provided a basic understanding of the first law of thermodynamics," Templeton snorted. "Her consumption changed it for her needs. When the time comes, she'll restore what I lent to her."

"With *her* energy," I pointed out.

"With *energy*," he stressed. "Period."

I had to trust Templeton knew what he was doing. If anyone understood what Nisha could and would do, it was probably him. I slid off the chair and crossed to the bar where he stood. I was tempted to ask for a glass of wine. I couldn't handle the hard stuff. "But when did this happen? Two days ago you door traveled into my home with the news about Blackstone."

"The night your mother was rescued from the warehouse." Templeton tossed back the last of his drink.

"But –"

"I've been able to use magic to reignite some door travel energy inside me," he cut me off. "It's not always accurate, but I've been able to work with it."

I let my hand wander to the top of the bar and rubbed the polished wood with my finger. "Your magic? You've been using your own magic to do it?" I lifted my head.

"No."

"I don't understand. Someone else's magic? You're using another person's magic?" We were standing close; I could see his pulse flutter in his neck. I watched the tiny movement, thinking about his words and the energy I felt when I was near him – the new vein of power I sensed when he delivered the news about Blackstone's murder. It was familiar... *because it was mine.* "Oh."

He inclined his head.

"You're using the piece of the Crimson Stone I gave to you. That's how you've been able to do it. But it's not the whole Stone, that's why you're having problems with door travel."

Templeton poured himself another thick finger of whisky. "You are partially correct."

"Then enlighten me."

He turned and put some distance between us. "Unlike you, I'm not foolish enough to carry a piece of the Stone with me everywhere I go. I didn't have it with me at the Courthouse today – I didn't want to risk bringing it with me. There's too much instability in the Empire. The Fringe's attack on the Courthouse proves it."

"Okay, I get that. But there's something else. I can't put my finger on it, but it's more than the piece of the Stone, isn't it?" What was he holding back?

"Yes." Another sip taken. His nostrils flared once, but he resigned himself to answering my question. "Because you carried the piece against your body for such a long time, you imbued your own door travel energy into it. It might not have been the case with any other Salesman, but because you also have some sort of..." Here Templeton faltered. He gestured with his glass. "Some sort of magical tendencies –"

"Abilities," I corrected.

"Fine, *abilities*. This enabled the Stone to open a two-way street between its magical properties and your magic. The piece of Stone you kept close stored up enough power for me to draw from when I need to door travel. And no, it's not always accurate. It's frustrating." He finished off the rest of his drink and grimaced.

"You're using my energy for your door travel," I stated. "And that's why you want the rest of the Crimson Stone."

Templeton lifted a shoulder. "I have my reasons beyond this impairment."

"I'm sure you do." I rubbed the back of my

neck with a dirty hand. "But Templeton, why? Why did you go to Nisha?"

"Because I knew she'd be able to tell you where Sebastian was keeping Lydia. Your mother was in danger. I didn't expect you would take off on your own after her," he huffed.

"No, Templeton." I closed the distance between us yet again. I touched the hand holding his empty glass. "Why did *you* go to Nisha to help me?"

A soft knock on the study's door startled us both. It opened and an older man wearing a perfectly tailored black suit stepped inside. He nodded to me before addressing Templeton. "I thought you'd returned, Mr. Templeton. It seems as though you and your guest have had an exciting day. I'll set out new clothing for you to change into. We have a few of Miss Audra's things and I believe we can find something suitable for your guest to wear while she's visiting."

Before Templeton could reply, I thrust out my hand to the kind gentleman. "Hi. I'm Emily, and I would love a change of clothes."

"Ah, so this is Miss Emily! Templeton has told

me about some of your travels. I think he worries about the trouble you find." He took my hand in both of his, giving it a gentle squeeze. "It is a pleasure to meet you," he finished before turning his head slightly and lifting an eyebrow. His gaze was fixed back on Templeton.

Templeton cleared his throat. He gestured toward me uncomfortably. "Mr. Archie, would you please find something suitable for her to wear?"

"Of course, Mr. Templeton," Mr. Archie replied, glancing down at my shoulder bag. Templeton noticed and picked it up, refusing to meet my eyes as he handed it to me. "And you would like me to show Miss Emily where she could freshen up as well?"

"Please," Templeton answered, his jaw tensing.

"I would be honored." Mr. Archie offered his arm to me. "Come along. Let's see how we can make you more comfortable."

❈ ❈ ❈

We exited the study and Mr. Archie led me

down a hall and upstairs to one of the guest bedrooms with a large, attached bathroom. As we walked, my head swiveled back and forth. I was mindful to keep my mouth from hanging open in utter wonder.

I knew Templeton was wealthy. Apparently, he was 'lord of the manor' wealthy.

The house was gorgeous – dark polished wood, elegant wall tapestries, immaculate marble floors. I could almost smell the long history and affluence. Brass lamps with tiny white shades were discreetly secured to the banister at each landing accompanying the wide staircase we climbed. As we drew nearer to each one, the light quietly clicked on.

The guest room Mr. Archie chose was the second door to the right of the staircase. The room itself was tastefully decorated, with a queen-sized bed covered in a maroon and gold duvet. The headboard was covered in padded, nut-brown fabric and arched high up the wall. The wardrobe, nightstand, and dressing table with chair complemented the room, yet were devoid of any proof of use. A rose-colored sofa was placed near a window, a soft blanket casually laid over one arm. The thick carpet was the color of rich chocolate and I looked down at the dust trail my clothes had left.

"I'm sorry, Mr. Archie."

"Nothing a vacuum cannot fix," he replied.

I declined a bath in the luxurious marble tub, explaining I'd simply freshen up. I felt weird about getting naked in Templeton's home. Changing into a set of clean clothes seemed like a more palatable choice.

Mr. Archie tapped on the bathroom door when he returned. "Mr. Templeton's cousin Audra is about your size. She keeps a limited wardrobe here, but I believe this will do. I will leave the clothing on the bed."

"Thank you," I called through the door. I'd washed off the dust from my skin and toweled it out of my hair. The healing scarf from Lucie was a tad dusty, but I wasn't going to give it up. I shook out the bits as best as I could over the bathtub before I shed my tee shirt and jeans. I peeked out the door. The coast was clear. Mr. Archie left behind a pair of white cotton pants and a long-sleeved, green and white striped shirt. The fitted fabric was soft on my skin. The boat neck ran from shoulder to shoulder. I carefully rewrapped Lucie's scarf around my bruised neck. I checked the mirror. I looked nice.

Mr. Archie had thoughtfully left a pair of tan ballet shoes alongside the bed. I stripped off my socks and tried them on. A perfect fit. I was Cinderella.

My hair was a different story. I dug into my shoulder bag and produced my travel brush and a hair band. I pulled my hair back into a ponytail. It would have to do.

A knock on the door revealed Mr. Archie's impeccable timing. He brought in a laundry basket for my dirty clothes. "You look lovely, Miss Emily."

"Oh, thank you. I appreciate everything you've brought for me." I picked up my sneakers and added them to the laundry basket. "Where is, uh, Mr. Templeton?"

"He'll be joining you shortly. He also wanted to freshen up. He asked me to make you comfortable in his study." Mr. Archie led me to the staircase.

"Mr. Archie, I'm not sure where we are. I mean, in the Empire?"

The man paused. "Ah, yes. The estate is northeast of Matar. It's about a two-hour drive from the city."

The estate.

"Does Templeton – I mean, *Mr. Templeton* live here alone?" Smooth.

Mr. Archie raised an eyebrow. "At present."

The trip back to the study was a short one. He offered to pour me a drink. I thought again about wine, but I opted for a glass of water. Mr. Archie retrieved a tall glass from the bar and sliding open a panel, revealed a discreet water and ice dispenser. He brought me the glass and invited me to rest in the wingback chair – he'd wiped off the dust I'd left earlier. He assured me Templeton would be along soon.

After Mr. Archie excused himself, I explored the room, first browsing Templeton's bookshelves as any guest might do while waiting on their host – even a reluctant one.

Bookshelves lined three walls. Many titles pointed toward an interest in history, and not only the Empire's. Some shelves were dedicated to ancient, Indian, Asian, European – both East and West – and North and South American histories, as well as texts on countries south of the equator. Others were packed with names of philosophers: St. Augustine, de Tocqueville, John Stuart Mill, Hobbes, and Locke. I noted the names of women as well, but only a couple were familiar to me, like Mary Wollstonecraft and Ayn Rand.

I scanned the next set of shelves, my fingertips gliding over the worn spines. Tomes representing world religions, ancient art, and magic – although the last bit seemed to only contain general topics. I wouldn't be finding any stash of Templeton's secret books on magic here.

My perusing led me to a section of fiction. His choice in authors didn't surprise me: Twain, Wilde, C.S. Lewis, Stoker, and Shelley. There was even a section of children's books. Next, poetry: Walt Whitman, Mary Oliver, Poe.

My path wound around several low tables before I found myself browsing the shelves behind Templeton's desk. Biographies. *Erotica.*

I let the latter be.

Turning away from the wall of books, I slid my finger along the gleaming edge of his wide executive desk, pushing the leather chair aside. I traced a path from the far end, slowing as I neared the middle. I stopped above the small rosette serving as the drawer's knob. I glanced up at the door on the other side of the room. I'd only take a peek. My finger moved lower, tapping it gently. I hooked the pad of my finger around the edge of the rosette and tugged. The drawer wasn't locked.

I met no resistance as I pulled it open. Pens and pencils were evenly placed in the narrow tray beside a thumb drive. Paperclips were sprinkled in the same tray's corner. An opened roll of breath mints sat at the other end. So incredibly ordinary.

Setting my shoulder bag on the desktop, I edged the drawer open even more. Beyond the pencils and mints, a Polaroid photo lay face down. I drew the stiff print from the desk and turned it over. A date was scrawled in a bottom corner. The year was smudged, but I could make out the word 'Summer.'

Two young men appeared in the image: one tall and unsmiling, the other grinning broadly – a gangly teenager in a tee shirt and baggy camo cargos. His lean arm slung up and over the stiff shoulders of his scowling companion. The photo had been taken outside on a sunny day.

Templeton and Rabbit.

Templeton appeared to be about 18 or 19 years of age. His face was young, but the unhappy countenance was that of an aged man. His hair was short. The angular lines of his face were already there – no latent boyishness to round out the future man's hardness. He wore a simple white, short-sleeved shirt and light dress trousers. Rabbit looked… Well, it *was* Rabbit. He looked young, but he was probably in his early thirties. But if a person didn't know any better, they'd believe a young teen was trying to hang out with an older cousin.

I knew the two men had a history, but I didn't know the nature of it or for how long they'd known one another. Rabbit always seemed amused by Templeton. And Templeton seemed… to not dislike Rabbit. It was probably about as close as Templeton ever got to having a friend. But here in this photo, even with Templeton's trademark sourpuss, there was a camaraderie – something tangible bringing the two together.

Like the person who took the picture. Was it another friend? A parent?

As I mused on the photographer's identity, my eyes were drawn back to the drawer. A second Polaroid photo, also face down, lay in the same space as the first. I withdrew it, hoping for more information much like a cardplayer draws from a deck praying for a winning hand. I flipped it over.

The photo was of my mother and me.

I blinked. Templeton had a photo of me as a young teenager. I was 13.

Swallowing, I lifted it closer to my face and studied it. I remembered this photo.

Someone had given my father a Polaroid camera as a gift that year. It was a bit of nostalgia for him, and we had fun taking silly pictures. The day marked by this photo was beautiful. It was summer and we were on a picnic. I wore a turquoise cami under a white tee shirt and a short denim skirt. I remember clearly choosing the cami because it was soft and light, hugging the slight, new curves starting to shape my body. You could see the color through the white shirt layered over it. My hair was down, and the breeze blew it across my forehead and to my right. I pressed against my mother's side, my arm around her waist and my left cheek against her right. The wind caught her strawberry-blond hair and blended into mine while she held her wavy locks away from her face with a hand. She wore her favorite capri pants with beads she had sewn in a swirling pattern down the sides of each leg. We were barefoot. We were laughing. We were happy.

This was the summer before my father was killed.

I held a photo in each hand. Now I knew the identity of the photographer who took Templeton's and Rabbit's picture. It was my father. It was the same person who snapped the memory of my mother and me on that glorious summer day.

The new question became: why did Templeton have a photo of us?

I examined the unsuspecting teen in the snapshot. Her life was going to radically change in only a few, short months. Her father would die soon.

And why did Templeton have this photo?

I didn't hear the door open, but I sensed him when he returned. "You have a picture of us – my mother and me." I raised my head.

Templeton didn't growl, scowl, or frown at me. Instead, he simply walked around the side of the desk and gently took the photos. I examined the side of his face while he looked at them. His expression gave away nothing.

"While I'm far from surprised, Emily, I'd appreciate it if you'd refrain from snooping when you're in my home," he said, his voice soft.

"You have a picture of me," I repeated. "Me when I was 13. Why do you have this?"

I saw the twitch in his cheek as he made to return the photos to the desk drawer. I placed my hand on his to stop him. He froze, his eyes shifting from the photos to where my hand had landed. I pulled away.

"Your father showed it to me," he answered. He reviewed the pictures.

"But why do you have it?" I didn't understand. It didn't make sense.

"Because…" Templeton faltered. "Because there wasn't time." He tossed the photos on top of his desk and ran his right hand through his short hair, causing a couple of locks to stand up. It was damp; he must have showered. His left hand, I noted, squeezed briefly into a fist. He tilted his head back and stared vacantly at his ceiling, the color in his eyes fading. "There was no time."

"What do you mean, Templeton?" There was something very bad about this discovery. I thought I'd learned enough today. I licked my lips. Templeton's energy – combined with the piece of the Crimson Stone I knew he now carried – was palpable. It grew in intensity. I could feel it swirling below the surface, but his rhythm had changed. Instead of the cool, controlled power I usually sensed, it became erratic, desperate.

"Templeton?" I asked again. I felt my own energy rising easily and pressing against his. I probed deeper, finding a layer of turmoil I never suspected. It made me dizzy – even nauseous.

"Don't," he said, suddenly pulling away and shooting a dark look at me. "Don't do that again, Emily."

"Then tell me." I ceased exploring his energy and picked up the two photos. "I'm guessing my father took this picture of you and Rabbit. But this one," I waved the photo at him. "I suppose it's believable my father would show this to you, but why would he let you keep it?"

Templeton snorted. "He didn't *let* me keep it."

"So, you stole it?" Even though a niggling

sense at the back of my mind warned me against baiting him, old habits die hard. It's what we did, after all. *After everything.*

"I didn't steal it," he snapped. "You have no idea what you're talking about." He turned and stalked around the desk to stand in the middle of the room facing away.

"Then don't you think it's time you told me?" My voice raised. "Templeton, look at me when I'm talking to you! I've earned at least that much today!"

He whirled around, his sharp features hard in his face. "You think I owe you more?"

"You're damn right!" I yelled. We'd thrown the doors wide open and I was not turning back now. Not after everything that had happened, from the moment The Book landed on my doorstep on my thirtieth birthday, to becoming a Salesman, to fighting Templeton for the Crimson Stone – to fighting Templeton on everything! To having my life saved by him more than once. To saving his today. I threw the photos at him. He jerked back as if I had struck him.

"Pick. Them. Up," he gritted out at me.

"Tell me the truth. All of it," I demanded. I

couldn't take it anymore. All the lies and secrets here in the Empire. The constant battling with Templeton. The Fringe's violence. The terror I felt when I pictured Sebastian's face. A roiling sensation grew in my stomach. I felt like I couldn't breathe, and my chest felt tight. I didn't deserve this. I didn't deserve to be attacked and made afraid. I heard a tiny crackling sound in my ears. I saw Templeton lift his chin. He sniffed at the air. We both could detect a scent of something burning. "I mean it, Templeton."

"You better pull back your angry energy, Emily," Templeton cautioned. "I won't let you burn my house down in a foolish attempt to get something you want. I will stop you and it will hurt."

I couldn't fully comprehend what was going on, but I understood it was my energy starting to burn in the room. It was the turmoil in Templeton bringing it to the surface. The suffering in the slice of energy I touched made me desperate to know the truth.

"Then tell me. I'm not asking again," I warned. I pictured the walls around us covered in flames. I would force him to tell me. My piece of the Crimson Stone in my shoulder bag pulsed and I saw a faint glow appear under his shirt.

Templeton lowered his gaze to the floor where the photos lay, and his lips moved silently. The fingers on his right hand twitched. A sharp pain sliced into the center of my forehead and I cried out. My concentration broken, I stumbled and knocked into the desk chair. It rolled backward but I managed to steady myself with one hand and remain on my feet. My other hand covered my forehead, and I closed my eyes tightly. The pain was horrible, but it left as fast as it came. I dropped my hand and slowly opened my eyes. Templeton remained still as stone, watching me.

"Tell me," I whispered. "Please tell me."

He sighed, the expression on his face changing from wary to weary. He shook his head, again lowering his gaze. Eventually, he shrugged as if capitulating to an internal dialogue. He looked up. When he spoke, his voice was low, a forced calm. "I was on the train."

I bit my lower lip, studying him. What did he mean? On the train? "Which..." My voice caught in my throat. *No, please don't say it.*

"Which train, Templeton?"

In the time I've known Templeton, I've never felt such an intense stare. His own breath became shallow. His lips were parted. He steadily worked the words from his mind to his tongue. "Your father's."

The sob came out of my mouth so unexpectedly it surprised both of us. He startled and I collapsed into the desk chair, gripping the arms. Templeton took one step in my direction before stopping. He lifted a hand.

"Emily," he began.

"You were on the train?" My voice grew higher. I pitched forward, shouting. "You were on the train!"

It was rumored Templeton had been seen on the train right before the explosion. For 18 years the rumor persisted – and now he was admitting it was true! He was telling me he was *there*. Why? Why was he on that train?

All the fears I had last year came rushing back. Did he put the bomb on the train? He said he didn't – but did he lie to me? Was I a fool to believe him after all this time? Trust meant nothing in the Empire!

I slammed both of my fists on his desk. "You

were on the train!"

Templeton raised his hands, his palms facing me. "Get a grip on yourself. I was summoned to the train. Your father requested I join him."

I climbed to my feet. The pain that sliced through my brain was completely gone and my mind felt crystal clear. "You're lying."

"I am not."

"You had something to do with the bomb," I accused him. My old fear was coming true. He must be guilty. He kept the fact he was on the train a secret for almost two decades for a reason.

"I did not," he hissed. "I would never play a part in Daniel's death."

"I lost my father on that train, Templeton!" I exploded at the sound of my father's name. I could feel the heat burning in my chest again. I jabbed my finger at him. "My father was murdered on that train!"

"Two people lost fathers when the train exploded," Templeton yelled back. Fury flashed in his pale eyes.

I sucked in a breath. What did he say? Oh no, please no. "You and I… We're not…"

"Related?" Templeton was horrified. "We

share no biology, Emily."

I shook my head. I was confused by the admission. Taking a breath, I pushed the burning feeling down. I had to keep control of myself. What was he saying? "Then I don't understand. What do you mean?"

Templeton flexed his fingers as he worked to regain his own control. "Did you ever wonder why your father was on the train, Emily? He's a Salesman. Why wasn't he door traveling?"

It wasn't unusual for a Salesman to travel by any of the typical means any other person would travel: car, train, plane. But if we could door travel, why wouldn't we?

"I guess, well," I stammered. "I didn't know about door traveling when he died. I didn't know he – we – could do that."

"But you know now," Templeton pointed out.

"Do you know why he was on the train?"

"Yes."

I'd had enough. I was exhausted from the day. "Why, Templeton? Tell me."

"Because he was escorting my father back into the Empire."

I'd never heard any mention of Templeton's father. His mother was the Salesman, and I knew his door traveling ability was inherited through her line. I knew nothing about his father. "Why would your father need an escort?"

"Because he had been banished from the Empire. He was your father's prisoner." Before he could explain, we were interrupted. Templeton's eyes cut to his butler as he slipped into the study.

"Mr. Templeton," Mr. Archie interrupted. "You have another visitor. Mr. Rabbit is here."

CHAPTER 13

Stepping around Mr. Archie, Rabbit appeared. He nodded briefly in my direction before switching his attention to Templeton.

Templeton, for his part, was clearly surprised to see Rabbit. His body seemed to lean back, his chin lifting as his head turned. He pressed his lips together.

"It's good to see you again, Mr. Rabbit," Mr. Archie added as he delivered a pointed look at Templeton.

Rabbit shifted, sparing a moment for the older gentleman. "It's good to see you, too."

"If you'll excuse me," Mr. Archie answered. He started to pull the door closed, but then he paused. "I'll plan on dinner for three this evening, Mr. Templeton."

Templeton made a sharp noise of disgust and turned his back on everyone. Mr. Archie merely gave a patient smile before slipping out of the room. The man was a saint.

"I thought it was time the three of us had a discussion, Templeton," Rabbit stated.

✳ ✳ ✳

After Mr. Archie left, Rabbit walked to the bar and poured himself a shot of something clear. He knocked it back, flinching as he swallowed.

"The Fringe blew up the Salesman Courthouse. I was on my way here when the network reported the attack." Rabbit's curious brown eyes flicked to mine. "And Emily is here. What did I miss?"

"We were in the building when the explosions hit," I told him. "We were leaving Justice Spell's chambers and BAM! The bombs went off."

Templeton swiveled around when I mentioned Spell. "Emily, what we learned from Spell needs to stay private."

"You've got to be kidding me?" I scoffed.

"I am not," he replied.

"What's going on?" Rabbit gave us both the once over as he worked to get caught up on what had happened. "What about Spell?"

"She's dirty," I said.

"She is *not* dirty." Templeton snorted as he dismissed my comment. "The Fringe is threatening her. She's trying to keep her family safe."

"She closed the investigation on my mother's kidnapping even though she knows who was behind it," I challenged him. I turned to Rabbit. "And guess who we saw coming out of Spell's offices today? Sebastian St. Michel and his mother. Isn't that a coincidence?"

Rabbit crossed his arms and looked at Templeton. "It doesn't look good, but what do you think?"

"Hey!" I interrupted. "I think it's pretty obvious – and Spell admitted the Fringe pressured the Court to do their bidding."

"I get that," Rabbit said. "Templeton?"

The corners of Templeton's mouth turned down. "I think there's more to the story. Spell's not corrupt. I believe her family is in danger."

"She should worry," Rabbit said. "Emily, we haven't had time to talk since you've been in the Empire."

I winced. "Yeah, I kind of shot our evening to hell last night. I'm really sorry, Rabbit."

He offered a sad smile. "It'll be okay."

Templeton observed our exchange, his eyes narrowing. "What did *she* do?"

I didn't like the way he emphasized 'she.' I

opened my mouth to tell him to shove it, but Rabbit jumped in.

"No big deal, Templeton. Leave it be." Rabbit attempted to put a button on the subject.

I, however, did not pick up on the clue to stop. "When I saw Nisha, she told me I had to deliver a message to Rabbit. She wasn't going to tell me who went to her on my behalf unless I agreed to do her a favor." I downplayed the agreement.

"You did what?" Templeton exploded, catching me off guard. He took two steps toward me. "Do you even have a fraction of a clue of how dangerous that was?"

"I do now!" I shouted at him as my temper flared again.

"Both of you, stop it," Rabbit tried to intervene. "This is getting us nowhere."

Templeton ignored Rabbit. "Did you deliver Nisha's message?"

"Templeton," Rabbit warned.

"I had to. She said she'd take my heart if I didn't." I felt the heat burning in my cheeks. The shame of my selfishness returned.

Templeton gave a little jerk and he turned on Rabbit next. "What was it? What did she make

Emily tell you?"

Rabbit shook his head no. "We're not going there."

"Emily, leave. I want to talk to you, Rabbit," Templeton ordered.

"No. We're not doing this. We need to focus on more important things right now." Rabbit remained cool.

"I'm not leaving," I added.

Templeton tensed, his head lowering as he pivoted back and forth as if he were searching for something. He zeroed in on his leftover Scotch glass and he snagged it. I stepped away, afraid he would throw it. The color in his eyes faded completely, leaving only a black rim around his irises. He gritted his teeth and he slowly set the glass back down. He refused to look at either of us as he stormed out of the study, slamming the door behind him as he left.

Rabbit winced.

"Damn," I breathed. "Why do you put up with that?"

"We were friends once." Rabbit kept his head down, but peered at me from under heavy brows.

"What happened?" I asked. "Why did the friendship end?"

"Why do friendships between men often go south?"

Ah, there it was. "A woman."

Rabbit nodded grimly.

"Who was it?"

Rabbit motioned to the leather wingback. When I declined, he took it. He sat forward with his elbows on his knees, his large hands loosely clasped. "That's where it gets interesting."

I lifted my palms, shrugging. "I'm not going anywhere. I've got time."

"We were young – well, Templeton was young. He was still new to being a Salesman. Nineteen. Although he was far from the typical teenager, he still had his share of raging hormones." Rabbit straightened, pausing to pinch the bridge of his nose. "I did not have the luxury of youth as an excuse for my poor judgment."

"You both liked the same girl? This scenario has played out a million times before, Rabbit."

"This was no ordinary girl," Rabbit replied.

"Oh? Help me out here," I said, rolling my

hand and encouraging him to continue.

He nodded, looking at the floor. "It was Nisha."

"What? You and Nisha?" Holy hell, was that how she knew Rabbit? Was this why he was afraid of her?

Rabbit leaned back in the chair, running both of his hands over the top of his head and through his unruly curls. "Yeah."

"One second." I lifted a finger. I retrieved Templeton's chair from behind his desk. I wheeled it across the room and faced it toward Rabbit before taking a seat. "Tell me."

Rabbit blew out a breath, his eyes traveling up to the ceiling. "I was, I don't know, probably around 37. I can't keep track of the years. Your father introduced me to Templeton. He told me about his powers, about how he was struggling to find his way. He didn't fit in. Templeton never had time for his peers, and he certainly was younger than the other Salesmen. There was nothing in common there. Daniel thought Templeton could use another friend, someone he could trust."

"And he does trust you, doesn't he?"

"As much as he'll ever trust anyone, I suppose." Rabbit said. He shook his head. "It's hard not to grow fond of him."

"Now that's crazy talk," I said.

Rabbit laughed. "I traveled a lot back then. I'd catch up with Daniel and Templeton when we were in the same cities. I think Daniel tried to give him some normalcy. And even though Templeton might not admit it, he needed your father. He needed *a* father."

"Yeah, speaking of –" I began.

Rabbit held up a hand. "Hang on, I'm not done. You said earlier you wanted answers. Just listen, Emily."

I nodded.

"And then Daniel was killed. Templeton went to dark places after that – in his head and literally."

"He wasn't already there?" I asked snidely, pointing to my temple.

"He went darker. He was already practicing magic, and he's horribly curious." Rabbit coughed. "You two are a lot alike."

"I'll forgive you for comparing me to him," I replied. "But go on."

"When you start practicing dark magic, you will attract dark beings."

"Like Nisha."

Rabbit put his finger to the tip of his nose. "Templeton's interest grew. She started to teach him her magic, kept him close to her. They became lovers."

I blanched. "He slept with her?"

"So did I." Rabbit's face was stone.

My mouth popped open. "Rabbit, how could you do that?"

"Well, hormones, Emily. My body was that of a teenager's – maybe 17 or 18. You've been around teenage boys. They're stupid walking bags of horny chemicals."

"But you weren't a teenager – your brain was a grown man heading for 40."

"Yeah, but again, a brain under the influence of hormones. Nisha was otherworldly in her beauty. Seductive, impossible to resist," he defended himself. "Anyhow, I was trying to hold onto Templeton. With Daniel gone, there was no one to watch out for him – no one to keep Templeton out of his own way. And that's how I met Nisha. She was dangerous, but exciting to me. I knew better, but I wanted her."

"And that's when you slept with her." I crossed my arms.

"I defended my actions to myself by believing if I was sleeping with her, she would leave Templeton alone. In a way it worked."

I didn't understand. "You mean she stopped seeing Templeton?"

"Not totally, but she had less time for him. He found out why and…" Rabbit waved his hand. "In the meantime, the Rabbits around me saw a change in my behavior. Nisha's wickedness influenced me. I couldn't see it, but my friends could. I did things I'm not proud of during that time. Eventually, the Tortoise came to me. He helped me see the truth."

"You need to tell me more about him," I said. "But first tell me the rest. Did you dump Nisha?"

Rabbit curled his upper lip. "What do you think?"

"No?"

"No. I wanted to, but I could not stop seeing her. Emily, I was compelled. Spellbound, like Templeton." He puffed out his cheeks and blew out another breath. "She likes having a pool of men to… please her."

"I think that's enough detail."

"Yeah," he said, giving his head a shake. "I

knew we both had to get away from her. I asked what I could give to her for my freedom. For Templeton's."

I felt a chill slide up my spine. "What did you give up in return, Rabbit?"

He fidgeted in the chair and the leather creaked under his weight. "The love of my firstborn child."

I drew in a sharp breath, my hand going to my mouth. "You did what?"

"The irony is I thought I was pulling one over on her." His face dropped. "I didn't think she'd ever be able to collect payment. The joke was on me."

"I don't understand."

"Emily, one in three male Rabbits is sterile. Some believe now it's more like two in three. I can't have children. I've known this since I was young. Rabbits have big families, and they get their males tested as soon as they come of age. I fall into the 'no kids' camp. I thought Nisha's terms didn't matter because I knew I couldn't have children."

But Rabbit said the joke was on him. "Rabbit, was the fertility test wrong? I mean, did you end up having a child?"

My friend's eyes became watery. "A daughter," he whispered.

I could sense his heartache. "Oh, Rabbit." I pulled the desk chair closer and reached for his hands. "But how could she not love you?"

A tear broke free, and he pulled one of his rough hands away. He wiped at both of his eyes with the palm of his hand. "She doesn't know I exist."

I listened as Rabbit told me his saddest tale. Because he was deemed sterile, in Rabbit culture he was likely to remain a bachelor. He claimed he wasn't overly bothered by this, and he dated Rabbits and non-Rabbits alike. Since he didn't need to use anything for birth control, he didn't always make the wisest choices when it came to protection. Then, in a weird twist of fate, he managed to get a non-Rabbit woman pregnant. This didn't go over well with the woman's fairly affluent parents. In the end, she married another after a month-long courtship. Rabbit's daughter called this other man 'father.'

"She'll be 17 in April," Rabbit finished. He fidgeted with a dime-sized hole in the leg of his jeans. "She's beautiful."

"You see her?" I asked.

"I don't see her in the way you think. But I know where she is." He barked out a sharp laugh. "In the end, the debt to Nisha was paid. But she collects it over and over."

Rabbit went on to explain how Nisha not only fed on the magic of others, but the pain they caused themselves. As if not being able to be with his daughter wasn't enough, Rabbit's ongoing heartache nourished Nisha's power.

I continued to hold onto one of his hands. We sat silently for a few minutes before I spoke. "And Templeton? He's no longer spellbound either?"

Rabbit shook his head. "Nope. But he was furious with me for interfering in his private business. I also knew he was angry because Nisha favored me." He swallowed. "She still does."

"And then I go off and make a deal with her." I hung my head. "Oh, Rabbit. I'm so sorry."

"Hey," he let go of my hand and lifted my chin. "She played you."

"Well, I won't let you down again. I promise."

This time Rabbit genuinely laughed, and it sounded good. He dropped his hand and smacked my knee. "Emily, I know you mean well, but no promises, okay?"

"I feel like I should be offended," I sulked. "I can keep a promise."

"I'm only teasing," he assured me. I knew he wasn't, but I'd do better. I'd fix things between us.

"I don't even know if I should ask this, and I get it if you don't want to tell me, but the message I gave to you from Nisha… I couldn't understand what I said to you last night. I don't know what it was."

"It was magically encrypted," Rabbit told me. "But I understood it."

"Are you going to tell me what it was? What she said?"

He let his head tilt to the side, letting his gaze wander across the room. "She told me if I came back to her, she'd give my daughter's love to me."

My chest tightened. "What are you going to do?"

Rabbit slowly returned his eyes to mine and shook his head. "Nothing."

❧ ❧ ❧

Rabbit and I spent the next hour trading information. He knew about Blackstone's murder – of course – and was knee-deep in gathering information with the rest of the Rabbits in the network. While they didn't know Blackstone personally, they certainly understood the gravity of the situation. Rabbit was particularly concerned about the North Door being compromised.

"I know the Empire is supposedly guarding it," he said. "But I'm bothered by the Fringe taking aim at one of the Empire's directional doors. Why now?"

There were three other official directional doors leading into the Empire from the east, west, and south. Rabbit was concerned the others would be targeted by the Fringe, too.

"Do you know where they are?" I asked. I only knew the location of the North Door.

"We have ideas," he said. "We're watching different spots to see if the Empire beefs up security. That'll be a clue."

"I'm not sure I understand the whole point of the Fringe taking the doors, though. The Fringe is made up of Salesmen – and they can door travel. The directional doors are one-way doors into the Empire. Well, except for one day of the year when you can go either way. Why would the Fringe be interested?"

"The network believes the directional doors are not only Empire-related. We think the doors might be able to go to other places in the universe." Rabbit regarded me. "We don't believe you need to be a Salesman to use them, either."

"Another Rabbit once told me the same thing. This opens up a whole other bag of tricks," I said. "Have you been to these other places?"

He shook his head no. "I used to travel more, but mostly I keep to the Empire now. I spent some time in Europe. As for the other possible planes of existence, no."

"What do you think these other places are?"

"Not sure. Different concepts of the universe and what's real." Rabbit shrugged. "This would be a good subject to bring up to Templeton. But probably not today."

"One thing at a time," I agreed, but I thought about Rabbit's words. Blackstone had once described the Empire as a concept – but a place with cities and people. I was still trying to wrap my head around it.

We were quiet, each lost in our own thoughts. He startled me when he spoke again. "How's your neck, Emily?"

I lifted my hand and touched the scarf. "It doesn't hurt. This is a healing scarf from Lucie."

"Let me see." He loosened the material, pulling it away gently. "It's lightening a lot faster than if you didn't have Lucie's magic working on it."

"Light enough to go without a scarf in front of Jack?" I checked Rabbit's reaction.

"Sure. If you want him to kill Sebastian."

"I want someone to…" I let my voice trail off. I cleared my throat. "I want to stop him. I want to hold him accountable."

Rabbit let go of the scarf and I adjusted it. "Emily, something occurred to me about this –" he motioned to my neck "– and Blackstone."

I froze. "You think Sebastian is the one who strangled Blackstone?"

Rabbit nodded. "I think it's possible."

"We never got to talk last spring," I shuddered. "Everything in the warehouse came to a head in an instant."

"We're not going to talk about it," he told me.

"That's fine with me," I agreed. I didn't want to picture my friend and the other Rabbits preparing to... well, do what they did to Simon. He deserved punishment for the killings he committed, but the whole scene made me uncomfortable. Sebastian escaped that night, leaving Simon to the Rabbits' wrath.

But what if he hadn't gotten away? I felt my lips curve wickedly. Hopefully he wouldn't get as lucky the next time we faced off with him.

"Emily?" Rabbit prodded.

"Nothing," I said, pushing my unholy wishes aside. "Sebastian, yeah. What do you know about him? Is he really an important part of the Fringe? Or a wannabe?"

"Oh, he's got some power," Rabbit confirmed. He rose to his feet and stretched. "You ready for a drink?"

"Is Templeton's house the party place?" I joked.

Rabbit laughed as he picked up various bottles and read the labels. "Hardly."

"I'll still pass. I need a clear head. Took too much in today," I said.

He settled on another shot of vodka. He

leaned against the bar's counter. "I think you know Sebastian comes from a wealthy family. The St. Michel name goes back several hundred years. The money comes from banking primarily, from what we can tell. You said you met his mother today?"

"When they were leaving Spell's offices. Odette – she's a real pill. I hadn't met her before, but she knew Templeton." I waved a hand, indicating the lavish space surrounding us. "I guess I'm not surprised."

"Templeton's family is also pretty old and moneyed." He rocked the empty shot glass between his fingers.

"This Odette seemed like a real snob, but at least now I know which parent is the Salesman. Sebastian inherits his legacy from his mother," I said.

Rabbit held up two fingers. "Inherits from both parents. His father's a Salesman, too. They don't like to 'marry outside of their own kind.'"

"I guess I'm not surprised," I replied. "Does it make him doubly powerful or something?"

"As a Salesman? Nah. But don't get me wrong, Emily. The St. Michels have a lot of power.

And I believe they're supporting Fringe activities. Sebastian's got quite the reputation as being untouchable. He likes to pull strings to get what he wants. It's what his family does." Rabbit rubbed his chin. "The difference is Sebastian is more hands-on than his elders. It's a game to him. He likes displaying his power – and money. He's also somewhat of a playboy."

"Yeah. I bet." I snorted. "Rabbit, do you think the St. Michel family is the head of the Fringe?"

"Anything is possible," he answered. "I think it's more than one family, but every instinct tells me the St. Michels are right at the top. All the information we've gathered since the kidnapping has threads leading back to their name."

"Do you think we can take them down?" I asked. I wanted to know if I was completely off my nut.

His boyish face lit up. "We can absolutely try. You have a plan?"

"Working on it," I said. "And we need the third piece of the Crimson Stone. We've got to find the Tortoise."

"I think I know where to look next. You want to come with me?"

"Try to stop me."

We were interrupted by one of Mr. Archie's soft knocks. He stepped inside the study. He raised an eyebrow at Rabbit. "Please don't spoil your dinner with too much vodka, Mr. Rabbit."

Rabbit chuckled. "I've yet to turn down one of your meals, Mr. Archie."

The man smiled. "I'm setting out the hors d'oeuvres now. Would either of you like to freshen up before dinner?"

"I should wash my hands." Rabbit winced at his cracked knuckles.

"Do you remember where the nearest restroom is?"

"I do."

"Then I'll return in a few minutes." Mr. Archie stepped back out.

"Did you come here a lot?" I asked as Rabbit started to leave.

"Enough." Rabbit paused at the door. "Templeton was with you when Sebastian and his mother came out of Spell's?"

"Yeah, we were on our way to meet with her," I told him.

"What did Templeton do when he saw Sebastian?"

"He grabbed him by the shirt and put him up against the wall," I said, picturing the scene in my head for the hundredth time.

Rabbit's dark eyes glittered. "Good."

CHAPTER 14

Rabbit returned from washing up at the same time Mr. Archie came back to the study. He led us through Templeton's home into a grand dining room. The long table could have easily sat two dozen guests. I doubted it ever saw more than two people dining at a time.

"You think that's for Templeton?" I gestured to the high back chair at the end of the table. A dinner setting, minus a plate for the main course, was placed on the table in front of it. I snickered. "Should I sit in it?"

Rabbit's eyes rolled toward me. "I don't think today's the day for it."

I grinned but left the chair alone. Two other settings appeared to the right and left of Templeton's. At least we weren't sitting 10 feet apart. I scoped out the plates of hors d'oeuvres on the buffet. Mr. Archie made sure Rabbit had plenty of vegetarian choices. I snagged a stuffed mushroom cap and a square of prosciutto-wrapped cheese. Both were heavenly.

"Does he eat like this every day?" I wondered aloud. "Or is this because of us?"

"He has a penthouse in Matar," Rabbit said absently as he placed various crudités on a plate. "There's a dining club near it. He likes to have dinner in one of their private rooms."

"Alone?"

Rabbit shrugged. "Probably."

"That's sad." I added another mushroom to my little plate and took a seat to the left of the table's head. "He told me some things today, Rabbit."

Rabbit sat down in the chair across the table. "Anything you want to tell me?"

I rubbed my lips together and thought about it. "Yes, I do. But I don't know if I should yet. I need more answers from him. We were having it out when you got here."

"How did you get here?" Rabbit asked. "Or more to the point, why are you here?"

Yet another secret from Templeton I was reluctant to share after our massive blowup in his study. And yet, that's what kept getting us in trouble. We all had pieces of the bigger story, but we didn't always know the other person's part in it. I popped the last of the mushroom into my mouth and chewed.

"I door traveled from the Courthouse

through the same door as Templeton. I focused on 'home' – and I think he did, too. We both ended up in his study. I can't begin to understand all the ins and outs of door travel." I wiped my fingertips on my napkin and avoided making eye contact.

"I'll let whatever it is slide for now," Rabbit said, his nose twitching. He bit into a carrot stick as he studied me.

The sharp snap echoed in the room and triggered a thought. "Rabbit, you've been here, what, almost two hours? Why haven't I heard your phone buzz once?"

"I'm on radio-silence," he said. "After today's bombing, the network went nuts. We also discovered we were being hacked again. Unless it's crucial, we're all keeping a low profile."

"It's the Fringe? Is that what you think?"

"Yup. It's been happening all year. We've been concerned about a different kind of attack – a technological one." Rabbit leaned back in his chair, resting his head. "We're not that surprised. We've managed to stay ahead of them for years, but they've been slowly catching up. They're moving faster than the Empire's tech team." He added a pair of air quotes to 'tech team.'

"But why is the Fringe targeting the Rabbit network? To what end?" I asked.

"Oh, everything from getting more information to circumventing the technology the Empire has in place to monitor door travel," he replied.

"Makes sense I guess," I said as a movement at the other end of the room snagged my attention. Templeton entered the dining room. He made a face at the buffet as he passed, skipping the hors d'oeuvres.

"Rabbit's filled me in on what's been happening since the bombing – well, at least with the network," I finished as Templeton uncomfortably sat at the head of the table.

Templeton regarded me for a moment, before abruptly turning toward Rabbit. Again, he said nothing. If I didn't know better, I'd have thought his jaw was wired shut.

Rabbit didn't let him suffer. "There was a total of three bombs detonated at the Salesman Court today. We confirmed it was the Fringe, but they claimed it from the get-go. Deaths are in the teens, so far. There'll be more. They're still digging out. All the justices have been accounted for. Some weren't even in the Empire at the time of the explosion, like Jo. She's home in New York City."

"Was it a random attack or was there a target?" Templeton finally spoke.

"Seems random," Rabbit answered as he salted a piece of celery. "There weren't any notable court cases scheduled."

I leaned forward, putting my elbow on the table, and rubbed my chin. "It's weird though. Sebastian and his mother were in the building. If the Fringe is behind it, why would they bomb the building when two of their leaders were inside?"

"I suppose if the St. Michels knew about it ahead of time, they could door travel out before the bombs went off," Rabbit said. "But door traveling in and out of the Courthouse is monitored. Did they have time to get from Spell's chambers to the main entrance at the front of the Courthouse?"

"Funny you should say that," I said. "I bypassed the Courthouse entrance and skipped the metal detectors by door traveling straight onto Spell's floor. If any bells and whistles went off, I wasn't aware. I saw no ramifications."

Templeton sipped from his water glass.

"Did you come in through the Courthouse entrance?" I asked him.

He nodded, his contemplation on the glass in front of him. I could almost hear the wheels turning in his head.

Mr. Archie appeared, bringing our dinner on a quiet silver cart. I gaped at the great platter sitting on top: roast duck served on a bed of saffron-scented rice. Now, I hadn't been in Templeton's home *that* long. This menu was already in play before Mr. Archie knew Templeton wouldn't be eating alone. *My how the other half lives,* I thought.

Mr. Archie first served us smaller plates consisting of a baked pears and fennel salad, dotted with crumbled blue cheese. For Rabbit, Mr. Archie had 'whipped up' a pasta and cheese bake with spinach and pesto *pangrattato*. That dish he set near Rabbit. I wondered if it would be rude to ask for a serving.

Retrieving a plate from the dish warmer on the cart's lower shelf, Mr. Archie turned toward me. "Shall I serve you, Miss Emily?"

"Um, yes, please?" I watched as he selected

several pieces of the duck's breast and laid the thin slices on the plate. He added a portion of rice, topping the grains with toasted slivered almonds. I pulled the napkin into my lap as he set the dinner plate in front of me. He went on to serve Rabbit a sizeable helping of the baked pasta, before setting a dish with roast duck in front of Templeton. Mr. Archie provided each one of us with a glass of white wine, setting the bottle on the table near our reluctant host. He then excused himself after promising to return shortly.

"Wow," I said breathlessly. "This looks incredible. Did Mr. Archie cook all of this?"

"I have a cook, but yes, Mr. Archie often prepares meals." Templeton poked at a piece of fennel. When he realized I was watching him, he raised his head. "Why are you staring at me?"

Rabbit snickered from the other side of the table.

"This is very strange." I considered my plate before cutting a piece of the duck and taking a bite. It was heavenly.

"What is strange?" Templeton continued. "Roast duck?"

"No," I replied. I pointed at him with my fork. "You. Eating."

Rabbit grinned into his glass of wine.

"Such a child," Templeton grumbled and stabbed a chunk of the baked pear.

I ignored him and lifted my chin, peering down my nose across the table at the casserole dish sitting near Rabbit. "It's sort of a fancy mac and cheese, right?"

I could almost *hear* Templeton's eyes roll in his head.

"Give me your plate," said Rabbit as he held out his hand. I beamed a happy smile at him as he added a serving of the pasta by the roast duck.

Templeton mumbled something about 'the death of me.'

"Thank you," I said, as Rabbit passed my plate back. The three of us ate in silence for a few minutes. As much as I was content to concentrate on one of the best dinners I'd ever had, I couldn't stand it. I lifted my head. "Okay, let's not talk about anything that's going to set anyone off, but can we discuss what we're going to do next?"

Rabbit chewed and nodded, sneaking a

glance at Templeton.

Templeton set his fork to the side of his plate before putting his napkin to his mouth. He refolded the linen. "I plan to speak with Spell privately."

I wasn't sure what I expected, but it wasn't that. "Why bother?"

"She's likely to share more with me if I'm alone." Templeton smiled meanly. "She doesn't like you."

"The feeling's pretty mutual at this point," I sneered. "Rabbit? What do you think?"

"Well, like we talked about earlier, we need to find the Tortoise. Then we'll have all three pieces of the Crimson Stone." Rabbit pointed a finger at Templeton. "Yours included."

"The Tortoise? So that's who you gave it to for safekeeping. Interesting." Templeton inhaled through his nose. He shook his head. "The trouble is, even Rabbits can't usually find him."

"Rumor is he's back in the Walled Zone. I've checked a few of his haunts over the summer but found nothing. I'm starting to pick up on new chatter across the network." Rabbit bobbed his head toward me. "Emily's going with me. It would be good if you'd join us. You could door travel in once we get a better idea of where the Tortoise is staying. I'll have the network pass a message to you."

When Rabbit mentioned door travel, Templeton's eyes flicked to me. I remained silent. "It's an option," he said.

"If we do this, would we be going through Matar?" I asked Rabbit.

"Yeah. I'd like to bring some muscle on board since we're going into the Walled Zone," Rabbit replied. "Why?"

"I had a couple of thoughts," I said. Both men listened as I went on to explain what I'd been cooking on in the back of my brain.

The first thing I needed to do was go back to Kincaid. I'd door travel to Tara's and we'd call Anne to join us. I wanted to talk to Jo and I'd ask her to door travel to me after I filled Tara and Anne in on everything they needed to know. I also wanted to learn if Tara had discovered anything in the letters Blackstone gave her to go through before he was killed. I wanted to check with Anne about keeping my mother out of Jack's hair.

And I needed to see Jack. I'd figure out how to do it without being forced to reveal my run-in with Sebastian.

When I was finished in Kincaid, I'd door travel back to Lucie's. That's when I'd try a bit of my own magic – but I needed Templeton's help.

Rabbit nodded as I shared my ideas. Templeton watched me thoughtfully. When I mentioned needing him for the dreamwork I planned, he shook his head before I could elaborate.

"I don't think you can do this, Emily. First of all, you don't have a connection, a personal reference point for the Tortoise. I can't imagine you'll be skilled enough to pull him into your dream without it. You don't have the experience." Templeton pursed his lips, turning the idea over in his head.

"That makes sense but let me finish." I pushed my dinner plate to the side and leaned in. "Rabbit has a connection to the Tortoise. I want you to pull Rabbit into your dream. Then I want to meet you in that same dream. Be where I can find you – like in your study. Using Rabbit's connection to the Tortoise, we pull him in and ask him where he is. Easy peasy."

Rabbit lifted an eyebrow. "Is any of this possible?"

Templeton tapped his long fingers on the tablecloth. After a moment, he shrugged. "I suppose it's not impossible. I could keep the environment stable."

"And I want to do this from Lucie's house," I added. "She's 'boosted' my magic before with some of her own energy. I think she could help."

Templeton was surprised. "You've worked magic together?"

"Not a lot," I answered. "But she helped me when I activated a bunch of Whispering Flower seeds before. She's always available to teach me. She'd want to help us now."

"Lucie's a good lady," Rabbit said. He used his fork to swipe another bite of pasta directly from the serving dish. "She's a lot of fun."

Templeton's head swiveled toward Rabbit. "You're spending time with her?"

Rabbit coolly assessed Templeton's response. "She's worth getting to know."

"We're getting off-track," I interjected. "We're also running out of time, and I want to get back to Kincaid. Let's pick a time to try the dreamwork. Rabbit, are you going to stay here tonight?"

"Do I need to find a different place to bed down?" Rabbit asked Templeton.

Templeton snorted. "Of course not. Mr. Archie has one of the bedrooms prepared for you."

"Alright. Let's say 11 o'clock. It'll give me plenty of time to do the things I need to do," I said. "Rabbit, would you send a message for me? I know you're not using the network right now, but can you get a message to Tara and tell her I'm coming? I'm guessing she's at *Pages & Pens*. She's usually there late during the week. Ask her to call Anne, too."

Rabbit nodded. "Not a problem. And Jo?"

"No, I'll text Jo from Tara's bookstore. I'm assuming she's still home," I said.

"What about Jack?" Rabbit's gaze floated to the scarf around my neck.

I touched the soft fabric and tried to make a joke. "Yeah, maybe tell Tara to ask Anne to bring a turtleneck. Hopefully we're having Kincaid's typical chilly fall weather and wearing it when I go home won't seem weird."

"Will do." Rabbit pulled his phone from his jeans pocket and reached out to the network.

My message would be sent.

"And on that note," I said, pushing my chair back from the table. "I should be going. I need to get my shoulder bag from your study, Templeton."

"I'll walk you there." The Salesman stood and we circled the table toward the dining room door. We were met by Mr. Archie.

"I was coming to see if you were ready for dessert," he told us. "We have Black Forest cake this evening."

I heard Rabbit make a sound of pleasure as he continued to study his phone.

"You have no idea how tempting it sounds," I told the kind man. "But I have to head for home. There are important things I need to do tonight."

"Then I will wish you safe travels, Miss Emily." Mr. Archie gave a slight bow. "Please come stay with us when you have more time."

I nodded, feeling Templeton's hand on my shoulder blade as he nudged me forward. We didn't speak as we returned to his study. I had a feeling he was turning something over in his mind, and I didn't want to interrupt. Once I'd retrieved my shoulder bag, he held up a hand.

"I want to try something." He reached for me. The serious expression on his face gave me pause.

"You're not going to try some sort of Vulcan mind-meld with me, are you?" I asked lamely, resisting an urge to pull away.

The corners of his mouth quirked up. "I wouldn't have pegged you for a sci-fi fan."

"Jack watches T.O.S.," I explained with a shrug. "But yeah, not my speed."

"Hold still." Templeton slowly unwound the silky scarf from my neck. "Lift your chin."

"What are you doing?" I asked, but I didn't pull away.

"Trying to make it easier on you tonight. Don't move. It won't hurt." Templeton inspected my neck as his fingertips stroked my skin. His blue eyes faded as they always did when he was angry or used magic. I could feel a cool energy everywhere he touched.

"What are you doing?" I asked again. I hated it when he didn't answer my questions.

"Applying a glamour," he replied. "I don't know how long it will last. I'd still take the scarf if I were you, but I think I can disguise the bruises for a short period of time."

"Thank you," I whispered. His eyes flicked from my throat to mine, then back to his ministrations. A memory bubbled up. It seemed like eons ago, but Templeton also once grabbed me by the throat. I barely knew who he was at the time, and he'd disrupted the proceedings recognizing me as a Salesman. The Fringe attacked that day, too. As Templeton fled the chaos of the courtroom, I'd grabbed his sleeve. He reacted by putting me up against the courtroom wall and telling me to go back home. Templeton was just as capable of violence as Sebastian. And yet, he'd put himself in danger to help me more than once. I struggled to reconcile the different versions of this man.

His hand slipped away, and he scrutinized his work. "It's done." He picked up Lucie's scarf to hand to me. I reached for it, but he pulled it back and examined it. "She has a distinct signature in her magic. I don't know much about the Bellerose witchline, but I assume it's thinning like the others."

"I don't know anything about that," I said, reaching for the scarf. He handed it over and I wrapped it back around my neck loosely. I nodded. "Thanks again."

"You are welcome." He sighed, scanning the room to avoid looking directly at me.

"I didn't tell Rabbit about your door travel issue," I said. "But you should probably let him know tonight."

Templeton didn't reply but motioned to the door. "Give Ms. Parker-Jones my regards."

I put my top hat on my head. "I'll see you later tonight, Templeton." He and I still had much to discuss, but it would have to wait.

I turned toward the door leading out of his study and pictured the backroom of *Pages & Pens*. I hoped Rabbit's message made it and Tara was there waiting for me.

The energy rose easily in my chest, and I stepped on through, leaving Templeton's estate and returning to Kincaid.

❋ ❋ ❋

Tara was indeed still at *Pages & Pens*. She saw Rabbit's message and also texted Anne – who was on her way. As I door traveled into the back room, Tara shot out from behind her desk and hugged me.

"We've been worried!" Her arms wrapped

around me, and she squeezed. "What's been happening?"

I peeled my best friend off me and flopped down on her couch. "You would not believe the half of it."

"I've got all night." Tara stood at the end of the couch, her hands on her hips. "Wait, have you been shopping? Those are some nice threads."

"Ironically, yes, I have been shopping." I briefly flashed back to Big Rabbit browsing racks with me at the secondhand store. "But this is a borrowed outfit. I needed a change of clothes. There was an incident."

"There always is," Tara replied as she lifted my feet and sat down. "Huh. These ballets are an expensive label. Who are you hanging out with these days?"

I waved a hand. "Doesn't matter. When is Anne getting here? I don't want to tell the same story twice. Plus, I've got to see Jack."

"He's climbing the walls. Want to text him?" Tara held out her phone.

I shook my head. "Not yet. Listen, while we're waiting for Anne, can you tell me anything you've learned since I've been gone? Anything in those letters from Blackstone's library?"

"I *did* find something. Hang on." Tara moved my feet and retrieved the box of official Empire letters. "There were notes written on some of the correspondence – almost like journal entries. I think they were left for Blackstone, but I wonder if he ever even saw them."

I sat up. "You think they're important?"

"Tell me what you think." Tara sifted through the pages. She'd slipped them into clear plastic sleeves. "Here."

The pages she handed me were old and yellowed, but not so old that they were brittle. I skimmed the handwriting until a handful of words caught my eye – *Empire's official directional doors.* "Do these letters and notes give the locations of all the doors?"

"Not quite. They list the *possible* locations," she said. "Basically, the notes indicate where the Empire was hoping to place the directional doors."

"This is useful." I set the letters on the table. "Rabbit told me today they had an idea of where the doors could be. I should show him these and we can compare. We're worried, Tara. Rabbit told me the directional doors might not only be portals for the Empire. He told me he thinks other places beyond the Empire might be a part of this, too."

Tara's mouth popped open. "Get out?"

"And he thinks the Fringe is on a mission to take control of all four," I continued.

"Makes sense. Why wouldn't they?" Tara's phone buzzed. "Anne's here. I need to unlock the door." Tara left the room to let Anne in through the front door of the bookstore. I picked up the pages and letters from the box and scanned them for more information.

"Emily!" Anne cried out, rushing to me. She pulled me into her embrace. "I've been trying to keep track of you through the tea leaves. Yesterday I had such a bad feeling. In the cup I saw a demon standing on a top hat."

I hugged her back. "Yeah, that sounds about right."

Anne released me as Tara sat on the end of the coffee table. I blew out a breath. "I don't want to go into it, but I had a run-in with Sebastian yesterday. It wasn't pretty, but I got away." I reached for one of Tara's hands and one of Anne's. "Listen, I'm okay, but this is not something I'm ever telling Jack. It was a close call and Sebastian will get his. But that's it. No more discussion about it."

A concerned Anne looked to Tara, who shrugged. "If that's what you want?"

"It is. I learned a lesson. No more barreling in unprepared." I let their hands go. "But there are a few things I want to tell you. Then we need to get Jo here."

"Tonight?" Tara wrinkled her nose.

"Yes, it's important. The Salesman Court's been compromised," I said. "And bombed."

"Bombed?" Anne shook her head. "When?"

"Earlier today," I said. "I'm surprised you didn't know." Anne had many friends and family living in the Empire.

"No, I tried the Empire service earlier, but the operator said it was down." She lifted her palms. "It happens sometimes. I thought it might be related to Rene's murder and the attack on the North Door here in Kincaid – that maybe they were slowing down messages to better monitor what was coming from here."

"I don't know anything about the Empire's service, but the Courthouse was attacked. I was with Templeton and we got out." I didn't tell my friends about his door travel issue. It was too much to go into and I didn't have a lot of time. "The Fringe claimed credit."

"Damn," Anne said. "It's coming to a head, Emily. You need to be careful."

"Before we text Jo, I have a few more things I want you to know. I've hooked up with Rabbit and Lucie, and even Templeton is sort of on board. Rabbit confirmed Sebastian's family does have influence in the Fringe. He wouldn't say they were the only ones at the top, but they're definitely up there. Rabbit still needs to get his piece of the Crimson Stone. We're going to attempt to find the Tortoise through dreamwork tonight," I finished.

"We?" Anne repeated.

"Templeton agreed to work with us – at least for the time being. He's going to pull Rabbit in, then I'm going to try and join his dream. Using Rabbit's relationship with the Tortoise, we're going to try to get to him. If we can find him, we can get the third piece," I explained.

"And Templeton still has the piece he took from you?" Tara asked.

"Oh, yeah. He's definitely got it."

Tara's shrewd brain caught a clue. "Something we should know?"

"Another time," I said. "Also, I found out today Spell is being influenced by Sebastian's family – or by some part of the Fringe."

"I don't believe that!" Anne shook her head. "No. I don't see it at all."

"She admitted as much to us today, and I saw Sebastian and his mother coming out of Spell's chambers," I told her. "This is what I want to share with Jo."

Anne's shoulders drooped. "How could she give in to them?"

"They're threatening her family. I still think she should've fought against them, but…" My voice trailed off. "But we still have Jo and we need to let her know."

"We do," Tara agreed. "What else?"

"Um," I twisted my lips to the side, thinking. "Right. My mother. Anne?"

"I brought her into the *Brew Too* and she's making a mess."

"Sounds about right," I nodded. "I'm going to owe you big."

"Oh, yes. You will," Anne replied.

"Let's get Jo here," I said as I stood. "I'll explain what's going on with Spell, but everything else let's keep to ourselves. We don't want to put Jo in an awkward spot. She can't be held responsible if she doesn't know what we're doing."

"Agreed," Anne said. She rose from the couch. "I'm going to make tea." As she passed, she glanced at my outfit. "Oh, Emily, I was in such a rush I forgot to bring you a turtleneck – but you're not going to need it. It's quite balmy tonight."

I reached up automatically and touched the scarf hanging loose from my neck. I cleared my throat. "It's okay. You're right. I won't need it."

"I do love the shirt you're wearing, though. It looks like the one I gave to my niece Audra for her birthday this past summer," Anne finished.

Her words hit me like a ton of bricks. "Your niece? Audra?"

"She lives in the Empire. Lovely young woman." Anne picked up the tea kettle and started to leave the back room.

"Hold on there, Anne," I ordered. She stopped and Tara gave me a funny look. "Audra?"

"Yes. What's the matter?" Anne set the tea kettle back down.

"It's a very long story," I began. "But in a nutshell, I ended up in Templeton's home in some pretty dirty clothes following the blast at the Courthouse."

Anne winced.

"What am I missing?" Tara interjected.

"I had to borrow something to wear. Templeton's Mr. Archie was nice enough to let me borrow a shirt and pants left there by Templeton's cousin. *Audra.*" I knew in my heart it wasn't a coincidence. Anne often advocated on Templeton's behalf. He'd visited her in the past. She told me she was with him all those years ago in Anwat on the horrible Eve of Silence. The night he whisked my mother away from Sebastian's men, he brought her to Anne's home in Kincaid. "Anne, your niece is the same Audra, isn't she?"

"Yes," she confirmed. "She is."

"Ohmigod," Tara clapped a hand over her mouth. "Are you Templeton's mom?"

"No," Anne and I answered at the same time. Anne stayed silent, so I continued. "Anne's not a Salesman. But her mother is."

Anne heaved a big sigh. "It wasn't my secret to tell, Emily. Templeton doesn't want people to know I'm related to him – and hold on.

It's for my benefit, not his. Templeton's not a popular person in many of the magical communities in Matar."

"You're Templeton's aunt?" Tara pulled a lock of hair to her mouth, an old habit she resorted to when she was completely caught off guard.

"I'm Templeton's aunt," Anne nodded. She leaned against the hutch's counter and rearranged the teabags Marley had tucked into a basket. "My older sister, Gavina, is a Salesman – she's the firstborn child in my family. She's also Templeton's mother. We have another sister, Catriona. She's Audra's mother."

"Gavina and Catriona?" Tara repeated. "Those are two mouthfuls. You lucked out with Anne."

"It's actually Annag," Anne replied.

"I stand corrected. Not so lucky."

I would've scolded Tara for being rude, but I was feeling perturbed myself. I'd known Anne for going on a year, and I cared deeply for her. She'd become such a good friend. She knew and respected my father. *Oh.* "And that's how you met my dad. It wasn't the other way around, was it? You didn't know my father first."

A wistful smile returned to Anne's face. "I met Daniel through Templeton, yes. And that's also how I met Rabbit."

"But why all the secrecy? I mean…" I lifted my arm and let it fall back uselessly. I was hurt.

"Like I said, Templeton chose to keep the information private. And if he's never told you, Emily, then I take it to mean he'd still prefer not to have the information out there. There are things he wants to keep to himself, and that's certainly his right. I personally don't care how others in Matar's magical community perceive me, but I respected Templeton's wishes." Anne picked up the tea kettle a second time. "Take it up with him. I'm going to get some water."

Tara turned to me, unblinking. "Can you believe that?"

I snorted. "After everything else I learned today, this is only the half of it."

"You've got to tell me," she whined.

"I will," I promised. "But we don't have time now." I held out my hand. "Can I use your phone? I want to text Jo."

She handed it to me. "She's under the name Bossy Legal Chick."

In spite of myself, I laughed as I texted a message to Jo, explaining where I was and that it was an emergency. I asked her to door travel in from Downstate. I flicked a glance at Tara. "I don't suppose you also have a bombshell you'd like to drop on me today?"

She tapped her lips with a finger, thinking. "Well, there is one."

"Let 'er rip," I said, my attention back on the phone screen. The message status changed from 'Delivered' to 'Seen.'

"I made out with Jack back in college before introducing you to him."

CHAPTER 15

I lifted my head. "Seriously?"

"Seriously, but it was like kissing a relative. Neither one of us was into it." She shrugged. "Are you hungry? I'm hungry. Should I order takeout?"

"And you're telling me this now... because?" Wait a minute. Tara and Jack kissed?

"I figured my confession would be overshadowed by all the other drama. The timing felt right." She took the phone from my hand. "Thai food?"

"No, thank you," I automatically answered. "Um, I already ate."

Junior Justice Jo Carter chose that moment to door travel into *Pages & Pens* by way of a broom closet door. She stood there, top hat in hand, wearing pajamas and a robe.

"I see you've dressed for the occasion." I motioned to her nightclothes.

"It's been a long day." Jo's mouth thinned into a line. "But I'm glad to hear from you. I've tried to text you, but your phone is off."

"You should probably sit down," I suggested,

motioning to the couch. Tara quickly scooped up the letters we had sprawled across the coffee table and slipped them back into the plain white box. She carried it away and over to her desk.

"I have a feeling sitting isn't going to help much," Jo said, lowering herself onto the couch. "I wanted to talk to you about Blackstone. I'm sorry, Emily. He was a good person."

"He was." I puffed out my cheeks and blew out a breath. "Why didn't I hear from you about his death? I had to hear it from Templeton."

"No one was allowed to disseminate any information. I'm still not allowed to talk about it outside of official discussions. I can't tell you anything." Jo leaned her head back into the cushion. "But I'm guessing you know a lot by now. I'm also assuming you've been running around the Empire."

I cringed. "Well, yes. And don't worry, you don't have to keep it a secret. I saw Spell right before the bombs detonated. She knows I violated my grounding."

Jo lifted her head. "You were in the Courthouse?"

"Right before the crap hit the fan. Templeton was also there. So was Sebastian St. Michel and his mother," I said.

Surprise flitted across Jo's face. "You were all together?"

"No, not in the sense that we all intended to meet." I put my palms together and touched my praying hands to my lips. I needed to succinctly explain this to Jo.

Jo waited for me to continue. When I didn't immediately speak, she glanced at Tara. "I know you were close to Blackstone. I'll probably want to talk to you in the next couple of weeks. I'm sure the Empire will want to debrief with you on any work you were doing on behalf of the Record Keeper. I'll make sure it's me who checks in with you."

"Thanks," Tara said sadly. "I miss him. Let me know when you want to talk."

"I'll text you." Jo looked to me expectantly. "Emily?"

I nodded. "Okay, I'm just going to fire it all out there – ask questions when I'm done."

"Fine. Get on with it." Jo waved a hand.

"I heard about Blackstone's death a few hours after it happened. I hated sitting around and waiting – especially since Templeton knew the North Door had been tampered with."

It was Jo's turn to wince. "I'm not surprised, but I was hoping we could keep it under wraps."

"Templeton told me," I said. "But the Rabbits know, too. It's not a big secret. Anyhow, I decided to ignore the Empire's door travel grounding and headed for Matar. I needed to catch up with Rabbit to see what he knew and maybe even come up with something to do to help." I glossed over that part and kept talking. "Anyhow, while I was looking for Rabbit, I had a run-in with Sebastian. He attacked me, but I got away."

Jo's face remained expressionless. "Did you report the attack? Are you okay?"

"I'm fine," I told her. "It could've been a lot worse, but yeah, I'm okay. And yes, I did sort of report it."

"Sort of?" Jo cocked her head to the side. "Is there a report on record with the Empire guards?"

"Nope. Here's the deal. After this went down, I decided to confront Spell."

"Emily, confronting a Justice of the Salesman

Court is a good way to get arrested. Plus, you don't have permission to travel – I'm sure Spell knows you're violating the restriction placed on you. I doubt she thinks you took the train into the Empire." Jo's attention skipped to the door as Anne brought the tea kettle back in.

"Oh, she knows," I said. "I arrived at the Courthouse and met up with Templeton on Spell's floor. When we got to her door, Sebastian and his mother were coming out of Spell's chambers. Templeton had words with Sebastian and Spell ordered us into her office. Sebastian and his mother left, but something had gone down before we got there."

"Do you know what?" Jo asked.

I shook my head. "No, I don't. But when I told Spell about the attack, although I know she believed me, she didn't move on it. When I pressed her about arresting Sebastian for kidnapping my mother *and* for attacking the Empire guards in Vue, she put me off."

"Well, Emily, she can't talk about any investigations with you – and she's probably not privy to all of the details," Jo argued.

"Unfortunately, that's not the case. The short story is this: Spell said she was told if the Empire didn't drop the investigation, her family would be in danger. She admitted once the investigation was halted, the threats stopped." I watched Jo for her reaction. As a lawyer, she developed a good poker face.

"I see." She frowned, turning her head and rubbing the back of her neck. She glanced back in my direction. "I was not told about any orders for the investigation to stop. Let me look into it, Emily. I'm not saying they haven't been shelved, but I was one of the victims in the attack in Vue. Given my role with the Salesman Court, I'm surprised I wasn't told."

When Jo used the word victim, Tara snorted. Jo had bloodied the nose of one of the attackers that day. She had been roughed up, but she gave as good as she got.

"Find out what you can," I encouraged. "But keep it on the down low. I don't know who you can trust." I hesitated. "I hope you still trust me."

Jo gave a short, mirthless laugh. "I do. But try not to make anything worse."

"I'm working on it," I replied.

"That's what I'm worried about." Jo climbed to her feet. "The bombing today freaked out my family even though I wasn't even in the Empire when it happened. I'm going home to spend time with my daughter and husband. Is there anything else I should know?"

"Um, I don't think so." I pretended to think. "Nope, that's all I have. I wanted to let you know about Spell. And, you know, maybe something should be done about that?"

Jo nodded. "If she's been influenced by anyone and compromised her integrity as a justice, you are absolutely right. She shouldn't sit on the bench. I sympathize. The violence is terrifying – I'm terrified. But Spell took an oath. If we start picking and choosing –"

"Then why even bother claiming the Salesman's Court upholds the law?" Tara put it out there.

"Exactly. Ugh, I hate this." Jo picked up her top hat and placed it on her head. "And obviously you got out of the Courthouse unscathed, Emily. Thank goodness. You left before the bombs went off?"

"Sounds about right." I smiled. Jo did not. Instead, she walked over and gave me a hug.

"Please be careful," she told me. "I don't know what you are going to do but think it through.

I'll pass along anything I find out to Tara, okay?"

"Thanks, Jo." I said. "And watch your back. You're not an average Salesman, you know?"

She laughed. "Right back at you." She glanced at Tara and Anne. "Ladies." Jo walked to the broom closet and door traveled home to New York City. The door shut softly behind her. Her door travel energy was disciplined, and Jo always traveled gracefully.

"Well, that's done," Tara said. "Poor Jo. I'd be scared."

"She can handle herself," I assured Tara – but I did worry. I hoped Jo could find an ally. There were a couple of justices who she might be able to turn to for help. Then again, I would have counted Spell among them until today.

"Emily," Anne interrupted. "Are you going home now?"

"I'd better. I have to talk to Jack and let him know I'm okay. Don't tell him I talked to you guys first. It'll only make him worry." I held Anne's gaze. I was still angry with her. No, that wasn't it. I was hurt. And yet, Anne was there for me through some of the worst times I'd had in the Empire. When I needed help, she stepped forward immediately and never complained. She kept Templeton's secrets like she kept mine. I supposed it was fair. "I'm sorry I got angry, Anne."

She lifted a shoulder. "I'm not surprised. I'd be upset, too. I'd thought maybe it would've come out when your mother was missing. To be honest, I was hoping you and Templeton would've settled into some sort of friendship by now." She shook her head. "You're both a little headstrong."

"A little?" Tara quipped.

The events of the day played across the private movie screen in my brain. Templeton's face flashed across it several times – in the Courthouse hall, in his study, over dinner. I suddenly became aware of the cool glamour on my neck. I could sense his magic was still strong.

"Friendship? No," I said. "But let's say what we have these days isn't too bad."

❈ ❈ ❈

I told Tara and Anne I'd have Rabbit keep in touch before I said goodbye and door traveled from *Pages & Pens* and through the front door of the home I shared with Jack. It was after 9 o'clock and my mother was curled up reading on the couch with the three Furious Furballs. William and Mischief didn't even bother to lift their heads. Mystery mouthed a silent meow.

Mom looked up. "I'd get up but…" She gestured at the cats draped over her body.

I shook my head, grinning. "It's okay." I dropped a kiss on her forehead. "I'm sorry I didn't come home last night. I didn't get to connect with my friend until very late. It made sense to stay in Matar."

"Hmm. I don't know about that," she answered. "But I'm not the one to convince."

"Speaking of Jack," I said. "Where is he?"

"I think he's upstairs listening to music. He had his headphones on." Mom waved her hand toward the stairs. "A gin martini was in his hand the last time I saw him."

I was sure the martini was the only thing helping Jack keep his sanity. I walked up the stairs and found him sitting in my office, my chair tilted back and his eyes closed. I touched his arm, mouthing 'sorry!' when he jumped and opened his eyes.

He pulled the headphones off and stood up, pulling me into his arms and burying his face into the side of my neck. I felt the scarf shift and hoped like hell the glamour held. He took a deep, shuddering breath. "I'm glad you're home. There hasn't been a message since last night."

"I know," I answered, letting him hold me. "I wanted to send you one, but there was a lot going on today."

He leaned back and searched my face. "Are you home for good?" The hope on his own face crushed my heart.

"No," I answered. "But I wanted to see you and tell you what's going on." I took his hand. "Come into the bedroom so we can both sit down."

Jack followed me and closed the door when I motioned for him to do so. I climbed up onto our bed and sat holding a pillow, my legs crossed. He joined me, scooting closer and placing another pillow between his back and the headboard. "I wanted more than anything for you to say you weren't leaving again." He reached for my hand.

Jack wore a green tee shirt over another

long-sleeved shirt and a pair of red and black plaid pajama bottoms. He looked solid, comfy. He looked like home. I abandoned my pillow and curled up against him under his arm. He hugged me and kissed the top of my head.

"This is what's been going on," I began. I told Jack about staying at Lucie's and looking for Rabbit. I skipped over how I traveled to the Rabbits' bonfire space and the experience with Sebastian. I did tell him I'd been sent a giant Rabbit to watch over me while I waited for Rabbit to come to Lucie's. He gave me a squeeze and said 'good.'

I didn't want to tell any of Rabbit's secrets related to Nisha, so I skipped over that debacle as well. I was starting to feel more than a little guilty. I switched to the story about seeing Templeton and running into Sebastian and his mother. I glossed over the conversation but shared how Templeton had 'shoved' Sebastian. I felt Jack tense.

"And then what happened?" he asked calmly. He stared straight ahead.

"Well, here's where it gets interesting," I said.

Jack scowled. "I'm not going to be happy, am I?"

"No," I admitted. I wiggled free and moved onto his lap, my knees pressed into the mattress alongside his thighs. I put my hand to his chest. I could feel his heart beating and it felt good. "Justice Spell broke up the 'incident' between Templeton and Sebastian, then ordered us into her office. Well, ordered Templeton and me. Sebastian waltzed away with his mother."

"I don't get it." Jack ran his hands up and down my arms.

"Apparently, Jack, the Fringe has threatened Justice Spell's family, and she caved. She closed the investigation into Mom's kidnapping *and* the other Fringe-related crimes happening around it." I drew circles on the front of his shirt with my fingertip. "I couldn't believe it."

"She knows what they can do, what they've done." Jack's hands didn't stop moving. They were now on my shoulders gently squeezing. "She was on the bench with your father, Em. She saw all the violence. She's probably scared."

"I'm sure she is," I agreed. "But this is her job. She's supposed to uphold the law."

He nodded. "Yeah. It stinks. Does Jo know about this?"

I licked my bottom lip. "She's been informed. She'll let Tara know if she finds out anything. She's walking a fine line."

Jack's fingertips slid down the silky ends of the scarf. He looked at me hopefully. "Is that all?"

"Oh, how I wish I could say yes," I told him. "First of all, I'm sitting here in front of you. I'm clearly okay."

He stiffened. "What happened?"

"After Templeton and I left Spell's chambers, the Fringe bombed the building."

Jack didn't make a sound, but the color left his face

"And as you can see, I'm fine."

Jack let go of the scarf and rested his palms on my thighs. "Yes, you've said that. You got out in time."

"Technically."

He blinked. "Explain."

"The explosion happened when we were in the building. Then we door traveled out of there." All of this was true.

"You weren't hurt at all?" I could feel the tension rolling through Jack's body as he worked to keep his composure.

"I was not." I needed to get us to a better part of the story. "Afterwards, I met up with Templeton and Rabbit. We talked about what we're going to do next."

"Which is?"

"Believe it or not, dreamwork. We need to find the man Rabbit gave his piece of the Crimson Stone to. I think this is our best bet. Even Templeton is sort of on board."

"What, now you two are buddies?" Jack's voice developed an edge.

"I wouldn't say that," I replied. "But yeah, I need his help."

"Doesn't everything come with a price in the Empire, Emily?" Agitated, Jack stirred. I rose up onto my knees, cupping his face in both of my hands.

"Hey, everything comes with a price. Period. Right now, the cost of doing nothing is greater than any risk. I truly believe that." I leaned in and brushed my mouth over his. He didn't pull away. I considered it a win.

"How long are you staying?" he whispered.

"I've got to go, but I'll send a message." I pressed my forehead against his. "Please don't hate me, Jack."

His hands slid up to my hips. "I don't hate you. I'm scared for you."

I straightened. "I'll be okay. I'm not going it alone."

"Do you want me to take a train into the Empire?" He asked suddenly. I was surprised.

"No, I need you to keep babysitting my mother," I said.

He groaned. "It's only been a couple of days and it feels like a year."

I laughed. "Hang in there. Let Anne take off some of the pressure."

"You're going to owe so many people."

"I already do." I looked around our bedroom. It would be easy to stay, but I couldn't. "I've got to go to Lucie's. I need to bring her up to speed. I'm hoping she can help."

"I thought you were staying with her? Doesn't she know all this already?"

"Oh, I am. But I haven't seen her since this morning." I slipped off Jack's lap and hung my legs over the side of the bed. "I need to say 'bye to Mom before I leave."

Jack brushed his hand through my hair. "She's reading on the couch."

"I saw. I came right upstairs."

Jack gave me a soft smile. He played with one of the ends of the scarf. "What's up with this? You don't wear scarves."

"I do sometimes. I borrowed this from Lucie." I stilled as he ran his finger along the fabric covering my neck. His fingertips brushed my skin.

"Are you cold? Your neck is like ice."

"It is?" I replied, gently pulling away and standing. "Weird. I don't feel cold. Must be Lucie's witchiness or something."

Jack tilted his head. "What's that mean?"

"It means I have no idea," I answered. "But I've got to go. Kiss me then walk me back downstairs."

✳ ✳ ✳

My heart tightened in my chest as I kissed Jack one last time before door traveling through my pantry door into Lucie's kitchen. The brownstone was quiet, but Lucie left a low light on over the sink. I flicked the switch for a brighter one.

A note on the counter caught my eye. Lucie had written:

Hey Emily – I'm out with Basha this evening. I'll be home later. I told Big Rabbit to take the rest of the day off. Hopefully you've reconnected with Rabbit and things are better between you two. I'll talk to you when I get home.

Damn. I'd hoped to count on Lucie when I started the dreamwork. Looks like I was going it alone – at least until I caught up to Templeton and Rabbit.

This would be interesting.

CHAPTER 16

It was 20 minutes before 11 o'clock and I made myself comfortable in Lucie's spare bedroom. I'd hoped she would return early, but she didn't. This new guy certainly kept her busy.

"She deserves to have someone in her life, too," I said aloud to myself. Sighing, I reached over to dim the light on the nightstand. I didn't want to fall asleep immediately, but I did want to be relaxed enough to slip into dreamwork swiftly. My plan was to zero in on Templeton's study – as well as slide into the dream he'd be creating for Rabbit. In a sense, I was hoping to walk into the room and find slices of their subconscious waiting for me. Then I was going to have Rabbit feed me the images and feelings he had about the Tortoise. I'd use those to reach out across the night and bring the elusive Tortoise into the room for a visit.

I would be making this up as I went along.

A large part of magic, at least for me, was rolling with ideas on the fly. There were definitely rules for certain spells and methods – and probably a lot of practices I didn't understand – but I seemed to manage. I was hoping tonight would be no different.

The night was a perfect fall evening. The weather was even warmer than expected and I'd left the window open a crack to let in the fresh air. Being in the city, it was never fully dark outside. The branches from a sidewalk pear tree swayed back and forth, and I watched as its shadows danced across the wall. Ignoring the shiver skipping down my spine, I adjusted my position. I'd kept my outfit on – I didn't feel like showing up inside Templeton's dream in my pajamas. He always had something to say about my nightclothes. I felt my eyebrows pull together. He was so damn judgmental. Wouldn't it be funny if he and Rabbit were sitting in the study wearing pajamas when I got there? I smirked. Matching pajama sets.

Rabbit probably slept in the buff. Templeton would be the pajama type. Or maybe not? I didn't want to envision either of them in their skivvies. Why was I thinking about this? I needed to center my thoughts on Templeton. My mind wandered to our last interaction, to how he'd helped hide the bruises on my neck. I could feel the cool touch of his fingers, and I realized I could conjure the woodsy scent of his soap if I focused on it. My eyes fluttered and my thoughts meandered. I should start thinking about Templeton's home. I yawned. *His estate.* I wondered how big it was. Mr. Archie said Templeton was the only one living there, but if Anne's niece Audra visited, maybe others did, too?

My thoughts swirled in my head when I remembered Mr. Archie leading me from the spare bedroom where I changed my clothing and back to Templeton's study. I could hear my footsteps as I walked, echoing in the silence. The scent of furniture polish was stronger now. The lights were low, but I could see my way. Somewhere in the darkness, I heard Templeton's voice call my name and I turned.

The hall leading to his study appeared at my left and again I heard Templeton's voice. It tugged at me as I stepped into the hallway. This time only one door appeared at the end. When I reached it, I pushed it open, letting myself into the room.

Templeton and Rabbit sat at a table playing

chess as a comfortable fire crackled in the fireplace nearby. A few lamps lit the room, but they couldn't penetrate the shadows along the edge.

"You took the long way in," Templeton noted as he advanced his knight, jumping a pawn in the process.

"I took the only way I knew," I replied. I watched as Rabbit's eyes caught the flickering light of the fire. They were completely black.

"Your visit to Kincaid went well?" Templeton watched expectantly as Rabbit lifted a hand, but the other man abandoned his move before touching a chess piece.

"It did. Your aunt says hello." I raised an eyebrow as Templeton lifted his head. I pulled on the hem of the shirt I wore. "Anne bought this for Audra."

Templeton didn't acknowledge the familial relationship. Instead, he pushed his chair back from the table and stood. "Rabbit."

Rabbit pulled his attention away from the chess board. "Are we ready? Is she here?"

"He can't see me?" I hadn't expected this.

"Apparently not. But he said you pulled him into a dream before." Templeton examined

Rabbit's face, searching his features.

"It was by accident. Last year." I crossed to Rabbit's side. "Rabbit? Can you hear me?"

Rabbit's nose twitched. "I can sort of hear her voice, but she sounds like she's far away."

"Let's see if we can align our subconscious selves better." Templeton put his right hand on Rabbit's left shoulder. "Relax. Emily is going to put her hand on your other shoulder. Don't be alarmed if you feel it."

I listened to Templeton's instructions and placed my right hand gingerly on Rabbit. He flinched and his eyes turned in my direction, but he looked right through me. It was unnerving. "Why are his eyes all black right now?"

"Hyperaware. It's a reaction to being pulled into my dream. He's asleep and he's feeling vulnerable," Templeton replied.

"Rabbit?" I leaned in. "Can you hear me now? I'm right here." Without making a conscious decision, I pushed out a slip of my energy to touch my friend.

"I can sense her." His boyish face broke into a grin. "I can't see or really hear her, but I can feel she's nearby."

"It will need to be good enough," Templeton said. He glanced around the room. "I can only hold this environment stable for a short time, and I believe it'll become even more fragile when you try to contact the Tortoise."

"Then let's do this. Tell Rabbit to picture the Tortoise as clearly as he can inside his mind and to pull up his feelings for him – bring them to the surface." I ran my hand down his arm and clasped his right hand in both of mine. Rabbit shuddered and goosebumps raised on his arm.

Templeton relayed the message, and I closed my eyes, relaxing again. Instead of trying to push my energy out, I tried to draw Rabbit's into me. I cleared my mind and took several deep breaths. Each time I breathed in, I envisioned Rabbit's energy like a white light glowing over his skin and flowing toward me. I could feel his big hand tremble between mine.

"Easy, Emily," I heard Templeton warn. "You only need a few impressions and feelings from Rabbit. Don't pull at him like that. Stay receptive."

I nodded, letting go of the glow from Rabbit's energy so it would instead ebb and flow with his thoughts. That's when I saw an image of an older man taking shape on the wall of my brain. It was fuzzy, but as Rabbit's breath deepened, the lines of the figure became clearer. Colors filled in.

The man sat hunched on a stool, his legs bent with his knees pointed in opposite directions. He wore tall, rubber-soled garden boots which traveled up his legs, stopping a couple of inches below his knees. Gnarled hands were folded in his lap, and mud had splattered on his work pants right above his boots. His brown wool coat was well-worn. On his head perched a dusty green hat with a wide brim. The man's full beard ended halfway down his chest – a dark brown swatch streaked with much gray. His unruly hair was long and hung over his shoulders. It was lighter than his beard. His eyes were bright and sparkled with curiosity. Like all Rabbits, they were a deep brown.

With this image came Rabbit's feelings for the Tortoise. I could sense a profound respect for the older Rabbit with an intense desire to find him. I latched onto those feelings and let them bloom inside my chest. I held Rabbit's hand tightly as another spasm ran through his body. My eyes remained shut as I pushed out across the universe and imagined the Tortoise walking into Templeton's study.

And, of course, he did not stroll in at my bidding.

"Emily." I could feel Templeton's warm breath on my ear. "He's here."

Opening my eyes, I peered past Rabbit. There, sitting across the room on a stool, was the same man I conjured in my head. The Tortoise didn't walk in like I expected – he simply appeared. I swallowed. We did it.

"I'm guessing if you called me to this space, it must be important." The Tortoise spoke kindly, revealing a set of crooked teeth.

"It is," I answered, afraid to move a muscle. I was afraid to even blink. My heartbeat raced.

"Settle yourself," Templeton murmured at my side.

"You're not a witch," the Tortoise continued as he studied me. His sparkling eyes drifted to Templeton next. "But you have inherited magic in your blood, don't you, Salesman?"

Templeton didn't answer.

"Mr. Tortoise?" The old man refocused on me.

"My name is Emily Swift. I'm a Salesman, too. I'm also a friend of Rabbit's." I nodded my head toward my friend.

"The young man isn't looking very good, now is he?" replied the Tortoise.

I risked a glance at Rabbit. He swayed on his feet. "No, he isn't, and that's why I have to be quick, sir."

The Tortoise lifted a hand. "Tell me."

"We need to find you. We need to know where you are. Rabbit's been looking, but he's been unable to locate you. We need the piece of the Crimson Stone he gave you. I have a piece, Templeton has a piece, and we need the third one. We're going to reunite all three," I finished.

"For what purpose?" he asked.

"The Fringe attacked and killed the Warden of the North Door," I told him. "Then they tampered with the North Door directly. They've also bombed the Salesman Courthouse. Their violence is increasing. People are in danger – my friends and family are in danger. Rabbit said they're also trying to hack into the Rabbit network. We need to stop them. The Empire isn't doing its job and it's getting worse."

"And you want to use the Crimson Stone?"

"Yes, I think so. I don't know how else we can do it," I admitted.

"Hmm." The Tortoise turned to Templeton. "And what is your reason for wanting the Stone?"

"I'm only in this room to assist Rabbit and Emily," Templeton answered smoothly. "That is my purpose here."

Templeton's answer didn't exactly fill me with glee, but I pressed on. "Please, Mr. Tortoise. My father was Daniel Swift. He was on the Salesman Court and –"

"I know who your father was, child. A rare ally of the Rabbits. A good friend to your Rabbit here." He tilted his head to the side and evaluated me. "I suspect you are the same."

A lump formed in my throat. "I try, but I don't always do such a good job."

The Tortoise surprised me by chuckling. He stood and slowly walked his arthritic body to Templeton's desk. He leaned over it, choosing a fountain pen. He looked up. "A piece of paper?"

"Inside the upper right-hand drawer there is a notepad," Templeton answered.

The Tortoise pulled out a piece of paper and

wrote a line. He returned the pen to its holder and left the paper on the desk. "I'll be there tomorrow when you arrive," he said, leaving the desk behind as he passed us. He paused, eyeing an ashen Rabbit as his head began to droop. "It seems I need to go now."

I nodded. "We'll be there tomorrow."

The Tortoise continued across the room and eased back onto his stool. "I'll have boiled coffee for you." He pointed a knuckle at Templeton. "Wake Rabbit up."

"We will," I answered as the subconscious slice of the visiting Tortoise faded away. I purposely let go of the energy I collected from Rabbit and heard a sharp snap. Rabbit's hand yanked from mine, and he crumpled. Templeton managed to keep him from falling completely to the floor. He swore.

"Let's get him to a chair," he grunted, supporting Rabbit's deadweight. The two of us carried Rabbit to the wingback chair by the fireplace. Rabbit's head lolled from side to side.

"What's happening?" I knelt by the chair and reached up, patting Rabbit's cheek. "Come on, Rabbit. Wake up!"

"Stop it!" Templeton slapped my hand away.

"He needs to truly wake up. Go, get out of here now so I can release him from this dream."

"But –"

"Now!" Templeton hissed. He held Rabbit by the wrists and pressed them against the unconscious man's chest. "We'll talk tomorrow."

I backed away, watching the scene unfold. I'd used a lot of Rabbit's energy to conjure the Tortoise. I didn't realize I'd put him in danger. I wiped my hand across my mouth. Templeton was right. I needed to go. But I also needed to know what the Tortoise wrote on the paper – what if Templeton took off without us? Turning, I hurried to the desk. The Tortoise left directions specifically for Rabbit:

11.37.4.65.12.86.

Because we were all dreaming, I knew I couldn't take the paper with me. I pushed my shirtsleeve up my arm before grabbing a pen and writing the numbers on my skin.

"Emily, I swear if you don't leave right now," Templeton threatened from the other side of the room. He kept his grip on Rabbit.

"Take care of him," I begged, stealing one last look at my weakened friend before fleeing Templeton's study.

* * *

I ran down the hall, hurrying through several rooms before I realized I didn't know where I was going. Even more unnerving, I wasn't waking up.

"Crap," I swore. I pulled on my lower lip. I needed to get out of Templeton's dream – assuming I was still in it. Maybe I was back in mine? I rushed through his large home until I found a door leading to the outside and stepped out into the autumn night. The air was cooler in the countryside, but not cold. I walked forward, squinting into the shadows as I headed for a line of trees.

The grass underneath my feet was wet and I could hear my own footsteps rustling through the slick blades. I checked over my shoulder. Templeton's home was gone. Instead, I was surrounded by moonlight and trees.

"Okay," I soothed myself. "I'm probably in my own dream now. I'll walk and wake myself up."

No such luck.

The path wound around a slight rise of land, and I crossed over the crest, heading down into a clearing where a bonfire danced in the center of a circle. I hesitated. I was back at the Rabbits' bonfire space in the woods. It was like the night Tara and I visited – except there were no Rabbits here. I was alone.

I sucked in a long breath through my nose. I prayed I was alone.

"I'm dreaming," I reminded myself out loud, my voice quivering. My eyes wandered past the raging fire, and I could make out the ghostly outline of the outhouse building. I shivered, putting my fingertips to my throat. My skin no longer felt cool. Templeton's glamour was wearing off.

I approached the fire, my gaze skittering across the perimeter of light surrounding it. How had Sebastian found this sacred space? What did he want with it? I walked a path to the right of the flames, circling and wondering what the Fringe planned to do here. Whatever it was, they'd pollute this place.

"Well, pinch me." Sebastian's low voice cut into my thoughts.

Rattled, I jerked backward as the dangerous man appeared, rounding the fire from the other side. We stood facing one another. "It's only a dream," I blurted out.

"A dream?" He smiled wickedly, spinning and peering out into the darkness, the fire at his back. His arms rose, his body stretching upward and casting a long shadow over the ground. "But it feels like more than a dream, doesn't it?" His fascination swung back to me, his face hardening as the firelight danced across his cheek. "Doesn't it, Emily? It feels real. We're both here. I like it."

I pulled in a breath and took another step back. We were not having a repeat of the last meeting at this place. "It's a dream and I can wake up."

Sebastian paused. "But I'm not sleeping. I'm... Well, I'm on my way to bed, but I'm not going to sleep." He ran a hand over his chest.

"I'm sending you back," I told him.

"But you're sleeping, aren't you?" He ignored me, leering. "Somehow you're doing this and now we're together. Emily, are you dreaming of me? Did you want to see me again?"

"Not on your life," I answered, keeping my distance. I needed to wake up. *C'mon, Emily, wake up,* I ordered myself silently. "You're a sick man, Sebastian. You're going to pay for everything you've done. That's a promise."

"So, it is true," Sebastian continued. He inspected my body as if he were looking for evidence. "You do use magic. Is that what Templeton wants with you? Is this what makes you valuable to him?"

"We're done here," I replied, as I retreated. *Wake up wake up wake up,* I chanted in my head.

"What's on your arm, Emily? Is it a tattoo?" He faked a grab and I flinched. "Magical writing?"

I pulled my shirtsleeve down and attempted to cover the directions leading to the Tortoise. "Keep your filthy hands off me."

"I can put your magic to good use," he growled. "Come here!"

Sebastian leapt toward me again, his hand almost catching my arm. He stumbled over the rocky ground as he pitched forward, and I took advantage of the lucky break: I smacked my palms against him and shoved him into the fire.

Sebastian's scream pierced the still night air. I gasped as I sat up in Lucie's spare bed, shaking and covered in a thick sheen of sweat. My heart thudded in my chest, and I pulled the covers around my body, willing myself to calm down. I rocked myself back and forth, telling myself I was safe.

I drew in one last trembling breath before easing back down onto the mattress. I knew I would not get another minute of sleep before tomorrow arrived.

❋ ❋ ❋

I was wrong.

Sleep eventually came to save me, and I was deep under when Lucie shook my shoulder in the morning.

"Emily," she prodded. "I think you overslept. It's after 8 o'clock. Rabbit and Templeton are downstairs waiting for you."

"What?" I sat up so quickly I almost head-butted Lucie. She jerked back. "What do you mean they're here?"

Lucie grimaced. "When I got home this morning, they were sitting on my stoop. Well, Rabbit was sitting on a step and Templeton was leaning against the door. He's his usual chipper self," she added dryly.

I slid out of bed and rummaged through the bag of secondhand clothing I'd picked up when I was with Big Rabbit. "On the stoop? Why? Why didn't Templeton –?" I caught myself. Maybe he couldn't door travel in? Or, had Lucie raised the wards again?

"I have no idea," Lucie answered as she surveyed the spare room with her hands on her hips. She turned to me. "Why are you wearing clothes? Did you sleep in them?"

"It's a long story," I said. I changed my shirt as I took note of hers. I snagged my deodorant from my shoulder bag and reached under my clean shirt to swipe it across my armpits. "Wait, did you just get home? You look like you've been wearing those all night."

"Oh, good grief. I can't wait until all of you are out of my house," she grumbled. "Between you and Templeton, I'll never get a moment's peace about my love life." Lucie left the room and I heard her clopping down the stairs. *Love life?*

I finished changing into a clean set of clothing before hurrying through a routine of using the bathroom, brushing my teeth, and running a brush through my messy hair.

Templeton's glamour had worn off, but only a light bruising was visible. I wrapped the scarf around my neck. Maybe later today the bruising would be completely faded. I pulled my hair into a ponytail as I descended the stairs. Voices drifted up from the kitchen.

Lucie made a pot of coffee while Rabbit explained our plans to meet up with the Tortoise. I was relieved to see he was well. After last night, I wasn't sure how he'd feel. He was pale, but Rabbits were very fair skinned. It was hard to know if he was still feeling the effects of the energy I took from him last night, or if it was my guilt making me worry about his health.

Templeton barely graced me with a nod before resuming his scrutiny of Lucie. She was clearly ignoring him. I wondered what I'd missed. She'd mentioned her love life upstairs. Hmm. Another long night with Basha? When the other two weren't around, I'd have to get details.

"Hey," I said as I put my arm around Rabbit's waist and gave him a side hug. I leaned my head against his shoulder. "Are you okay?"

"I'm fine," Rabbit assured me, tilting his head and looking down into my face. "It was more draining than I thought it would be. Once I was out of the dream, I felt better."

"What happened?" Lucie asked as she set a mug of coffee on the countertop in front of him. She didn't offer any to Templeton.

"Emily drew too hard on Rabbit's energy. She's undisciplined," Templeton answered before I could explain. "I thought you were going to work with her last night. You could have guided her better."

Lucie turned to me. "What's he talking about?"

"You weren't here when I got back from Kincaid," I said. I explained how I thought she could help by lending some of her witchy energy to the dreamwork we did. "But in the end, we didn't need it. Don't listen to him." I motioned toward Templeton.

"Do you always stay out all night?" Templeton cut in. He glared at Lucie.

She rolled her eyes. "I'm so done with you already today."

"Enough." I fired off a warning look at Templeton. "Both of you. We need to get to the Tortoise as soon as we can." I held out my arm with the inked numbers.

Rabbit held up a piece of paper. "Got it already."

"I wasn't sure if Templeton would take off without us," I countered. The moody Salesman snorted. My turn to ignore him. "Rabbit's filled you in?"

Lucie nodded. "Pretty much."

"I'd like to get going as soon as we can." I rooted around in one of Lucie's kitchen cupboards before holding up a box of toaster tarties. "Can I take these?"

"Sure," she said, waving a hand before leaning over the counter and resting it against Rabbit's forehead. Templeton's eyes narrowed as he watched her. "Are you sure you're feeling up to another adventure? You look peaked."

"Completely fine," he grinned. "Trust me."

"I want you to come with us," I said to Lucie. "I think the more magical people we have when we get all three pieces of the Crimson Stone together, the better."

Lucie paused to think. "I can come with you. I don't have anyone scheduled for a reading today. I'll send a message to *Coffee Cove*. I can ask them to hang a sign on my door saying I'm out of the office."

"Rabbit, you know where this is?" I pointed again at the numbers written on my arm. "How long will it take to get there?"

"You're not door traveling?" he asked.

"Um, no." I risked a look at Templeton. "How did you two get here?"

"Templeton hired a car to drive us in. It was waiting for us first thing this morning. We got an early start," Rabbit explained.

"Do you still have it? The car?"

"No," Rabbit replied. He started to text. "I can get us transportation though."

"Or I could drive," Lucie interjected.

"You have a car?" I was surprised.

"Of course. It's parked in a garage two blocks from here. Let me change my clothes and then I'll go get it." She shrugged. "It's no problem."

"Fantastic." I gestured toward Rabbit. "Anything we need to do ahead of time?"

He shook his head. "No. It'll take us about two hours. Maybe less."

"We'll get gas on the way out of Matar," Lucie added as she grabbed a set of keys from a drawer. "You or Emily can ride shotgun." She pointed at Templeton and twirled her finger at him. "You can sit in the back."

"I'm quite comfortable being chauffeured by you, Miss Bellerose. I assume this vehicle of yours has enough leg room?" Templeton smirked.

Lucie made a sound of disgust before exiting the kitchen.

"I don't know what it is with you two," I said to Templeton, throwing my hands up in the air. "But you better table it before we get into the car. I can see her tossing you out and leaving you on the side of the road somewhere if she gets mad enough."

Templeton's mischievous smile remained on his face long after Lucie left, but he didn't add anything more to the conversation.

Rabbit shook his head at the Salesman before turning toward me. His nose twitched. "How about hitting me with one of those toaster tarties?"

CHAPTER 17

We waited outside for Lucie to return with her car. I had to admit, it felt weird having Templeton ride along with us. A part of me was surprised he wasn't relying on door travel – even if it was somewhat problematic for him right now. I assumed he wasn't taking any unnecessary risks. And maybe he thought he'd have a better chance of walking away with all the pieces of the Crimson Stone if he was there when we caught up with the Tortoise.

"Why didn't you answer the door earlier?" Templeton asked out of nowhere.

I turned. His arms were crossed and he leaned against the railing leading up to Lucie's front door. I made a face. "Because I was sleeping."

"I tried to reach out to you," he continued. He waved up at Lucie's brownstone. "I couldn't even sense you inside."

"I don't know," I said. "Maybe Lucie's wards blocked you from poking into her house when she's not here."

"She's not blocking me now," he grumbled.

I looked at Rabbit and pointed to Templeton, mouthing: *what's with him?*

Rabbit shrugged. "He didn't get enough beauty rest last night."

Templeton shifted, turning his back toward us.

"I was worried I wouldn't be able to sleep." I moved down a step and sat by Rabbit as he scrolled through a couple of old messages on his phone. "After I left Templeton's dream, I walked into my own. I ended up at the bonfire spot."

Rabbit lifted his chin. "What happened?"

"Nothing at first, but I think I might've accidentally pulled Sebastian into my dream." I didn't even need to look up to know Templeton's expression. The man could go from annoyed with everyone to angry with me in less than two seconds. "It surprised the hell out of me. Sebastian was unhinged as ever."

"He didn't try anything, did he? I mean, I know it's a dream and you have some control," Rabbit said.

"It's more than a dream," Templeton interrupted, scanning the street. His top hat dangled from his left hand. "It's letting someone into your own private thoughts. And once it's done, it's easy to do again. You need to get better control of what you're thinking about during dreamwork, Emily."

"I wasn't trying to pull him in," I defended myself. "But he did realize it was more than a dream for him, too. That bothers me."

"It should," Templeton scolded.

"What happened?" Rabbit asked.

"He said creepy things and then tried to grab me. He's consistent." I gave an involuntary shake. "But he missed this time. I shoved him into the fire."

Rabbit frowned and grinned at the same time. "Did it hurt him?"

"And then what?" Templeton prompted from above before I could respond to Rabbit.

"He screamed and luckily I woke up. I didn't want to wait around to see what happened next." I tilted my head back to look at Templeton. "Since it was only a dream, I'm guessing nothing happened to him – that his subconscious snapped back into his body when I woke up?"

Templeton's eyes tracked a blue and black RAV4 Hybrid as it slowed. "That's accurate. He probably felt a little of the aftereffects today, but it's not as if he were truly burned."

Lucie double-parked the RAV4 and beeped the horn. Rabbit and I climbed to our feet and Templeton followed. I heard the doors unlock as we hit the sidewalk. Rabbit reached for the back door, but I told him to sit up front and give Lucie directions.

I clambered into the back and slid across the seat to make room for Templeton.

"Alright kids," Lucie said. "No backseat drivers allowed." She glanced in her rearview mirror, her eyes lingering on Templeton before meeting mine. I shrugged. Lucie shifted into drive, and we pulled away from the curb.

Rabbit explained the route we'd take out of Matar. Lucie stopped for gas, tossing a newspaper in the backseat between Templeton and me when she returned. He waited until she faced the windshield before picking it up.

Hitting the highway, we headed northwest. The directions the Tortoise left for Rabbit would guide us to the foot of the Walled Zone. I'd never been in this part of the Empire.

"Doesn't he worry about the Fringe since he's right by the Walled Zone?" I leaned forward between the seats.

Rabbit shook his head. "The Tortoise doesn't worry. But we should be on guard once we're there. With the attack on the Courthouse yesterday, it's a good idea to watch our backs."

"Is there anything new about that?" I asked. Rabbit's phone was still fairly quiet. It did buzz from time to time, but nothing like it normally did.

"The Empire isn't saying much, but the news reports have a lot of talking heads voicing opinions," Rabbit said. "But the Salesman Court confirmed they are still 'holding the bench' and those responsible for the bombing will be held accountable."

"Unless you're the St. Michel family," I said wryly.

The newspaper rustled beside me. "Junior Justice Jo Carter is quoted on the front page."

I leaned over to Templeton. He pointed. Under the photo of a bombed Courthouse, Jo was quoted. I read it aloud so Rabbit and Lucie could hear. *"The Court will not stand idly by while terrorists attack the center of our government. Whoever is responsible for this violence will be found and they will be arrested. They will be brought to trial. The Salesmen sitting on this bench will not be deterred or influenced by outside forces. We are here to uphold the law, not to succumb to the radical elements of our Salesman ranks. It does not matter who you are. If you are tied to this attack in any way, you will be held accountable."*

Rabbit whistled low.

"The gloves are off," Lucie said.

"That's our Jo," I added. "It says to turn to page three for more."

Templeton opened the paper and the news report continued under a black and white photo of Jo. Standing behind her with grim expressions stood Justices Howard Manchester and Norford Smith. Justice Spell was nowhere to be seen. I skimmed the rest of the article.

"At least we have Jo on our side." I sat back in my seat. "Hey Rabbit? There's this man named Kirby. One sec." I rooted around in my shoulder bag. I still had the phone number. I held out the slip of paper to Rabbit. "Can you get a message to him? See if he can provide some covert protection for Jo's family in New York City. Tell him Emily Swift's requesting his help – that Sadie from PA mentioned he might be able to do something like this. But make it clear Jo and her family can't know."

Rabbit took the paper. "Well, what do you know? Emily has connections to muscle."

I smirked. "I have many layers."

"Like an artichoke. So much work, so little reward," Templeton deadpanned over the paper.

Lucie laughed. Templeton raised his head, surprised.

"Even you can't ruin my good feeling about Jo. I trust her. She won't let this go," I finished.

Rabbit gave a nod. He ran his thumbs over the phone screen, starting the chain to get a message to my Aunt Sadie's mysterious Kirby. "What about your mother and Jack?"

I didn't know why I was reluctant to have someone watch over my house and loved ones. I hesitated. Maybe it was because once I did it, it proved I *believed* they'd be attacked.

"Do it, Rabbit." Templeton said quietly. He kept reading the paper. "If this man isn't available, I know someone."

Rabbit went back to his texting. "Got it. Hey Lucie, take exit 12. We'll head up route 21."

"Sure," Lucie said. She bobbed her head toward his hands. "Aren't you worried about using the network? Aren't you all mostly on radio-silence?"

"We are," he said. "But a few of us have set up a series of relays in the chain. Even if the Fringe hacks in, they're only getting a fragment of the message."

"Crafty," Lucie replied. She steered the RAV4 toward exit 12.

"It's our business," Rabbit winked. He fished a pair of wireless earbuds out of his pocket and fumbled with his phone. "We've got an hour's drive on 21. I'm going to plug in and chill if no one cares."

"Be my guest," Lucie said.

A few seconds later, *Rhino Vomit* blasted into Rabbit's ears.

"I can't believe he's not deaf yet," Lucie said. She checked her rearview mirror, her fingers on the radio dial. "You two care if I turn on the Empire's Public Radio station?"

"Go for it," I said as the newscaster's voice droned through the speakers. We rode along without speaking. Through the window, I watched the trees and yellowing fields fly by. The sunny autumn weather in Matar was left behind. The morning turned gray. It looked like rain.

Templeton kept reading beside me. I'm certain on some level it was to avoid conversation with the rest of us. I glanced over at him. As always, he was impeccably dressed, wearing a pair of tailored black trousers and a deep blue, long-sleeved dress shirt – although the top button was left undone. His dress coat was folded on the seat between us. He'd moved his top hat from his lap when he started to read the paper. It sat between us as well. His face remained expressionless, and I studied the sharp angle of his jaw. He no longer wore his sideburns long. His short, dark hair waved slightly at the nape of his neck.

"What?" he finally acknowledged me.

"Did you tell Rabbit about this yet?" I motioned to his top hat.

Templeton's eyes stayed on the paper, and he gave his head a barely perceptible shake. I turned back to the window. I didn't know what Templeton planned, but eventually he'd have to admit his power for door traveling was limited. I rested my head against the window as the rain began to fall.

✻ ✻ ✻

Lulled by the sound of rain beating down on the roof, I dozed. I woke to Rabbit directing Lucie through a series of turns. Templeton had refolded the paper and watched the scenery pass with a bored expression. Lucie's RAV4 slid when she took a corner too fast. It was muddy.

"Sorry about that," she said, palming the wheel in the opposite direction. "We're off the beaten path."

She was right. A dirt road wound through the woods we now drove through. We bounced around.

"Not much longer," Rabbit promised. Five minutes later a modest cabin appeared at the end of the road. It was pushed back against the tree line. A soggy, overgrown vegetable garden sat to the right. On the left, a chicken coop. A thin line of smoke rose from a chimney.

"I'll try to park where there aren't any puddles, but it might be impossible." Lucie stopped in front of the cabin. "Is he home? I don't see any other vehicles."

"The Tortoise doesn't drive," Rabbit answered. He glanced into the back seat at Templeton's top hat. "I'd leave the hat here. The rain is brutal."

"Maybe roll up your pant legs." Lucie cast a look over her shoulder at Templeton and pressed her lips together. A flash of amusement in her eyes gave her away.

"Your concern is touching," he replied, opening the car door and rising out into the poor weather. He crossed from the RAV4 to the porch in several long steps.

"Luckily my people really don't melt under a little water," Lucie joked before dashing up onto the porch by Templeton. Rabbit and I bounded after her. We shook off the rain while Rabbit tapped on the door.

"It's open," came a strong voice from inside. Rabbit pushed the door, and we crowded in after him.

The cabin was warm, with a woodstove in the corner taking the rainy day chill out of the air. Wet clothes hung on a rack near it, the smell of drying wool permeating the cabin. An old tabby cat resting in a bed near the stove perked up when we entered. It slowly stood and stretched, arching its bony back. The kitty gingerly stepped out of the bed and sauntered over to Rabbit. He squatted down and patted its furry head. "How ya doing, Rex?"

"Thank goodness it's not called Rabbit," Lucie whispered as she leaned close. I saw the corners of Templeton's lips quirk up briefly.

The Tortoise's kind eyes landed on Lucie. "I see you brought somebody new with you."

Lucie stepped around Rabbit and crossed over to the older man. She held out her hand. "Lucie Bellerose. I hope we're not intruding."

"Of course not," the Tortoise said, taking her hand in his. "Rabbit, leave Rex to the two Salesmen. Bring their witch a chair from the back."

I loved the Tortoise's bluntness. Judging by her expression, Lucie did as well. She raised an eyebrow but chuckled. "For the record, I don't belong to anyone," she teased. "But if you're offering?"

The Tortoise patted her hand. "I might be a bit long in the tooth for you." He led her to the table where four chairs already sat.

"Thank you for being so gracious, Mr. Tortoise," I said, taking a chair. "Especially after we brought a piece of you into our dream last night."

The Tortoise wobbled around his cozy kitchen. Rabbit returned with a chair for Lucie and was next enlisted to grind up coffee beans. In the meantime, the Tortoise cracked an egg into a bowl – then he dropped the shells in with the egg. He crushed them with a fork while he scrambled the yolk into the whites. He waited for Rabbit to finish grinding the beans, then added the grounds to the egg and crushed shell. "You want the piece of the Crimson Stone Rabbit gave me for safekeeping."

"Yes," I replied. "We need it to put an end to the Fringe once and for all."

The Tortoise added a spoonful of water to the strange mix of ingredients, then began mashing everything together into a paste. "You had the Stone in your possession last year, didn't you?"

"I did." I gestured to Templeton. He'd taken a seat to my right. "They were separate but hanging from one necklace. Templeton reunited them. There was a fight, and the Stone flew loose. I grabbed it –"

"– and used it," Rabbit chimed in.

"And used it," I repeated. "And I want to use it again. I have one of the pieces, and Templeton has one, too. I've been able to do some magic with only the one piece and it was pretty potent."

"Tell me why you didn't keep the Stone when you had all the pieces together last year," the Tortoise said. He added the coffee paste to a pot of simmering water. He set a wind-up timer for 10 minutes.

"At the time I thought it was a better idea to separate the pieces. It's a lot of power in one gemstone. I didn't think one person should have that much power." I stole a glance at Templeton. "And I wanted to keep it hidden from the Fringe. It would be harder for them to find if it were in three different places."

"But now that's changed?"

"Yeah." I looked down at my folded hands resting on the table. "The Fringe's reach is growing. This week they came to Kincaid and messed with the North Door. They killed my friend, Mr. Blackstone, in his own home. The Empire has not done much to stop them. We found out the bench has been compromised. In a way, the Fringe is forcing my hand."

"Hmm." The Tortoise stirred his pot of murky water with a wooden spoon. He pointed the utensil at Rabbit. "Come stir this until the timer goes, then pour the coffee into this metal pot. Leave room. I'll need to add cold water." The Tortoise left Rabbit to his chores and sat down in the chair across from me. His warm eyes sparkled. "I would bet you're not easily forced into anything."

"Maybe 'forced' isn't the perfect word, but here we all are," I said.

"The piece of Stone Rabbit brought me is not mine to keep," the Tortoise said. "You are certainly welcome to take it back."

Relief at his words washed over me. For a moment I thought he'd refuse to give it to us. "Thank you, sir."

The Tortoise turned to Templeton next. "You're Rabbit's friend John Templeton, correct?"

"I'm Templeton," he confirmed. I felt around with my foot under the table to kick him for his habitual hostility. Lucie beat me to it – I saw her twitch and Templeton startle when her foot connected with his shin.

"And you're content to let Emily have the Stone?" The Tortoise raised two bushy eyebrows.

"While my confidence in Ms. Swift's abilities is not as great as her own, I think there is an opportunity to wound the Fringe by proving a connection to one of the more prominent families in the Empire. Typically, I wouldn't involve myself, but she can't seem to stay out of trouble." He finished the last bit with a dismissive wave of his hand.

"Then why do you help her?" the Tortoise asked. All eyes turned to Templeton.

His mouth opened to speak, then he abruptly shut it.

"Sebastian says I'm your pet," I said. I felt a pang of hurt in my chest when I spoke. I hated those words. After what I'd seen in Templeton's study, I feared maybe it was true.

Templeton's jaw tightened. "That jab was at me, not you. I do not think of you as a pet."

"Then is it only because I've had pieces of the Crimson Stone?" I turned to Lucie for support. She lifted her palms as she shrugged. I returned my attention to Templeton. "What am I missing? What am I to you?"

He didn't answer, but the Tortoise spoke. "Your father was also called John Templeton, wasn't he?"

Templeton gave a curt nod. The color drained from his irises. His eyes roamed the room – the instinct to seek a door for escape surfacing. I held my breath, waiting for Templeton to try to flee. He didn't.

The Tortoise stroked his beard, watching Templeton. "I know who your father was, son. He practiced magic – *black magic*."

Lucie let out a little *'oh.'* Templeton met her gaze, but still said nothing.

Templeton had admitted to me in his study that my dad was escorting his father back to the Empire. That his father was my dad's prisoner on that damn train, but for what he didn't say.

"It's why he was banished from the Empire, wasn't it?" I asked. My voice trembled when I spoke. Lucie's eyes widened and Rabbit's nose twitched.

Templeton raised his right hand and rubbed the back of his neck. He focused on the tabletop. "It seems you know things, Tortoise."

The old man's mouth worked thoughtfully under his beard. "I'm a Rabbit. We know most things. I know all things."

Templeton barked a laugh, startling everyone but the old man. "Then you know why I want the Crimson Stone."

"What's going on here?" I looked past the Tortoise to Rabbit, who stood distractedly stirring the coffee simmering on the stove. The rich aroma chased away the smell of the Tortoise's drying clothes. "Rabbit?"

He shook his head. "I don't know any of this, Emily."

"Rabbits deal in information." The Tortoise rose from the table. He gave Templeton a pointed look. "But I do not deal in secrets. I do, however, suggest you tell your friends yours." He paused and pointed a knuckle at me. "This one deserves to know since you believe she's tied to the Stone." The Tortoise shuffled into his kitchen, retrieving ice from his freezer and placing the cubes in a new pot. He added cold water and set it down on the counter by the empty coffee decanter.

Templeton also rose to his feet. Before he could take a step, I reached out and snagged his shirtsleeve. "Please don't go."

He didn't pull away. "I don't want to sit."

"Then stand. But tell me what the Tortoise is talking about," I said. Lucie observed Templeton, her eyebrows pulling together. Rabbit abandoned his kitchen duty, moving to the table, but he didn't sit.

Templeton licked his lower lip – a nervous response I never would've expected from the man. He wouldn't look at me. He concentrated instead on Rabbit. "My father commissioned the creation of the Crimson Stone. Alice White's father made it for my father, but he didn't know for what it would be used. He didn't know what kind of magic my father practiced."

To Rabbit's credit, the shock of Templeton's admission didn't register on his face. Templeton's secret, however, sliced into my stomach. Did he know this when we were all in Vue on that horrible night? He had to have known!

"Who's Alice White?" Lucie asked, cutting into the room's tension.

"She was a shopkeeper in Vue. She was killed by Tahl Petrovich last year because he wanted the Crimson Stone. Her father was a jeweler – and a magic man of some sort according to Tuesday. We figured out he'd created the Stone, but we thought he did it for his daughter." I pushed my chair back and stood, feeling angrier. "Alice hid the Stone in her antique store. That's where we found it. That's where Petrovich shot Templeton."

"And Emily used the Stone," Rabbit said, the shine in his eyes growing as he realized there was more. "She surprised you when she did, but it's more than that, isn't it, Templeton?"

The kitchen timer buzzed, surprising us. The Tortoise snickered as he poured the hot coffee in the stainless-steel coffee pot, grounds and all. He then slowly added some of the ice water. Using two ratty potholders, he carried the coffee pot to the table, before returning to the kitchen for cups.

"You know the prophecy," the Tortoise said to Templeton, a crooked smile appearing through the mass of hair on his face. "You believe you are the night to the light."

Templeton didn't respond, but the lines in his face hardened. Whatever the Tortoise was referring to, he'd struck a nerve with the tight-lipped Salesman.

"And," the Tortoise continued as he poured the steaming liquid into the cups, "you think Emily is the light."

"I'm the what?" I interrupted.

"There is a prophecy," the Tortoise said. He hobbled over to a writing desk and retrieved a sheet of paper and a pencil. Returning, he sat and began to write. "Templeton's father set it in motion when he had the Stone made."

I bent and squinted at the handwriting. The Tortoise didn't write familiar letters. The words consisted of flowing lines, looping across the page. It wasn't any language I recognized. I glanced at Rabbit; he shook his head. Lucie tilted hers to the side as she leaned forward in her chair.

"This is an ancient language," she said.

"Can you read it?" asked the Tortoise.

Lucie shook her head. "No, but I think I know this word." She pointed. "It's used as a symbol in my witchline."

"And what do you think it is?"

Lucie raised her eyes. "It means 'light.'"

The Tortoise sat back in his chair. He nodded. "You are right."

"What does the whole thing say?" I asked.

The Tortoise turned to Templeton. "I believe you are familiar with this language?"

Templeton studied the paper. "I know the prophecy."

"Seriously, Templeton. How about bringing the rest of us up to speed?" I was getting tired of all the beating around the bush. A part of me recognized Templeton *was* getting pulled apart after all this time, but there couldn't be any more unknowns. "Is someone going to tell me what this says?"

"It means 'The night protects the light. Their heir sets fire to the stone.'" Templeton answered. Lucie's head jerked up. I saw her lips move as she repeated the words silently. Templeton turned away and walked to the window, wearily fixing his gaze out into the gloom as the rain grew in its intensity.

I stilled, my breath stolen. These were the same words appearing in The Book. These were two of the lines Evangeline revealed to me from the pages of my father's journal. "I know this," I managed to squeak out as I sank into my chair.

Templeton spun back around. "You know the prophecy?"

Now all eyes were on me. I nodded. "A new message appeared in my father's journal this week." There was no need to explain Evangeline at this point, but I'd tell Lucie later the message was brought to me by the disembodied witch.

The Tortoise tapped the tabletop with his twisted fingers. "Do you have it with you now?"

"I do." I dug through the shoulder bag at my feet. The Book was still safely nestled inside. I recovered it and placed it on the table. I kept it shut, giving Templeton a sidelong glance. "But I don't let a lot of people look at it."

The Tortoise nodded. "Of course. But would you show us the page where the lines appear? That's all we want to see."

Templeton moved to my side. I sensed his energy, though weaker than usual. It curled toward The Book.

"No need to do that," I said quietly. Everyone watched as I opened it. I turned through several places, before finding the passage. I pushed The Book to the center of the table for everyone to see.

"There is more to the prophecy," Templeton whispered as he leaned over me. He lifted his hand as if to touch the page, but never completed the act.

The Tortoise seemed pleased. "Read it aloud,

Emily."

"Okay." I swallowed, taking a deep breath before reading.

A traveler is born.
The night protects the light.
Their heir sets fire to the stone.

Lucie's hands came together, her fingers barely woven together as if in prayer. She raised them, pressing her forefingers to her lips. Brows drawn together, she remained silent.

Rabbit cleared his throat. "Tortoise, are you saying Emily is to bear Templeton's child?"

"No!" I said, slapping the table with my hand. "Not a chance. No way." I jabbed a finger at Templeton. "I am not having any part of *that*."

The Tortoise raised his hand to stop my outburst. "The translation you have is not quite accurate." He reached a bony hand forward and placed a fingertip on a line. I felt The Book vibrate, but it didn't seem alarmed by the Tortoise's touch.

"What's the inaccuracy?" Templeton asked. His eyes had narrowed.

"This word." The Tortoise's fingertip slid to the word 'heir' before he pushed the paper he'd written upon earlier alongside The Book. His other hand hovered over the sentence he'd written in the old language. He pointed to one of the squiggles. "Translated, this is not 'heir.' The closest translation you would recognize would be 'successor.'"

"Whoever translated the phrase went with a word they better understood," Rabbit surmised.

"Perhaps," agreed the Tortoise.

"Wait, what exactly is the difference?" I asked. I'd relaxed after learning the prophecy wouldn't require me to, er, know Templeton more intimately.

"One who follows another," Templeton answered, preoccupied with the lines in my father's journal. "It doesn't require there be any blood relation between the two. But the first line in Emily's book is nothing I've known as part of the prophecy."

"I'm the traveler, right? That's why I have this message?" I tapped The Book's page and looked to the Tortoise for confirmation.

"There's... I think I know some of this," Lucie interjected. I noted she'd`lost color in her cheeks. She picked up the Tortoise's pencil with a shaking hand. On the paper she wrote:

A traveler is born.
The night protects the light.
Their heir sets fire to the stone.
A shadow is cast.

"I was already familiar with the second and fourth lines. There's a passage…" She faltered. She wouldn't look up from the words she'd written. "I knew lines were missing, words that were supposed to be between the light and shadow lines, but I didn't know what they'd be. I didn't know about the traveler line Emily was given. I never saw the 'heir sets fire' line."

"But where have you seen this before?" I asked, reaching for her. She was still gripping the pencil. I gave Lucie's hand a gentle squeeze. I didn't understand why she was troubled.

Lucie rubbed her lips together, moistening them. "In a book of magic passed down to me through my witchline. The writing inside indicates more than one author. Spells in French, English, and Latin appear."

"Okay," I replied, trying to encourage her. "Go on."

"The parts of the prophecy are written in

two different sets of handwriting in my book. The first in Latin, the second in French." Lucie stopped again, pulling her hand away from mine. She seemed to be struggling with something and touched the 'light' line with a trembling finger. I checked Templeton's reaction. He focused on Lucie, realization rippling across his sharp features.

"The word for light in Latin is lux," he said softly. "Lucie is the French derivative of Lucia. The Latin name Lucia is derived from lux."

It took a moment for me to catch up to Lucie and Templeton's interpretations. *Oh.* I was the traveler, but Lucie was the light!

A traveler is born.
The night protects the light.
Their heir sets fire to the stone.
A shadow is cast.

But the Tortoise had said Templeton believed he was the night? Why? Before I could ask, the Tortoise pulled the paper back. He flipped it over. The first four lines he wrote were in the original ancient words of the prophecy. The next four were in Latin. And finally, the last four lines were in English. The Tortoise had made changes:

A traveler is born.
The knight protects the light.
Their successor sets fire to the stone.
A shadow is cast out.

He changed 'night' to 'knight' and added the word 'out' to the last line.

Rabbit grinned. He clearly understood something I did not. "You knew it was 'knight' with a 'k' all along, didn't you Templeton?"

"My surname is derived from a particular area in Wales. It's believed a religious house of the Knights Templar was once located there. My line stems from this region." Templeton refused to look away from Lucie. She stared at the table.

"I need to talk this through," I said.

"I need some air," Lucie said at the same time, rising suddenly and hurrying to the cabin's front door. She slipped outside, shutting the door behind her.

Templeton made as if to follow, but Rabbit blocked his path. "Give her space, Templeton."

When these two very different men faced off, I was always struck by the differences between them. And yet, even when they were both angry, there was a history they shared that often informed how they behaved. This was one of those times.

Templeton acquiesced, turning to me. "The stone in this passage is clearly the Crimson Stone. Your birth as the traveler advanced what my father set in motion. If Lucie is the light, we need to make sure she is kept safe."

"And the Crimson Stone?" I asked. Here we go, he's going to argue he should keep it.

"It should remain with me. My father is the one who commissioned its creation."

"You will give it to Lucie," said the Tortoise. "Her magic will keep it hidden until the successor appears."

"The prophecy doesn't say to give it to the light," Templeton objected.

"Nor does it say the knight should keep it," the Tortoise scratched his head while he considered the words. "No, I'm predicting you and Emily will give the Stone to Lucie. And she'll be able to keep it safe from those who'd use it for their own gain. Even you, Templeton."

I had to admit, if there would be any one person I'd entrust the Crimson Stone to, it would be Lucie. But there was one last line in the prophecy. "Tortoise, what about the last line?

You changed it."

The four of us looked back to the paper where the Tortoise had written, 'A shadow is cast out.'

The Tortoise took his time in responding. He shrugged. "I believe it means the evil growing here in the Empire might be defeated."

CHAPTER 18

The rain hadn't stopped. It came down in a straight sheet, filling the dirt road we'd traveled with deep puddles. I stepped out onto the covered porch to check on Lucie.

"Hey," I said, joining her on the far end. "Are you okay?"

Lucie lifted one shoulder in a shrug. "I guess. I needed time to think. I felt like everyone was looking at me."

"We were," I said.

She rolled her eyes. "Nice."

"You know, I'm a little jealous." I leaned against the rough wood of the railing. A slip of wet air gusted against my face. "Fancy prophecy and you get to be the 'light.'"

"Oh, brother," Lucie muttered.

"I'm used to everything being about me." I couldn't keep a straight face and bumped my hip against Lucie's.

"You're a piece of work, Emily Swift."

"Although, I am relieved I don't have to sleep with Templeton. And how did Rabbit put it? Bear his child?" I teased and bumped my hip against Lucie's a second time.

"The prophecy indicates a *successor*, Emily. No crawling under the covers with Templeton required," Lucie stated.

"Speaking of getting between the sheets," I began. I ignored Lucie's groan. "Another full night out with Basha? I'm having a hard time believing last night was another innocent cuddling session."

Lucie couldn't hide her dreamy smile. "Yes, I was with Basha."

"And?"

"Get over it, Emily." Lucie shook her head, but her face gave it away. She was happy.

"So, if the kissing was... What did you tell me? Excellent? If that was hot, how was everything else?" Between the downpour and needing to escape the tension in the cabin, Lucie was stuck on the porch with me.

Her eyes never left the rain. "Everything was excellent. I like him. A lot. I like how he makes me feel."

Lucie's voice had grown softer. I examined the side of her face. "And that is?"

"Sexy. Special."

For a moment I didn't know what to say. I

was caught off guard by her confession. Lucie *was* sexy – in body, mind, and spirit. She was confident, quick-witted, and kind. She was the whole package. I didn't understand why she would need someone to make her feel special. "When do we get to meet Basha?"

"I'm not sure now," Lucie sighed. "I mean, I need to learn what it means to be the 'light.' And then there's Templeton."

I nodded, turning back to the rain. I thought about both of them – how they interacted. They were constantly poking at one another. Lucie held her own with him. Scratch that. Templeton managed to hold his own with her. *Hmm.* "Lucie, if you hadn't met Basha, would you like Templeton?"

She didn't answer right away, picking at a loose piece of wood on the railing. "I don't dislike him, but he's work. And I don't fully trust him."

That I understood. In fact, in the back of my brain I was picking apart what I'd learned inside the cabin. One thing stood out: Until a few minutes ago, Templeton thought I was the 'light.' He also thought we'd have an 'heir' – and that does require getting naked. Before finding out Lucie was the 'light,' what was Templeton expecting from me? What I learned today didn't exactly give me the warm fuzzies. Templeton was still working for one person: himself.

Eventually we'd have to talk about what he had thought would happen between us. I was not looking forward to it. In the meantime, another thought bubbled up. "Do you believe this prophecy is true? I mean, it's only true if you believe it, right?"

Lucie abandoned the splinter she worked free, using her index finger to flick it out into the rain. "I do believe it – especially because the prophecy appeared in more than one place. Four of us had lines from it. The Tortoise clearly knew them all. I might not have known the two lines in my book were a part of a prophecy, but I can't discount how strange it is to have them. There is definitely a connection."

The cabin door opened, and Rabbit appeared. He joined us, putting his arm around Lucie and dropping a friendly kiss on her forehead. "Congratulations. You've just won a major role in a prophecy."

That brought out a laugh and she pushed him away. "Alright, that's enough."

Rabbit grinned. "Seriously, though. I've been checking the network and there is major flooding in a few areas. If we don't get going soon, we're going to be sleeping on the floor with Rex tonight."

"I'll pass," I said. "Lucie? Are you ready to go back in? We still need to get the Tortoise's piece of the Crimson Stone."

"Yeah, I'm fine." She wiped her hand over her face. "I'm over it."

Rabbit didn't seem to be convinced, but he held the door for her as she went back into the cabin. When I followed, he placed his strong hand on my forearm. He whispered into my ear. "This is not a bad thing."

I hesitated. "What do you mean?"

"It's a gut feeling," he said. "I've learned some things about where Lucie lived before moving back to Matar. She was sent to study in a remote part of France under a powerful witch called Guillaume. From what I've picked up, he's a strict magical teacher. Brutal even. If Lucie can handle whatever the Congress of Empire Witches throws at her, she'll be able to handle how the prophecy plays out. She'll be able to handle Templeton – and the Crimson Stone."

His last words jarred me. "You think she should use it?"

"I'm not saying that. But I think she should be the one who keeps it."

"Why her?" *And not me?* I thought.

"Because she has the maturity and magical skills to keep it safe. And Templeton will, well, he'll watch over her whether she wants him to or not," Rabbit finished.

"Guys?" Lucie called from inside the cabin.

"Coming," I replied. I needed to find out more about Lucie's time in France. Anne had even mentioned something about it. And what the hell was the Congress of Empire Witches? More conversations for later.

✽ ✽ ✽

The Tortoise brought an antique jewelry box to the table. I recognized it as the one I found in Vue the night I gave Rabbit a piece of the Crimson Stone to hide. The Tortoise opened it, revealing the very same piece. A tiny tongue of flame flickered inside the Stone. A faint hum drifted up from my shoulder bag on the floor. Another hum answered it – this one came from Templeton's mid-section. Everyone looked at his stomach.

Templeton sighed, tugging his dress shirt up. Around his waist was a narrow band of leather. A discreet pocket was built into it and sat above the front of his right hip. The humming increased. He unsnapped the flap holding the pocket shut, pulling out a cloth envelope made of plain, white cotton. I recognized it. It was the fabric I'd used when I'd sewed the packet together. Templeton had kept it.

"I wouldn't guess you'd be the type to wear a girdle," Lucie said, eyeing the leather. She sucked in her cheeks to keep from smiling.

Templeton sniffed, but the corners of his mouth twitched. He let go of his shirt. "I figured this was safer. I didn't want it rolling around in my pocket."

The piece of the Crimson Stone pulsed red inside the cotton pouch as he held it. I retrieved the tan soapstone box holding the third piece of the Stone from my shoulder bag, opening it and setting it by the jewelry box. I removed the cloth I'd wound around the gemstone. It tingled against my skin, and I gently placed it on top of the cloth.

Rabbit pulled a pocketknife from his jeans, opened it, and passed it to Templeton, handle first. Templeton cut along the seam of the cloth pouch he held and pulled out the final piece of Crimson Stone. He laid it on the table next to mine. All three pieces pulsed in rhythm, each gemstone containing its own flickering flame. I could sense the power running between them – the ebb and flow of the energy took on the appearance of a conversation. Before I could ask if anyone else could see it, Lucie spoke.

"They're talking to each other," she said.

"I think so," I agreed. "Can you see it, Rabbit?"

He shook his head. "No. Tortoise?"

"No," the Tortoise answered. "But I don't deal in magic."

I knew Templeton could see it. He watched the Stones communicate. "Do you understand what they're saying?"

"They're telling each other stories," he said. He stroked each one with his finger, his eyelids sliding shut. I could feel Templeton's power growing inside him. The Stone could fill the gaping hole in his power Nisha created when she took his door travel energy from him. I couldn't blame him for wanting the Stone for himself.

But that's not why we were here. We needed the Stone to beat the Fringe. "Can you reunite the pieces?"

Templeton opened his eyes. Each piece sat in its own setting of silver, with tiny hooks on the sides. When the three pieces were brought together, they formed the Crimson Stone. When I first found it, the Stone was in three pieces hanging from a silver necklace. The necklace was gone, but the pieces could still be joined together.

We watched as he picked them up and hooked the pieces together. He whispered a spell over them. I saw Lucie watching his mouth – perhaps trying to determine what he was saying. The pieces flashed a ruby-colored light, casting the entire room in a red glow. The Crimson Stone was formed.

"Whoa," Lucie spoke in a low voice. "I can feel it."

I nodded. "This is why I separated the pieces.

It's too powerful in the wrong hands."

Templeton retrieved the cloth from my soapstone box and wrapped the whole Crimson Stone in it. He placed it in the jewelry box the Tortoise had kept safe.

"Now what?" I asked.

"Now we hit the road," Rabbit replied. He turned to the Tortoise. "The rain is bad. I'm worried we'll get stuck on the road."

"It wouldn't be the first time," said the Tortoise. The old man turned to me, leaning against the table. "You have what you need now. You and your friends should be on your way."

"Thank you for…" I lifted my hand and waved it in the air. "Everything."

The Tortoise nodded as Rabbit gave him a hug goodbye. The old man peered at Templeton over Rabbit's shoulder. "Take care of each other. You can learn a lot from a Rabbit."

Templeton merely inclined his head. He picked the jewelry box off the table and handed it to me. I added it to my shoulder bag. It was getting heavy. I'd have to do something about that.

It was still raining, and we slid in the mud

as we sprinted the short distance to Lucie's vehicle. The sky had grown dark even though it was midday. I buckled my seatbelt. It was going to be a slippery ride out of there.

Lucie took the road like a professional. She was a serious driver, but at least she didn't have the wheel in a death grip. A few times we slid – and I did yelp once or twice – but she spun the wheel and navigated the more treacherous parts with confidence.

"Anyone else hungry?" Lucie asked as we left the dirt road, pulling onto a paved one. We were still out in the middle of nowhere.

"I could eat," said Rabbit. My stomach grumbled. The toaster tartie had lasted as long as it was going to. I'd sipped some of the Tortoise's coffee, but it was cold by the time my lips touched the cup.

"We'll stop at the first decent place we see," Lucie promised. Rabbit took up the job of providing guidance on which way to go as she drove. A few times I felt the vehicle hydroplane. The weather hadn't improved.

We'd only traveled about 15 minutes before we saw red flashing lights in the distance. I leaned between the seats. "Accident?"

Rabbit was already texting. "Maybe, but there's more than one flooding issue being reported across the network."

Lucie slowed as we neared the scene. Empire guards and their vehicles blocked the road ahead. She lowered her window until a splash of rainwater blew in and she inched the glass back up as a guard approached. "Can we get through?" she called through the narrow opening.

The guard shook his head. "Flood took out a portion of the road. It's going to be closed until they can get someone in to fix it. Won't be anytime soon."

"Crap." Lucie blew out a breath. "Is there a detour?"

"You're going to have to turn around and find a different route," the guard replied.

"Fine," Lucie said. We didn't have a choice. "Is there a place where we can get something to eat near here?"

The guard motioned to the road behind us. "Go back that way and hang a right in about three miles onto Banks Road. *Wayside Inn.* They have pub food."

"Perfect," said Lucie. She nodded her thanks

and turned the RAV4 around. We headed for the inn.

※ ※ ※

The *Wayside Inn* wasn't anything special to look at from the outside. We'd parked on the right side of the building and entered through the front entrance. It wasn't that exciting on the inside, either. The person at the dingy reception counter directed us to the left toward a portion of the inn called the *Wayside Pub*.

It was empty except for us. We chose a round table near the bar. Since all of us were soaked to the bone, Lucie asked for bar towels so we could wipe off some of the wetness clinging to our bodies. I was surprised when the barkeep gave us a stack. Lucie tossed him a wink when she thanked him. He brought us a pitcher of beer and took our orders. We all ordered burgers and fries – except for Rabbit. He ordered a veggie burger and a blooming onion.

"Well, this has been a day." I offered up a grim smile to the tired faces sitting around the table. "Rabbit, did you come up with an alternate route for us?"

"Yeah," he said. "It's going to add another hour of driving and hopefully we won't run into the same issue." He motioned to Templeton. "You don't have to stay. You can door travel out of here before we get back on the road. I'll get a message to you when we're back at Lucie's." Rabbit pointed a finger at me. "You don't have to stay with us either. But stay in one place for once. We can regroup when Lucie and I get back to Matar."

Templeton took a sip of his beer. He didn't look up. Damn him. He's going to have to come clean about his door travel issue sooner or later.

"You know what? I'm going to stay with you guys. I'm guessing even Templeton is on board for the rest of the road trip – he'll want to keep an eye on the Crimson Stone. And maybe we can decide what our next steps should be." *Merry early Christmas, Templeton*, I thought.

"Suit yourself," Rabbit said. He rolled his shoulders, giving his wet curls a shake.

My gaze fell back down into my drink. The wind howled outside and the door behind me leading directly to the outside of the building slammed as someone pushed it open.

Lucie's attention flitted to the door in response and her face lit up. "Basha!"

I turned in my chair, surprised at Lucie's outburst. A tall man, with shaggy dark hair stood shaking off the slick rainwater. It ran down his face and over his leather jacket. His brown eyes lifted. He was surprised to see Lucie, but his mouth slid into an evil grin as his eyes surveyed the room and met mine.

Sebastian.

❊ ❊ ❊

Lucie rose from her chair, taking a step forward. The joy on her face was unmistakable. "What are you doing h–?"

Before she finished her sentence, Templeton was on his feet, his long fingers catching her arm at the elbow. He yanked her back toward our table and her hip smacked into it. Beer sloshed over the sides of our glasses. Rabbit had jumped up at the same time as Templeton, sending several chairs over backwards as he pushed forward and advanced toward Sebastian.

"Templeton, knock it off!" Lucie shouted. She

struggled to shake free of his grasp, but he jerked her backward again and she stumbled. I scrambled out of my chair and caught her around the waist. "What the hell is wrong with you?" she yelled at him.

Two large, rain-drenched men entered the pub behind Sebastian. I recognized one of them. He'd held a gun on me when I was captive in Matar. He shook his head as he pulled out a handgun and pointed it at us, stopping Rabbit in his tracks. Mr. Gunman's eyes met mine and the corners of his mouth turned down. I admit the first thing running through my head was not *'he has a gun!'* but instead, *'he doesn't look very happy to see me.'*

Sebastian, however, looked ecstatic.

Lucie stopped fighting to get free when she saw the gun. I released my grip on her.

"Basha? What are you doing?" Lucie took a tentative step. I saw Templeton flinch. I knew he'd grab her if she tried to go any further.

"This isn't Basha," I told Lucie. I motioned to the sneering man at the door. "This is Sebastian."

"No, it's not. That's not..." she faltered. She sucked in a breath and shook her head. "He's

Basha." But I could see it in her face. She realized I was telling her the truth.

"But it *is* Basha, isn't it Templeton?" Sebastian sauntered closer. He lowered his head and clocked Rabbit, watching as the other man rocked from one foot to another. "Put a gun on that one," he ordered the second man hovering behind him. "You know how unpredictable wild animals can be."

"I still don't…" Lucie stopped. She blinked several times. I saw her swallow hard. *Don't cry*, I pleaded with her silently. *Don't give him the satisfaction.*

"Basha is a derivative of Sebastian," Templeton said, his pupils shrinking as he watched Sebastian roam the room. "It's what his sycophantic friends call him."

"Ooh," Sebastian tsked. "Still touchy after all these years? You need to get over it, Templeton."

I wasn't sure at what Sebastian hinted, but since I'd witnessed the interaction between Templeton and Sebastian's mother, I realized the two had more of a history than I'd first thought.

Sebastian continued to prowl around the

room. With two guns trained on us, no one dared to move. Rabbit's glittering eyes had switched to solid black. He looked as though he were wound tight and waiting to spring at the man pointing the gun at him. I could see Templeton's fingers flexing out of the corner of my eye. I knew we were both thinking about the Crimson Stone.

"Lucie," Sebastian exhaled as he stood in front of her, tilting his head to the side. He lifted his hand and stroked her cheek with the back of his finger.

"Don't," she flinched. "Don't touch me."

Sebastian ignored her and ran his fingertip along her jaw. His warped gaze crawled over her shoulder and he stared, unblinking. "You're both so different," he addressed me. "Lucie didn't put up a fight. She was more than willing."

Templeton's arm shot out and he knocked Sebastian's hand away from Lucie's face. The two Fringe lackeys swung their guns back and forth as Sebastian swore, and in the brief disturbance, I grabbed my shoulder bag from my chair, slipping it over my shoulder. I plunged my hand inside it and stilled.

"Give me that," Sebastian waved his hand at one of the gunmen. He took the weapon and pointed it at Templeton's head. "Just how many pets do you need to fill the void, Templeton?"

That did it. "I'm not his pet!" I yelled.

Sebastian's focus swung to me again. "Now, she's the one who excites me, but you better get to her first, Templeton. I have plans for your Emily."

"You're not touching either of them," Templeton said evenly.

"Well," Sebastian shrugged and lowered the gun – but only slightly. "It's a little late for Lucie. But don't worry, she liked it. You don't mind coming in second, do you Templeton?"

Lucie called Sebastian a very bad name. Then she spat in his face.

Lightning fast, Sebastian pressed his gun against her forehead. Everyone froze. He wiped his hand across his cheek. "That wasn't very ladylike. But what witch is?" Sebastian ran his tongue over his teeth, making a sucking sound as he studied Lucie's face. "Templeton, remember the way your hound whined after I shot her during that stupid hunt? I had such bad aim back then, I had to shoot her a second time. Then a third." He laughed again before his expression suddenly stilled. His finger hovered by the trigger. "But I'm a much better shot now. *Pow.*"

Lucie shuddered.

All the color disappeared from Templeton's eyes. His irises were completely white leaving only a band of black ringing them. His pupils were down to pinpricks. His lips moved silently. I managed to work the lid of the jewelry box open and was trying to get my fingers on the Crimson Stone. Whatever Templeton was doing, the Stone was reacting. I could feel the heat pouring off it.

"Okay, three hamburgers and a veggie one for the Rabbit!" the barkeep announced as he spun into the room, the food tray held high. The swinging door slapped against the wall. Sebastian and the other gunman reacted by pointing their guns toward the noise. Lucie took advantage of the break and shoved Sebastian. Rabbit went for the man with the gun. Once more Templeton grabbed Lucie by the arm, flinging her behind him and over the chairs Rabbit had knocked aside. Her head smacked into a chair leg and she crumpled.

In the confusion I grabbed the Crimson Stone – it burned in my hand – and dropped my shoulder bag to the floor. My fingers stayed wrapped around the Stone. Templeton tackled Sebastian, and the gun went spinning out of the insane man's hand. I went after it but froze when I heard a gunshot. The man struggling with Rabbit had fired his gun into the ceiling – parts of it rained down on them. Rabbit banged the man's arm into the wall as he tried to get him to drop the weapon.

Templeton and Sebastian pounded each other relentlessly as they rolled across the floor. Templeton managed to get the upper hand for a moment, beating Sebastian's head against the floor before the other Fringe brute pulled him off. Sebastian scurried to his feet, slamming his fist into Templeton's stomach.

Distant sirens alerted Sebastian to the Empire guards approaching and he backed off panting. He gritted his teeth at Templeton before his eyes tracked across the room to find me. His mouth split into a perverted smile before he lifted his chin once and blew me a kiss. He dashed through the pub door behind him.

It took me only half a second to realize he didn't go outside. He'd door traveled.

The Crimson Stone was on fire in my fist. I felt the power filling my body and lifting my hair. Static snapped through the room. I made a beeline for the same door.

Templeton wrested free from the Fringe member who held him. He delivered a punch to the man's jaw as I reached for the doorknob, the energy crackling at my fingertips. I felt my door travel energy shooting through my body and connecting with the door's receptive counterpart.

I heard Templeton yell for me to stop.

I centered in on my destination.

Sebastian.

CHAPTER 19

I landed hard but on my feet in a low-lit hallway. My first thought as the door shut behind me was that I'd somehow door traveled back to Templeton's home. The surroundings reeked of wealth. Then I noticed Sebastian turning around at the end of the hall. Of course. I'd followed him to his own house. I'd landed at the St. Michels' estate.

The shock of seeing me in his hall wore off fast. "Well, look at what we have here. Putting some kind of magic behind the door traveling, are we?"

"You were easy to follow," I said. He came closer and I could see the blood dripping out of his left nostril. His lower lip was swollen, and fresh blood seeped from a cut when his face twisted into a hungry leer.

"Easy to follow?" he mused, running his tongue back and forth through the blood on his lip. He stopped before he reached the spot where I stood. "Interesting. You focused on me as the destination, didn't you?"

I lifted a shoulder. The Crimson Stone vibrated in my hand. It wasn't glowing yet, but its energy was starting to play with mine again. I clutched it tightly. "That's me, thinking outside the box."

"Yeah, you are special," he tipped his head to the side as he appraised me. "But you have bad taste in friends. Templeton's annoying, but you're now hanging out with Rabbits? Emily, you should stick to your own kind."

He was baiting me, maybe even stalling. I suppressed the dark feeling rising inside me. "I do stick to my own kind – my 'kind' is made up of good and loyal people. Now, what did Templeton say? Your friends are sycophants? Will they stand by you when we take your family down?"

"Threatening my family?" He put a hand to his chest. "A woman after my own heart. Are you willing to do anything to get to me?"

The Crimson Stone pulsed, snagging his attention. "Yes," I answered.

Sebastian immediately realized what I held in my hand. "You have the Crimson Stone. You brought it here." His voice lowered. "Let me see it, Emily."

"Oh, I want to show you the Crimson Stone,"

I said. The deep anger I'd felt over the past few days bubbled up. The heat twisted in the pit of my stomach, stretching up and gripping my heart. The air crackled and I could smell something burning.

I lifted my arm, raising my fist to reveal the magical gemstone. I felt the air around us grow warmer as the energy overflowed my hand. Calming my breath, I let a tendril of the Stone's energy drift out and snake toward Sebastian. He watched, fascinated. I pushed it again, zeroing in on his left cheek. The flame grew inside the Stone in my hand. Mustering every ounce of control I had, I flicked the energy – it licked the side of his face, burning him. Sebastian yelped, stumbling backward.

His shaking fingertips touched his cheek. "You little –"

"Sebastian?" An elderly voice called out from farther down the hall. The energy of the Crimson Stone snapped back into my hand and the flame inside shrunk. I dropped my arm, still squeezing the gemstone.

Sebastian glowered at me, stepping to the left as a frail woman came into view. Her right hand trailed along the wall as she walked; her left she held raised in front of her chest. "Right here, Grandmother." He took her hand, gently bringing her forward. Drawing her close, he kissed the top of her head. "I'm right here."

"I smelled something hot. I think something is burning," she said. Her trembling hand stretched upward toward his face. He turned his head away to prevent her from making contact. "And I heard voices."

Sebastian blinked slowly, his eyes rising to mine. "It's my friend, Emily. She's here to visit me."

"Emily? Who is Emily?" His grandmother held out her hand. "Can she come closer?"

"Let my grandmother 'see' you, Emily. Come here." Sebastian's upper lip curled.

I watched the old woman's fingers twitch as she waited. Shoving the Crimson Stone deep into the front pocket of my jeans, I cautiously stepped forward. The grandmother's eyes were clouded, and she stared into the air past me.

"Closer," Sebastian whispered. "Let her touch your face."

My body ached with the tension filling it, but I took another step, keeping a wary eye on Sebastian. His grandmother ran her fingers over my skin, from my cheek to my chin, over my lips and along both sides of my nose. Her fingertips were featherlight as they skittered around my eyes and over my eyelids as I squinted. She reached higher, touching my forehead. Her hand brushed over my hair once before she lowered it.

"She's very pretty, isn't she Sebastian?" his grandmother said, tilting her head up as if she were in fact seeing the wicked man's face.

"Very pretty." His voice took on a huskier quality.

I backed away, fighting an involuntary shudder. This had gone on long enough. Sebastian adjusted his grandmother's position and now she stood in front of him, facing me. Smirking, he wrapped both arms around her and rested his chin on the top of her head. There was no way I was touching him behind his human shield.

"Can you stay for dinner tonight?" The grandmother rested against Sebastian.

Disgusted, I could barely look at the man. "No, ma'am. I have to leave." I turned toward the door I'd traveled through.

"We'll finish our discussion later, won't we? Do you want me to come to Lucie's? Or should we find someplace else to meet since I'm guessing she and I just broke up?" he taunted.

I stopped and tossed a black look over my shoulder. "Tell you what, Sebastian. I'll come find you. It'll be a surprise – but we'll pick up right where we left off."

I door traveled out of the hallway before he had a chance to reply.

❋ ❋ ❋

Lucie was my last thought as I left Sebastian's house. I stepped from his hallway and into her kitchen through the pantry door. My heart hurt for her. I crossed to the line of barstools and climbed on the nearest one. I folded my arms on the countertop and laid my head down.

I should've killed him. The thought sickened me, but I couldn't keep watching this man hurt people... *Destroy people.* I shut my eyes and felt the tears burn through my eyelashes as they leaked out.

Briiing-briiing! The phone for the Empire's

service rang twice in Lucie's cupboard. I sat up too quickly and my head swam. Steadying myself against the counter, I slid off the barstool and opened the cupboard door. The phone rang again, and I answered it.

"Hello?"

"This is the Empire's messaging service. Please hold for a message." The sound of ticking and chimes followed.

A voice with no semblance of inflection came on the line. "I have a message for Ms. Lucie Bellerose. May I please speak with her?"

"Ah, this is Lucie," I said into the receiver. I hunted through Lucie's kitchen drawers for a notepad and pencil.

"Ms. Bellerose, I have a message from one Ms. Tara Parker-Jones. The message is as follows: 'Tell her I found another letter she needs to see right away.' This completes the message, Ms. Bellerose," the Empire's operator concluded.

I'd stopped rooting around the drawers when I heard Tara's name. "When was this message sent?"

"The message was received at 11 o'clock this morning. This message was brought to you by the Empire's award-winning tier two operator team," the voice informed me.

"Oh-kay," I replied. *Weird.* "Thanks."

"You are welcome. Goodbye." The line went silent. I would never get used to using the Empire's service. I missed my own phone.

I ran my hand through my hair. I wanted to know what Tara had found, but I had to get back to the *Wayside Inn*. I assumed the rest of the Fringe ran like Sebastian when they heard the sirens, but I couldn't be sure. I'd travel through the front door of the inn instead of directly into the pub in case the drama was still happening. I made sure the Crimson Stone was pushed as far as it could go down inside my jeans pocket and headed for the pantry door. A banging on the front of Lucie's brownstone stopped me. Shouting followed. What the –?

Warily, I crept from the kitchen toward the banging. Big Rabbit's face pressed against the side window by the door, his huge hands cupped around the sides of his face to shield his eyes while he looked inside. I heard him yell my name.

"Good grief." I hoped Lucie didn't have a neighborhood association. At this rate we were going to get her in trouble. Hurrying to the door, I unlocked it. Big Rabbit burst in and picked me up in a bear hug.

"Check the house," he barked as a dozen Rabbits streamed in after him.

I wriggled, trying to get free. "It's okay! I'm the only one here. You can put me down."

Big Rabbit reluctantly lowered me. "This is her," he said to several Rabbits standing by. "Tell Rabbit we got her. She's unharmed. Tell him we'll stay here. Let the rest of the network know she's been found."

"What's going on?" I spun around and watched as two Rabbits came back down the stairs. Everyone had moved so fast. Now they all crowded around us, eyes completely black and glittering. Their noses twitched.

"Rabbit messaged the network. He said you took off after Sebastian and were in danger. But you're here. You came to Lucie's," Big Rabbit finished.

"Ah..." My eyes roamed the faces around me. I recognized several from the group of Rabbits who attended the bonfire last spring. "Well, yes and no."

Big Rabbit hung his head. "Rabbit's not going

to like this."

"He won't be the only one," I said. "But where are they? I mean, Rabbit was with Lucie and Templeton. Are they okay?"

"They're okay. They're still driving," he said. "There was a fight? With the Fringe?"

I nodded and explained what happened at the *Wayside Pub*. I omitted the part about Sebastian posing as someone else and using Lucie. That was something they didn't need to know.

"Bad, bad things happening," Big Rabbit said. "Once Rabbit gets here, we'll figure out what to do next." He turned and headed for the kitchen.

Here we go again, I thought. "Hey, Big Rabbit? Does everyone want pizza?"

❋ ❋ ❋

I handed over my credit card with instructions to order enough for everyone. Then I excused myself to go 'freshen up' upstairs.

"Oh, no you don't," Big Rabbit said, catching my elbow as I tried to leave the kitchen. He turned to a female Rabbit. "Can you please make sure she doesn't take off?"

My mouth popped open. "I don't believe you!"

Big Rabbit waved a big finger at me. "You get people in trouble."

I glared at him. The female Rabbit put her hand on my other shoulder. "Men, huh?"

I took a closer look at the woman.

"Oh! It's you!" I shook off Big Rabbit and hugged the woman standing beside me. This was the female Rabbit who helped me when I was searching for my mother in Matar. She was one of the Rabbits who swarmed the warehouse to rescue me from Sebastian and his men. She was also one of the Rabbits who beat Simon for murdering another female Rabbit.

A thin scar ran from the corner of her eye and down to her jaw. It was new. She saw me looking at it. "Fringe. We've been fighting them in the south. It's changing from a technological battleground to a more hands-on one."

"They're getting worse," I nodded. I jerked my thumb toward the hall leading to the stairs. "I only want to use the bathroom."

"Let's go," she fluttered her hand.

My shadow followed me upstairs. At the top, I turned into the spare bedroom. Standing in the middle of the room, I decided to come clean – I had a feeling she'd agree to help me. "Look, I got a message through the Empire's service from my friend Tara back in Kincaid. She found something in a letter from the office of the Warden of the North Door. She has a whole box of letters, and some reference the directional doors. Her message said she found something new. It must be important. I need to go to her bookstore and then I will be coming straight back. Rabbit's going to want this information. We all need it."

The female Rabbit listened, bobbing her head as she considered what I said. She didn't spend much time thinking about my request. "Go. But come right back to this room. I'll hold Big Rabbit off if he comes looking for us."

"I will." I paused, realizing I still wasn't using my top hat during door travel. I was violating Empire rules right and left. *Pfft.* I didn't care. "I'll be right back."

I leaned toward the closet door as I raised my energy. The Crimson Stone answered mine with a comforting pulse of its own. We were aligning our energies every time I used it. I touched the doorknob and stepped on through to the back room of *Pages & Pens*.

❖ ❖ ❖

Marley stood by the hutch unwrapping a plate of frosted cupcakes. The frosting was a toxic shade of neon orange. He raised his head when I stepped out of the closet.

"Wait, were you in the closet?" Tara's assistant pointed to the door behind me.

"No, I was not. Is Tara here?" I asked.

"Yeah, you were in the closet," he replied, absently scratching the top of his head. "Right?"

"No. Where's Tara?" Ignoring poor Marley, I made for the door leading into the storefront.

"I'm right here," Tara said, appearing in the doorway. She motioned to Marley. "Okay, Cupcake. These are not the 'Emilys' you're looking for. Go help the customer out front before I energize your behind."

"There are so many things wrong with what you said," I told her.

"I can't keep all of Jack's movie quotes straight," she replied, still ignoring her bewildered assistant. She closed the door behind Marley as he left the back room complaining about not being a member of the club. "Lucie gave you my message?"

"Sort of. What'd you find?" I trailed after her as she headed for her desk.

Tara picked up a plastic sleeve with a sheet of paper inside. "Remember how I said a handful of the letters were from Blackstone's predecessor? This is one of them. I'm going to cut to the chase, Emily. There's a fifth directional door."

"What? How can there be a fifth one?" I pulled the sleeve from her hand. A lot of the thin handwriting had faded. Tara pointed to a line.

"Start here," she directed.

"*A door leading straight into the Empire is rumored to be in the Walled Zone. If this is true, a fifth directional door has been established. The direction of this door is said to be from Above.*" I read the sentences aloud. "What does this mean? From above?"

"And it's capitalized," Tara added.

"Above… like heaven?"

"Do you believe in heaven?" Tara looked surprised.

"No more far-fetched than the Empire," I answered. "But I wonder what it means."

"Here." Tara reached into her desk and retrieved several other plastic sleeves. "These are the letters I already told you about. Rabbit might recognize some of the landmarks listed. They might even point to the other directional doors."

"Thanks," I said. I tapped the edges of the sleeves carefully on the desktop, aligning the pages. "He's on his way to Lucie's. I'm meeting everyone there."

Tara chewed on her bottom lip, shrewdly evaluating me. "How's it going?"

"Peachy."

"That bad?"

I blew out a breath. "It's bad."

Tara leaned closer, her eyes zeroing in on my neck. "Do you have bruises?"

My hand flew up and I realized the scarf had come loose, exposing my throat. How long it had been like that, I didn't know. "Oh, yeah."

"Emily?" Tara squeaked. "What happened?"

"Wait," I pleaded. "Do you have a mirror? I want to see."

Reluctantly, Tara dug out a palm-sized mirror from her top desk drawer. She handed it to me. "Is that what Sebastian did to you?" she asked.

I used the mirror to check my neck. "It looks pretty good. Lucie's healing scarf has really helped."

"Emily?" Tara's voice developed an edge. "Answer me."

I set the mirror down on the desk. "Yes. He grabbed me by the throat. I got away. That's it."

"You can't keep doing this," Tara said, sinking into her desk chair. "You're going to get killed. Like Blackstone. Holy hell, Emily! Blackstone was strangled." Tara's hands flew to her mouth.

Tara wasn't thinking anything that Rabbit and I hadn't already considered. How did he put it? Sebastian might come from a family at the top of the Fringe heap, but he was 'more hands-on' than others. It was a game to him.

"I don't know if he's the one who actually did it," I said. "But it wouldn't surprise me either."

Tara's phone buzzed with a new text. She picked it up. "It's from Jack. *'Heads up, we're coming in.'* Oh, crap, they're here! I told him he could bring Lydia by again!"

"I've got to get going. I can't be seen," I said, heading toward the closet door, the plastic sleeves in my hand. "I don't have time, there's too much going on back at Lucie's. Wait... Marley!"

"Dammit!" Tara swore as she rose from her chair. "I'll grab Marley and make sure he keeps his mouth shut. You get out of here! Be careful. Go!"

I gave a nod and zipped through the back room's closet door, making my escape. I stepped into the spare bedroom upstairs in Lucie's brownstone. The female Rabbit sat on the bed, flipping through a book of poetry.

She pointed her chin at the protected letters in my hand. "You get what you need?"

"I did," I said. "Anybody miss me?"

Someone tapped on the door. Big Rabbit called my name.

I winked at the female Rabbit and opened the door. "Right here."

He seemed so relieved I felt guilty. Well, it had to be done. "We ordered pizza," he said. "We even got one with pepperoni for you."

My heart melted. "You take good care of me, Big Rabbit."

He blushed but threw a particularly curious look at the woman sitting on the bed. "What have you been doing up here?"

She wasn't impressed. "Girl talk… *Big Rabbit.*"

I couldn't resist. "You know, like about… girl underwear."

He held up a hand. "I've heard enough." He spun on his heel and went back downstairs.

"He's one of my favorite Rabbits," I chuckled.

The female Rabbit nodded. "He's a good man."

✼ ✼ ✼

The pizza arrived before Rabbit, Lucie, and Templeton returned to the townhouse. I halfheartedly ate a slice with the others, listening to their chatter. I'd relaxed but worried about what we'd be up against next. I was eager to share the information about a fifth directional door with Rabbit – and Templeton. I wondered if it would be news to the Salesman.

I wiped my hands clean and left the others, choosing to curl up on the sofa in Lucie's front living room while I waited. I chose a book discussing telekinesis from one of her shelves. The Crimson Stone was either granting me the power to blast someone away from me, or it was amplifying the abilities I already had. I read through the passages, absorbing as much as I could. Different Rabbits popped their dark-haired heads in periodically to check on me, but they seemed to realize I was staying put. *For now.*

A short time later, my eyes were crossing from all the information I'd read. Closing the book, I honed in on a gray figurine in the center of Lucie's mantel. It resembled a woman, but the miniature statue lacked any features. Her two arms curved upward in the shape of a Y. The legs were posed tightly together, the feet blending into a square base. The figure's hips were exaggerated, and a spiral was carved into her belly. I let my eyes relax and my vision blur. My energy built slowly, almost wearily, in my chest. My arms tingled. I lifted my right hand, encouraging the energy to reach out. I guided it as the Crimson Stone hummed reassuringly in my jeans pocket. I curled my fingers and the energy swirled around the figure. I raised my hand slightly, and the statue raised off the mantel.

The sound of keys in the front door alerted

me to my friends' arrival. I took great pains to lower the figure back to the mantel and stood up, stretching and waiting. Rabbit appeared first, his angry eyes combing over me. He said nothing. Lucie was right behind him. She had a bruise at her right temple where she'd hit her head at the *Wayside Pub*. She waved tiredly at me before craning her neck toward the kitchen. "Good grief, are they multiplying?"

"It's a party," I joked lamely.

Templeton was the last person through the door. He took one look at the crowd in the kitchen and made a sharp right into the living room. He handed me my shoulder bag. "It's all there."

His lower lip was split in the middle and he had a dark bruise under his left eye. His top hat was missing, and his short hair stuck up at odd angles. The four of us stood silently, the tension thick in the air. Eventually, I spoke. "Yelling at me isn't going to help."

"Or make a difference," Rabbit sighed. He pulled me to him, wrapping me in his embrace. The knuckles on his right hand were scraped and swollen. "This time, I was really scared for you, Emily. That's saying something considering everything you've already been through."

"I wasn't," I admitted as he released me. "I was very angry." My eyes flitted to Lucie. "For all of us."

"You left him alive?" she asked. She pressed her lips together and I saw her cheek twitch.

"Yeah, I did." I took a deep breath and proceeded to tell them everything that happened when I followed Sebastian to his house. I didn't leave anything out. For once, Templeton waited until I finished before asking questions. He wanted to know more about the energy I pushed out when I burned Sebastian's cheek.

He nodded when I described how it felt. "Good. You're controlling your magic better. Your anger fueled it."

"Be careful of that," Lucie argued. She shook her head at Templeton. "She's got to be careful when feeding her magic with her feelings. What she chooses matters. You know that."

"And you know very well how you can mold angry energy into something advantageous," he countered.

"Right now, we'd rather not hear from you,

Templeton," Rabbit cut in. "Your little omission was the icing on the cake today."

Templeton glared at Rabbit.

"What omission? *Oh.*" I winced.

"Yeah," Rabbit replied. They knew about Templeton's door travel issue.

"He couldn't follow you," Lucie told me. "And that meant you were alone with Basha." Lucie's voice caught in her throat. She swallowed. "I mean, Sebastian. Rabbit was furious."

"I was terrified," Rabbit corrected. "Now I'm furious. And I still don't know what's going on with…" Rabbit gritted his teeth. "Him. He won't tell me why he can't door travel."

"Enough," I said, lifting my hands. "There is pizza in the kitchen. Rabbit, go eat. Templeton, suck it up and go get a piece of pizza, too. Take it into Lucie's back yard if you want to be alone. You're obviously not going anywhere right now. But you and I are going to talk at some point. Just the two of us."

Before Templeton could argue, I turned to the table by the couch and picked up the letters from Tara. I handed them to Rabbit. "Letters from a previous Warden of the North Door. Tara found these in a box from Blackstone's library. There's a reference to a fifth directional door – in the Walled Zone."

Rabbit glanced up at Templeton. "Do you know about a fifth directional door?"

Templeton shook his head. "I do not."

"You two go now," I said, reaching for Lucie. "I want to talk to Lucie alone. But save her a couple of slices of pizza."

CHAPTER 20

Lucie closed the door behind the men before sitting down on the sofa. Her bright blue eyes were wet with tears. "I'm so sorry, Emily."

"What? Why are you sorry? You have nothing to be sorry about." I sat on the coffee table and faced her. "You did nothing wrong."

"But I didn't want to see it." She hung her head. "I had this gnawing feeling about Basha, and I ignored it. I was having too much fun and didn't want to spoil it. But I knew something was off."

"None of this is your fault," I told her. "You understand that, right? This is all on him."

Lucie raised her head. "He had a cut under his right eye – it was bruised. I asked him what happened, and he said something about a boxing ring at the gym where he works out. Said his 'buddy' caught him off guard. But it had to be from when he attacked you."

"How would you know he was lying? He made up a believable excuse," I said.

"And he lied to me about his name." She looked down at her hands as she picked at her thumbnail. "He said it was Basha Michaels."

"Again, how could you guess who he was?" I wanted to convince her she did nothing wrong. Sebastian used her. It was a game to him – a sick one.

"And then last night I…" Lucie's voice trailed off and she covered her face. "I can't believe what happened, how he fooled me – how I *let* him fool me. I'm so ashamed."

"Okay, that's enough." I slid forward and pulled her into my arms, hugging her. She sniffled and I felt her body quake. I rubbed my hand up and down her back. "Please don't say that. You did nothing wrong."

Lucie sucked in a shuddering breath, pulling away and nodding. "I'm sorry, Emily."

"Didn't you once give me a hard time for saying a bunch of 'sorrys' when I didn't need to apologize?"

That brought a half-hearted smile to her lips. "Yeah, I guess I did."

"We're going to take Sebastian and the Fringe down. You'll get your chance to get even," I told her.

"Maybe," she said, twisting her mouth to the side. "I'd rather not see him ever again. But I'm glad you served him a taste of his own medicine today. You had control of your power and used it against him. *You* had control of the situation."

"Until granny arrived," I said. "Poor woman. He hid behind her."

"He knew it would bother you," Lucie guessed. "I bet it was a lot of show. It would've been different had Templeton followed you."

"Oh, right. Speaking of…" I grimaced. "What happened after I followed Sebastian out of there?"

"That," Lucie began as she wiped her cheeks with her fingers, "was ugly."

"I bet. What happened?"

"I was getting myself off the floor when you door traveled out of there. I heard Templeton yell for you to stop. He was still wrestling with one of Sebastian's men. The sirens were getting closer, and the two Fringe members broke away and door traveled right out of there. Rabbit started shouting at Templeton to go after you, but Templeton didn't budge. He just stood there. I thought Rabbit was going to have an aneurism. He shoved Templeton against the door you went through. Obviously now we know why Templeton didn't go after you."

Lucie took a breath and continued. "Next thing you know the Empire guards are bursting into the room and they have their guns out. The three of us throw our hands up and the first thing the guards do is cuff Rabbit."

"Holy hell!"

"You said it. Rabbit switched from yelling at Templeton to being as still and silent as a stone. He didn't even blink. He was beyond angry. Meanwhile, I'm trying to explain how we were attacked by the Fringe." Lucie ran a hand over her head and combed her fingers through her hair. "Thank goodness for the barkeep. He told the guards we were customers and that he'd seen other men fighting with Templeton and Rabbit. That's when the guards believed me."

"Does it get worse?" I hated to ask.

"Of course," she replied. "The guards eventually take the cuffs off Rabbit and tell us we can leave."

"They didn't cuff Templeton? Or you?"

Lucie blinked. "Nope. Only Rabbit."

I couldn't even begin to imagine how livid Rabbit must've been. "And then what happened?"

"I was feeling woozy." Lucie pointed to the bump on her temple. "I handed Rabbit my keys. The two of them said nothing until we got out to my car. Rabbit suddenly turns around and shoves Templeton. For the record, Rabbit can get pretty creative in his swearing. Rabbit's eyes went to solid black, and he kept pushing Templeton until his back was up against the vehicle. Then Rabbit grabbed the front of Templeton's shirt and started banging him against the side. Templeton didn't even put up a fight. He just took it, Emily. Then Rabbit screamed something like: *'Why won't you go after her? What's wrong with you? He's going to kill her!'* Templeton shouted back that he couldn't go after you, that he can't door travel without the Crimson Stone. He said something else to Rabbit – something I didn't catch – and Rabbit threw a punch, but he purposely missed Templeton and hit the side of my car. And then he punched the same spot over and over right by Templeton. It was terrifying. Templeton didn't even flinch."

My mouth hung open. I remembered Rabbit's swollen knuckles when he hugged me earlier.

"How did it end?"

Lucie sighed. "Rabbit suddenly stopped. He looked at me, told me he'd get my car fixed, and then got in and started the engine. He sat there texting the network to get everyone looking for you. I told Templeton to get into the back seat and I sat up front. Rabbit spent some more time on his phone before shifting into drive and heading for Matar. That was the longest freakin' ride home of my life."

"And Templeton didn't explain why he couldn't door travel?" I asked.

"No." Lucie shrugged. "He didn't say a word until we got home. Rabbit found a parking spot out front and here we are."

I nodded, chewing on my lower lip. "It's my fault Templeton can't door travel."

Lucie lifted an eyebrow. "Oh, hell. Now what?"

I explained how Templeton made a deal with Nisha to help me find my mother when she'd been taken by the Fringe. I told Lucie at first I'd thought Rabbit was the one who went to the dangerous priestess for help, but how I found out it was Templeton instead.

"After the Courthouse explosion, I confronted him," I told her. "I knew something was off. He admitted he lent his door travel energy to Nisha for a year. He realized he could rely on the one piece of the Crimson Stone he had – the piece he took from me. He can draw from its magic. On top of that, he uses the power I'd added to it when I was wearing it earlier this year. It's not one-hundred percent accurate, though. Remember how he had problems door traveling out of your kitchen the other day? But for the most part, it's been enough to keep him going."

"Wow." Lucie shook her head. "Yet another reason why he wants the whole Crimson Stone."

"That and the whole prophecy thing," I said.

The two of us sat silently, musing on all the information we'd exchanged. Lucie nodded as if coming to a decision. "How much longer is this deal with Nisha supposed to last?"

I did a quick count on my fingers. "It's been less than six months since my mother's kidnapping. He's got at least half a year."

"We need him to be at full capacity for everything we want to do," Lucie said. She rubbed her bottom lip with the pad of her fingertip.

"Think about today, Emily. What if it would've been a different scenario playing out between you and Sebastian? Templeton couldn't get to you. None of us could. But if he'd been able to door travel, you would've had backup if you needed it."

"I don't know how to fix this for him," I admitted.

"I might," Lucie sighed. "How hard is it to find this Nisha?"

"Oh, no," I said. "And you all think I'm nuts? No way. You do not want to mess with that."

"You're right, I don't. But sometimes you need to do what you don't want to do for the greater good. Right? That's what you're doing – that's why you're going after the Fringe." Lucie paused. "Wait, would Rabbit be able to find Nisha?"

"Yeah, about that…" I wasn't going to spill the beans about Rabbit's history with Nisha, but I told Lucie he wouldn't be up for helping us find the priestess. "He has a good reason for avoiding her."

Lucie gave me a quizzical look but let my comment slide. "Well, we'll see. Let me cook on my idea. In the meantime, let's go find out what the small army of Rabbits are doing in my kitchen."

"You should eat," I said.

"I don't have much of an appetite." A shadow briefly flitted across Lucie's face, but then she clapped her hands once and stood up. "Alright, enough of my wallowing. I should probably check on Templeton, too."

"Why don't you let me do that?" I offered. "I'll take him a piece of pizza. He probably didn't get one."

Lucie nodded as she opened the door and we stepped out of the living room and into the brownstone's entryway. "You know, Emily, when the message came in from the network saying you were safe and sound, I turned around and looked at Templeton. I've never seen such relief on a man's face. He was terrified for you, and he was helpless to do anything."

* * *

I grabbed a slice of the pepperoni pizza as well as a meatless slice with black olives and green peppers, balancing both on paper plates.

The whole group of men and women huddled around my Rabbit as he pointed to portions of the letters I'd given to him. He directed different Rabbits to investigate the various passages and references. Lucie's kitchen was now a hub of the Rabbits' network. Their thumbs were a blur as they slid across their phone screens.

I stepped outside, shutting the door on the chattering and buzzing behind me. The air was chillier and it would be dark soon. Templeton sat at the round table Lucie kept in her back yard, his arms crossed over his chest and his long legs stretched out in front of him as he leaned back in the chair. His eyes were closed, but I sensed he wasn't sleeping. I set the pizza down on the table and sat in the chair across from him.

"I don't eat pizza," he said, his eyes still closed.

"Who doesn't eat pizza?" I asked. "Maybe you should. Maybe you'd lighten up if you lowered your dietary standards."

A faint smile floated over his lips, but he kept his eyes shut.

"Come on. I won't tell anyone," I teased. "No one has to know Templeton ate wondrously greasy pizza and enjoyed it."

Templeton shook his head but finally opened his eyes. He sat up and looked at the two plates. "Which one is yours?"

"Neither. I already ate. I didn't know what you would like," I said.

He chose the slice with the olives and peppers.

I fished a paper towel out of my back pocket. "Here. It really is greasy. I wasn't joking."

Templeton let out a quiet groan but took the paper towel. He took a bite of the pizza and winced. His split lip probably didn't care for the tomato sauce.

"I'm sorry about today," I said. "Lucie told me everything that happened at the *Wayside* after I left."

Templeton focused on his pizza, saying nothing.

"But I had the Crimson Stone and I didn't want Sebastian to get away," I said. "I knew I could take him."

"You don't need the Stone to do that, Emily," Templeton said. He patted his mouth with the paper towel. "You have enough ability without it. The Stone simply makes it easier for you to use your magic."

"I'm not so sure," I argued.

"I am. My father had it made. I know what it can do." He sat back in his chair.

"Fair point," I replied. "I know we have a bunch of things to discuss, and we can't get to everything –"

"Not everything is up for discussion, Emily." The edge returned to Templeton's voice.

"You thought I was the 'light' in the prophecy." I looked around the yard. Everything was bathed in an autumn-orange haze as the sun set. I swallowed. "What did you intend?"

Templeton tilted his head back. "I 'intended' to keep you safe."

"And what about the heir part?"

"We now know the translation was a misinterpretation."

"But you didn't until today." I waited.

He took his time in answering, choosing instead to eat more of the pizza. Minutes passed. "Your father was afraid he wouldn't be able to keep you safe. His work in the Empire put his family at risk. After he was killed, the spotlight was no longer on your family – on you. But you turned 30 and your door travel energy matured. And you're... *you.*" He shook his head. "You're a magnet for trouble."

"I'm not yours to watch over," I told him. I tried to understand what he was telling me.

"I made a decision after Daniel died," Templeton continued. I startled at the use of my father's name. Templeton didn't seem to notice. "I resolved to keep an eye on you to make sure you weren't targeted by the Fringe when you became a Salesman. If you were, I would step in if you got in over your head." He smiled wryly at his plate. "And you were a little entertaining at first."

I pointed at him. "Don't start."

"But then, the hunt for the Crimson Stone surfaced. I didn't expect that. It changed everything. The Stone belongs to me – to my family. When I saw you use it in Vue, I witnessed your power. I believed you were part of the prophecy. And you are. Now that I have all the lines, I understand you are the traveler."

"And Lucie's the 'light,'" I finished.

He nodded. The shadows had crossed into Lucie's yard, but I could still see his pale eyes shimmering. "But that doesn't mean I won't continue to make sure you're safe."

I didn't know what to say.

※ ※ ※

We sat wordlessly for a while, content to think our own thoughts about all we'd learned. Templeton ate both slices of pizza. Eventually, I said we should go back inside. He was reluctant but followed me. When I asked him if he planned on staying the night – although I could NOT imagine him parking it on Lucie's floor – he said he'd call a car to take him to a place he had in Matar.

Oh, right. *His penthouse*.

We returned to the kitchen where the Rabbits worked. I noticed Lucie and Rabbit weren't with the others. I touched my female Rabbit friend on the shoulder.

"Where are Lucie and Rabbit?" I asked.

"Um," she looked up and around. "I think… Hey, Rabbit? Where's Rabbit?"

Big Rabbit was working on another slice of pizza. He swallowed before daintily wiping his lips with a paper towel. "I think they went outside. Out front. I saw them talking on the sidewalk. Rabbit didn't look happy, but I figured as long as Emily hadn't run off, we didn't need to worry."

I tilted my head. Uh-oh. What was Lucie up to? "When was this?"

"About a half-hour ago?"

My eyes cut to Templeton. He pulled a face. I headed to the front of the townhouse where I opened the front door and looked up and down the street.

No Lucie. No Rabbit.

Templeton joined me. His gaze roamed the sleepy street. "Lucie's vehicle is gone. Do you know what's going on?"

"I have a bad feeling I do," I answered.

"Tell me."

"You're not going to like it."

"I never do."

"Well," I began. "How about you show me where to find Nisha and I'll tell you on the way?"

CHAPTER 21

"A taxi will be faster," I argued when Templeton wanted to call for a car. I'd grabbed my shoulder bag from the living room, opting to leave my top hat and The Book behind in the spare bedroom. I needed to lighten my load. I returned the Crimson Stone to the jewelry box and forced it to the bottom of my bag. I wasn't crazy about taking it with me, but with all the pieces reunited I didn't dare leave it behind. Looping the strap over my head and across my chest, I balanced the bag on my hip. Templeton's top hat had been left in the back of Lucie's car.

We hustled down a block before a taxi came into view and I flagged it down. Templeton gave an address for a building near the center of Matar. Mindful of the driver, I kept my voice low and explained how I believed Lucie convinced Rabbit to take her to Nisha – that Lucie thought she might be able to help Templeton. He was not happy with me for revealing the reason behind his inability to door travel.

After making a comment about 'stupidity becoming contagious,' Templeton clamped his mouth shut and fixed his gaze on the night outside the window. Dinner time traffic packed the streets, and it took our driver extra time to get downtown. When he finally pulled the taxi to the curb, Templeton handed the driver several bills. I waited on the sidewalk.

"She lives here?" We stood in front of a mammoth luxury high-rise building.

"In the penthouse. Wait here." Templeton strode toward the lobby doors.

"Ah, no," I replied, keeping on his heels.

The doorman greeted Templeton by name while he held the door open for us. The sound of a whistle and a sharp 'Emily!' being called from the street behind me caused me to stop.

Rabbit stood leaning against a signpost. His arms were crossed, his hands tucked under them making his biceps bulge. When he didn't move from his spot, I crossed the distance between us. I saw Rabbit's eyes shift past me and raise. Templeton had followed.

"Where's Lucie?" I asked at the same time Templeton demanded to know why Rabbit brought her to Nisha.

"Like I could've stopped her," Rabbit dismissed Templeton. "She just would've found someone from her circle to bring her here." Rabbit turned to me. "She's inside. She asked me to wait for her here. She didn't want me to go with her. Did you...?" His voice trailed off.

"I told her about Templeton's deal and how he can't door travel because of it. I said you didn't like to be around Nisha. That is it. Period," I stressed.

Rabbit's jaw tightened, but he nodded. He made eye contact with Templeton. "I can't believe how stupid you are. Lucie told me about the deal you cut with Nisha. What were you thinking?"

Templeton lifted a shoulder. "I seem to remember you weren't coming through with details on where to find Emily's mother. Someone had to step up and help."

Rabbit pushed off the signpost and I jockeyed in between the two men. *Damn, Templeton!* Couldn't he keep his mouth shut for once? I faced Rabbit. "We're going to lose this battle with Sebastian and the Fringe if you both keep fighting each other."

"Templeton's meddling, all his lying, has made everything worse," Rabbit asserted.

"That's not entirely true and you know it. I'm not defending all the crap he's pulled," I said. I heard Templeton snort behind me. "But he's come through for me. And he's here now. We need him." I could sense Templeton's intense gaze as it landed on my back.

"He's here because he can't door travel and he wants the Crimson Stone," Rabbit challenged.

"Yeah, I know that's a part of it, but it's not the whole story," I answered. Rabbit's eyes tracked to the high-rise doors, and Templeton and I turned at the same time. Lucie appeared, nodding at the doorman as he held the door for her. She startled at seeing the three of us on the sidewalk.

"I wasn't expecting to see you," she said as she joined us. I realized she was speaking directly to Templeton. "But your timing is good. Nisha's expecting you."

Templeton's features hardened. "What did you do?"

Lucie lifted her chin. "I paid your debt."

"With what?" Templeton hissed.

"Not discussing it with you," she bit back.

Rabbit reached for her hand, searching her face. "Are you okay?"

"I'm fine. Oh, she's not one I'd want to play in the pool with, trust me," Lucie said. Her attention flitted to Templeton. "No one should. But she's waiting for you now. I'd make this your last visit to her."

Templeton didn't respond to Lucie, but stepped closer, studying her face as if he could determine what she'd traded with Nisha. Rabbit visibly tensed at the Salesman's move. Templeton shook his head in disgust before walking away and disappearing into Nisha's building.

I watched him go. I didn't exactly fear for him, but I worried. Lucie told Rabbit we could all go back home – that Templeton wouldn't need a ride after meeting with the otherworldly priestess.

Rabbit texted the network while Lucie drove. I sat in the back seat and held Templeton's top hat in my lap while I stared unseeing out the window. I tried to remain positive. He'd be okay.

Good grief, now I was worried about Templeton!

This week couldn't get any stranger.

❃ ❃ ❃

Back at Lucie's, Rabbit rejoined the others in the kitchen. Lucie stood in the entryway, unmoving.

"You okay?" I asked. "Do you want me to ask Rabbit to make everyone leave?"

"No, it's fine," she replied. "I need to shower." She abruptly turned and headed upstairs to the second floor. I let her go. Maybe later she'd tell me how she paid Templeton's debt.

In the kitchen, Rabbit gathered updates from the network. Most of it didn't make sense to me, but several Rabbits were particularly animated when relaying their information about tracking down financial transactions.

I looked around the room. All the pizza boxes were gone, and someone had taken the trash out. The dishes had been washed. Clean coffee mugs were stacked in a short, triangular tower on the countertop. I even caught the scent of fresh lemon. Someone mopped Lucie's floor.

"What's next?" I asked Rabbit. We moved away from the others to talk more privately. It was getting late.

"I'm going to bed down here on the couch. The others have places they can go for the night, but a couple will hang around outside to keep an eye on things. With Sebastian knowing you're here at Lucie's, it's a target." Rabbit shook his head. "I didn't see it coming – the whole Lucie-Sebastian thing. He was a step ahead of us."

"Lucie feels horrible about not making the connection," I said. "She liked him. I mean, she liked the person he pretended to be."

Rabbit wiped his hand across his mouth. "I gave her some space. I knew she was seeing someone, but she was kind of tight-lipped about it. I mean, I get it. Her dating someone isn't anyone's business. I was tempted to check into who she was seeing – you know, to make sure he was a decent guy. I could have. I should have. But I wanted to respect her privacy. And now I regret not going after any information."

"You did the right thing," I assured him.

"Did she tell you what she gave to Nisha?" In spite of himself, Rabbit shivered. "I have a bad feeling."

"I do too," I said. "But no. I don't have a clue." I sighed. "I'm going upstairs to shower after

Lucie. Do you need anything from me?"

"Nah, I know where everything is." Rabbit patted me on the shoulder before telling the other Rabbits to start packing up. Everyone would return in the morning.

I climbed the stairs to the spare bedroom and flopped down on the bed. Feeling low, I focused on the ceiling, realizing I hadn't reached out to Jack once. I closed my eyes and groaned. I was too exhausted to do anything.

I awoke sometime later. Rolling over I checked the clock. It was late and the house was quiet. Still, I could see from my vantage point that the lights remained on downstairs. I climbed out of bed and changed into my pajamas. I'd shower in the morning.

Downstairs, I saw Rabbit sitting alone in the living room, pouring over the letters and his phone. He hooked his thumb toward the kitchen. I nodded.

Lucie sat on one of the barstools, sipping a glass of red wine while she watched her pantry door. She gestured to the bottle when she saw me. "Help yourself."

"Thanks," I said, retrieving a glass from her cupboard. "Feeling better?"

"The shower was nice," she answered. "Felt good to wash off that woman's energy."

"You can do that? It can be –"

"Figure of speech," Lucie interrupted. "But I can see why Rabbit's bothered by her. She's a deep well of dark magic."

I let her remark about Rabbit go. "Can I ask what you gave to Nisha? I mean, it's not my business, but it sort of is, maybe?"

Lucie shook her head and chuckled into her wine glass. She swirled the ruby liquid. "You are lucky I love you, Emily. But even if I told you what I traded, you wouldn't know what it was. It wouldn't mean anything to you – or to Rabbit for that matter."

"But I know exactly what it is." Templeton stood in the kitchen in front of the pantry door. He'd entered so silently, so swiftly. I briefly saw a swirl of blue-colored door travel energy around his legs before it dissipated.

"Dammit, Templeton!" Lucie put her hand to her chest. "I'm going to put a bell on you." She paused, her hand lifting to her mouth. She pulled on her lower lip. "In fact, I think I have a spell I can use."

He scowled at her, stepping toward the counter. "Don't change the subject."

"She wouldn't have told you what I gave to her. You're bluffing," Lucie insisted.

"Normally Nisha wouldn't share details of a transaction. But she wanted to reveal what a prize she'd picked up tonight." Templeton's voice dropped dangerously low.

"It was mine to trade." Lucie's eyes narrowed to glittering slits. She sipped her wine.

"Okay, someone has to tell me what it was," I said. I heard Rabbit come into the kitchen behind me.

"What's going on?" He gave Templeton the side-eye. "I'm guessing you're back up to full power?"

Templeton didn't acknowledge Rabbit. Instead, he addressed Lucie. "When the Congress of Empire Witches learns of this, you will be punished." Templeton spit out the last four words.

"Lucie? What is he talking about?" Rabbit's nose twitched.

Lucie muttered something about expecting a simple life in Matar. She glared at Templeton. "Guillaume gave it to me. Directly. If you know what *it* is, Templeton, then you know who *he* is. The Congress is the least of my concerns. I'd appreciate it if you kept this to yourself."

Rabbit mentioned the same name when we were at the Tortoise's cabin. "Who is this Guillaume?" I asked. No one answered and Rabbit gave me a nudge.

"And you don't think he'll find out?" Templeton was incredulous. His hands landed on the countertop across from her and he leaned angrily toward Lucie. "I can't believe you'd do something so foolish."

"I'll deal with him when he does," Lucie snapped at him. She threw back the last swallow of her wine before abandoning her barstool. She started to leave the kitchen. At the doorway, she whirled around. An orange-red glow coasted over her skin. She stalked toward Templeton and poked him in the chest when he faced her. "You know what, Templeton? You're a real prize. I don't know how you think *this* is going to work, but I have news for you, you don't want to push me." When Lucie said 'this' she waved her finger back and forth between their bodies. "I don't need your lectures or your judgment. And I will *not* be told what to do. Especially by you."

For his part, Templeton didn't move a muscle. A beat passed. Lucie spun away from him and stormed back out of the kitchen. When she reached the bottom of the stairs, she shouted from the other room. "And you're frickin' welcome!"

Rabbit let out a low whistle, but then couldn't hide his grin. "She does have a bit of a temper, doesn't she? Of course, you have such a way with women anyway."

Templeton snorted. "Joke all you want, but Lucie's put herself in a bad position."

"With Nisha?" I was trying to keep up.

Templeton gave his head a shake. "Guillaume."

I was dying to ask who Guillaume was, and why he mattered, but I'd had about enough. I couldn't take anymore tonight. But Templeton could door travel again. That was a good thing.

Rabbit cleared his throat. "I have something I want to show you. Earlier Emily gave me letters Tara found. I think there might be a couple of questions you can answer for us since you're a Salesman." Rabbit held up a finger when I opened my mouth. "Not a ding, Emily. Templeton knows more of the Empire's history, and he might even have resources we can use."

I nodded. "Oh."

"I'll be back." Rabbit left to retrieve what he wanted to show Templeton.

"I'm going to bed," I announced. "You're coming back here in the morning, right?"

Templeton's lips parted, and he nodded. I wondered if the look of surprise slipping across his face was because I asked if he planned to return, or if he was surprised to realize he would. "Yes. I'll be here."

"Good." I rinsed my wine glass out in the sink, eyeballing his clean clothes. He must've returned to his estate before coming to Lucie's. "By the way, what did Nisha do to you? Your door travel energy is in color now. It's a blue – really intense. I saw it when you arrived."

Templeton frowned. "Why do you think it's different?"

"Because it's blue."

"It's always been blue."

It was my turn to be surprised. "I've never seen any color."

"Well, now you do." He ran his hand down his shirtsleeve. He hesitated at his wrist, rubbing his fingertips on the cuff. A late-night lint hunt.

I rolled my eyes and set the glass on the counter, only pausing when something occurred to me. "Wait, does my energy have a color, too? Can you see mine?"

The corners of Templeton's lips curved slightly, and he continued to examine his sleeve. "It's green. Vibrant."

"Huh." I nodded as I took in his words. "Alright, I'm going to bed. Goodnight, Templeton." I met Rabbit in the doorway. "Are you two going to be okay down here without a referee?"

"It's all good, Emily," Rabbit assured me as he watched Templeton. "I'll see you in the morning."

❖ ❖ ❖

All the drama was draining, but in the end it made me sleep like the dead. A part of me worried I might slip into dreamwork – then accidentally pull in unwanted people. But by the time my head hit the pillow and I settled under the covers, I was out like a light. *All night.*

This time I didn't oversleep. I had time to

shower and even time to dry my hair with Lucie's blow dryer. I checked my neck in the mirror as I blasted my head with heat. If I looked carefully in the right places, I could maybe see a hint of a bruise, but for the most part, Lucie's scarf did the trick.

I pulled on my jeans and drew a long-sleeved tee shirt over my head. I could hear a low din of voices downstairs. The Rabbits had returned.

A chorus of *'mornings!'* and *'hey, Emily'* greeted me. There were a couple of new friendly Rabbit faces, but it was largely the same crew as the day before. Big Rabbit stood at the stove making pancakes. Lucie plated them as he served each fresh batch. She passed me an empty plate. "If ya can't beat 'em, join 'em."

"Pretty much," I said. "Where's Rabbit?"

"He took off with someone to bring back a couple of vans. He said he needed to meet up with a few people." Lucie set the maple syrup on the counter. She pointed toward her dining room with a butter knife. "At least the room is getting some use."

I peeked around the corner. More Rabbits.

"They really are multiplying," I stage-whispered to Lucie.

"You have no idea," came a voice at my side. The female Rabbit with the scar ate her pancakes while she stood. "I have 17 brothers and sisters."

"Good grief," Lucie grimaced. "Your poor mother!"

"It's not uncommon, but yeah. Too many mouths to feed." She took a big bite of her breakfast.

Lucie's face softened. "Well, my kitchen is always open to Rabbits."

"Thanks," she replied, her own face lighting up. "We've been lucky with Rabbit's friends. Not all Salesmen and witches are friendly."

"Why is that?" I blurted out. "I don't get it."

The woman raised one shoulder briefly as she worked a fork through her pancake. "Who says hatred makes sense?"

"Order up!" Big Rabbit sang out. I headed for the stove and took a short stack, soaking the cakes in butter and syrup. Big Rabbit leaned down. "I was going to put blueberries in them, but she's not a fan."

"Who?" I asked.

He tipped his head toward the female Rabbit.

Then he blushed.

I sucked in a quick breath. "Ooh, you like her!"

"Shh, shh, shh!" He waved a spatula at me.

"She doesn't know?" I pursed my lips.

"Don't say anything – don't!" He plastered a grin on his face. "Hi, Rabbit."

"Can I get a couple more pancakes?" the female Rabbit held out her plate to him.

"For you? Anything!" Big Rabbit's face colored again, and he turned back to the pan.

I left the two Rabbits to figure it out for themselves. Someone deserved to have a happy relationship.

Jack. I had to see him. A message through the Empire service or the Rabbits would not cut it. My neck was healed. I could go home.

I finished my breakfast and told Lucie what I planned. I'd be right back.

I grabbed my shoulder bag with the Crimson Stone inside but left my top hat behind.

I stepped through Lucie's pantry door and into my home.

✻ ✻ ✻

Jack sat at the dining room table, drinking coffee and tapping away on his laptop. He startled when I stepped out of our pantry. I hesitated, giving him a wave with my hand as I set my shoulder bag on the floor. "Hey."

"Hey," he said, standing and crossing to me. His hair was damp, and I could smell the shampoo he'd used. It was a comforting scent. "I'm not even going to ask if you're home to stay."

"That's probably wise," I replied. "But I had to see you."

"Anne's been relaying the Empire's news to me as she gets it. They've stopped regular travel in and out of the Empire. Apparently, door travel is still possible." Jack's focus went to the empty space right above my head. "Where's your top hat?"

"I left it at Lucie's. You know I don't need it. And they can't stop us from door traveling." I glanced into our kitchen. I felt strangely out of place. I needed to change that. "Is there coffee?"

"Plenty." Jack's hand stroked my arm. "What's wrong? I mean, what *else* is wrong?"

My lips twisted in a rueful smile. "Good one."

"Do you have time to sit down and talk?" Jack's fingers curled into my shirtsleeve. He tugged on it. "Over coffee."

"I can stay for a while. Um, where's my mother?"

"Anne was here bright and early. Lydia's 'helping' at the café. Personally, I think she's on a mission to drive everyone crazy so we'll take her back home." Jack pulled me to him, pushing my hair aside and nuzzling my right ear. For a moment I stiffened, then remembered the marks Sebastian had made were gone.

"We're alone?" My eyes drifted closed.

"Yes," Jack whispered. His lips touched the skin under my ear.

"Then I don't need coffee."

❋ ❋ ❋

I left Kincaid an hour later. When I arrived at Lucie's, I noted the Rabbits were wound. Something big had happened.

"What the hell?" I asked as I stepped into an excited throng of Rabbits. I was going to start calling the trips between places and Lucie's kitchen pantry The Pantry Express.

"Got me," Lucie said, drinking a cup of coffee as she leaned against her sink. "They found something. They're trying to get Rabbit back here."

"Big Rabbit? What's going on?" I called across the room. He held up a finger, asking me to wait. I grabbed a clean mug off the counter. "Is there any more coffee? I haven't had any yet."

"Self-serve," Lucie pointed.

"What's up, Emily?" Big Rabbit met me at the coffee pot.

I fluttered my hand, pointing right and left. "Everyone's all charged up."

"Breakthrough. Two, in fact. We're downloading the financial transactions of at least three dozen Empire muckety-mucks. Two are on the Salesman Court, the rest are in different branches of government. But we've been able to trace the money to Ivanov Transport – and even farther back."

Ivanov Transport. Sebastian used those warehouses when he kidnapped my mother. "Farther back to where?"

"Several wealthy families."

"Are the St. Michels one of them?"

"They're funneling the most money through

Ivanov Transport," Big Rabbit confirmed.

Jackpot. "What are we waiting for?"

"Rabbit will want to see this," he answered.

"But I know someone who should see it right now." I went on to tell Big Rabbit who Jo Carter was. "We need to get her here to see this A.S.A.P."

Big Rabbit seemed unsure. "Emily, she's part of the Salesman Court."

"I would trust Jo with my life. She can hit them from the inside while we get them from the outside. I don't know if she's here in the Empire or at home, but we've got to get her this information right away." I gave him my best toothy grin. "Please?"

Big Rabbit was torn, but he caved. "Give me a minute. We'll find her. What should I tell her?"

"Give her this address and tell her we have the proof she needs to clean up the Salesman Court."

* * *

Jo Carter arrived at Lucie's at the same time Rabbit returned with the new transportation. The other Rabbits were skittish around Jo at first, but her interest in what they'd found and her perceptive questions earned respect fast. That, and two of the Rabbits recognized her as the Salesman who once executed a fierce palm strike against the nose of a Fringe member. She sat in the dining room surrounded by laptops and printers – and Rabbits. They were arming her for a different kind of battle.

Big Rabbit briefed my Rabbit on what they discovered before switching to the other exciting piece of information. There was some sort of dead section in the Walled Zone. The Rabbits couldn't access it through any of their technological tools – they couldn't hack into anything in this hidden region. It was on a strip of land owned by Ivanov Transport. It'd been purchased within the past six months.

"We know the Fringe has kept a presence there for many years. If the fifth directional door is in the Walled Zone, we think we should look here," Big Rabbit finished.

Rabbit agreed. "But do we know why we can't get a look at what's there first?"

"No. It's obscured by something. We're working on it though." Big Rabbit paused. "Should we get on the road? Head in that direction?"

"Yeah, let's start. Let's get packed up and head west." Rabbit looked around the room as he spoke. "I met up with representatives from three other clusters this morning. They're going to meet up with us on the way. Let's get them the message." This meant other Rabbit colonies were joining us. Good. We'd need the numbers.

Lucie spoke up. "It might be helpful to know a friend of Sebastian's has a cabin west of Matar. He took me there." She bit her lower lip. "You guys should put it on your radar."

"Do you have an address?" Rabbit asked.

"No, but I can tell you how we got there. That might give you an idea," she said.

The kitchen grew quiet and the Rabbits in the room turned their heads toward the pantry, noses twitching as a hatless Templeton entered. I was glad Lucie didn't raise her wards against him but knew if he kept giving her a hard time, she probably would. I couldn't blame her.

The Rabbits went back to their work. Templeton registered Jo's presence in the dining room but headed in our direction instead. He joined us, standing near Lucie and soundly ignoring her. Lucie tensed but refused to move away.

And Lucie called *me* childish.

Rabbit launched into an update, sharing what we now knew.

Templeton listened to Rabbit, scowling when he heard the name Ivanov Transport. "Vlad Ivanov's family has been involved in organized crime for decades," he said.

"The Ivanovs are entrenched," Rabbit agreed. "We're beefing up protection for Jo and her family."

"She still doesn't know, right?" I glanced in Jo's direction. She was sorting papers as Rabbits handed them to her.

"Nope," Rabbit replied.

"There's more, though," I prompted Rabbit. "Tell him about the dead space in the Walled Zone – the place Ivanov Transport owns."

Rabbit explained the difficulty the network was having when trying to break into any of the technology in that particular section of the Walled Zone. Templeton pondered what Rabbit outlined. "Let me see your phone."

I was surprised when Rabbit so readily handed it over to him. Templeton held the phone in the palm of his left hand and hovered his right one over it. I watched as he pressed his door travel energy around it, the dark blue wrapping around both of his hands. I assumed I was the only one who could see it.

"Tell someone to message you directly right now," Templeton instructed. Rabbit motioned to one of his crew.

Nothing happened.

"Again," Templeton ordered. Another message was sent and not received. Templeton pulled his door travel energy back, no longer concealing the phone behind it. A moment later the two missed messages buzzed into Rabbit's phone.

"What just happened?" asked Rabbit.

"I think I know. He blocked your phone from receiving messages sent by your network with his door travel energy," I answered for Templeton. "I think this means the Fringe is using their energy for door travel to block anyone from finding them."

"Because they're hiding the fifth directional door?" Lucie mused.

Templeton smirked. "Or maybe the directional door is leaking energy and that's obscuring everything. The Fringe tampered with the

North Door. They've probably done worse to this one – if it is in fact there."

"Either way, it's good to know what we might find when we get there," I said. I clapped my hands together. "I know you're getting the show on the road, Rabbit. You guys get a head start. I want to run something by Templeton. We can catch up."

Templeton shot me an irritated look and Rabbit tipped his head to the side. "Really?"

I nodded. "Really. And Rabbit, can I borrow one of the network's phones?"

CHAPTER 22

Several Rabbits heard my request and laughed.

"I'm serious," I said. "This way we can find you and door travel to wherever you are when we know it's safe to catch up."

"I don't know, Emily." Rabbit discreetly glanced around the room at his brethren. "We don't hand out technology."

"Maybe that should change?" I waved a hand. "Discussion for another day. Templeton?"

I beckoned for him to follow, and he reluctantly fell in line behind me. I found the Rabbit who worked with Lucie to determine the address of the cabin Sebastian took her to when he was acting as Basha. We got a surprise – it wasn't a friend's cabin after all. The name on the deed was Sebastian St. Michel.

"Weird," I said. "Why would he tell Lucie it belonged to someone else? It doesn't make sense."

"Unless he didn't want her showing up unannounced," Templeton suggested. "If she thought it was his friend's cabin, she'd be less likely to go there without an invitation. If she knew it was his, she might've paid him a surprise visit."

"I guess. What a jerk. He really hurt Lucie." The minute the words were out of my mouth, I regretted it. Lucie wouldn't appreciate me talking about this with Templeton.

"He's always been a cruel person," Templeton said absently as he reviewed papers the Rabbits had printed and left on the counter.

I decided to take advantage of Templeton's split attention. "How long have you known him?"

"Since we were children. He was spoiled then, too." Templeton licked a finger and paged through a second pile.

"Your families knew each other then?" I hoped no one interrupted us.

"Yes. He and I attended the same prep school." Templeton stopped reviewing the pages and lifted his head. "Why are you asking me these questions?"

"It's clear there's a long history between you two," I pointed out. "I wondered how much of it happened before I met him in the warehouse last spring."

Templeton took his time before answering.

"As I said, I've known him since childhood. Our mothers were in the same social circles. What you see in Sebastian now was there then – arrogance, entitlement, a predilection for depravity. It gives him pleasure to hurt things. He feels powerful."

I thought about Sebastian's reference to shooting Templeton's dog. "How long have you known he's been part of the Fringe?"

"I've had my suspicions about the St. Michels family for a while, but it's been of little concern to me, Emily. I'd see Sebastian at various functions I've been forced to attend over the years, but we've had limited interaction." Templeton picked up a discarded pencil and circled lines in the data he reviewed. He added a few dates and handed the paper off to a passing Rabbit. "These large transactions coincide with election dates in the west. Double check which officials own these accounts. Make sure Jo Carter gets the information before she leaves."

The Rabbit gave Templeton a funny look but took the page.

"Sebastian is a fly, but when he finds a wound to put his fingers in, he'll keep doing it – it entertains him." Templeton continued, his gaze roaming the room until he found Lucie. "She'll be a target now. He probably enjoyed messing with a witch. He might've been surprised to find us at the *Wayside*, and he probably wasn't done using her yet, but now he'll flip the game. When it amuses him, he'll find a way to hurt her again."

Now we both stared in Lucie's direction. "After talking about it with Lucie, I realized Sebastian knew right when I landed in Matar. He was dropping her off when I arrived here. I couldn't see him through his car's tinted windows, but he could see me on the sidewalk. But even before that, I think he was using her to get to me."

"It's what I assume," Templeton said. "I'd like to ask her how she met him, what she may have told him without even realizing it."

"I don't think that's a good idea," I told him.

"Agreed." Templeton refocused on the papers in front of him. "She'll need to get over him first."

❋ ❋ ❋

Before I reconnected with Rabbit, I told Templeton my plan. I wanted to door travel to this cabin Lucie visited. I thought it might be useful to look around if it belonged to a friend of Sebastian's. Now that I knew he owned it, I was convinced we'd find something useful there.

Templeton listened. "No one here will want us going there alone."

"That's why we can't tell them," I said.

Templeton's eyes lit up. He was on board.

"But I was serious about wanting a phone. We need to stay connected to the network." I spotted Rabbit and motioned for him to come over.

"He'll lend you one," Templeton said.

"How do you know?" I asked.

"Because he indulges you." He gave Rabbit a thin smile.

"I don't indulge her." Rabbit's brows drew together.

"So, I'm getting a phone?" I grinned.

Rabbit slipped a compact device into my hand. "Put it in your pocket and don't pull it out it in front of others. Templeton, you'll have to show her how to use it."

My mouth popped open. "You have a phone?"

Templeton smirked.

"He used to, but I had to shut it off." Rabbit rolled his shoulders before twisting his head from side to side. I heard his neck crack. "He abused the privilege."

"Ah, Junior Justice Carter is preparing to leave," Templeton said, turning away. "If you'll excuse me. Let me know when you're ready to go, Emily."

"What's he talking about? Where do you think you're going?" Rabbit searched my face. "I'll know if you're lying."

I laughed. "I'm not running off by myself. Templeton's going with me. He agrees we should visit some places and gather information only we can get to right now. That's why I want the phone. I want to be able to find you and catch up. Make sure you're near a door so we can travel to you."

Rabbit sighed. "Well, part of the truth is better than none. But keep in touch with me. The phone is on silent – it won't buzz. I don't want to give you away if you're sneaking around. You'll know you have a new message because the phone will grow warm for a moment."

I hugged him. "Thank you."

"It's only because you're not going it alone. I'm glad Templeton is going with you."

"I'm as powerful as he is, you know." I lifted an eyebrow. "Magically speaking."

"I know you are. But you need to know what to do with your power." Rabbit avoided eye contact for a moment. "Your heart is as strong as Daniel's was. He'd be proud of you. Frightened for you, but proud."

I felt the tears well up. "Thank you for saying that."

Rabbit nodded. "Listen, we're going to meet up with the other clusters on the way into the Walled Zone. Once we're together, we'll wait for you and Templeton. If we can surround this hidden place, and if we can shut off whatever is blocking us, it'll be easier to find out what they're hiding when we swarm in. But we'll wait for you two before we move."

"Sounds like a plan. And you're bringing Lucie?"

"She's still hurting, but she's ready to go. Half of her doesn't want to see Sebastian – assuming he's there. The other half of her is itching to make him pay."

"Let's hope that's the Lucie who shows up today." I felt Templeton's impatience floating across the room. "He's ready to go."

"Be safe," Rabbit called after me.

"Do you know where you're going?" I asked Templeton. I was traveling light but bringing the Crimson Stone. It was deep in my jeans pocket. The phone Rabbit gave me was in the other. My top hat sat on the bed in Lucie's spare bedroom alongside my shoulder bag.

"I have the address. Do you know anything about the cabin? I'd rather not walk in through the front door in case anyone's staying there."

"Lucie mentioned a glass atrium on the side of the cabin."

"That's what we'll aim for then. It's an acceptable risk." Templeton's door travel energy began to rise. A silky blue stirred around his body. A white glow shimmered around the pantry door. It hummed.

"Not traveling with an official hat?" I mocked him. It was strange to see him without one.

"What makes you think any of my hats are official?" Templeton taunted. His pale eyes faded even more and he door traveled out of the kitchen as the air around him flashed.

"Hats?" I repeated. Good grief, all this time he wasn't even using an official top hat? Frustrated, I glanced away from the door and caught Lucie's eye. She gave me a haunted smile and a thumbs up.

My heart broke. It was unfair. Just yesterday she was so happy – she had met someone who made her feel special. And now she was forced to crawl through the misery of knowing she was used. I knew she felt stupid. No matter what I said, she was going to feel that way.

She was going to hurt for a while.

When I took down Sebastian, I'd make him pay for what he did to Lucie, too.

My door travel energy grew as I pulled it up in my chest. I could see a bright green tendril drift away from me and flirt with the white trails seeping around the pantry door.

Forcing myself to drop the bad feelings I had, I now marveled.

It *was* vibrant.

* * *

It's a little disconcerting to land in a place you've never been before. Strike that. It's a lot disconcerting.

I stepped into a large bedroom, immediately retreating, my back pressing against the door of the closet I'd used for traveling. *Crap.* Assuming I was in the right cabin, I'd missed the atrium.

My heart fluttered in my chest as I took in the room. At least I was alone. The décor held a decidedly masculine flavor, with colors trending toward gray and black. I tiptoed across the carpeted floor, circling the king-sized bed. A pair of men's jeans and a white tee shirt were tossed on the bedcover, but the bed itself was made. A door to the *en suite* bathroom sat opposite. I continued, easing the bedroom door open and peeking out through the crack. The long hallway was empty, and the stairs were at the end to my right. I crept out, listening warily for any indication of people below as I descended the stairs. Nothing.

The stairs brought me into a huge living room. Couches and chairs filled the comfortable space. A massive fireplace took up most of the far wall. I walked to the center of the room and slowly turned in a circle. A frightening, chestnut-colored bear skin rug hung on another wall, the head still attached, its mouth frozen open in a roar. Wide windows were placed in the wall at the front of the room letting in the mottled light of the late morning.

Arguably I stood in a log cabin, but it was a cabin on steroids.

There were no photos or anything to indicate I was indeed in Sebastian's cabin, but I'd go on faith I'd landed in the right spot. I needed to find Templeton.

The living room blended into a dining area with a long table, the wide top made from a slice of tree trunk. I passed into the kitchen, but he wasn't there either. A door to my far right led to the outside where the land sloped downward to a lake. But again, Templeton was nowhere to be found.

I retraced my steps back to the living room, passing the stairs and searching in the opposite direction. It was brighter on this side of the cabin. I headed toward the light, passing an open door. I glanced to my left and saw Templeton sitting at a desk.

"What are you doing?" I stepped into the office.

"Seeing what *Basha* has been up to," Templeton snarked. He slid open a desk drawer.

"No one's here, right?" I crossed to a cabinet and tried a drawer. Locked. I'd have to find the key.

Templeton noted the barrier. "Spell it open, Emily."

"I don't know how to," I answered, raising my hand and trying to use my door travel energy to pull it open.

"No, not like that." He left the desk and stood behind me. His graceful fingers wrapped around my wrist, and he held my palm up. "Use your travel energy if you think it will help, but you can pull it open with your intention instead. Aid it with this." He whispered a string of strange words into my ear. I repeated them automatically, focusing on the locked drawer. It popped open. Templeton released me, returning to the desk and picking up where he'd left off.

"Huh. Handy." I'd have to remember this one. I started to run my fingers through the folders inside.

We spent the next 45 minutes exploring Sebastian's office. We found nothing that would give us an edge or link him to the Fringe.

The books lining Sebastian's bookshelves were a fraction of the size of the library Templeton kept in his study. I browsed them halfheartedly, skimming my fingertips over the spines while Templeton leaned back in Sebastian's leather desk chair. Frustrated, he ran his fingers through his short hair.

Toward the end of a row of hardbacks I noticed an older spine on the shelf. I squinted. The worn lettering listed the title as *Empire Tales for Children*.

It was a book of fairytales.

Oh, holy hell. My heart skipped a beat. Was this the missing book of fairytales stolen from Blackstone's office last year? I'd thought Templeton took it before we both went after the Crimson Stone. I'd eventually figured out the Fringe stole the book instead. And now Sebastian had it.

I pulled the book from the shelf and opened it, looking for proof. My breath caught in my throat. It was handwritten – just like the book stolen from Blackstone. I turned the pages seeking a reference to the Crimson Stone. I found it in a tale called *Three Pieces*.

"You discovered something." Templeton's

voice sounded unusually loud in the room.

I held the book up. "Blackstone's missing book of fairytales."

"Is it?" Templeton sat up and held out his hand.

I gave it to him. "I'm certain. It's handwritten and there's a fairytale in there called *Three Pieces*. I skimmed it. It references keeping a blazing stone safe by breaking it into three pieces."

Templeton found the section I referred to and read it silently. He turned several pages. "This book will be useful."

"It belongs to the Cooper-Hewitt Library in New York," I reminded him.

Templeton waved his hand, dismissing me. A moment later, a satisfied smile cut across his face. "This book is even more valuable, Emily."

I leaned in and read the title he pointed to: *Six Doors*.

"North, East, West, South," he read aloud. "So as Above, moreso Below." He paused. "It's a variation with which I'm not familiar."

"Are you thinking the same thing? That this 'Empire tale' is referencing the directional doors? And that there's a sixth one, too? A

Below?"

Templeton's jaw worked. "If I had more time, I'd visit the library at the Congress of Empire Witches. There might be useful information there. But it'll have to wait."

I pulled the phone from my pocket and tried to locate the texting app. Nothing on the screen made sense. I sighed and held it out toward Templeton. "We need to find out where Rabbit is. Can you show me how to use this thing?"

"My pleasure." Templeton stroked the screen and called up a keyboard. "He's programmed it so you can only message him. That's disappointing. I was looking forward to listening in on the network." He handed the phone back to me.

"I'd imagine it's a lot of noise," I said, texting Rabbit that we were almost done with our mission and asking where we should meet up. His reply came back immediately. They were still traveling, but he'd have an address soon. He told me to hold tight.

"Looks like we have time to kill," I said.

"We can spend it going through the book of fairytales," he replied.

"Sure." I had a sudden thought and grinned. "But let's do it in the kitchen. While we're here, we might as well take advantage of Sebastian's 'hospitality.' Hungry for an early lunch?"

* * *

I rooted through the refrigerator in Sebastian's kitchen. There wasn't much – milk, eggs, shriveled produce. I pulled out a container of leftover Chinese takeout, setting it on the counter. I lifted the lid and took a sniff. It didn't smell spoiled. I chewed on my thumbnail while I considered eating it.

"I wouldn't risk it," Templeton warned. He continued to flip through the book of fairytales.

"You're probably right." I closed the container.

"You can't possibly be hungry. Didn't you eat?"

"The Rabbits cooked up a batch of pancakes. I had a couple." I pawed through the cupboards looking for snacks.

"There's your problem," he said, his nose still in the book. "No protein."

"Jackpot. Energy bars." I pulled out a box and opened it. Grabbing a bar, I held it out to him. "Want one?"

"I'll skip the package of chemicals, thank you."

"Suit yourself." I tore open the wrapper and took a bite. "We should get all the information we need before returning the book to the Cooper-Hewitt Library. We probably don't have a lot of time now, but we can take it to Tara for safekeeping."

"No." He turned the book sideways as he studied the handwriting.

"No? I think it will be safe with Tara. In fact, she'd be having a fit that we're being this casual with it now."

"I meant no – as in the book is not going back to the Cooper-Hewitt Library." Templeton lifted his head. "I'm taking it."

"What? No, absolutely not. Blackstone stole it from the library. It should be returned," I argued.

"And then the Fringe stole it from Blackstone – that's why Sebastian has it." Templeton closed the book. "And now I'm stealing it from him."

"Seriously, Templeton. It needs to be –"

"No." He strode toward the door leading into a cellar. "Stay here. I'll be right back."

"Where are you going?" For a moment I thought Templeton was taking the book to the cellar. I realized too late he was door traveling. "Oh, no you don't!" I abandoned my energy bar on the counter and tried to catch his sleeve. He was gone.

"Gah!" I slammed my hand up against the door. I couldn't believe him! I stopped. Honestly, I wasn't surprised. I mean, what did I expect?

I decided not to follow him, trusting he'd be right back. In the meantime, I had a brilliant idea.

Returning to the refrigerator, I grabbed the carton of eggs and swiped an onion from the crisper. A drawer of cutlery was easy to find, and I cut the onion in half before tossing the knife into the sink. There were several bedrooms upstairs, but the one I'd landed in had to be Sebastian's. I'd leave him a couple of parting gifts.

Once back in the monochrome bedroom, I paused at the foot of the bed. My fingers touched the abandoned tee shirt and I could smell the cologne I'd come to associate with him. A flash of Sebastian's wild eyes tore through my mind, and I jerked my hand back. My heart thumped against my chest. I was right. This room was Sebastian's.

My eyes flicked to the bathroom.

Sebastian had both a shower stall and a separate bathtub with all kinds of fancy knobs and jets. Turning on the overhead light, I found what I was looking for in the shower.

After I removed the top from the shampoo bottle, I picked apart the layers of the onion, blinking back my tears as the sulfur gas wafted upward. I poked slices into the open bottle. When I thought I'd added enough, I screwed the top back on and returned it to the shower stall. I rubbed the onion over a bar of soap.

Childish? Yes. Satisfying? *Oh, yes.*

Before leaving the bathroom, I rubbed the onion over his toothbrush and wiggled a couple of thin slices into the tube of toothpaste as well. I added a slice to a bottle of his hair gel.

I had five eggs in the carton. Two ended up deep in the toes of a pair of expensive-looking cowboy boots. The other three I added to the pockets of various clothes I found in his closet. I tossed the egg carton behind a stack of shoe boxes.

The phone in my pocket grew warm and I checked the screen. Rabbit sent the address of where they were waiting. I'd leave as soon as Templeton got back. I texted Rabbit a thumbs up and pocketed the phone once again.

I had a slice of the onion left and crossed to the nightstand by Sebastian's bed. As I slid the drawer open, a bottle with clear liquid rolled to the front of the drawer.

"Ew, gross," I said aloud after reading the label. I looked at the piece of onion in my hand, then back at the bottle. Did I dare touch it?

"What are you doing?" Templeton hissed behind me.

I panicked, dropping the onion and slamming the drawer shut. "Don't sneak up on me!"

A second slam sounded downstairs. Someone was in the cabin.

"We need to go – now!" Templeton ordered through gritted teeth. He shoved me toward the closet door.

"Wait! I have an address." I dug for the phone

in my pocket.

A man's voice called up the stairs. I didn't know if it was Sebastian or someone else.

"Emily, go! I'll follow you." Templeton pushed me toward the closet door a second time.

"But you need the address!" I held up the phone's screen and opened my mouth to give him the information, but it was too late. Templeton let go of me and rushed toward the bedroom door as someone began to push it open.

Templeton put his shoulder into it, slamming it shut. Whoever it was on the other side swore.

"Leave!" Templeton grunted as the person bashed against the closed door.

I spit out the address, knowing Templeton didn't hear me. His body jerked with each slam. Behind me, the closet door hummed as I pressed my door travel energy toward it. I shouted for him to follow me before zipping on through the other side to join the Rabbits.

CHAPTER 23

The address I'd focused on allowed me to enter an abandoned airplane hangar. It was crawling with Rabbits. At least 50 pairs of eyes turned toward me as I lurched through the door. Several men I didn't recognize rose from their chairs, their posture suggesting they did *not* like my surprise entrance.

"Hold up!" Rabbit weaved through the crowd and met me at the door. "Good. I was worried about you. Where's Templeton?"

I gestured to the door, fear growing in my chest. "I don't know. I mean, are there more doors into this place? Something happened and we had to get out of there fast. Templeton was trying to hold them off – or him off, or someone off." I was blabbering.

"Slow down," Rabbit put his hand on my shoulder and squeezed. "Where did you two go?"

"We went to see if we could find anything at Sebastian's cabin," I told him. I looked past Rabbit. "Templeton didn't have the address to come there. I'm hoping he can pinpoint me and follow. But are there more doors? Maybe he came in a different way?"

Rabbit's fingers flexed on my shoulders when I admitted we'd been searching Sebastian's cabin. He lowered his chin and released me. "Check the other doors," he ordered a group of Rabbits who had gathered around us. "We're looking for an arrogant Salesman."

But it wasn't necessary. The door behind me flew open and Templeton stumbled through. Before anyone could react, he pirouetted and hovered a hand over the doorknob as the door slammed shut. He cast his spell, his chest rising and falling rapidly while he worked to catch his breath. He turned and glared at me.

"Not my fault," I said, lifting my hands.

"What did you do?" Rabbit asked Templeton, pointing toward the door we'd both used.

"Locking it against door travel." Templeton rubbed his forehead. His hair was mussed, and his shirt was untucked, but he didn't look like he took any new hits – at least there wasn't any fresh evidence on his face. "I doubt Sebastian is skilled enough to latch onto our travel energy and follow us, but I'm not taking any chances."

"It was him?" I shuddered.

"It was." Templeton looked up at the ceiling and sighed. "There was no lock on the inside of the bedroom door. To leave, I had to let go. When I did, Sebastian busted in. He interrupted me as I was beginning to door travel out of there. We struggled."

"But you got away." Lucie appeared at his side.

Templeton's attention snapped to her. "I did."

Rabbit wasn't amused. "You want to tell me why you two were in his cabin?"

"We thought we might find something useful – and we did," I said. Around me, Rabbit noses twitched. "Um, let's go someplace more private."

"There's a room in the back." Rabbit led us past other Rabbits, several dismantled vehicles, and computers and laptops in use or in various states of repair. Some sort of horrid death metal music echoed from a distant corner.

Lucie brought us bottled water and the four of us sat down at a table covered with maps. We told Rabbit and Lucie about what we'd found at the cabin. Both listened without speaking, but I could see Lucie wasn't comfortable. Her experience in the cabin had been vastly different than ours. Her experience was a lie; ours was not.

"What is the passage in the book of fairytales?" Lucie asked when we'd finished.

"North, East, West, South. So as Above, moreso Below," Templeton replied.

"The 'moreso' is throwing me," Lucie said. She motioned to Templeton. "In the witchlines I know it's 'as above, so below.' Another mistranslation?"

"Possibly, but I'm inclined to believe it's intentional. But I don't know what it means," he said. "I assume it means whatever is in the Above, it's to a greater degree in the Below."

"But what *is* the Above and the Below?" I asked and waited. And waited. No one answered right away.

"In many witchlines, the above is the metaphysical – usually something divine in nature. The below refers to the plane we exist on. This." Lucie lifted both hands, gesturing to our surroundings.

"Heaven and Earth?" I asked.

"If it makes it easier for you to wrap your

head around it, sure. But I'm not convinced the phrase you read in the book of fairytales is the same thing." She turned to Templeton again. "I want to see this book."

He nodded. "I will get it for you, but I'm returning it back to my study before we go from here. I'm not carrying it with us into the Fringe's domain."

"You'll have time," Rabbit cut in. "We're waiting on a few more Rabbits, but we want to go into this dead zone after dark. We've done a good job of establishing a perimeter." He pointed to one of the maps. "We'll approach it from four sides. The plan is mostly reconnaissance and disabling whatever they're using to block us, but we'll happily engage if it comes to it."

"It might," I said. I leaned back in my chair. "How far are we from Sebastian's cabin?"

"About an hour and a half's drive, maybe more. We're inside the Walled Zone." He pointed out our location on the map. "We're less than an hour from the dead section we found."

"He'll probably be door traveling, but even if he isn't, Sebastian still has plenty of time to get from his cabin into the dead zone before nightfall," I said. "If he's there, I'm going for him."

"If that happens, we'll have to take the fifth door," Rabbit said. He pulled a couple of the maps together. "The question becomes, what do we do with it when we have control of it?"

"We figure out what it is," Templeton answered. "I think we can presume it's a one-way door into the Empire like the four other official directional doors."

"But from *where*?" I stressed. No one could answer me. "Something's bothering me. In the official Empire letters Tara reviewed, she said there were handwritten notes about where the Empire was hoping to *place* the directional doors. If the Empire was choosing where the directional doors should go, then wouldn't they know about these others? Wouldn't they exist because the Empire put them there?"

"Unless someone else established these directional doors," Lucie mused. "Maybe the Fringe found the two the Empire didn't find. Now they're trying to open doors into planes other than the Empire's four directional doors."

"Six doors are referenced in *Empire Tales for*

Children – I wonder who wrote the book," I said.

"A seer, perhaps," Lucie answered.

"I have to get back to the other cluster reps," Rabbit said, standing. "You guys keep working on this. I'll let you know when we're getting ready to get back on the road."

Templeton also rose, moving toward the room's door. "I'll retrieve the book of fairytales."

"Put on more appropriate shoes," Rabbit commented wryly. "Something with grip on the soles."

Templeton snorted and door traveled out of the room.

Rabbit suppressed a laugh. "I didn't dare suggest he switch to jeans."

"Perish the thought," Lucie added. "Alright, we do have some time to kill. Let me show you around, Emily. While Rabbit is doing his thing, you can meet a bunch of new Rabbits."

Rabbit held the door for us as we rejoined the growing contingent of Rabbits in the hangar. "By the way, does anyone else smell onions?"

I hid a smile.

* * *

Rabbit assembled a sizable army of Rabbits to take farther into the Walled Zone where the dead section hid its secrets. The first set of Rabbits would serve as high-tech warriors searching for weaknesses in the technological barriers set up by the Fringe to keep others out.

Other Rabbits, known as the 'perimeter group,' would surround the dead zone on foot and watch for who – *or what* – was going in and out. They were on standby for a third group of Rabbits who'd sneak into the Fringe's compound, and as Rabbit put it, run a reconnaissance mission while disabling anything they found working against us. My Rabbit would be in this last group with Lucie. If they were compromised, the perimeter group of Rabbits would swarm in as backup to help.

Templeton and I planned to follow on the heels of Rabbit and Lucie's group. Rabbit would send us the coordinates of a building we could use for door travel once he was inside. I wasn't sure how that would work, but I learned Templeton would be able to read the string of numbers Rabbit would send. *Figures.*

Because the vans would be packed with Rabbits, Templeton and I would stay behind in the hangar until it was time to go. Templeton would door travel first, and I'd zero in on him and follow. Good plans are important. I hoped we'd have good luck as well.

Waiting. Oh, how I loved to sit around and wait.

I checked out a few of the electric vans Rabbits were loading for the trip. Aluminum baseball bats and two-by-fours were loaded into the backs of several, accompanied by thick loops of chains. A couple of Rabbits examined sets of brass knuckles as they tried them on. Their glittering eyes flicked up to mine as I passed. I was strangely uneasy. These Rabbits didn't look friendly.

"Um, this is awkward, but do you have guns?" I asked Rabbit while I cringed.

Rabbit raised a thick eyebrow. "Emily, Rabbits are pacifists. What do we need guns for?"

Right.

After the tour, Lucie read through the book of fairytales Templeton retrieved. The tale called *Six Doors* was short. In it, a clever young girl roamed the Empire searching for openings to other realities and concepts across the universe. Whenever she found one, she weaved a tapestry of energy from the fire in her hands and placed it over the opening separating the planes to make sure nothing unwanted could slip into the Empire. During her search, she named the six doors she found, calling them North, East, West, and South – and of course, the Above and Below doors. The girl never revealed what was on the other side of any of them, but whatever was on the Above side, there was more of it on the Below side. This we believed.

North, East, West, South.

So as Above, moreso Below.

We theorized the patched openings existed before the Empire claimed them as their own, turning them into the four official directional doors. We wondered if the Empire leadership even knew about the Above and Below doors.

Sebastian had the book of fairytales. He knew.

Blackstone once had the book of fairytales. He had to have known, too. Did he tell the Empire leadership?

The same book containing the tale of *Six Doors* also included the tale called *Three Pieces*. Were these two connected? The fire in the young girl's hand – was it the fire from the Crimson Stone?

Lucie and Templeton argued the possibilities, agreeing and disagreeing with one another during an intense discussion. Eventually they stopped questioning each other, both studying an open page.

"Oh," Lucie breathed. "It's a key. The Crimson Stone is a key. The girl in *Six Doors* used it to lock the openings she found. If the Stone can lock them, it can unlock them, too. That's why the Fringe wants the Stone."

"Wait," I interrupted, lifting a hand. "Two things. The Crimson Stone was commissioned by Templeton's father, and this book of fairytales must be older than the Stone. Secondly, if the Stone is the key, how did the Empire open the doors without it?"

"It's possible the author was a seer, like Lucie said earlier," Templeton theorized. "The story doesn't need to be historically sound. Its intention might be to convey how to solve a problem. Many of the Empire's legends only have grains of the truth in them. As for the Empire opening the doors the child supposedly closed, perhaps the Empire found a different way to do it."

"Her tapestry of energy could've been sliced open by a powerful being." Lucie rubbed her lower lip with a fingertip. "But we're slipping deep into conjecture. I think if we find the fifth door and it's been opened, we should try to close it with the Crimson Stone."

Templeton huffed. "Don't you want to know what's on the other side?"

She hesitated. "Yes, but under controlled conditions without the Fringe breathing down our necks."

"I think we can all agree to that," I said. "I have the Stone with me, and we'll see what we find. You'll tell Rabbit about this during the drive to the dead zone?"

"I will and speaking of…" Lucie motioned toward the door.

Rabbit had popped his head in. "Do any of you have gluten or peanut allergies?"

"Um, I don't." I glanced at Lucie. She shrugged and shook her head. "Why?"

"Because *your* Big Rabbit's making batches

of peanut butter sandwiches for everyone to eat on the road trip. *Everyone*," Rabbit emphasized.

"I like peanut butter," I said.

"Great. Come get yours. We're packed up and ready to go. Lucie, the van leaves in 10 minutes. You're riding with me," Rabbit finished.

"Okay, this is it," Lucie said. We hugged. "Be careful."

"You, too. Hopefully we can find you easily," I said.

Lucie eyeballed Templeton. When he said nothing, she touched his arm and told him to stay safe before leaving to catch up with Rabbit.

"Smooth, Templeton," I said. I picked up the book of fairytales and handed it to him. "Better put this someplace safe. I'll meet you back here in 45 minutes."

He took the book. "Where are you going?"

"I'm going to take a walk." I put my hand up. "Don't worry, I'm not going anywhere. I only want to clear my head. I'm going to eat my peanut butter sandwich outside in the quiet where I can think."

※ ※ ※

And that's what I did. I didn't wander far from the hangar after the vans of Rabbits left. I sat at a beat-up picnic table and ate my sandwich and drank my bottled water. At one point I felt Templeton's eyes on me, so I knew he was checking to make sure I was still there. But he let me be.

I took the Crimson Stone out of my pocket and studied it. The Stone hummed faintly when I stroked it, but I didn't bring it up to full power. After a while, I put it back in my pocket and instead practiced lifting the empty water bottle off the top of the picnic table. I waved it slowly back and forth through the air. It wasn't that hard to do. My door travel energy seemed to bolster my control when I dipped into it.

It was getting cooler – and later. I was eager for Rabbit to text me a location. I hadn't told anyone I was frightened about what we'd find, and I wondered if they were scared, too. Rabbit didn't seem to be, and Lucie looked determined. Templeton looked annoyed.

I stayed outside for a few more minutes enjoying the calm around me before the phone in my pocket grew warm. I fished it out and read the message: *Get ready. Soon.*

I texted back a thumbs up and left the picnic table. The wind picked up, sending the dried leaves under my feet into a whirling dervish. I wondered what the rest of the night would bring.

❋ ❋ ❋

Templeton waited in the hangar, nosing through some of the equipment the Rabbits left behind.

"Are you interested in this stuff?" I asked, motioning to the abandoned benches and technology.

"I'm curious about everything, Emily," he said. "Aren't you?"

"Probably not everything, but the Rabbits' network is fascinating, I'll give you that." I watched him tap on random keyboards as he walked. "Templeton, it's no secret the Empire – well, specifically Salesmen – and Rabbits don't get along. I mean, the Rabbits are treated like second class citizens half the time. But you're not like that, are you?"

Templeton rummaged through boxes of discarded equipment. "I judge beings individually, Emily."

"And that's why you're friends with Rabbit," I said.

"We're not friends," Templeton dismissed me. "Rabbit was Daniel's friend."

Whenever Templeton said my father's name, it shook me. "Were you my father's friend?"

He paused, his hand hovering over a box of leftover Rabbit equipment. He blinked. "Daniel was my mentor. I respected him."

The phone in my pocket grew warm again. I pulled it out and read the string of numbers Rabbit texted to us: *14.75.3.16.70.1.*

"It's showtime," I told him.

CHAPTER 24

Templeton door traveled ahead of me, and I followed him immediately, barely allowing him time to land in the dead zone infiltrated by Rabbit and his crew. I could even catch tendrils of his travel energy in front of me as I whipped from the hangar to a building in the Fringe's territory.

We entered at the back of a warehouse lit only by the glow of emergency lighting and exits. No surprise – Ivanov Transport owned the place. They probably used the facility for storage. Rabbit and two others stood waiting for us.

"Where's Lucie?" I asked in a hushed voice.

"She's on the other side of the complex with another group of Rabbits." He assured us she'd be as safe as if she were with us. Big Rabbit was watching over her. Templeton seemed uncomfortable with this development, but we had other things to worry about first.

"What do we know?" I asked.

"It may say Ivanov Transport on the deed, but this place is definitely being held by the

Fringe. I don't have a final count yet, but there are at least 50 Salesmen."

"Is Sebastian among them?" I asked.

"No reports of him yet, but it doesn't mean he isn't here," Rabbit replied.

"I predict he's here," Templeton said. "He's agitated after finding someone in his cabin. He'll come here. He's worried."

I didn't say anything, but I agreed. In fact, I could almost sense the psychotic Salesman. My own energy was becoming hypersensitive. I wondered if this was what Templeton experienced? While I sort of liked it, it also made me uncomfortable. It was like always being connected to a current of high-octane energy – but you had to decipher the messages rolling through it. You had to figure out what was safe and what was dangerous.

Rabbit went on to describe the footprint of the place, which included four large warehouses facing a sparsely lit quad. That space was open except for a tent in the center. Several trailers were parked on the opposite sides of the warehouses. The whole place was surrounded by a high fence with razor wire. When I wondered how they got through, Rabbit snickered and asked if I ever heard of Rabbits being effectively kept out by fences.

Rabbit and his two crew members reached for their phones at the same time. Rabbit swore. "Compromised."

"Notifying the perimeter group," said the Rabbit next to him. "Swarm?"

"Tell them to delay 10 minutes." He looked at me. "Here we go."

❋ ❋ ❋

The five of us exited and crept along the side of the building. Above, a single floodlight snapped on and we could hear voices yelling across the expanse. Templeton's fingers dug into my shoulder, and he jerked me backward.

"Stay with Rabbit," he ordered into my ear.

"Wait," I said, whipping around and reaching for him as he blended into the shadows. "Where are you going?"

He didn't answer – he was gone. *Damn him!* I scrambled to catch up with the three Rabbits slinking alongside the wall in front of me. We crouched low as the floodlight passed overhead. Rabbit put his hand on the top of my head and pushed. "Keep down."

I didn't need to be told twice. We waited and I leaned into Rabbit. "Did you find out if the fifth door is here?"

"No," he answered, scanning the empty space behind me. "But the tech group is working on breaking into their intranet. Last message said they were through the first wall blocking them. Did Templeton take off?"

"What do you think?" I followed Rabbit's lead as he and the others rose and advanced again. The sound of yelling on the other side of the quad increased and we heard a few whistles – followed by a couple of gunshots.

"Let's move it!" Rabbit ordered and we scurried in the opposite direction of the noise, away from the action and toward a second warehouse for better cover. Inside we found two rows of tractor trailers. "See if you can find keys in these things," Rabbit commanded his men while fishing his phone from his jeans pocket. "If we need to start crashing through the Fringe line, we will." He looked down. "Excellent. One of my crew accessed a computer on the inside and dropped a firewall for the tech group. They hacked in. They're downloading everything they can find."

"Anything about the fifth door?"

"Hang on." He thumbed a message. A few seconds later a reply came back. "So far no references to a door."

"Damn." The noise outside the warehouse was escalating. The fighting raged between the buildings and my breath quickened. I knew this would happen, but it was still terrifying.

But amid my swelling anxiety, something niggled at the back of my mind. The arrangement of the buildings seemed strange. Why was there a grass yard surrounded on all sides by massive warehouses? It was out of place for the complex. Were they hiding something? Protecting something? "Rabbit, what did you say about a tent?"

"There's a tent in the middle of the quad. A big one. I couldn't get a good look, but it might only have three sides on it. Hang on." He texted again and we waited. The reply came back. One of the tech group Rabbits accessed an electronic copy of a bill of lading for the tent. It was delivered to the complex only two weeks ago.

"There's something in that tent," I said, jab-bing my finger at Rabbit. "One guess as to what it is."

"It's possible," he answered. "We'll see how close we can get, but we might have to wait until we've fully taken control."

Rabbit whistled to the other two Rabbits, and they responded with shrill chirps of their own. We left them behind, stealing back outside. Another floodlight swept back and forth across the quad lighting up fistfights and, in some cases, beatings. Fists pounded against flesh.

"We've got to get those lights out." Rabbit winced as we shrunk back into the shadows yet again. He texted with one hand. "The perimeter group of Rabbits is starting to swarm. I'm ordering a contingent to the rooftops. Those lights have got to go."

"How will you see? I mean, I get it, but…" My voice trailed off and I recoiled at the blast of another gun. The shooter was close.

"We're Rabbits, Emily. We can see in the dark." He waited for the light to pass by, and we broke into a run, seeking a place where we could better see the front of the tent. A spotlight unexpectedly roamed the ground in front of us and we each split off running to the side – Rabbit to the right and I to the left. I didn't realize we'd been separated until I stopped alongside a warehouse wall to catch my breath.

"Oh, freakin' great," I muttered. I eased forward in the shadows; my hand stretched out in front of me as my fingertips grazed the warehouse wall. Ahead a door opened, revealing men's voices. I instantly recognized Sebastian's.

"Put these animals down," he growled at his men as he stomped out of the building. "I want this whole damn place lit up like a Roman candle! We need to see how many of them are in here. And I want double protection on the tent!"

I remained flattened against the side of the building. In my pocket, I felt the Crimson Stone begin to hum. *Please, not yet,* I begged it silently. Sebastian's tall frame was backlit as he stalked farther into the quad. A moment later, a loud explosion thundered from outside the enclosure, sending fire into the night sky and Fringe members racing. I hoped the blast was the work of the Rabbits.

The detonation echoing, I saw Sebastian and his men pull back. Sebastian's silhouette contorted violently, his arms waving at his men as he shouted. Transfixed, I watched his body twist as he raged. He moved like a demon.

Both Rabbits and Fringe zigzagged in and out of the roving beams of light. More gunshots rang out and I saw two people fall to the ground. Two others pivoted, backtracking and picking up the fallen. They raced for the shadows. *Rabbits.*

My eyes darted back and forth as I scanned the chaos. I'd take advantage of the explosion. I made a dash for the center of the quad. Again, a floodlight waved across the ground. Another one followed, lighting up Lucie as she ran toward me, her arms pumping. A Fringe member spotted her and gave chase, rapidly closing the gap. A pale arm reached from the shadows and clotheslined the man before he could catch Lucie. He was dragged screaming into the darkness as the floodlight flashed by.

"Lucie!" I yelled, waving as I ran. "This way!" I'd retreated, heading back to the side of the warehouse. Another floodlight blazed to life from a rooftop. Lucie and I huddled together against the wall.

She swore a blue streak, leaning over to catch her breath. "We found explosives," she panted. "Then we blew up a tractor trailer."

"Add it to your resume," I answered, scouting the space around us.

She coughed and wiped her mouth with the back of her hand. "Glad you find this funny."

"I don't," I replied. "But listen to me. I saw Sebastian – he's here. He wants the entire place lit up. We've got to get these lights out for the Rabbits."

"Give me one second." Lucie lifted a finger. "Let me get it together."

"No pressure, but hurry," I told her. "And there's more. Rabbit and I think the fifth door is in the tent in the middle of this place. Rabbit says it looks like there are only three sides. We should go for it."

Lucie nodded, rolling her shoulders before rubbing her palms together. "Let's do it. But first let me take out a couple of those lights."

She bent at her knees, keeping her feet together and lifted her hands, still summoning her own energy. As her arms rose, she pulled her hands apart and revealed a glowing ball.

Lucie reached higher and her body bounced as she took aim at one of the floodlights. At the flick of a wrist, the ball of energy popped out of her hands, arced through the air, and smashed into the light, snuffing it out.

"One down," she said. She repeated the action and took out a second light.

"Basketball player in high school?" I asked. It was an impressive display.

She snorted. "Last girl picked in gym class – but I loved to learn new spells. Mastered that little trick years ago."

"Paid off. Come on." We threaded our way through a murky portion of the quad, heading for the tent. Two floodlights still rotated overhead, but we were able to reach the back of the tent without being seen. Rabbits and Fringe members fought at the front. Two brawls leapt closer, fists driving into faces and stomachs. Bloodied faces roared at each other. Lucie and I plastered ourselves against the canvas wall. The Crimson Stone in my pocket started to hum again. I felt its heat intensifying.

I inched forward, fixated on my goal. The fifth door was inside the tent. I could feel the door travel energy saturating the air. It was like nothing I'd ever felt before. It was both intoxicating and menacing.

Lucie pressed up behind me. "Can we get inside?"

"We're going to try," I said. We padded forward; eyes wide as bodies thrashed around us. The sound of wood striking flesh seized my ear, followed by a man's grunt as he took a hit to the stomach. *Another one for the Rabbits,* I thought. I wrapped my fingers around the edge of the tent, pulling myself around and into the light. My hand dove into my pocket as the heat of the Crimson Stone swelled. Lucie slipped in, standing a couple of paces behind me. In front of us, a shimmering silver rectangle stretched upward from the ground, making the door at least seven feet tall. It was over three feet wide.

"It's the Above door," I heard Lucie breathe.

I held the Crimson Stone in my hand. I looked at it. My door travel energy wrapped the Stone in a green ribbon. Everything felt... *activated.*

"I think we should close it before anyone sees us." The energy spiraled up my arm. Goosebumps covered the back of my neck. "Lucie?"

I swung around to find an ugly man with a

missing eye grasping Lucie, a hand around her neck holding her against his chest. His other hand slapped across her mouth. She struggled, kicking her feet as he lifted, choking her.

"Let her go!" I shouted, lunging forward. The Crimson Stone glowed in my hand. The man reared back, and Lucie managed to clock his crotch with the heel of her sneaker. It was enough to make him loosen his hold and she broke free, dropping to the ground.

The sound of two hands clapping together slowly brought everything to a halt. Sebastian stood to the side with three of his men – who kept their guns trained on us. "You girls should take your show on the road. I'd buy tickets to watch you fight all sorts of monsters."

The one-eyed man made another grab for Lucie – a mistake. This time she was ready and threw a handful of stones and dirt into the man's face. She shoved him and he fell backward. She spun toward Sebastian. The reddish-orange aura Lucie wore when she was angry darkened as it slid over her skin.

"Enough!" Sebastian shouted. "Shoot them if they move toward the door." His head rolled back and forth, as he pointed at the rooftops, once again raging. "And where are the damn lights? How many times do I have to tell you idiots? I want to see everything around us!"

"Feeling surrounded, Sebastian?" I mocked him. I squeezed the Crimson Stone. The firepower in my right hand felt very good. My own power coursed through my veins, matching it. When the time came, I would draw upon the Stone to magnify mine.

Sebastian zeroed in on the Stone. "Brought me a present?"

"I can't wait to give it to you." I brought my hands together and transferred the Stone to my left hand. At the same time, Sebastian's order was finally obeyed, and more floodlights powered up around the quad. Some sat at ground level, and my breath caught as I took in the sheer number of Rabbits and Fringe members battling around us. The odor of sweat and fresh blood filled my nostrils. I saw my Rabbit running in our direction with a dozen of his crew, his hand gesturing to the right and left as Rabbits broke off to the sides planning to surround the tent. Rabbit raced directly toward us with two others. My eyes cut to the left and I saw Big Rabbit slam a Fringe member to the ground with one hand before he raised his head and screamed.

I followed his line of vision. Two stories up, a Rabbit fought fist-to-fist with one of Sebastian's men. The two skirted the edge of the roof. The Rabbit threw a hard punch with her right arm, knocking the man back. In his place stepped another, swinging a pipe.

He connected.

She fell.

"No!" I reacted, throwing my right hand up toward the woman. My palm vibrated as I held the woman still in midair, her body writhing.

Sebastian took advantage of the situation, charging for the Crimson Stone and knocking it from my left hand. I stumbled but didn't break my concentration, holding the woman as still as I could. Sebastian dove toward the Stone and was body checked from the side as Templeton burst onto the scene. The two men rolled across the ground. Sebastian's gunmen maneuvered to get a clear shot, pushing against each other. Lucie clambered after the Crimson Stone.

Placing my full intention on the suspended

Rabbit, I lowered her as gingerly as I could into Big Rabbit's upraised arms. He snatched her from the air, cradling her against his chest before disappearing out of the light and into the night.

Lightheaded from sustaining a high level of energy across the quad, I turned to see Rabbit and his men trading punches with the three gunmen. From the inside of the tent, Lucie clutched the Crimson Stone in her left hand. The blackening blood-red glow she wore on her skin rolled over her body as Templeton and Sebastian circled each other at the opening of the tent. Templeton's eyes were colorless; his body tensed as Sebastian went in for another strike.

As Sebastian attacked, I heard glass breaking throughout the complex as warehouse windows shattered and floodlights sizzled out. The air smelled like burnt matches. At first, I thought the Rabbits set off another explosion, then I realized it wasn't a bomb that blew.

It was Lucie.

Gripping the Crimson Stone with both hands, Lucie kept pouring her own energy into it. She crouched; her lips pulled back as she bared her teeth. Something was building and I was afraid.

The firepower in her hands mushroomed and a new shockwave rolled from the witch and across the entire complex. Everyone was knocked to the ground – everyone except for Lucie.

Ears faintly ringing, I placed a hand on my knee and pushed myself back to my feet. Rabbit rose from the ground at my left. His eyes now a solid black, his beat-up hands flexed as he zeroed in on Sebastian. Climbing to his feet on the other side of Rabbit, Templeton warily assessed Lucie.

Sebastian staggered to his feet by the fifth door, battered but laughing. "Lucie, baby, in a different time and place, we were meant for each other."

"I will kill you, Basha," Lucie whispered. She rose from her crouched position, lifting the Stone again and tapping into the power effortlessly. The space inside the tent filled with its crimson glow.

Rabbit's focus flipped to our friend. "Lucie, that's not who you are. That's not what you do."

She didn't reply.

The energy in the Above door by Sebastian swirled.

"You know what's in the Above?" he taunted her, his hand stroking the energy radiating out of the fifth door. "I do. I've seen it. It's filled with fierce beings, Lucie. They're beautiful beasts. But watch your step. If you anger them, if you break their laws, they'll turn into monsters and rip apart everything in their path. *Everything*." Sebastian sucked in a deep breath, his eyes rolling up as he quivered. His fingertips continued to dance across the opening of the fifth door. "They'll make powerful allies – or enemies." He suddenly focused on Templeton. "You'll be no match for them."

"Do you know what's in the Below?" Lucie's voice cut into the air. She didn't give Sebastian a chance to answer. "No? Maybe we should find out." Lucie steadily lowered her hand and directed the Crimson Stone's energy toward the bottom of the door. Templeton swiftly crossed to Lucie, anticipating her intention as he slipped behind her. His hand drifted toward her left hip. As his fingers made contact, sparks erupted. His right hand locked onto her other hip and he braced himself. He enveloped Lucie in his powerful blue door travel energy.

"As Above moreso Below," Lucie chanted. A long shadow stretched out from the bottom of the fifth door. The magic sizzled on the ground and the black energy popped upward. As she concentrated, aided by Templeton, the ground split open. A hint of something decaying past the opening wafted up.

"Holy hell, it's the sixth door," I murmured, covering my nose and resisting the impulse to draw away from the gaping hole.

Shocked, Sebastian instead leaned toward the sixth door, gawking into the darkness. He licked his lips. "You opened the Below door," he marveled.

The fury expanded inside my chest as I watched Sebastian. I wanted him to be punished – I wanted him to feel real pain. More than that, he needed to be defeated.

If there were beings who could turn themselves into monsters in the Above, did that mean there were *always* monsters in the Below? Because *'moreso Below'*?

Sebastian *was* a monster. That's where he belonged. If he remained in the Empire, even if he were to be arrested, there was no guarantee he'd ever pay for what he'd done. The violence may not have always come directly from his own hands, but the blood belonged on him. His hands were dripping with it.

Sebastian needed to be thrown through the door Lucie opened. I edged forward, avoiding Rabbit's touch as he stretched for my arm. I raised energy from the same well I'd developed over the last few days, holding out my right hand palm-first toward Sebastian. My fingers splayed, I pressed my energy out at the depraved Salesman, and he stumbled. Still, he avoided falling.

"You little –" he snarled, spinning around to face me. Hatred rolled off him in thick waves.

"You monster," I shot back, straightening my arm and pressing my energy as hard and fast as I could against his body. It nailed him right in the chest and he floundered backward. I realized he was trying to raise his own door travel energy – a smoky gray swirled around his waist as he reached for the Above door. "Oh, no you don't."

Lucie and Templeton held the sixth door open as I blasted a third and final surge of my energy at Sebastian. It ripped through his chest, and he screamed as the door travel energy from the Below door snagged his and forcibly yanked him through. I heard him scream my name once before the sound of his shrieking abruptly turned to silence.

"Close the door!" I pressed my palms together to stop the energy from pouring out of me. I shuddered as it circled back into my body.

Templeton's hands dropped from Lucie, and she stepped closer to the two doors. She hesitated, a frown pulling her eyebrows together as she considered the openings before her. She knelt, pulling the Crimson Stone to the center of her chest. She bowed her head, the aura surrounding her body dropping its shadowy hue and switching to a shade of red. The air around her sparkled.

The shadow of the sixth door – the Below – started to cave in on itself and drew back under the bright shine of the fifth door – the Above. When it was gone, Lucie kept the Crimson Stone in her left hand, still holding it tightly to her chest, but raised her right hand. Her palm touched the opening of the fifth door.

I could feel Rabbit strain at my side as he resisted the urge to rip her away from the opening. Templeton's door travel energy was rising again. If Lucie was pulled through the fifth door, I knew he would chase after her.

Lucie's steady hand stroked the surface of the fifth door. The Crimson Stone's flame pulsed rhythmically against her chest. Realization washed over me. It matched the beat of Lucie's heart.

The fifth door shimmered but began to shrink toward its own center. I watched as it reduced to the size of a thumbnail before completely winking out. The door to the Above was closed. Lucie swayed and Rabbit was at her side in a flash. He helped her to her feet, his arm sliding around her waist. Her head dropped to his shoulder.

"We've got it under control out there," Rabbit said to Templeton as he guided a dazed Lucie from where the doors once appeared. She kept a tranquil Crimson Stone pressed tightly to her chest. "I'm getting her to a van. She needs to go home. She needs to rest."

Templeton opened his mouth to argue but didn't. He gave a curt nod, but his expression gave away his true feelings.

Squinting, I examined the empty space where the two doors had been. There was nothing to indicate they ever existed. I ran a hand across my forehead. "How do you think the Fringe knew about this?"

Templeton watched Rabbit and Lucie disappear into the inky night as they picked their way across the quad where Rabbits directed each other with flashlights, whistles, and shouts. They rounded up the remaining Fringe members. Templeton answered, but his thoughts were clearly elsewhere. "They've been looking for some time. I'll need to examine the book of fairytales more thoroughly. Perhaps that's where they found the information leading them here."

"Maybe." Rabbits across the quad tied up the leftover Fringe members, forcing them to kneel in a line. Big Rabbit came around the side of the tent. Before I knew what he planned, he enveloped me in a big bear hug. He smelled like grass and sweat. "Ow!"

"Sorry," he sniffled into my hair. "Emily Swift, I owe you my life for what you did today."

I wriggled in his arms, my legs dangling. "You don't owe me anything! But can you put me down?"

He lowered me and took both of my hands in his. They completely covered mine. He bent to look me directly in the eye. "If you ever need anything from me – any help or information – all you have to do is ask. I will be there for you."

I was about to tell him not to worry about it, but I had an idea. I glanced at Templeton. His arms were crossed over his chest, and he regarded Big Rabbit with a curled lip.

"On second thought, Big Rabbit, there *is* something you can help me with. Let me catch up with you in a few minutes," I said. The massive man nodded, squeezing my hands gently before leaving me alone with Templeton.

"There's nothing left here for us – we should go." My arms flapped uselessly. Noting the frustration still lining Templeton's face, I tried for a little bit of levity. "Heading home to the grand ol' estate?"

He scowled. "We need to discuss the Crimson Stone."

"No, Templeton, we don't. Not tonight, anyway. It's safe with Lucie and that's where it's going to stay for now," I said. I rubbed my forehead. "But we will talk about it. All of it – including these doors and how to keep them shut."

Templeton's eyes narrowed. "I want to know what's on the other side of both. It's foolish to remain ignorant."

"Well, I can tell you what's on the other side of the Below door," I said as I began to leave. "Sebastian. With any luck, the monsters already found him."

CHAPTER 25

I enjoyed the autumn afternoon in a quaint town located south of Matar called Becket. I sipped my plain latte – topped with a bit of whipped cream, of course – in a tidy café tucked into the corner of the bookstore. From my vantage point inside *Becket Books*, I watched a pretty teenager chat as she bagged a purchase for an older woman.

Earlier, I bought a magazine at the same counter. The teen's wide smile was beautiful, and her warm, brown eyes sparkled as she rang up my order. When a coworker offered her a cookie from the café, she pushed a thick lock of wavy black hair behind her ear and told him: *I could eat.*

Her name tag read 'Celeste.'

"And you think this is a good idea, why?" Templeton's disdain snaked into my ear from above.

I looked up. It had been two weeks since I'd last seen him. We all met at Lucie's three days after the battle in the Walled Zone. The four of us – Templeton, Rabbit, Lucie, and I – needed to make a decision regarding the future of the Crimson Stone. In the end, Lucie made the decision for all of us.

"You know who she is, don't you?" I challenged as he sat in the chair beside me.

He appraised the girl behind the counter. "Who do you think she is, Emily?"

"She's Rabbit's daughter," I answered softly. "But you already knew this."

He gave a brief nod. "The question is, why are you here?"

"I guess I wanted to see her, to find out if she's happy." I tracked Celeste as she danced around her coworker. She laughed, giving him a shove when he reached for her cookie. "I know what it's like to grow up without a father. And Rabbit... Rabbit's wonderful."

"The girl has a father," Templeton replied. He picked up my magazine and scoffed at the title. "The man her mother married raised her. By all accounts, he's a good parent. The child's unaware she doesn't share his biology."

"But what if..." I waved my hand uselessly. "What if someday she finds out and wants to know who her biological father is? How will she know where to look?"

Templeton admonished me. "You know better than anyone. If a Rabbit wants to be found, she will find *him*."

"I guess." I frowned at the drink in my hand. "You're right."

"I'm always right," Templeton smirked.

"Are you going to Blackstone's memorial service?" I changed the subject.

Templeton sighed. "If my calendar is free."

"Lucie will be there." I bit my lower lip.

"Why is that relevant?"

"Because I think you like her," I said to him.

"I don't... *dislike* her." Templeton huffed. He refused to look at me.

Leaning back in my chair, I considered the man who'd puzzled me for nearly a year. I studied him: the short, dark hair; the palest blue eyes I'd ever seen; the sharp angles of his face; the long line of his nose. The bruises he'd gained from the recent fights we dragged him through were gone. Templeton's surly – but handsome – aristocratic expression gave him away. "I can't believe I'm saying this, but you should ask Lucie out. Take her to that fancy dining club Rabbit says you haunt."

Templeton sneered. "I'm not in need of your

advice."

"Suit yourself." I finished my last sip of coffee and stood. "But I'll save you a seat at the service in case you show up."

* * *

That first night in Anne's apartment after Rene Blackstone was killed, Tara had written: *Goal – Take Down the Fringe.* Did we do that?

On some level, yes. But evil like that never completely goes away. Still, we had massive wins.

The Rabbits provided Jo Carter with the ammunition she needed to bring charges against over three dozen members of the Empire's leadership – including four members of the Salesman Court. This didn't include Justice Beverly Spell, however. Before she was charged, Spell resigned from the bench. She petitioned the Court as a simple Salesman, requesting banishment from the Empire instead of a trial. The Salesman Court agreed.

I was deeply saddened by Spell's choices, but I couldn't hate her. She was desperate to protect her grandson from the Fringe.

And speaking of Junior Justice Jo Carter, she was made a full justice, taking over Spell's seat. Four other junior justices were fast-tracked into the remaining four seats on the prestigious Salesman Court – handpicked by Jo and Justices Howard Manchester and Norford Smith. Those three leaders also drove the investigations into several wealthy Empire families – including the St. Michels. They found more than enough evidence to arrest and charge dozens of prominent members from the ranks of the Empire's highest Salesman society. Odette St. Michel was among them, as was her husband. I learned things happen differently in the Empire. Even before the trials began, the Empire seized all material goods and land owned by the families.

With the rapid action being taken by the Empire, former Justice Tahl Petrovich finally ran out of luck. After a swift trial, he was found guilty of murder and treason. He was sentenced to death but submitted an appeal. The trial for Simon – also known as 'Speedy' – began. I predict he will be found guilty of murder as well.

Ivanov Transport was no newcomer to being

investigated by the Empire. Templeton predicted they would weather this storm – he was probably right. The Empire did seize the company's holdings in the Walled Zone, including the space where we closed the fifth and sixth directional doors.

The Rabbits disappeared right after the battle in the quad, taking with them anything of value and – I assume – the bodies of the Fringe who didn't get away. No body, no crime. Although, Big Rabbit was easily found when I called in 'the debt' he owed me. I never would've found Celeste without him. Rabbit's daughter was a surprise to Big Rabbit, but he understood the need for secrecy. He swore on his honor he would never reveal my Rabbit's loss to anyone.

Rabbit and Lucie spend a lot of time together. They are great friends, but sometimes I worry he looks at her the same way Templeton looks at her. But I'm probably wrong.

Three days after the major battle in the Walled Zone, we all met at Lucie's. None of us denied that Lucie was the 'light.' None of us could argue against Templeton's claim on the Crimson Stone. His father had commissioned the creation of it, after all. We also agreed that separating it into three pieces and sending it in three different directions like I'd done the first time around carried its own risk. The Stone should remain intact. But it was still dangerous to hold onto it with the pieces reunited.

In the end, Lucie made the decision for all of us. She claimed the Stone since she was the one who used it to close the fifth and sixth directional doors – the Above and the Below. Rabbit and I agreed. Frankly, I was relieved. I'd had enough of the Crimson Stone to last a lifetime. I didn't want it.

Templeton was not at all happy, and the two argued. Eventually, they came to an agreement: Lucie would cast a spell to put the Crimson Stone to sleep. Templeton would then be allowed to keep it at his estate – but he could not use it unless Lucie awakened it.

As Lucie sang a soft lullaby over the Stone, casting a spell while her fingertip stroked the surface, I snuck a peek at Templeton. His eyes were a little bit bluer than usual.

With the short-term fate of the Crimson Stone decided, Lucie and Templeton agreed they should begin their research into the book of fairytales – specifically in relation to the Above and the Below directional doors. We needed to know more about the beasts and monsters Sebastian claimed were on the other sides.

I'll admit it, once in a great while I still feel a prickle creep down my spine and look over my shoulder. Sebastian St. Michel was sealed in the Below and was probably dead. Lucie didn't talk about him, of course, but before she declared the subject off-limits, she told me how she'd met him.

Last summer, Sebastian – *Basha* – began to frequent *Coffee Cove* where Lucie read cards. It started out with harmless eye contact with an attractive man drinking coffee when she arrived in the afternoon. Then came the occasional 'hello.' She noted he favored tables near her reading room door. Eventually their small talk progressed to hints of a mutual attraction before diving into full-on flirting.

One day Lucie saw the name 'Basha' written in the book where she listed her schedule outside her door. He penciled his name into several back-to-back slots. When Sebastian sat down for his reading, he abruptly reached across the table and put his hand on the deck of Tarot she planned to use. He teased her about reading cards and said he believed people created their own fates. She told him in the end that was true – but to pull a card anyway. He turned over the top one: Three of Swords.

Heartache.

He hung his head, peering up at her at with a devilish smile. He apologized for being so cheeky. He 'confessed' he'd experienced his own share of heartache, but he was still willing to take chances. Then he asked her out to dinner, sitting back in his chair and lacing his fingers behind his head while he waited. Lucie admitted he'd charmed her by then. Warning bells were ringing inside her head, but she didn't heed them – she didn't want to. After the weeks of flirting and teasing, she was smitten. She wanted to go out with him. Whatever it was setting off her internal alarm system, surely she could handle it. She said yes.

Later, after learning her Basha was actually Sebastian, when Lucie pulled the same deck of Tarot down to use for a client, she realized *every* card in the deck had turned to the Three of Swords. The Tarot tried to warn her, but she ignored it.

The deck is no longer in her collection.

A sad truth surfaced as Fringe members were identified and arrested: Sebastian was present when the North Door was compromised in Rene Blackstone's home. When Blackstone confronted the invaders, he was attacked. Those arrested claimed Sebastian himself strangled Blackstone. They might be lying to save their own skins, but after my experience with the deranged man, I'm inclined to believe it's true.

With the dismantling of the Fringe's leadership, the Empire moved to strengthen its four directional doors. The Empire, although charting a new course with fresh leadership, needed to establish a new status quo. It was understandable. There had to be some stability following the shakeup and changes.

And what about me? I returned home.

Home to Jack, our three Furious Furballs, my best friend Tara, and my dear friend Anne – who I now knew to be Templeton's maternal aunt.

My mother, to everyone's delight, is happily

back in Western New York where she works on her art. This past year of craziness made me realize that there IS something I inherited from this Meta Muse: Courage.

The Book – capital 'T,' capital 'B' – still sits on a shelf in my office. I page through my father's journal every so often to see if there are new messages from the witch Evangeline. We never did determine who spelled my father's journal long before it landed on my doorstep almost a year ago. Sometimes you have to live with the unknown.

Why my dad was bringing Templeton's banished father back into the Empire on that ill-fated train 18 years ago remains a mystery. I still want to know why, but I have a feeling it's going to be a long time before I can get Templeton to drop his guard again.

Jo and I talked about my role moving forward with the Empire. My 'grounding' was lifted, and I was approved as a full-fledged Salesman. I was allowed to door travel – unaccompanied by a Senior Salesman – and was no longer the bane of the Salesman Court. Jo did stress the Empire's laws required all Salesmen to use an approved top hat when door traveling. Traveling without one could result in a rescindment of the Empire's permission to door travel.

Pfft.

While I was extremely grateful for Jo's advocacy on my behalf, I was also tired. I opted out of the Salesman stipend I'd receive if I worked for the Empire transporting magical and mundane items for others. I decided to remain plain ol' Emily Swift – albeit the one who could travel from place to place, simply by stepping through a door.

I was ready for my new life as a Salesman – one that included my friends from the Empire, but one that didn't demand more than I was willing to give. I was a different person after all we'd been through, but a person I liked. I had a lot of people to thank for that.

Even Templeton.

EPILOGUE

The memorial service for one Mr. Rene Blackstone was held at a beautiful stone church in Kincaid. The autumn day was exceptional, with the cerulean sky providing a brilliant backdrop for the red, yellow, and gold leaves pressed up against it. I shielded my eyes in the sun and looked around as men and women milled about in the yard. Newly-minted Justice Jo Carter delivered a loving and moving eulogy for the late Record Keeper and Warden of the North Door. During the service, Tara read one of her favorite poems by Rainer Maria Rilke. It was one of Mr. Blackstone's favorites as well, she told those gathered for the celebration of his life. The poet's encouragement to *"... love the questions themselves, like locked rooms and like books written in a foreign language..."* matched the two bibliophiles' souls perfectly.

Tara received an invitation the day before the service, hand-delivered by Jo. Although the North Door was still being evaluated, the work Tara and Mr. Blackstone previously submitted to the Empire was extremely valuable and it needed to continue. Combine that with Tara's vast knowledge of rare books and the Empire was not eager to lose such a valuable brain. The Salesman Court offered Tara a position as Record Keeper for the Empire. She accepted. She would move into 1221 Northgate Way before winter.

At first, I was surprised Tara agreed to live at Northgate as it was there Blackstone's life came to an end. But Tara being Tara, she told me she would not let death own the library for a moment longer. She was taking it back for Blackstone – and for herself.

I breathed deeply, pulling in the crisp afternoon air. I was glad to be out of the church. The cloying scent of hyacinths overwhelmed me. I surveyed the yard and noticed Jack engaged in a conversation with Rabbit. The two men stood against the low stone wall surrounding the church's garden. They bent their heads over Rabbit's phone while he pointed to something on the screen. Jack nodded and laughed, matching Rabbit's broad grin.

Before I could join them, I felt a cool breeze drift lightly across the back of my neck – I'd pulled my hair up in a twist, leaving my tender skin exposed. Teasing tendrils from a familiar energy charged with consistent power encircled me. I could scarcely make out the blue hue as it vibrated in the air. The initial caress was followed by a sharp poke of energy against my back. I sighed.

Templeton.

Turning, I peered up into the faded eyes of the man who understood such a unique part of me with an intimacy no one else would ever share. He didn't smile, of course, but he didn't break his gaze from mine as he looked down his nose.

"Did you even attend the service?" I asked, annoyed.

"Yes."

"I didn't see you."

"You were looking?"

I blew out a breath. "No. But I didn't feel you either."

The corners of his mouth quirked up. "Do you –"

"No." I held up a finger. "Don't."

"I was simply going to ask if you could still sense when I'm close," he chided me. "It's possible the longer you're outside the Empire, the more your awareness of other energies will lessen."

"Oh," I said, twisting my mouth to the side as I mulled over his words. "Yes. I can still sense you. I don't try to, though."

"I suppose it's too much to expect it to lessen just because we're not near each other regularly. No matter," he finished, waving a hand. I watched as he became distracted by the right cuff of his suit jacket. His pupils shrank to pinpricks, and he lifted his left hand.

"Let me get that for you," I said, reaching out and grasping his hand. Although he didn't pull away, I felt Templeton stiffen as I made a show of leaning in and examining the cuff for a stray piece of lint. Finding nothing, I instead picked off some imaginary fluff and flicked it into the breeze. I looked back up, biting my lip to prevent a grin.

Horrified, Templeton gawped at his jacket cuff. He blinked several times.

"You're all set now," I said, letting his hand go and giving his arm a pat as if we were the best of chums.

Rendered speechless, Templeton's lips pressed together.

"Well, I'd better get back to Jack. Let's try not to run into each other for a while. With the Fringe being dismantled and me stepping away from any official Salesman duties, I don't think we have much of a reason to see each other anytime soon," I said.

"No, I guess not." Templeton shifted his attention, scanning the scenery behind me.

He was searching for a door.

"Goodbye, Templeton," I finished.

He barely acknowledged my last words. Instead, a shadow of satisfaction flickered over his mouth as his eyes landed on his target. "Yes, goodbye, Ms. Swift." With that, he stepped around me and strolled across the yard. I turned to watch his departure. When he veered away from the building's side door, I was surprised to see him instead approach a group of Salesmen and witches chatting off to the side.

Lucie tilted her head at Templeton's arrival. He appeared to excuse his interruption, placing a hand on her elbow. Her expression curious, she allowed him to lead her away from the others.

Templeton's back was to me, but I could tell

Lucie was listening to him speak. A moment later a flicker of surprise flashed across her face. She nodded. Templeton touched her arm before abruptly turning and walking back toward the door. He didn't pause to look back at either of us but left, effortlessly door traveling from here to there – wherever there was – in an instant. Lucie watched him go, a bewildered expression on her face. She shook her head before she caught me watching from across the yard. Looking from the door to me, she lifted her hands and shrugged.

Before I could cross to her, a hand touched my shoulder. I jumped.

Jack lifted his eyebrows. "Everything okay?"

"Yeah, I guess," I answered, casting one last look at the door Templeton disappeared through. Lucie returned to the group she'd been chatting with before the interruption.

"What do you think, then? Are you ready to go?" Jack asked.

"I am, I just..." My voice trailed off as I watched Lucie lean toward our friend Anne and whisper something into her ear. Lucie gestured to the door Templeton used. Chewing on my bottom lip, I turned to Jack. "You know, it's nothing. But…"

"But what?" Jack drew me closer. His finger traced the curve of my jawline before he dropped his right hand and lifted my left. He kissed my palm before turning my hand over. With his thumb, he rubbed at the engagement ring I now wore on my finger.

I melted into his warm, brown eyes and decided to let it go. Whatever Templeton had planned, it didn't concern me. I shook my head. "You know what, Jack? I think it's time for someone else to pick up the story."

The end.

Coming in 2022: the first book in the
Bellerose Witchline Series!

ACKNOWLEDGE-MENTS

To my husband, Gordon – the man who lived with months of chaos and picked up the slack nearly every day. Thank you for reading every line of this book twice – and sometimes even three and four times. Thank you for acting out scenes with me in our dining room. Thank you for tolerating my obsession with a certain rock band while I wrote this book. Thank you for loving me. I'm still not sure what I did to deserve you, but I'm grateful for the life we've created every single day of it.

To Jill Elizabeth (Jill-Elizabeth.com): I'm so glad that writing group was not for us. Has a decade passed? I can't imagine writing the Door to Door series without you. Your insight, feedback, and kindness helped me produce three books I am very proud of publishing. The support you've generously given to me – and to Emily, Templeton, and the entire crew – is priceless. I don't know how I'll ever be able to thank you… but thank you.

To Jennifer Brasington-Crowley (author of the fantastic Raven Song Series): Thank you for letting me send Rabbit and Lucie to a *Black Talons* concert so Lucie could crush on Raven Xerces. I'm so happy you said 'yes!' to letting me include references to your character and his rock band in this book – and I'm incredibly grateful for your friendship. And the teeth.

To my readers: YOU are making my dreams come true when you buy and read my books. As an independent, self-published author, reaching new audiences relies a lot on word-of-mouth. To those who tell others about my books, thank you. It means so much. To those who take the time review my book on Amazon and Goodreads - THANK YOU!

To my @WriterTracyBrown Instagram writing community friends, and in particular, you fabulous #IndieAuthors. (You know who you are...) You are truly the best bunch. Thank you for being so welcoming and supportive!

…and finally, to the unexpected muse who showed up as I wrote Emily's last book. You fed the well and I drank deeply from it. Wherever you are now, I hope your unparalleled talent and creative energy have finally found lasting peace.

FIND T.L. BROWN ONLINE

Website and Updates

Visit WriterTracyBrown.com to learn more about the Door to Door Paranormal Mystery series and to connect with the author in all of her social media channels.

Sign-up for the Door to Door Mystery Series Newsletter.

T.L. Brown Insiders Group (Facebook)

You are invited! If you like to have FUN when you read, this is the group for you! We talk about reading, new stories, and upcoming books. Get previews and enjoy author videos.

Join: Facebook.com/Groups/TLBrownInsiders

T.L. Brown on Goodreads and Instagram

Follow on: www.Goodreads.com/TLBrown and @WriterTracyBrown

BOOKS IN THIS SERIES

Door to Door Paranormal Mystery Series

The Door to Door Paranormal Mystery Series is a set of exciting, fast-paced mysteries by author T.L. Brown.

Door to Door (**Book One**)
First in series published in October 2020!

Two worlds collide when Emily Swift turns 30 and her late father's journal lands on her doorstep...

Seventeen years after Emily Swift's father died, a door is opened to a new world, an Empire led by peculiar men and women called Salesmen – transporters of magical items. These Salesmen have the unique ability to travel from place to place, and even world to world, simply by stepping through the "right" door.

Now that Emily is 30 it turns out that she can "door travel" too, stumbling unplanned into kitchens, bathrooms, and alleyways as her connection to the Salesman Empire is revealed. Fueled by the cryptic notes and sketches in her father's journal, Emily discovers the real reason behind his death: he was targeted and assassinated by the Fringe, a terrorist group of rogue Salesmen.

After an attack that leaves an innocent woman dead, a rare book containing clues to the whereabouts of the Crimson Stone is missing. Emily is charged with getting it back. As she races through the Empire, she pursues John Templeton, the mysterious Salesman with extraordinary abilities, who seems to both help and undermine Emily at whim.

With new friends Anne Lace and the boyish Rabbit, she tracks Templeton, but the Fringe is not far behind – as two new murders prove. Along the way, Emily struggles to balance her desire to find out who killed her father against the task of recovering the legendary stone. The internal journey of reconciling the father she hardly knew, with the great leader she'll never know, forms the foundation for a fast-paced race to keep powerful magic out of violent, fanatical hands.

***Through the Door* (Book Two)**
*Relationships tested, friendships built,
secrets revealed, sacrifices made...*

Salesman Emily Swift is back – *and so is Templeton!* After learning about her supernatural abilities and finding the Crimson Stone, thirty-year-old Emily Swift returns home to Kincaid to rebuild a normal life with her boyfriend. As she struggles to get a handle on her "door traveling" energy, a strange warning squawks from her car radio: a rogue, terrorist group called the Fringe is still watching her.

Before she can figure out if the message is from a friend or foe, Emily's quirky mother, Lydia, goes missing – and resurfaces in the Empire! As Lydia travels from city to city in this peculiar world, a wake of chaos is created. Add the murder of a hated art critic and a kidnapping into the mix, and things go from bad to worse. The Fringe believes Emily knows where the magical Crimson Stone is hidden, and they'll stop at nothing to get their hands on it.

Friends Tara and Rabbit join Emily as they race against the Fringe to catch up with Emily's wandering mother. Will Emily's nemesis, the mysterious Templeton, join her in rescuing Lydia? What will it cost her? Is the price too high?

Doors Wide Open (Book Three)
The third and final book in the series!

Emily Swift: Reckless, unruly, unreliable... brave and big-hearted.

My name is Emily Swift and I'm a Salesman – one who's currently persona non grata with the Empire's leadership. I'm technically grounded, but I can still travel from place to place simply by stepping through a door. Any door.

I've been told I'm overconfident and take foolish risks. Allegedly, I'm unreliable. I've been accused of fibbing – okay, lying – and holding back the whole story if I think it's the right thing to do. But here's the deal: I'm not the only one who's been less than truthful. I've been lied to, misled, attacked, held captive by a crazy terrorist, and even had to rescue my mother from kidnappers.

The Fringe – a rogue group of violent Salesmen – just murdered a friend and tampered with the North Door. I'm going to do whatever it takes to bring them down, and I'm counting on my friends for help.

I'm even taking a chance on Templeton... Because this time I'm busting all the doors wide open.

ABOUT THE AUTHOR

T. L. Brown is the pseudonym for the author who writes the Door to Door Paranormal Mystery Series. She was born in snowy Western New York where she developed a love of reading and writing. She holds a Bachelor of Arts from the University of Pittsburgh in History - Political Science.

After college, she moved to Rochester, New York and began to write a story about an average 30-year-old woman who found herself caught between two worlds: the known one and a new, often dangerous place known as the Salesman Empire. That character became Emily Swift.

Ms. Brown now lives with her husband in the beautiful Finger Lakes of New York State dreaming up new stories and quirky characters that make life all the more interesting. She believes that magic exists; you just need to look in the right places.

Made in the USA
Middletown, DE
17 November 2021